# Sugar & Gold

Emma Scott

Copyright © 2017 Emma Scott

All rights reserved

Cover art by Melissa Panio-Petersen

Interior formatting by That Formatting Lady

No part of this eBook may be reproduced or transmitted in any form or by any means, electronic or mechanical, including photocopying, recording or by any information storage and retrieval system, without written permission from the author.

This is a work of fiction. Any names or characters, businesses or places, events or incidents, are fictitious or have been used in a fictitious manner. Any resemblance to actual persons, living or dead, or actual events is purely coincidental.

# Acknowledgements

I owe so much to so many who helped make this book come to life.

Thank you to Melissa Panio-Petersen for your tireless work and your gorgeous covers. I am spoiled and blessed to have you, and literally don't know what I'd do without you.

To my amazing formatter, Angela Bonnie Shockley, who always works under the gun and who yet manages to make the inside as beautiful as the outside. I know I'm your problem child; thank you for not killing me. Xoxo

Thank you Joy Kriebel-Sadowski, Grey, Robin Hill, and Kathleen Ripley for going over (and over, and over) the m/s and making it shiny and clean—despite my best efforts to keep messing with it and dirtying it up again.

To Suanne Laqueur for always knowing exactly what to say, exactly when I need to hear it, and for recommending the best 'staying sane' podcasts. Let's always be us.

To Irene Oust, for your Russian language expertise, spasibo!

Thank you, my intrepid beta readers, whose feedback and support was invaluable in making the book what it is: Lisa Ackley Aiello, Jeannine Allison, Heather Bentley, Melissa Brooks, Annette Chivers, Sasha Lambert Clements, Dawn Dairymple, Liezel Felix, Dawn DeShazo Goehring, Saffron Kent, Desiree Ketchum, Alissa Laroche, Alison Mackie Lazewski, Julia Lis, Alissa Marino, Danielle McGregor, Kasey Metzger, Michelle Morrison Monroe, Joanne Goodspeed Ragona, Trisha Rai, Steph Simmons, Meg Thornton, Mari Tee, Tijuana Turner, and Becca Zsurkan.

Thank you to my editor, Jennifer Livingston, who brought so much more to the project than mere editorial expertise (though there was a ton of that too). It was meant to be.

A huge thank you to Shannon Fahey, a walking encyclopedia for the world of poker. You have added so much to Nikolai, and I'm so grateful to you for sharing your incredible expertise and experience with me.

And thank you to this book community—the bloggers and readers who do so much with every share, tag, mention, review…You make this happen and I cannot thank you enough for what you do, because a simple, "Hey, I read this book and liked it. Give it a try," makes an author's world go 'round.

# Playlist

*Criminal*, Fiona Apple
*Hey Baby*, Dmitri Vegas
*Stay with Me*, Sam Smith
*Trouble*, Cage the Elephant
*Blood in the Cut*, K.Flay
*Keep Going*, The Revivalists
*Yellow*, Coldplay
*Lost on You*, LP
*Wish I Knew You*, the Revivalists

# Dedication

For Robin, with a gratitude greater than thank you.

# Prologue

The man bolted upright from sleep. The night was thick and still as the houseboat rocked beneath him. He tried to grasp the dream that danced at the edge of his awareness. Images crossed his eyes like ghosts. A darkened highway. A shadowed figure kneeling on the roadside. And rain. So much rain. But the rest of the dream slipped through his mind like sand through fingers, leaving only a few remnants behind that he could see clearly.

*Highway 23*
*Margo Pettigrew*
*A gratitude greater than thank you...*

As with the other dreams of this kind, he didn't know what any of that meant, but knew he would. Eventually.

He turned to his wife sleeping beside him and kissed her. She stirred, and her hands slid protectively over the swelling roundness of her belly.

"I have to go," he whispered.

She blinked in the dimness, brushing the dark hair off her face as she sat up. The line of a scar divided her left cheek perfectly in half. "Go...?" Her sleepy eyes found the digital alarm clock that read 3:21am. "*Now?*"

The man nodded. "Now."

"Why?" She sat up. "And where?"

"A dream," he said simply. "I'm not sure where yet." He cocked his head as if listening to a voice only he could hear. "East. I have to go east. And I have to take the truck."

He got up and turned on the lamp, casting the small room in yellow light. He drew on jeans and a shirt. The houseboat rocked lightly as he crossed to the small dresser for extra clothes that he then tossed on the bed.

"Wait," she said. "You can't...You can't leave me. Leave *us*." She hugged her middle with both arms. "What if something happens to you?"

The man stopped and turned to face her. His blond hair glinted gold in the light. Swiftly, he moved to sit beside her on the bed. "I won't be in danger, I promise. But I have to go. I have to help someone."

"Who?"

"I don't know yet," he said. "I'll know him when I see him."

"Why does he need your help?"

Her husband shrugged, a small smile over his lips. "Love," he said. "For love."

She sat back against the pillows, her dark eyes full of worry. The man reached for her, took her face in his hands and pressed his forehead to hers.

"Remember what I told you last time?" he said. "It's still true. I swear it, baby. It's still true."

"You will always come back to me," she whispered, closing her eyes and holding his hands that held her.

"Always," he said. "I swear it."

He finished packing while she watched.

"How long?" she asked.

He paused, listening. "Six days," he said finally.

"You have the next six days off from the fire station," she said. "Was that planned?"

He smiled ruefully. "Is it ever?"

She answered with a dry smile of her own but it faded quickly. "I thought you were done with the dreams. I thought that was over."

"I did too," he said. "But this is important. I have to go. I feel…"

"You feel…what?"

"If I don't go, he'll miss her. They're lost in the dark."

"Who are they?" she asked, then waved her hand. "Never mind. You don't know until you know."

"Exactly."

He slung his packed duffle bag over his shoulder and walked with her to the front of the houseboat. There, he held her close and his hand found his way to her belly and their son, six months along.

"I'll be home soon," he whispered against his wife's dark hair. "I love you."

"I love you, too." She pulled away to look at him fiercely, her scar stark against her skin. "Promise me. Say it again."

He kissed her and ran his finger down the shiny seam on her cheek.

"I will always come back to you."

Then he stepped out onto the deck and the darkness swallowed him without a sound.

# Part I: The Devil in Me

*ken (kɛn) (n) : range of knowledge or perception*
***Synonyms:*** *awareness, vision, understanding, consciousness...*

# Chapter 1

## Nikolai

"When did it start, Nik?"

"I can't remember. Since forever."

"Can you sense what I'm feeling right now?"

"Yes. It looks like brownish-orange dust and smells like ... wet leaves."

"What does?"

"What you're feeling. I can see it. You don't believe me but you're excited because you've never seen this before. It's new."

"And you call it your ken?"

"I don't know what it is. I tried to look it up in a dictionary and found that word. I can't find anything else."

He scratches a note. "You've always been able to do this? To 'see' feelings?"

"Yes, it's nechistaya sila. Right, Mama?"

He glances at my mother, then back to me. "What does that mean?"

"I have the devil in me."

"Do you think what you can do—the ken—is wrong?"

"I don't like it. I don't want it. Can you make it go away?"

"I think this treatment might be able to do just that. You don't have the devil in you, Nikolai. Your brain is making you think you can sense what others are feeling."

"But I can see the dust ... I can taste it..."

"Hallucinations, that's all."

"And you're going to shock them out of me?"

"Something like that." His smile is ashen fumes and makes me think of lies. "Think of your brain as a computer and it has a little glitch. Turning it off and on helps to clear out the glitch. The current will act as a sort of reset."

"You're going to turn my brain off and then back on?"

"It's just a way to help you understand the process."

"I don't know..."

"The medication isn't helping, is it?"

"No. I hate it. It makes me numb."

"I think this treatment is much better suited to your particular affliction."

"So I am sick? Dad said I was, before he left. Sick in the head."

His smile tightens and he answers like he didn't hear. "What do you think, Nikolai? Are you ready to give it a try?"

"I guess."

"Very good." He looks to my mother. "If you'll sign the consent on his behalf..."

"Mama?"

She looks away from me. Maybe she'll look at me again if I do this.

They lead me into another room and have me lie down. They give me a shot of something in my arm and put a mask over my face. I inhale the gas and it makes me lighter than air. I float up toward the ceiling and in a blink I'm looking down. I'm sleeping. They attach sticky pads with wires trailing behind them to my forehead. They put a stick in my mouth.

The doctor with the lying smile hits a button and nothing happens but for my foot that's sticking out of the sheet - it trembles a little, like it's cold from being left uncovered.

A second later, my thoughts are cut into pieces. Lightning tears through me, blinding, ripping and burning. I see a flash like chaos and then everything rots to the gray of dead flesh.

I scream at my sleeping body.
NO! STOP! PLEASE!
Nurses and doctors, who'd been sitting calmly, are darting around now. The slow beeping of my heartbeat is now as fast as the white bolt that tears through me until it's all one loud noise, one horrific pain...
WAKE UP!
The doctor shuts off the machine. The lightning crackles away to nothing and I fall down, into myself.

My eyes open and I suck in air as if I hadn't breathed in years. Agony thunders in my head. Voices crowd around me.

"He was under full anesthetic..."
"Severe tachycardia..."
"Impossible..."

I sit up to more confused cries. I rip the electrodes out, then peel the sticky pads from my forehead; tear the tubes out of my arm.

"Nikolai, please calm down..."

I throw the thin sheet off. The floor is cold beneath my feet as I run. Hands try to grab me but I slip away. The pain pounds like a drum, driving me on, through the door. I run headfirst into the blinding white light of day that stops me like a brick wall. I throw my arm up to shield my eyes. Rough hands grab me around the shoulders and drag me back.

I fight them, but they're too strong, and the light is so bright...So bright...

"You still with us, Nik?"

I blinked hard, and wrenched my gaze from the single bulb hanging over the table. It took a second for the memory to dissolve and reality to appear, like a scene from a TV show fading out and opening on a new one. The fourteen-year old kid in a hospital gown was recast as a twenty-four year old, covered in tattoos, and bulked up with muscles because fuck me if anyone was going to lock me up again.

"Our new buddy Nik has gone bye-bye," said Paulie.

Atlanta. The poker game. I sat up in my seat and snorted a dry laugh. "Still here, cleaning you chumps out."

Laughter from the other six guys met my shit talk, though it was tight and mirthless. They didn't like me. They all had chip stacks of varying sizes in front of them, but mine was the largest.

We were in the basement of Paulie's pawnshop, downtown Atlanta, Georgia. On the main floor above, desperate people hawked their family heirlooms or Grandma's best piece of jewelry to eke out a little bit of money to keep going. To pay the utility bill or to score their next fix. Below, it wasn't much different.

Paulie ran a Texas Hold'em game three times a week where some of the players gambled with the rent or grocery money. $15 and $25 blinds and a $250 buy-in.

I could've found stakes like this anywhere, in any underground poker game in almost any town. And I did, on my endless crisscross of the country. But I wanted a big city. The endless days on the road took their toll on me. I needed people.

*I just can't be this damn close to them.*

Atlanta was too much. I'd been a fool to think I could handle it. It felt like the entire city, not just the pawnshop, hung over my goddamn head. The onslaught of all that life hit me like an acid trip that wouldn't quit. So many people filled with so many emotions. They screamed their lives at me in a riot of colors, and filled my mouth with the bitter taste of their bad memories.

Sweat trickled down my neck even though Paulie had the AC churning against the heat of Georgia in the summertime, and my head ached as if a hammer were pounding from the inside. I was at the bottom of the sea, with the crushing weight of the water pressing down on me...

I lifted the corner of my two cards with my thumb. A deuce and a four, both hearts. The flop had the ten and seven of hearts, and Jack of diamonds.

I let the cards lie, and kept my face impassive. Flush draw wasn't a bad hand. Lots of possibilities for a win and then I was out. Atlanta was too much. I had to get the fuck out of here.

"Hearts, hearts everywhere, what a crock of shit," said the big guy—Oliver—on my left.

*Liar.*

That was Oliver's tell. To make a cryptic comment about the cards at every play. It threw the others off; who the fuck actually *tells* a tell? Sometimes he was bluffing, sometimes not. I could always read him. I could read all of them. Even without my *ken*, I could read them like a book. With my *ken,* I was unbeatable. In my twenty-four years of pseudo-life, this was the only goddamn thing it was good for.

"So Nik," said Paulie, chewing around his cigar. "What do you do for a living?"

*I cheat at poker.*

"I'm a salesman," I said, striving to keep my voice normal. The bet came to me. Normally I'd check to reel them in, but this time I saw the big blind and raised it fifty bucks.

The table collectively inhaled and the smoke reflected in the overhead light shifted to sickly, suspicious shades of grayish-green and the piss-yellow of fear from a young guy named Eli on my left. The $250 buy-in was more than he could spare but he'd played anyway. To a lot of guys, poker was stronger than heroin.

"Motorcycle parts, was it?" Angus asked. He'd been my 'in' to the game. I'd met him on an online game, got to chatting, and earned an invite here. My usual M.O.

"Yeah, motorcycle parts," I said, taking a long draw from my beer bottle.

Angus saw my raise, and dumped the chips on the pile instead of sliding them across the table.

"Fuck's sake, Angus, quit splashing the pot," Eli said. He worked at the pawnshop, and was, in my esteemed opinion, a moron. It was probably obvious to everyone, not just me, that Angus' tell when he was bluffing was to splash the pot.

"Mind your business," Angus told Eli, giving me the side-eye. "Got to keep up with Nik here, who's been on a helluva run all night."

"*All night*," a guy named Will snapped.

He sat directly across from me, and was all hard edges, flinty glances, and suspicion packaged in a lanky frame. The kind of guy who'd draw a knife on you if you surprised him—a natural born asshole who couldn't take a joke if his life depended on it.

I'd seen his kind before—watching the action like a hawk, and keeping tabs on who had the blinds with anal-retentive diligence. I hated him immediately.

He sized me up for the hundredth time that night, taking in my tattoos that covered my arms and neck, and the 10-gauge silver talons that pierced my ears.

"*Hoax* and *pawn*," he said, reading the tattoos between the first knuckles on each of my hands. "What's that mean?"

"That's a secret I don't tell until the third date."

The table guffawed in a cloud of smoke, noise, and color. Will seethed.

Paulie dealt the turn. A six of hearts, and I had my flush.

Oliver whistled between his teeth, and folded. "It's Valentine's Day for someone, but sure as shit ain't me."

Judging by the dull gray around me, no one else had anything good either. Eli, who was too stupid to know when to fold, tried a bluff only a blind man might miss. Three other guys checked, and then the bet was to me.

"Action's on you," Will said, as if I didn't fucking know that.

Will was watching me closely. Despite his being a grade-A asshole, he was a good player; no tells. Except to my *ken*. From the subtle taste of his doubt, I could tell he had an okay hand but that he was wondering if mine was better. Without the *ken* I would have played conservative and guessed he had the better flush. The *ken* showed me he didn't.

I should've just gone all-in, forced everyone else to fold but my head ached like a bastard, and I didn't like the way Will watched me; how his suspicion curled around him thicker than smoke.

"Twenty," I said.

Will saw my twenty and raised fifty. I fought against the pain in my head, the relentless pressure that made my head pound.

"You don't look so good, Nik," Will said with a smirk. "Second thoughts?"

"None." I called his fifty, and took another sip of beer. I felt an itch under my nose and rubbed it with my hand holding the beer. The tattoos on the back of my hand were smeared with red.

*Fuck.*

Paulie dealt the last card, the river. Five of clubs. A garbage card to everyone, including Will. But pride was making his bets; he was in too deep to back out now. The others checked or folded. Will went all-in.

"Dumbfuck," Oliver said. "Nik's got the flush. Why're you pissing your money away like that?"

"He's bluffing," Will said. "He's going to fold like a lawn chair."

I surreptitiously put a cocktail napkin to my nose, careful to keep the blood from showing. It wasn't a lot. If I got out of there quick enough...

"Raise," I said. I didn't need to move my chips into the pile; they were all mine now.

"Fucker," Will said, slamming his palm on the table.

"Told you," Oliver sniffed.

I flipped my hearts over and reached for the pot. Three hundred dollars' worth, which brought my night's winnings to well over six hundred. "Cash me out," I told Paulie. "I'm done."

"The fuck you are," Will said. "You can't just take that much bank without giving us a chance to win it back."

"Yeah, I can," I said, dully, stacking my chips quickly into towers. "I'm coming down with something. Heading out."

Paulie cashed me out in silence, and the small basement felt the way the sky does before lightning strikes, prickling the skin on the surface.

"I don't like you," Will said, jabbing his finger at me like a knife.

"Feeling's mutual."

Will was a grinder like me. A guy who played for a living. I'd probably wind up sitting across from him again someday, and have to watch my ass. He knew I cheated, he just didn't know how. I had to dab my nose again and Will saw the bright red on the white napkin. He narrowed his eyes and rapped his fingers on the empty felt in front of him.

I left the basement through a side door that led up a staircase to the street, riding on a current of resentment and anger from below.

Outside felt no less suffocating than the basement. Atlanta was roaring and I had to get the fuck out of there. I stashed my winnings into one of the two side bags on my Bonneville T100 motorcycle—a 2012 model pushing more than 90k miles—and shrugged into my black leather jacket. I put on my helmet and the visor dimmed the world to gray.

With a spray of gravel, I tore away from the pawnshop, into the early morning just after dawn, and out of Atlanta. The leaden sky threatened rain.

A storm was brewing. A big one.

I imagined it coming down out of the sky, like a huge fist, sweeping me up into its grip and crushing me until there was nothing left.

I drove on and on, and my thoughts wandered into dangerous territory. They'd been doing that a lot lately, on my endless back-and-forth across the country.

It would be so easy to let the bike drift over the line where cars whizzed past me going the other way. To close my eyes and set the motorcycle head-on into the path of a rumbling semi, its air horn blowing in panic because it was too big to get out of the way in time...

Sometimes I thought the only thing stopping me was that I might hurt someone else. Other times, I didn't care, and my wandering thoughts pulled the handlebar along with them, toward that center divide. Or I'd grip the throttle and push the bike faster and faster, until the road was a gray blur that could tear me to shreds; the highway patrol would have to scrape me off the asphalt piece by piece...

The gruesome image was oddly comforting. I didn't want to die but this wasn't living. I wanted an end.

**Savannah, 3 miles**

The sign whipped by in a blur. I pushed my motorcycle past 75 mph, to outrun the coming rainstorm, and put as much distance between me and Atlanta as I could. Signs for Savannah told me to get off the 16 West, but I stayed on until they pointed the way to **Garden City, pop. 8905.** Savannah was too big. I'd drown there, especially after Atlanta. Garden City was small enough.

Even hundreds of miles and four hours later, I could feel Atlanta clinging to me like the sweat and grime of a long road trip. I needed to get back to zero. To dig under the noise and feel *something* that was truly mine. Even if that something was pain.

Before food or even a motel, I found a tattoo place in Garden City, tucked into the corner of a small strip mall. I coasted my Bonneville into the front of *GC Ink and Piercings* and took off my helmet.

Despite the dark gray of storm clouds gathering above, the green of summer was vibrant and alive in the numerous trees that filled the space between shops and the road, and in the grass along the front. Humid air trapped the electric buzz of the cicadas; an unending song of

Georgia in June. Unlike human life, animal life, for whatever reason, didn't assault my every goddamn sense—and the several other annoying senses no one else seemed to have but me. I liked the constant noise of the insects in the South. Like the buzz of a tattoo needle.

Inside the tattoo place it was mercifully cooler, and looked like a barbershop; white floors, dark chairs, plain walls but for framed artists' samples. Two artists were working. A third approached me as I shook out of my black leather jacket and set it and my helmet on a bench near the door. The guy was big and bald, with a red dragon snaking up one arm and disappearing under his shirt.

I could see he was bored and wanted to get the fuck out of Georgia. A gray-green haze of pot smoke infiltrated his thoughts, dulling his urge to skip town.

"What'll it be?" he asked, as if he were a bartender. His gaze swept over the ink of my hands and arms, up my neck, then to the silver talons in my ears. "I can do ink, but our piercing guy is out today."

"Tattoo," I said.

"Right-o."

He led me back to his station, a small cubicle with framed samples of his work all over the wall. On the way, we passed the other tattoo chairs. The customer in the next station over was trying his best not to show it hurt too much. The younger woman in the other was having second thoughts but was too far in to stop now.

"You got any idea of what you want?" the guy asked me.

The words, "Doesn't matter," almost escaped me but I pulled them back. Except for the *pawn* and *hoax* tattoos, the rest of my ink meant nothing. The design wasn't important. It was the pain I wanted.

*Needed.*

My gaze shot around his station, grazing over his samples. I found a Japanese koi fish, bright orange and pink, curling around itself, its scales almost iridescent. I pretended to study a few other samples, then looked at the guy.

"I was thinking of something Japanese," I said. "One of those…what do you call them? The giant goldfish?"

"Koi," the guy said, and moved to tap the sample on the wall I'd seen. "Something like this?"

"Yeah, that's it, man," I said. "That's exactly what I had in mind."

He frowned. "No variations?"

"Make it more orange than pink," I said. "And maybe a Japanese character overlaid on one side in black."

"Which one?" the guy asked, his annoyance thick in his voice. Dull fumes slightly stung my inner eye, the *ken*. "There's like...*a lot.*"

*How about Fuck This Bullshit,* I thought.

"Endurance," I said.

"Can do. I'm Gus, by the way."

"Nik," I said. "How much is this going to run me?"

Gus shrugged. "How big do you want it?"

I held my hands out, as if I were holding an invisible cantaloupe.

"'Bout one-eighty," he said.

"Done."

Despite the way Atlanta tried to drown me, the money I'd won off Will and Co. would add nicely to the $20,000 I had in my bank account—my only tangible connection to the real world. I kept two grand in cash on hand for expenses, plus a $3000 prepaid Visa, fully loaded for online gaming. Point is, I could afford a bigger tattoo, but I was running out of naked skin. I was tatted all over my neck, my entire chest, most of my back, down both arms, and over my hands and fingers. I had only a few on my legs but at this rate, I was going to be decorated full-body long before I hit thirty.

*Then what the fuck will I do?*

The idea of another six years of enduring this goddamn *ken* was going to drive me insane. If something didn't change quick, I wasn't going to make it to thirty. Hell, I wasn't going to make it to twenty-five.

"Ready?" Gus asked, jolting me from my thoughts.

"Yeah, sure."

I took off my black t-shirt and showed him the only patch of blank space I had left on my back—a swath under my left shoulder blade that carried down to my waist.

"Anywhere here is good," I said.

"Right-o."

I stretched out on the chair, resting my head on my arms and closed my eyes, as if I were lying on a beach somewhere, dozing under the sun. Gus readied his ink and needles. He tried to make some small talk about the dozens of other tattoos that decorated my skin, but my responses were short and blunt; he got the message quickly and shut the hell up.

His gloved hand touched my skin, increasing the connection between us, but the latex helped. The buzzing needle helped more, muting the whispers of his thoughts; the colors and tastes of his life. But it was the pain that erased them completely.

The needle bit into my skin, and I concentrated every bit of my awareness there, to feel every second and half-second in between. Tattoo pain was perfect—not unbearable, but not weak either. This artist wasn't particularly gentle, and I relished each stinging moment. It was *my* skin, *my* pain and no one else's.

For nearly two hours, I was free.

When he finished, I lay still for a few moments, reveling in the throbbing ache along the left side of my back.

"Hey, buddy. You fall asleep?"

"No," I muttered against my arm. "I'm…here."

*I'm still here.*

I felt better. Cleaner. I'd bought myself some time. I sat up and grabbed my shirt.

"You maybe want to *see* it?" Gus asked, a smoky cloud of suspicion curling up around him. I got that a lot lately. He was worried I was going to bolt without paying.

For his sake, I took a glance in the mirror. The guy was good. A snarling koi fish glided over my raised, red skin, its scales shimmered in iridescent orange. A black sigil was overlaid on one side. It might have been Japanese for 'endurance' like I'd asked for. It might've read, "The bearer of this tattoo is an asshole." All the same to me.

"Yeah, looks great," I said. As Gus put a bandage over it, I fished out my wallet, and handed him two hundred dollar bills.

"Thanks," I muttered. I threw on my shirt and strode out, hooking my black leather jacket over one shoulder.

Outside, the storm clouds were bunching together like a rugby scrum, ready to roll out. I thought about finding a motel, but there was a Fed-Ex in the same little strip mall as the tattoo shop. I figured I might as well find my next game while I was here.

In the shop, I rented the one computer in a corner so that no one could watch me and found an online poker site. Luckily, the store had no Wi-Fi restrictions and I was able to play. I fed the site the numbers off my prepaid Visa card and joined a game of Texas Hold'em on a local server.

Within minutes, a user under the handle of *TMoney1993* invited me to an underground game in Port Wentworth, just north of Garden City, night after next. I accepted and he PM'd me the address. He probably thought I was easy pickings.

*Sorry, TMoney*, I thought. *But I'm going to clean you out.*

"Sorry?" I muttered at myself in disgust, and logged out. As if a mental apology ever went anywhere. As far as I knew, the sense perception was a one-way street. Despite my frantic online research over the years, I'd never heard of anyone who could do what I could do.

Not one fucking person, anywhere.

---

The motel in Garden City was the same as every other motel I'd ever stayed at over the last few years. They all blended together: double bed, thin carpet, bathroom with its tiny bottles of cheap soap. Even the emotions of the people in adjacent rooms took on the same hues and flavors. I knew who was around me at all times: bored business travelers; parents straining to make the most of a cheap family vacation for their bickering kids; tourists who felt they had to see the world's largest ball of twine before they died.

That's if I was lucky.

Hopelessness and despair are black to my inner eye, and the more remote motels were often filled with the lonely and the desperate. The worst nights were those spent lying in a darkness deeper than the night, the shadowy pain of the person one room over seeping into my motel room like an inky black stain.

*So much misery in the world…*

And all of it shoved down my throat, every waking hour of my life.

I sat on the bed in the motel, listening to the thunder growling louder and the storm gathering power.

The new tattoo's bandage itched. I tore it off and relished the sting but it faded quickly.

*I can't keep doing this…*

I'd had the *ken* for as long as I could remember, and spent years going back and forth between hopeless resignation, and the raging urge to know what it was or if it had a purpose. Back and forth, back and forth, like my road trips across the country…searching for an answer or trying to outrun it.

I stood up and paced the small room. Outside the window, the trees swayed in the dark wind, and the first raindrops began to smatter the glass. My hand went to the Bowie knife I kept strapped to my belt. The dull throb of my newest tattoo was gone.

*It's not working anymore.*

More and more I wondered why I bothered with tattoos, or poker…or anything else.

*You need the poker money to live off of,* whispered a pathetic voice in my head; my own dying sense of self-preservation.

I wasn't *living.* I was on an endless road trip to nowhere. But I had $20,000 in winnings stashed in a bank for no fucking reason that I could tell, except that I had to keep adding to it, making it grow. The savings had become like the *ken;* something whose purpose eluded me. Some big buy-in, maybe? The biggest game of my life? The *last* game of my life? A poker game but with Russian Roulette-sized stakes?

If I won, I would keep going.

If I lost…

*You gotta get off this train of thought before you do something stupid.*

I took my hand from the Bowie knife and grabbed my jacket off the bed. I needed a club. A place where I wouldn't be alone. Where I could be surrounded by people, but their scents, colors and thoughts would be muted by the smell of cologne, pounding music and flashing lights.

I asked the bored-looking guy manning the front desk if he knew a place.

"The closest one's Club 91, just outside Savannah," he said. "Small, but cheap drinks." He gave me a funny look, his curiosity tingeing his words with a taste like citrus. "Can't imagine it'll be hopping tonight, what with the storm and all."

"One way to find out," I muttered.

# Chapter 2

*Fiona*

Business was slow at Garden City Greens. The gathering storm had thinned the traffic on Route 25 that ran along the nursery, and only a few customers strolled the outdoor aisles of plants, trees, and banks of assorted colorful flowers. At the far end, the stock boy, Marco, was up on a ladder, helping a customer amid the stacks of orange pottery.

I helped a regular, Mrs. Paulson, choose a four-foot tall pecan tree for her front yard. As I rang her up, the elderly lady asked me a million questions about the tree's care, the right soil, and the probability of squirrels overrunning her property to get to the nuts. I answered all of her questions until she ran out.

"You know your botany, don't you, dear?" she said finally.

I shrugged and smiled. "I like to take care of things."

"Mmm." For the hundredth time that afternoon, Mrs. Paulson's sharp eyes peered at my waist-length blond hair with its wide swaths of pink streaking through it. Under my Garden City Greens apron, I wore oversized men's coveralls—smeared with soil at the knees—Doc Marten boots, and a sleeveless button-down shirt that revealed the hibiscus tattoo on my right shoulder, and numerous woven bracelets that adorned both arms.

"I know, I look like a farmer who's just gotten back from a rave, right?" I said, grinning.

Mrs. Paulson pursed her lips. "A *what?*"

"Nothing." I hid a laugh and put on my brightest customer service smile. "Do you have someone to plant this for you, Mrs. Paulson?"

"My nephew and his wife are arriving tonight," the elderly woman said. "But for now, I'll need help getting it into my car, preferably before we get drenched."

"I'm on the job," I said.

"It must be awfully heavy," Mrs. Paulson said dubiously, her gaze drawn again to my skinny arms, then glancing about for someone else. "Maybe we can call the stock boy over…?"

I squatted, hefted the tree by the pot. "Lead the way."

I carried the tree out of the wooden structure of the nursery that smelled like rich soil and flowers, across the dirt parking lot. At Mrs. Paulson's maroon sedan, I wedged the tree behind the passenger seat at an angle. Its branches scraped the roof, but it fit.

I dusted my hands on my soil-streaked overalls. "You're all set, Mrs. Paulson."

"I had my doubts, I must admit," the older woman said. "You're such a rail of a girl."

*For God's sake, will you eat something? You're embarrassing me…*

I flinched at the sudden, ugly memory that popped into my mind like a sneering jack-in-the-box. It had to have been pushing ninety degrees but my skin broke out in sudden gooseflesh, and I rubbed my arms.

"I'm stronger than I look," I said to Mrs. Paulson, trying to hold onto my smile.

"Apparently so." She glanced up at the sky and the thickening clouds through a nest of wrinkles around her eyes. "I hope they send you home before this rain starts," she said, climbing into her sedan. "Don't want you to wash away."

I brushed off her little remarks, determined to let nothing and no one—not little old ladies or ghosts of the past—ruin my mood.

Back inside I went to the register where Opal Crawford, the manager, was doing some bookkeeping. Her tightly curled hair was kept off her forehead by a bright scarf and her linen apron was spotless over her turquoise blouse.

I leaned my dirt-smudged elbows on the dirt-smudged counter. "Mrs. Paulson said you should send me home early," I said, with a grin. "And you know what they say; the customer is always right."

Opal smiled, her teeth white against her warm, brown skin. "You might get your wish and then some. I'm expecting Mr. Carlson to call any minute and tell me to shut down the nursery."

My shoulders drooped. "For how long?"

"A few days if the storm is as bad as they say it's going to be."

I chewed my lip. "I'm all for cutting out a little early on a Friday night, but a few days off...? I don't want to lose the hours."

"Speaking of hours..." Opal grabbed a small stack of envelopes from the desk drawer beneath the register, found the one with my name and handed it over. "Thanks to Louisa being out sick, you had a bunch of overtime, but I don't think Mr. C is going to approve much more."

I took my paycheck and tucked it in one of the front pockets of my overalls. "I'm going to *need* more if we close up for several days." I leaned over the counter again, smiling slyly. "I heard Louisa had a relapse. Bad one. Highly contagious. Don't think she should come in for another two weeks..."

"She has a bad cold, not the black plague, and anyway, *no*," Opal said. "I refuse to be your enabler."

"My what?" I laughed.

"You know what," Opal said. "I'm not going to help you save money in order to hightail it out of the country any faster than you already are." She shook her head and made a *tsk tsk* sound with her teeth. "No, ma'am. Won't do it. Miss you too much."

I smiled fondly at my friend. Opal was married and ten years older than my twenty-three years. She was steady and calm while I bounced around the nursery, getting my hands as dirty as possible. Her stiff, linen Garden City Greens apron was always immaculately pressed and clean, while mine was perpetually smudged with dirt. "Our friendship doesn't make any sense," she liked to joke, but somehow we fit. She was my best friend. One of my only friends...

*Ungrateful bitch, what about me? Why am I never good enough?*

I flinched and fought back at the sneering voice in my head. Some days he was silent, and I came close to actually being the cheerful, happy person I tried to project. Other days—like this one—he haunted me, jumping out of the dark corners of my memory, like some sick game of *Gotcha!* I had to fight to keep my cheerfulness, as if I were constantly running under a darkening sky, trying to stay under a patch of sunshine.

*In Costa Rica, there will be only sunshine,* I thought and reached across the counter to nudge Opal's elbow. "You *are* my enabler. You're *enabling* me to make my Costa Rican dream come true."

She sniffed. "You're close aren't you?"

"Yeah, I am," I said and joy bloomed in my chest, casting out the bad memories like a bright light driving away the shadows. "It's looking like six more months and I'll have enough to get situated down there."

Opal started to say something then snapped her mouth shut. "No. Never mind."

"What?" I asked, though I thought I knew.

"Nothing." She brushed off a smudge of dirt I'd left on her sleeve, and went back to work at the register.

"Uh oh," I said, trying to keep it light between us. "You've got that Opal Crawford-mother-bear thing going on again. Every time I talk about Costa Rica—"

"I can't imagine why," she muttered, not looking up from tallying her receipts. "Definitely not because you're all of twenty-three years old, moving thirty-four hundred miles away to a foreign country where you don't speak the language. *All by yourself.* Nope, nothing to do with *that*."

"I'll be fine," I said. "More than fine. It's what I want. A little piece of land surrounded by jungle, with the mountains at my back, and the beach at my feet. How many places on earth have all that?"

Opal raised her rich brown eyes to fix me with a look that was deeper than playful protectiveness. "I just want to know that you're moving there for you," she said slowly. "Not to put more miles between you and *him*."

I froze and then tucked a lock of long pink hair behind my ear. "Why can't it be both?"

Opal's thoughtful look deepened, a clinical, sympathetic gaze with a thousand thoughts behind it. She was going to night school to get a degree in counseling and I know she considered me her extracurricular project, trying to get me to open up about *him.* My ex. Steve Daniels. I'd told her next to nothing about him, only that I'd had an ex (I let her assume he was an ex-*boyfriend*) and that it had ended badly between us. She knew there was more to the story, but I couldn't bring myself to tell it.

*It's too humiliating.*

I didn't want to say the words. To give them life and make those years married to a sociopath real. To admit that I'd been a naïve eighteen-year old, easily manipulated. To confess that he'd charmed me into a whirlwind romance until his charm slipped off like the mask it was, and the manipulative liar emerged to show himself. He lied to me, insulted and belittled me, destroyed my self-esteem and then cried in my lap that I was the only person who understood him. He'd kept control of the money, made me a prisoner, not only in my own house, but in my own *mind.*

Steve had emptied me out of all that I thought I knew about my own self, and filled me back up with doubt, loathing and the inability to trust my own feelings. Costa Rica was everything he was not—green and gold and full of sunshine.

*Find the sunshine…*

"Hey," I said brightly, leaning on my arms over the counter to balance, and kicking my feet up behind me. "I'm going dancing tonight. Want to come?"

"Your change of subject just gave me whiplash." Opal held my gaze a moment more, then let me off the hook. For now. "Since when are you going dancing?"

"Since this minute. Want to?"

"I can't tonight," she said. "Jeff is dragging me to bingo night at the Shriners. Can you believe that? Mrs. Paulson will probably be there for God's sake." She shut the register with a bang.

"Bingo? At Shriners?" I covered my mouth with my hand, sending dozens of woven, multicolored bracelets tumbling down my arm.

"Yeah, yeah, I know," Opal muttered. "But he's volunteering over there, and I figure an extra hand can't hurt."

"You mean, you couldn't resist helping out," I said fondly.

Opal waved that off. "I'm too old to go clubbing anyway," she said. "Too young for bingo at Shriners, too old to go clubbing. Does that make me middle-aged? Already?"

"Definitely," I teased, grabbing a broom to sweep the area in front of the register.

"I'm glad you're going out," Opal said. "Maybe you'll meet some nice guy, hit it off…" She shrugged, her tone straining to be casual. "You've been working here for almost two years and I've never seen you with anyone serious."

"I'm close to Costa Rica," I said quickly. "No sense in starting something now. Wouldn't be fair." I stopped sweeping and leaned on my broom. "On the other hand, it's been ages since I've known the company of a person of the masculine persuasion." I shot her a salacious grin. "A girl's got needs, ya know."

My friend's expression brightened immediately. "You hussy!" she said. "A one-night stand?"

I hesitated. I'd been mostly kidding about my 'needs' but the words spoken aloud had woken them up. It had been years since I'd been with a man. I'd been too focused on my escape from Steve and then saving up for Costa Rica, that I'd neglected that part of the human experience. My body felt neglected of a man's touch. People had one-night stands all the time. I could have one too…couldn't I?

Since escaping Steve two years ago, I'd vowed to live my life by *my* rules, which meant that I didn't have any. If I felt like doing something fun or exciting, I did it. I was done cowering in the shadows. I was going to live out loud. Why not have a one-night stand if I wanted one?

"Yeah, why not?" I said, sweeping up dead leaves from the ficus tree by the door. "One glorious, no-strings-attached night of passion? I could live with that."

A flush of heat swept through me. I could more than live with that, I realized. I missed the weight of a man's hands on my body, or being lost in a haze of ecstasy. Maybe all the whispering voices of the past would be drowned in the presence of someone else. A delicious stranger whom I wouldn't have to know for longer than a night.

"Yeah, I just might do that," I said. "Or see what happens."

Opal glanced at me. "How does a one-night stand work these days, anyway? You pick up some stranger and go to his place?"

"I'm no expert," I said. "But I think it should be at my place. The sun rises the next morning, I stay, he goes."

"Does he have to go?" Opal asked gently.

"Yeah, he does," I replied, holding her gaze, before turning back to my job, pushing the small pile of leaves around and around.

"Not all men are like Steve."

"I know," I said, "but I don't have the ability to tell the difference."

*You're so stupid…a silly little airhead…*

I shook my head and swept harder.

"I need to be in Costa Rica. Once I'm there, I'll be free to just…be. Once I find myself again….No." I shook my head forcefully. "Once I *reclaim* myself, I'll be able to date again. Maybe love again."

The words sounded impossible. The idea of putting my heart into another man's hands, to trust him like that, *felt* impossible.

"I want that for you," Opal said. "I just wish you'd stick around so I could see it."

"It will happen," I said for her sake, finding a smile. "Until then, the salacious one night stand will have to do."

Opal laughed despite herself. I knew she only wanted to help, but only making it to Costa Rica could help me. Getting out of the country could help me. Then I could stop looking over my shoulder every minute.

I'd be free.

"Whatever you want, Fi," Opal said. "I'm just saying, don't close any doors okay?"

"Okay," I said, because it was the easiest thing to say. Much easier than explaining that my life was my own now and I wasn't going to be so foolish as to give it away. Not ever again.

Opal had been right. Mr. Carlson, the owner of the nursery, called and ordered her to shut the place down until the storm passed. Opal hung up with him and turned to me.

"If you could tell Marco we're closing up shop, you're free to go dance the horizontal mambo with your tall, dark stranger."

"Did you seriously just say *horizontal mambo*?" I laughed. "I think bingo night is just your speed after all."

"Oh, hush up your face."

I rounded up the other employees and we closed the nursery. Opal gave me a hug in the parking lot next to my old blue Prius. The sky was a yellowish-gray above us, and grumbling with distant thunder.

"You take care now," Opal said, her mama-bear voice returning. "Don't do anything I wouldn't do."

"You're not leaving me with a lot of options," I teased.

She snorted. "Go. Have fun. Be safe."

I drove off the lot along Route 25, north to the outskirts of Garden City. My apartment complex was small and looked like a one-story motel surrounded by maple and oak trees, as if it were situated in its own little grove in the woods.

On the drive, I pondered my plans for the evening. The idea of a one-night stand sent butterflies fluttering in my stomach and a blush rising to my cheeks. I wondered if Griff and Nate would come with me; be my wingmen.

I parked in front of #4, got out and knocked on #5, glancing nervously at the sky as the storm clouds thickened. The sound of cicadas was a constant backdrop, nearly drowning out the sounds of traffic on Route 25, adding to the seclusion of the complex. I figured the rain was still a few hours off.

Nate Miller opened the door looking ridiculously handsome and preppy in a polo shirt and khaki pants. His short, dark hair was perfectly coiffed and gelled.

"Fiona, darling! Oh God, look at you, you're a mess." He gave me an arm's-length hug to keep the grime from my overalls off his clothes. "You're done hauling mulch and selling grubs for the day?"

"Indeed," I said. "I was wondering if you and Griff wanted to go dancing at Club 91 with me tonight?"

"Honey, I'd love to, but the ball and chain insists we see his friend's play down in Savannah. An experimental theater piece that I'm sure will be *thoroughly* ridiculous, but…" He heaved a sigh. "I promised I'd go."

Griffin appeared at the door, blond hair loose and curling around his ears. He was dressed up too, in stylish jeans and a silk shirt open at the collar. "That's right," he said, gazing at his husband adoringly. "Nathanial has promised to do his part to support the arts."

"*Arts*," Nate said, making air quotes around the word and rolling his eyes.

I laughed. "I guess I'm on my own then."

"For?" Griffin asked.

"Dancing at Club 91." *And picking up a stranger to take home for purely sexual purposes.* I bit my cheek to keep from laughing. A little tingle of excitement slipped down my spine. My life, my rules.

"Rain check, Fi," Griffin was saying. He gave me a peck on the cheek, then glanced at the sky. "Literally. This storm is supposed to be a big one."

Nate frowned. "Maybe you shouldn't drive."

"If you do, don't drink," Griffin added.

"Or call an Uber."

"Or call us."

I waved my hands and shook my head. "Geez, you guys are as bad as Opal. And by *bad*, I mean wonderful and amazing and I love you." I backed down the open walkway to my place, blowing them each a kiss. "Have fun supporting the arts."

"*Fun,* she says," Nate drawled. "Bye, darling."

"Love you, Fi!" Griffin called after.

At my apartment, I started to put the key in the lock when I heard a car honk. I looked up and saw Nancy Davis from #8 and her four-year old daughter Hailey backing out of the parking lot in Nancy's silver SUV. Hailey's little starfish hand waved frantically at me, her smile wide.

I waved back. I babysat for her whenever Nancy needed me too. I'd babysit for her every night if I could. There was nothing better than Hailey's sweet head tucked under mine as she fell asleep, or the smell of her hair, or the way I got to listen to her vocabulary grow with each passing day; a little child growing and learning and making her way in the world…

I'd told Opal that Steve had stolen my ability to trust my own feelings, but that wasn't the worst thing he'd taken from me. The one thing I'd wanted more than anything else.

The pain was swift, like a punch to the gut and I didn't know if it was remembered pain or imaginary.

I choked down a sob, and waved weakly at Nancy as they drove away.

"Goddamn," I whispered. I clutched the doorknob tight until the ache subsided, and I buried it deep before it sunk its teeth into me and ruined my night entirely.

I could run to Costa Rica, or Nepal, or the North Pole and it wouldn't be far enough. I could fill my life with acres of plants and fruit to grow, or care for a thousand animals and it wouldn't matter. The emptiness would still be there. Forever.

I sucked in a breath, unlocked the door and stepped into my little studio. I shut the door behind me and imagined I was shutting Steve and those awful years out too. I felt safe in my perfectly square-shaped apartment. The bathroom and my bed were situated to the right of the door, the kitchen was along the left wall, and a small living area was across from that. An old and expansive window framed a full view of the oak and maple trees that ringed the complex.

Aside from the super-cheap rent that allowed me to save up for Costa Rica, it was that view that sold me on the place two years ago. I could pretend I was already in my forest, far away from civilization, and surrounded by lush greenery and wildlife. And because the interior wasn't much to look at, I used dozens of potted and hanging plants as my décor.

Lemony Snicket trilled a greeting from his cage by the window. My little canary hopped from one bar to another and back again, his yellow wings fluttering.

I went to his cage and put my fingers to the bars. "Hello, sweet boy," I cooed. He pecked at them gently, once, before hopping away.

"Storm's coming," I said and unhooked his cage from the window. "I'll move you over here so you don't get scared by the lightning, okay?"

I set the cage on the kitchen counter, and whistled at him. He sang back. Outside, thunder rumbled distantly.

"Big storm," I muttered. "Maybe I should stay in after all…"

*Where did you go? Out? Alone? And you didn't ask me first?*

I clenched my teeth. "I'm going," I said. I turned to Lemony in his cage. "I want to go out, so I'm going out. And if I want to bring a man home, I'll do that too."

Hearing the words aloud helped to strengthen my resolve against the relentless ghost of my ex-husband. I wondered if he could be considered an ex-husband when I never actually filed for divorce.

"*Yes*," I answered aloud, and reminded myself that I'd mentally annulled our marriage a long time ago.

"A marriage," I told Lemony, "is supposed to be a pact between two people who love and care for one another. It's not supposed to be used to bully them, take their money, and trap them in their own home. Am I right or am I right?"

Lemony hopped back and forth.

I opened the fridge for some dinner. "He's far away and I'm here, and I'm going to bring someone home tonight because I'm a grown woman," I said, pulling a fresh head of lettuce, a bag of peas, and an ear of corn from my refrigerator. I set them on the counter, a small grin finding its way to my lips. "I apologize in advance, Lemony, for what you might witness tonight, but I need a little physical affection. Or a lot, actually."

A flush of heat swept over my skin, warming away the chill of Steve's voice echoing in my mind.

I chopped lettuce, shelled peas, and stripped the kernels off the cob with a knife, and dumped it all into a bowl. I poured ranch dressing on it and plunked into the stool at the counter to eat. The bowl was filled with a mound of greens and corn, but still…it was only a salad.

*That's all you're eating? Jesus…*

"Yes," I answered, forking a huge bite. I never had much of an appetite and my metabolism was fast. I could eat a ton of food and never gain weight—

*Anorexic bitch…*

I winced and the food turned to clay in my mouth. I swallowed with effort.

"How about some music?" I asked my bird.

I pulled up iTunes on my phone, and soon Fiona Apple's "Criminal" filled my small space. I liked that song. It was about a woman toying with a man's heart, not the other way around. I loved Fiona Apple; her rich voice, her smart poetry, her sound…

Even her name.

I ate every bite of my salad, even though I started to feel full before I was halfway done. I forced myself to finish, hating that the last bite felt like a defeat when it should have been a victory.

*No,* I thought, dumping the bowl in the sink. Tears stung my eyes but I blinked them back. *There's no victory or defeat; it's just a damn salad.*

Thunder boomed again, closer this time, and the sky was dark outside the window. I fought to find my good mood again; the desire to dance and have fun was still there. Like always, I just had to dig through the remnants of Steve's manipulations to get to it, like a coal miner covered in black soot and choking on ash, trying to find the diamonds beneath.

"Screw him," I muttered.

I headed to my little bathroom. Under the spray in my pink-tiled shower, I washed the grime of work off me, and hummed to myself, to keep the memories from sneaking back in. That was another reason I loved the loud noise and pounding music of a club—it drowned out the insidious whispers and filled me up with music instead.

I'd found my smile by the time I got out.

I wrapped one towel around my long hair, and another around my body, and perused my little closet for something to wear. I found a cotton lace slip dress that went to just above my knee and put it on. I didn't need a bra—my boobs were too small to bother most days—but tonight the choice was a conscious one.

*God, you look like a boy,* Steve laughed in my mind, in that offhanded way he had of saying something devastating with a smile on his face. *If you want to get some enhancements, you won't hear any complaints from me.*

"Shut up, asshole," I said, inspecting myself in the mirror. "What do you think?" I asked Lemony.

He chirped with what I had to assume was, *You look stunning.*

"Thank you," I said. It didn't escape me that I was imagining my pet canary saying nice things about me.

*Pathetic. You're too emotional. Grow a backbone for God's sake.*

I turned the music back on to drown out those words... I didn't know if they were Steve's or mine.

I brushed my hair so that it fell down my back in its soft, natural waves, highlighted in swaths of pink. I put on my dozens of woven bracelets, perfume, and a tiny touch of makeup that made my blue eyes stand out.

"You look pretty," I told the girl in the mirror. She almost believed me.

I flopped on the couch, my purse in my lap, and dug my driver's license out of my wallet. The bouncer at Club 91 was going to look at it. I turned it this way and that, watching the light catch the iridescence that was imbedded into it.

It looked so real.

There was my photo with the name Fiona Starling beneath it, and a date of birth. Not my date of birth, but close enough. The age was right, anyway.

My paycheck had fallen onto the couch. I picked it up and glanced at the numbers again, then opened my laptop and logged into my bank account. I had $13,000 saved up. $10,000 had come from the money I'd taken from Steve the day I left. I could have cleaned out the account and left Steve with nothing, but I only took what was mine; the money my father had left me when he died, and not one penny more.

I did some mental math with the numbers on my paycheck, subtracting for rent and expenses and added the remainder to my savings.

"Six more months," I told Lemony. "I figure we'll be at $15,000 in six months, and then Costa Rica, here we come."

*You wouldn't survive one day in the real world without me. And if you tried, I'd find you...*

I bit my lip and opened a Chrome window in an incognito tab. I glanced around, as if Steve or a cop or a detective could magically materialize behind me. My hands shook slightly as I typed a name and 'Duluth, Minnesota' into the search bar.

The only news item was the same one I'd seen a hundred times, from the *Duluth Courier*. It was two years old and hadn't been updated. I scanned the article quickly for the words that soothed my jumpy nerves and quelled the fear in my stomach...

*Investigators have called off the search...*

*Husband distraught...*

*"She just disappeared."*

I inhaled through my nose, my chin thrust forward, my urge to go out and have fun and be with a man if I wanted to, all came roaring back.

*No rules. Live out loud. Find the sunshine.*

I snapped the laptop shut.

"I'm stronger than I look."

# Chapter 3

## Nikolai

The rain, which was little more than a drizzle when I left the motel, had become a downpour as I pulled the Bonneville under an overhang of Club 91's small parking lot. Only a dozen cars or so filled the spots but I could hear the music pounding under the sound of pelting rain.

At the front entrance, I flashed the bouncer my ID and ducked into the smallish space. Two dozen people were dancing under an array of colored lights to electronica music. The heat was concentrated, like a greenhouse; the air conditioner was scarcely keeping it bearable, but I eased a sigh of relief. The music infiltrated my head with its pulse, driving out the flux of life that surrounded me. The lights that crisscrossed the floor muted the smoky colors and haze of the dancers. I almost felt normal.

At the bar, I took a stool at one end and ordered a bottle of beer. I sat backwards to lean my elbows on the bar and watch the crowd of hard-core electronica fans that weren't about to let a storm keep them from jumping up and down all night. They were clumped together, slowing down with the music, then getting amped up when the DJ let the beat drop.

Except for her.

A young woman in white danced by herself as if she were the only person in the club—or on earth. And for a short moment, it felt as if she was. I saw only her; the way her lithe, willowy body moved to the music. It was a pulsing, techno-dance beat but this girl swayed and undulated like a long coil of seaweed swaying in clear waters.

I thought it was the trick of the lights at first, but no, her hair was dyed pink. The color of cotton candy. It flowed down her back, almost to her waist, in long ribbons like silk. She was ballerina-thin, and her white summer dress highlighted the delicate swell of her breasts and brushed the tops of her thighs. Sandals wrapped around her ankles with straps of hemp. All the while, her skin glistened like diamond dust under the changing lights and reflected shimmers of iridescent pink.

I watched, transfixed, as she lifted her hair off her neck, eyes closed, a smile playing over her lips. For a handful of beats she danced like that, her breasts pushing against her dress, stealing my breath, then she let her hair fall to cascade down her back.

Without thinking, I grabbed a pen on the bar next to someone's credit card receipt, and a cocktail napkin. I watched the girl and my hand sketched her face on the napkin, her head turned up, her eyes closed, that sweet, easy smile…

I looked down at what I'd drawn in awe. I hadn't drawn anything—or painted anything—in years. I used to like to paint—I thought it might be something I could do with my life that had meaning. But the hospital burned it out of me. For long years, I hadn't even thought of touching a brush, yet here I was, sketching this girl.

But the pen's ink was black and she was full of color…

A guy moved to dance in front of her, close to her, and a sudden, crazy urge to knock the fucker on his ass surged through me. I set the drawing aside and grabbed for my beer, my hand clenching the bottle tight.

The woman's eyes opened and she was unsurprised to find she had a partner. The guy bent to shout something in her ear and she nodded, but her body language shifted slightly; a small retreat that only I noticed. I didn't need the *ken* to tell me she wasn't interested in more than dancing.

Her eyes found mine. Locked on mine. She was still looking at me when the guy put his hands on her hips and sidled closer to her. They danced pressed together, and as they turned, I saw his hand inch toward her ass.

I took a long slow pull from my beer, hoping the cold would quench the fire that roared in me.

*Why the fuck do you care?*

I didn't know why, only that I did.

They turned, and the woman cocked her head at me, a funny little smile on her lips. Her eyes still on mine, she abruptly left her dance partner to stare after her, and crossed the distance between us.

My pulse jumped in my chest, while at the same time a sense of calm washed over me, like a cool breeze on a stifling day. Instantly. It would have been shocking had it not felt so good. The woman's white dress clung to her body. Sweat glistened on her neck, and up close it was apparent she wasn't wearing a bra. I wanted to touch her, to take more of that serenity she exuded and keep it for myself.

*You're imagining things,* I told myself. But the calm was real. In a small, heated club with pounding music and the lives of other people swirling thickly, the instant this woman came near, it all melted away.

"Not a dancer?" she asked.

"Not much," I replied.

Up close, her eyes were the bluest blue. Sky blue, or cornflower, I'd heard it called. In the dim of the club they were electric, and met mine with a mix of nervousness and something like defiance, as if she were fighting to keep her confidence from being stolen away from her.

"I was hoping you would," she said, softly. "Dance, I mean. With me."

Her words should have been lost under the pulsing music but I heard every one of them, and the way she spoke…Almost shyly but meeting my gaze unflinching. It sent my pulse into rapid fits while my groin tightened painfully.

"Settle for a drink?" I asked, watching a bead of sweat trickle down her neck to disappear into the valley between her small breasts.

"I suppose that'll do," she said. "I'm Fiona."

"Nik," I said, and signaled the bartender over. "Whatever she wants."

"Cosmo with a cherry," she said. She sat on the stool beside mine, and swiveled toward me, crossing her long legs with an easy grace. "Cosmopolitans aren't 'in' anymore but that doesn't mean they aren't still delicious."

As the bartender set down a martini glass filled with pale pink liquid in front of Fiona, the guy from the dance floor appeared behind her.

"Hey!" his face was twisted with frustration. He shot a glance at me then glared down at Fiona. "Fucking rude to walk away, you know?"

She turned her head slowly, her voice stiff. "Free country."

"So?" the guy said. "Still fucking rude."

Fiona ignored him, meeting my eye then casting her gaze to her drink.

"Hey," the guy said, tapping her shoulder. "I'm talking to you…"

Fear flared up around Fiona, a quick flash that smelled of hot carbon. She recoiled from his touch in a way that caused rage to boil up in me with shocking speed.

She didn't like it and so I didn't like it. At all.

"*Hey*," I said loudly, jerking the guy's eyes to mine. I calmly set my beer on the bar. "You want to dance?"

"What?" The guy blinked stupidly. "Not with y—"

I shot off the stool and gripped the guy by the collar of his shirt. His shock curled around me as I drove him backward, taking long strides that forced him to backpedal. I steered him onto the dance floor, jostling other dancers out of my way, then hauled his face close to mine.

"If you ever fucking touch her again, I'll break your face."

I didn't wait for a reply; the sallow yellow of his fear—the color of piss—was vivid enough. I released his shirt with a final shove, and left him standing in the center of the dance floor.

At the bar, Fiona toyed with the cherry in her drink, a small smile on her lips. "Guess we won't be seeing him again."

I sat down next to her and took a pull from my beer. "I miss him already."

She breathed a genuine laugh and held my gaze. Everything about her was pink; her drink, her hair, the bright halo of glimmering dust that surrounded her.

Kindness, compassion, charity. Those were the feelings I associated with pink.

I hadn't seen it this strong in anyone in a long time.

Fiona clinked her glass to my bottle. "Thanks for taking care of my over-eager dance partner, Nik. And for the drink."

"Sure."

She sipped her Cosmo. "Not much of a talker, are you?" Her eyes were impossibly bright, her smile showing a broad mouth and full lips.

"Club's not a great place for talk," I said.

"True," she said, "but here we are."

*Here we are…*

A short silence fell.

"Nik," Fiona mused. "Nik, Nik," she said again, in a light, sing-song manner. "Short for Nicholas?"

"Nikolai," I said.

"Oh, I like that." Her colors warmed and sweetened, like an invitation, drawing me closer. "Are you Russian? You don't have an accent."

"My mother is."

"Do you speak it?"

"Yeah," I said. "I picked some up."

She scooted closer on her seat. "Say something in Russian."

"Like what?"

"I'm not picky. I can't speak a word so anything is going to sound good."

I thought for a second and then spoke aloud the only thought I had in my head.

"Ti samaya krasivaya devushka na svete."

Fiona's smile widened and the bright wisps of her happiness wrapped around me. I wanted to take in more of it. Which made no sense at all. With other women, their scents were so often cloying and unwanted like the air wasn't mine to breathe.

*What the fuck is wrong with you? Get a grip.*

I sucked down a long swig of beer. Fiona watched me, her eyebrows raised, then she laughed. "Um, Nik? You realize you're supposed to tell me what you said, right?"

I shrugged and my lips twitched. "Don't remember."

Fiona laughed again. "Liar."

We both took a sip from our drinks and let a little silence fall between us. A nice silence.

"That was lovely, your Russian," Fiona said eventually. "Whatever you said, it sounded…sexy."

My gaze swung to her eyes. "Yeah?"

She tucked a lock of hair behind her ear. "Yeah. I was going to say something harmless like 'unique' or 'exotic', but I'd rather be honest with you, Nikolai. I don't like playing games." Her brow furrowed slightly. "I don't like it at all."

I sensed a shadow starting to creep over her. Something old and full of pain. Driving it away suddenly became my only goddamn purpose in life.

"I guess you're not going to like me much then," I said. "I play games constantly. Every day."

A smile crept over her lips. "Is that so?"

"Sure," I said. "Omaha, Texas Hold'em, stud, draw, lowball, high-low split…"

She laughed, flaring pink again, and the shadow around her retreated. "A joke and a smile too. I was beginning to wonder if you ever smiled."

I shrugged. "It happens."

"And those games, they're all poker, right? You play poker every day?"

"Not every day. Most days."

"For a living?"

"No, I'm a…" I coughed. "I'm a salesman. Motorcycle parts. I travel a lot for the job, and finding poker games in each city is sort of my hobby."

My standard lie, though I hated laying it on her. I knew plenty of grinders who lived off their poker winnings, but that was for the love of the game. I played because thanks to the *ken* it was easy to win, and I'd never cared that it was cheating. It was the only way to put my strange ability to use that I knew of, and it allowed me to give a big *fuck you* to the universe for cursing me with it in the first place.

But lying to Fiona felt dirty. Even when haunted by bad memories she was luminous, while I was tatted and stained, as if the ink on my hands would bleed out and onto the white of her dress if I touched her.

She cocked her head at me, wearing a perplexed little smile. "You don't look like a salesman." Her eyes drifted over my tattooed arms and neck, to the talons piercing my ears. "When I think of 'traveling salesman' I picture a middle-aged guy in a suit with a suitcase full of encyclopedias."

"No suitcase," I said. "Catalogues and order forms."

"And you travel a lot?"

"Almost non-stop."

"That sounds lonely."

"You do something long enough, you get used to it."

"I know what you mean," Fiona said, a tinge of darkness around her words—that shadow started to creep back until she buried it. "But the poker makes it fun?"

"Breaks up the monotony of the road."

"Do you make a lot of money?" she said, then laughed, beautiful in her self-consciousness. "Sorry, I'm not asking for your bank balance,

I just meant, are you any good at it?"

"I'm really fucking good at it," I said.

Her eyebrows shot up and she nudged my arm with a laugh. "If you don't say so yourself."

"Maybe I feel like being honest with you too." I could feel where she touched me, a tingling heat that was slow to fade.

"I like that." She swirled her cherry around in her drink by its stem. "So are you in town, selling motorcycle parts, for very long?"

"Couple of days."

"I hope the storm doesn't put a damper on your business."

"It won't."

"You're lucky. At my job, we've been given the next few days off."

"You sound bummed about that."

"Every penny counts." She met my eye. "I'm moving out of the country very soon and want to save up."

I took a sip of my beer. I'd known Fiona for five minutes, but the idea of her moving any further away than her seat at the bar filled me with inexplicable dread.

*What the fuck is wrong with you?*

But it wasn't what was *wrong* with me, anymore. It was what was right. The girl exuded a calm that danced along my skin, and when I inhaled, it was like breathing in the scent of something delicious but far away. The thrumming life all around me grew quiet. For the first time, I felt close to peace, and I wanted more.

*If I touched her...*

"Nikolai?" Her blush matched the color of her drink. She rested her chin in her hand. "Not to sound cheesy but you're undressing me with your eyes."

I felt heat creep along my neck and a bumbling apology rose to my mouth. Instead, I held her gaze, leaned closer to her. "You want to know what I said to you in Russian?"

Her eyes were bright and I could feel her draw closer to me. "Yes. Tell me."

"I said that you're the most beautiful woman I've ever seen."

The deep pink of her darkened to red. Not the ugly red of hate or anger, but the heated red of intense want. Hers matched mine. I wanted that strange sense of peace she exuded, but I wanted to touch her too. To take her hard and lose myself in her completely.

Fiona held my gaze. "I don't think that's true, but the way you look at me…I can almost believe it. Like how you watched me on the dance floor. I liked you watching me, Nikolai. It was as if I could feel your eyes on me before I found you."

*You found me…*

Her gaze landed on the sketch I'd done of her on the cocktail napkin. "Is this…me?" She raised her wide eyes to mine. I braced myself for her anger or wariness, that some total stranger had drawn her while she wasn't looking. But she took the napkin in her hand gently, like she didn't want to damage it.

"This is me," she said.

"It's…just…nothing…"

"Not to me," she said. "Can I keep it?"

"Yeah, sure."

"You're talented, Nikolai."

I shook my head, took a sip of beer.

"And modest too," she said, tucking the sketch into her bag. "I'm going to be honest with you, Nikolai…" She stopped and cocked her head again. "What's your middle name? Is it Russian too?"

"Alexei," I said.

"I felt something was missing," she said. "I'm going to be honest with you, Nikolai Alexei, I don't take strange men home with me on the regular. Hardly at all, actually. Or…never."

My pulse was hammering in my goddamn chest. "Okay."

"And I came here tonight with a vague plan that I might do just that…if I met the right person. Just for one night…" She blushed as if she were shy but her eyes held mine, unwavering. "I felt kind of silly about it earlier, but now…"

"Now?"

She looked at me once, then twice before turning back to her drink. "I'm a little bit surprised at how I feel right now," she said. "I feel…like I want to get somewhere and be alone with you as fast as humanly possible."

I swallowed hard. "I could live with that."

Holy hell, if that wasn't an understatement. I'd never wanted a woman so badly in my life. My eyes couldn't stay off of Fiona; they swept across her body, her flimsy dress, and the sweat that glistened on her neck. The way her skin glowed in the neon light gave her an otherworldly appearance; pale and translucent but lined in pink. A few strands of her hair stuck to her cheek like spun sugar.

*I'll bet she tastes as sweet too…*

"It's not like me to pick up strange men at clubs," she said again. "It's…surprising."

Caution and wariness twined with the heat of her attraction that was wrapping around me, making it hard to think.

"What do you need from me?" I blurted.

She was in the process of taking a sip and laughed a little, spilling a rivulet of vodka and juice down her chin. "Helpful, aren't you? What do I need…?" she mused, dabbing a cocktail napkin on her lips, then down over the sweat that beaded on her chest. "Reassurance, maybe. That we've made the requisite amount of small talk."

"What we do, or don't do, is no one's business but our own," I said.

She nodded. "So long as we're on the same page. Do you know what I mean, Nikolai?"

"Yeah, I do."

"My place. One night. That's it."

I'd have agreed to cutting off my arm if it meant I could touch her. "Whatever you want," I said hoarsely.

Fiona's eyes went to my mouth, and her lips parted with a little sigh that I felt more than heard. The sweet heat of her desire for me thickened around me like steam.

"What I want…" she whispered, her gaze trailing over my chest, my shoulders, up to my eyes where she held my gaze intently. "I don't want to talk anymore."

I tossed a twenty on the bar and followed Fiona out of the club.

On the street, the rain was pouring down in sheets, hammering the concrete, each drop exploding as it hit the cars parked in the lot. The sound was almost as loud as the music had been. We stopped under the overhang on the sidewalk.

Fiona's assuredness slipped and she bit her lip, her eyes on the rain.

I looked down at this woman, my hands clenching into fists to keep from touching her. "We don't do anything you don't want," I said against the pouring rain. "Say the word, and I walk away."

I held her gaze and I felt when she knew I was telling the truth. Her smile returned, one side curving up, as she looked to the street.

"I have this philosophy, Nikolai," she said. "Life is short. You have to make the most of it, every minute of your life. Don't you agree?"

"I guess."

"I keep a kind of bucket list and I add to it every day, whenever I think of something I'd like to do but haven't yet. I add it to the list, do it, and then cross it right off."

The rain crashed down and Fiona stepped out from under the overhang and into the downpour. The water drenched her instantly, turning her white dress translucent. It clung to her body, revealing everything. She watched me watching her; her lips parted slightly and the deep red of her passion tasted like a lick of fire in my mouth.

"Tell me, Nikolai Alexei..." She lifted her hair off her neck, turning her face to the sky. "Have you ever kissed a stranger in the rain?"

"No."

"Neither have I," she said. "But it's on my list."

I crossed to her in three long strides. Every nerve cell in my body screamed to put my hands on her, to kiss her hard and taste the sweetness of her; to take that peace she exuded and swallow it down.

But she needed something else. A slice of reassurance to balance the pulsing need.

I took her face in my hands, the rain drenching us both. Her eyes were impossibly blue under the yellow streetlamps, and her mouth parted in a little gasp of surprise. I felt my own brows come together, searching her open face, as if I could find the answers to my questions in the curve of her cheek or the soft glow of her skin.

I gently laid my lips to hers, tasting rainwater, and then the sweetness of her. Even in a deluge of rain, kissing Fiona was like tasting candy under a sun at midday. Warmth and sweetness suffused me.

Fiona kissed me back, hesitant at first, and then she melted into the kiss. She explored my mouth with hers, tasting me with soft sweeps of her tongue, until she was satisfied.

"My place," she said, breathing quickly. "Now."

Fiona took her car, an old blue Prius. I followed her on the Bonneville to a small apartment complex. The building was old and plain, but backed against a small forest of trees that were heavy with rainfall, the wind dragging their branches across the sky.

Wordlessly, I followed Fiona to her apartment where she hurriedly found the house key from her ring. She stopped, turned to me before opening, her eyes bright, cheeks flushed. I could hardly breathe myself, and my hands itched to touch her.

"You must wear a condom, no exceptions," she said, her voice hard but breathy at the edges. "Okay?"

"Of course. "

"*No* exceptions."

"I got it."

"One last thing…"

"Name it."

She laid her hand on my chest, over my heart. "Don't hold back. What you are…this…" She pressed her hand harder. "I want this. You. The power of you." She looked up at me, her eyes dark with yearning. "I want all of it."

I nodded like the mute, mindless animal I was fast becoming, and she opened the door.

Inside, I was dimly aware of the smallness of her place that smelled green with plants or flowers. Fiona shut the door behind her and pushed my jacket off my shoulders as I moved close to her, as close as I could. Our lips were almost touching as we breathed each other in.

Our mouths brushed once, twice…and then crashed together. The sweet taste of her flooded my senses as she kissed me hard, demanding, her tongue sliding against mine in brazen strokes. Her hands wove into my hair at the back of my head and she pressed against me, moaning softly.

My body responded at once; my erection painful in my jeans. I filled my hand with her hair, pulling gently, then down her back, to her ass. She moaned and my hand slipped under the hem of her skirt, to slide up her thigh.

"Yes," she whispered against my mouth. "This. I want this…"

The heat of her desire burned away the last of my control. I slammed her up against the wall, my mouth crushed to hers, my hands roving, grabbing, taking. She kissed me back just as hard—with biting teeth and deep sweeps of her tongue. Everything I gave, she took—my rough hands, my mouth that mauled hers, my stubble that left her delicate skin red and swollen. Her body was mine but I felt how badly she wanted *me* too; how fearless she was under my onslaught. It jacked up my need for her. I thought I'd lose my fucking mind if I couldn't have her.

She had what I wanted—what I *needed*—and every touch brought me closer to it. Being inside her would be a miracle.

Up against the wall, I lifted her dress off of her, and tossed it aside.

She watched me take in her nearly naked body. I filled my eyes with the sight of her breasts, small and perfect.

"Krasivaya," I growled, and put my mouth on one nipple, sucking and nipping, while my hand found the other.

"What does that mean?" she asked breathlessly, but with self-consciousness tugging at her. Someone—some fucking asshole—had made her feel bad about her body before. Many times. It was ingrained in her now, and I wanted to fucking rip it out.

"You're beautiful," I told her fiercely. "Every part of you…so fucking beautiful."

I kissed any response she might have had, and tasted her instead, that sweetness that burned hot with her own desire. Her fingernails raked down my back, grasping, then tugging at my shirt. I pulled away long enough to tear it off and then kissed her again. Her arms went around my neck, her hips pressed against mine, and now—skin-to-skin—the connection I felt to her intensified until I was dizzy.

*Need you…*

Physical contact sometimes gave me a person's actual thoughts and I hated it. Hated the invasion. Not this time. Fiona's whispered thoughts were like feathery kisses in my mind. She wanted me too, just as I was, and I'd never wanted anything so badly in my life until that second—one fleeting second—where I'd die for her if I could just have this…

My hand slipped between her legs to find her panties, and they were damp under my fingers. I tore them off.

"Yes," she cried against my neck. "Yes, Nik, yes…This is what I want…"

I couldn't get my pants undone fast enough, and when I did, her hand was there, stroking me.

"Oh my God," she whispered, her eyes widening as she gazed down at me.

Through the red haze of my need for her, I remembered a condom. I yanked my wallet from my back pocket and fished one out just as my jeans fell to my ankles. I tore the wrapper with my teeth, spit out the corner, and rolled the condom down. I lifted Fiona, my mouth crushed to hers again, her legs going around my waist.

"Nikolai…" she breathed, "Now. Hurry…"

*Yes, now. Right now, or I'll fucking die…*

I pushed inside her, and my eyes fell shut, my face buried in her neck while the sensation of her tight heat wrapped around me, swamped me. The need for her, the intense *want* was like a ferocious addiction; she was the drug my body had to have. And that essence or lifeblood or marrow of her—whatever it was that silenced the chaos of emotion that perpetually raged in me—I had it. With this woman, deep inside her, skin to skin in a hundred places, her mouth breathing into mine with every kiss, her tight, wet heat clenched around me…I finally had it.

"This," I growled. "Just this…"

"Yes," she answered. "This…"

I drove into her, hard and fast, again and again, with nothing more than mindless want and ravenous hunger. I was a glutton for that peace, yet I took it with an almost violent force. I kissed her, a short, shallow mashing of my mouth to hers, and tried to slow down before I hurt her, or scared her. But Fiona…fucking hell, this woman. She was taking everything I gave and asking for more. Her fingernails scraped the bare skin of my back, then down, to claw at my waist, my ass, digging in and pressing me harder. I held her under her thighs like she weighed nothing, and her legs were wrapped so tight around me it felt like she'd never let go. I didn't want her to.

"Yes," she hissed, her mouth stealing a deep, hard kiss, before letting her head fall back against the door. "Just like that. Just like…oh God…Don't stop."

I pistoned against her until I was nearly there, and then slowed down to hard, driving thrusts, one after another, pounding into her body. She took all of me, and yet with every crash of my hips against hers, words begging for *more* fell out of her mouth, punctuated by cries that grew louder and louder.

Finally, I felt her clench around me, her nails digging painfully into the flesh of my shoulders, and I relished that pain, better than a thousand tattoo needles. My body devoured the pain as I felt like I was devouring her, taking and taking…

She came then, her teeth sinking into my neck for a hard second, and then she threw her head back and released a cry out of her throat. I felt my own climax tighten in my groin like a fist and then explode out, into Fiona.

She held me with arms and legs and a searching mouth that found mine just as I came harder than I had ever had in my fucking life. She took all of it, in her body, in her mouth, through her skin, and through the thick haze of ecstasy.

As the shudders rippled through us, I held Fiona against the wall, my breath gusting over her neck while hers was hot over my chest, her forehead pressed to my shoulder. For a few long moments, we just breathed and I reveled in the silence.

The absolute quiet of the world that now consisted of only her and me.

# Chapter 4

## Nikolai

We held each other, catching our breath as the aftershocks of our orgasms rocketed through us. Slowly, reluctantly, I eased Fiona's feet to the floor. I slipped out of her and a little sound of loss escaped her lips. She looked up at me, her eyes bright and unwavering.

"You are something, aren't you?" she said with a tired laugh. She brushed the hair that had fallen over my eyes, a gentle, sweet touch. Then she kissed me softly and gave me a playful push away, breaking our contact.

Her skin was red in swaths across her neck and chest where my stubble had burned her; her lips were red and swollen. I stopped her from walking past me, reached out to touch the cut on her lip that my biting teeth had left.

"I'm sorry."

She laid a fingertip to the stinging scratches on my shoulder left by her nails and smiled coyly. "I give as good as I get. Besides, you think I saw you at the club, tatted up and pierced, with that hungry look in your eye and thought to myself, 'He's going to be an angel in the sack'?"

Fiona laughed and let her palm cup my cheek, before moving toward the bed, kicking off her sandals as she went. She toed the torn remnants of her thong and shot me an amused smirk. "You're lucky this wasn't a favorite."

I slipped into the tiny bathroom off the kitchen, disposed of the condom, pulled up my jeans and reached for my shirt. I didn't want to leave, but it's what I did. It's what was supposed to happen.

"It's raining buckets and your clothes are wet," Fiona said when I came back out. She had slipped naked into bed and had drawn the sheet only up to her waist. She lay back on the pillows, her pink hair damp and fanned out, spilling over her breasts. "Beer's in the fridge. Or if you want something to eat, help yourself."

*Stay. Better than that motel.*

A good excuse—good enough to cover the fear that the second I walked out the door, away from Fiona, that raging din of other people's lives would roar up in me again.

It was quiet here.

I didn't want to go.

I got a beer from the fridge. "You want one?"

Fiona slipped down to lay on her side, her cheek on her pillow, watching me. "No, thank you. You wore me out."

I chugged half the beer and then set the bottle on the counter beside a birdcage. The small yellow bird inside stared at me with beady black eyes. I stared back.

"Yeah, it's coming down hard," I said, wearing my poker-face.

"Stay," Fiona said softly from the bed. "For the night."

That was important to her. One night only, take it or leave it.

I took it.

"I guess I could sleep."

Fiona reached her arm around and patted the empty space behind her. "I won't bite." She laughed as my fingers went automatically to the teeth marks on my neck. "Okay, maybe that's not entirely true. But can you blame me? You're delicious. But you're safe now. I'm going to pass out as soon as you turn out that light."

I flipped the switch, plunging her small place into darkness, and moved to the other side of the bed. I stripped down to my boxers.

"Good night, Nikolai," Fiona said, her back to me, her voice heavy. In the dimness, I could see a tattoo that poured down her back— a spray of wildflowers in brilliant colors, with an uncannily realistic bee that buzzed among them.

I turned my gaze to the ceiling. This part of the one-nighter was supposed to be easy. I got up and left or I fell asleep with the unwanted residue of the woman's emotions clinging to me like cheap perfume. Tonight was different.

I lay beside Fiona in the quiet, her side rising and falling evenly, but she wasn't asleep yet. The light of her awareness was dimming and flaring with thoughts. Instead of feeling assaulted or invaded, the taste of those thoughts was sweet on my tongue, and the colors of her emotions beautiful—not blinding—as they swept across the *ken*.

*Normal. I feel normal.*

Or as close to it as was possible for me. With Fiona, the *ken* wasn't a torture. That's the best I could ever hope for—short of it vanishing altogether.

*Why? Why her?*

"Nikolai…" she said softly in the dark.

"Nik. Just Nik," I said, fighting to keep my confusion from curdling to frustration. The mystery of the goddamn *ken* had added a new plot twist.

"Okay. Just Nik," Fiona said, her back still to me. "Your full name is beautiful. I can't promise I won't slip."

"No, forget it," I said, immediately feeling like an ass. "Call me whatever you want."

Fiona rolled over to face me, and the peaceful calm rolled over with her, erasing the frustration. The pink halo of her inherent sweetness filled my eyes. Her lips parted as if to say something, but she changed her mind, and laughed lightly, shaking her head against the pillow.

"Nothing. Goodnight…Nik." She turned away again.

*She wants more.*

Not the roughness of earlier, but something else. Softer touches, softer kisses. This was supposed to be her tawdry one-night stand and she didn't know how to ask for anything else.

Thanks to the *ken,* she didn't have to.

I moved closer to her, so close that I could feel the heat of her body along mine. I lifted the long, damp locks of her hair off her neck, and put my mouth on her skin between her shoulder blades.

She stirred, shivering slightly.

I kissed her again, open-mouthed, tasting her and breathing over her hotly. And again, along the stalks of wildflowers, my tongue swirled over the petals.

Fiona shivered and released a breathy little moan. "Oh, Nik…For me that's a…what do you call it? An erogenous zone."

Her voice fell apart as my mouth moved over her skin, kissing and licking, feather light touches or teeth grazing, until she was pressing herself against me, her skin broken out in gooseflesh.

I brought my hand to her waist, skimming over the curve of her hip, down her thigh and back up while my mouth continued to explore the bare skin of her back, igniting little fires that were red and orange in my mind, like sparking embers.

"What are you doing?" she whispered, pressing herself into my touch.

I didn't have an answer. Only a new need. She'd had something I wanted and I'd taken it from her, against the wall, with desperate hunger. Now the need was to give something back, to give instead of take.

Gently, I rolled her to her back and knelt over her, my hands and knees on either side. I bent to kiss her, softly this time, soothing the rough redness of my earlier kisses with my lips. I moved down her neck, over the marks I'd put there, and kissed them too.

Fiona's hands sunk into my hair. "Oh Nikolai, I don't know if I'm ready yet..."

I shook my head, dragged my mouth down her body. "This is for you," I said, between kisses over her breasts, down her stomach, lower... "Only you and nothing else." I settled myself between her legs and glanced up to find her watching me, breathless and ready. "Okay?"

She nodded mutely and bit her lip. Anticipation and desire mixed, yellow and red, and I felt her hips shift under me slightly, rising. Offering.

I put my mouth on her.

*Oh Jesus...*

I'd been so rough earlier, my need so intense, and now it reversed its polarity. I wanted absolutely fucking nothing else than to make her feel good, to soothe any ache away with my mouth and make her come so hard she'd forget her own name.

She tasted so goddamn good. A sweetness that was all her own. I had to restrain myself from getting rough again, from sucking her hard or grazing my teeth. But her hands found my hair and pushed me into her while her hips rose and fell. Breathy little sounds and moans fell out of her mouth as her head thrashed from side to side.

*More, more, more....*

It was her voice that echoed in the hollowed out place inside me that belonged to everyone but me. But she was there now and she filled it up with all that was *her* and I felt whole for the first time in my life.

*Who the hell is this woman?*

"Nik, oh my God..."

Her words brought me back and she came then, a sustained tensing of every muscle, her back arched off the bed, an agonized cry tearing out of her throat, sending it to the ceiling, her head thrown back. For me, it was a sparkling cascade of her pleasure and I filled my senses with it, instead of trying to shut it out.

I held on to her hips and pressed in—hard—to make it last. She began to shudder, and I backed off slowly, with long, slow sweeps of my tongue, easing her through it, until she sank, boneless, onto the bed.

"Oh my God," she whispered into the dark that hid my satisfied smile. I started to roll off of her, but Fiona's hands snaked out and grabbed my shoulders, pulling me up.

I kissed my way across the soft landscape of her body, up to her mouth, and kissed her there too. A goodnight kiss, as I was sure she'd want to sleep for a hundred hours. But the red pulse of her want was flaming up, and her tongue invaded my mouth with intention.

"I thought you were done," I whispered against her lips, even as my body began to respond to her.

"I want you inside me," she whispered back urgently, "while I'm still feeling...*that*. What you did to me. I want that feeling with you inside me..."

She reached to the drawer in the nightstand beside her for another condom while I slipped off my boxers. "Slowly, this time," she said, tearing the wrapper. "Deep and slow." She rolled it down over me, and arched her back again. "Can you do that for me, Nik?"

I nodded. I'd do anything for her if it meant more of that inexplicable tranquility.

I buried the thought in a kiss and then slid slowly inside her for the second time that night. A groan escaped behind my clenched teeth at the sensation of her. The hunger was there, but so was the give and take. Her want was a pulsing need that wrapped around me as hot and tightly as her body did.

I moved slowly, thrusting deep into her, being gentle the only way I could to make it what she wanted. Her legs cinched around my waist, and her arms around my neck: a trap I normally tried to avoid with women I fucked. It was too easy to become entangled in them, their emotions or their messed up memories. With Fiona, I wanted to live there.

My mouth covered hers, my tongue delving deep too, but also softly, sucking the plump juiciness of her lips…I tasted sugar and strawberries and a summer breeze over a field of wildflowers…

*What is happening?*

My thoughts broke apart as I felt her orgasm welling up from deep within—from where I was inside her—spilling out and around us both. My own came seconds later, stealing my breath with its suddenness, as if my body were chained to Fiona's—what hers did, mine wanted too, and so we nearly came together in a sweating, gasping crescendo; a sudden tidal wave over a placid lake.

I collapsed on top of her, my body melting against hers, and she held me close, her breath hot on my neck.

"Nikolai Alexei," she whispered and cupped my cheeks to look at me in the dimness. "Who *are* you?"

It was a question I'd been asking myself for as long as I could remember. I had no answer, but in that moment—as I saw only myself reflected in the cornflower blue of Fiona's eyes—a frightening, exhilarating thought streaked across my mind.

*I don't know, but maybe you do…*

# Chapter 5

## Fiona

Thunder crashed and Lemony chirped in his cage, both sounds drawing me from a heavy sleep. I sat up slowly, blinking in the dimness and glanced down at the man sleeping beside me.

Nikolai Alexei—Last Name Unknown—was beautiful. His strong body was packed with muscles that were covered in intimidating tattoos. His ears were pierced with wicked-looking curves of silver, like barbed warnings not to get too close. But not to me. His spiky armor to keep people at a distance didn't apply to me.

Nik's face contrasted starkly to the rest of him—boyishly handsome, with blue eyes and short dark hair that was longish in the front. A sweet face but drawn tight with intensity, his brows always furrowed, a hard glint in his eye…Except now, he slept peacefully, lying on his stomach, the sheets just covering him to his waist. His brows were unfurrowed, his breathing deep and even.

*Peaceful.*

I let my gaze wander over his body, the muscles of his back under smooth skin. When awake, his blue eyes were hard, and those muscles were tense, as if Nik were constantly bracing himself against an unseen enemy.

One tattoo on his back was new; the skin around it still red. A Japanese koi fish and a symbol in black. I wondered what it meant.

"Sexy as hell," I murmured, and smothered a laugh.

At the club, Nik's intimidating body was sexy as hell too. Some primitive part of me loved watching him in action, as he easily removed the guy who'd tapped my shoulder and deposited him in the center of the dance floor like a little child who'd been bad and had to sit in the corner.

I hated to admit it but I liked that. Watching Nik had sent hot shivers cascading down my spine to settle between my legs, and I'd known then that if I were going to go through with my one-night stand plan, Nikolai Alexei had made himself the prime candidate.

*Not to mention it felt really damn good to see a man have my back.*

Lightning crashed and Lemony *cheeped* nervously. I slipped naked from the bed and covered the birdcage with a towel to quiet him. On the floor next to the kitchen stool were Nik's jeans and his wallet, which he'd pulled out of his pocket from his mad scramble to get a condom last night. I picked up the wallet to put it on the counter, and a few business cards fell out.

They were plain with the silhouette of a biker on a Harley and in one corner, his name—*Nik Young*—and a phone number.

"Nikolai Alexei Young," I murmured. "Last name no longer unknown."

I tucked the cards back in the wallet but for one.

*What are you doing? In case your imaginary motorcycle breaks down and you need spare parts?*

I slipped the card into my bag by the door.

*A souvenir from my one-night stand,* I thought. *I'm allowed.*

But I already had a souvenir. In my bag, I found the cocktail napkin with the sketch of me on it. I hadn't been lying when I told Nik he was talented. The sketch was skillfully and beautifully rendered, especially for ballpoint pen on a napkin. But more than that, he'd captured something in myself I'd been feeling as I let the music move through me. A little bit of the peace and happiness I fought for every day.

I slipped the sketch into my nightstand drawer and climbed back into bed, carefully so as not to wake Nik. He didn't stir except to bury his face deeper in the pillow with a contented sigh. I stared at him unabashedly, drinking him in.

*"Who are you?"* I'd asked him. I don't know why—the intensity of three mind-blowing orgasms must have rattled my brain. But Nikolai Young was everything I wanted that night.

Part of me worried I'd feel vulnerable having this stranger in my house. I didn't.

I thought I'd be shy having sex for the first time in years. I wasn't.

My body still hummed from his touch; I could feel everywhere he'd been on me, and the ache was delicious.

I slid down into the bed and sidled up to this gorgeous man. A lock of hair had fallen over his eyes and I raised my hand to brush it away…

*I always knew you were a slut.*

I snatched my hand back, as if the whisper of Steve's voice in my mind had burned me. Nik flinched in his sleep at the same time, his brows coming together again, his lips drawing down in an angry grimace. I held my breath as his hands reached for me, found me, and pulled me in. I turned to my side as Nik wrapped his arms around me, my back to his front, and I felt the warmth of his sigh gust over my shoulder. Then he was still again, deeply asleep.

I held perfectly still, my breath caught in my throat, bracing myself for more of Steve's terrible commentary.

Silence.

I let my breath go and melted into Nik's embrace.

*Is this supposed to happen?*

There was no answer, only his arms around me and perfect sleep sucking me under.

When I blinked awake next, the wan, gray light of a rainy morning filled my small space. Through the window, rain smattered the glass in a constant, heavy downpour. Nik stood there in jeans, no shirt, watching the rain. I bit my lip. This was the morning after, where the last night's decisions could be examined in the naked light of day. Did he regret coming here?

"Cats and dogs out there, isn't it?" I asked from the bed.

"Yeah, it's bad," Nik said without turning.

"Bad for your work?"

"No," he said slowly, heavily. "I can still go."

*Because that's what's supposed to happen. One night.*

"Some coffee first?" I asked.

"Yeah, that'd be good."

I drew on a t-shirt and a pair of underwear, and started for the kitchen. I could have grabbed a pair of baggy flannel pants I kept under the bed but I didn't. I liked how Nik's eyes raked over my bare legs. He dispelled the doubt and uncertainty that Steve had planted in my heart all those years ago and that still bore rancid fruit. Nik didn't look at me with distaste or disapproval; as if my body *disappointed* him. Nik looked at me with fire in his eyes. He made me feel beautiful and sexy.

And it didn't escape me that he hadn't put his shirt on either.

*He's not in a huge hurry to leave,* I thought. *I can live with that.*

I started the coffee and pulled down two mugs from the cabinet. I'd never done that before in the two years I'd been here. Coffee for two.

"What about some breakfast?" I asked, my voice suddenly whispery. I cleared my throat. "I can whip up some eggs, bacon…?"

"I could eat."

He said it casually enough, but I could have sworn I saw the blue of his eyes light up.

I made scrambled eggs and bacon, and we ate facing each other with Nik sitting at one of the stools at the counter and me standing in the kitchen across from him. He hardly said a word, but wolfed his food down and chased it with black coffee. The silence grew long and he showed no sign of breaking it.

"You really are the strong, silent type, aren't you?" I said with a laugh.

"I'm not good with small talk," Nik said. "Too much time on the road, I guess."

"You said you travel a lot, but how much is a lot? Like a couple times a month?"

"More than that," he said. His voice was a clear tenor, but scratchy, as if it were rusty with disuse. "I go back and forth across the country, no breaks."

I frowned. "But you have a place somewhere, right?"

He shrugged, pushed his food with his fork.

"Nowhere?" I asked. "For real?"

"No point in paying rent for a place I'm never in."

I blinked, shook my head. "Your job keeps you *that* busy? What about family? The holidays…?"

"I don't have any family. My dad took off when I was ten and my mom's in a home. Mind's gone. Doesn't recognize me anymore. But poker is constant." He shrugged again, as if it were all no big deal, but didn't meet my eye. "Christmas in Vegas with poker buddies isn't all that bad."

"I'm sorry about your mom," I said. "Alzheimer's?" I waved my hands. "Never mind. I'm sorry. I didn't mean to pry."

"It's okay. She's being taken care of."

"I'm glad. But the rest…I just can't imagine not having anywhere you can…That you…"

"Call home? Someday, maybe." Nik's lips curved up in a small approximation of a smile. "Right now, it's not in the cards."

A short laugh burst out of me, and I rolled my eyes. "Puns are awful."

"Too bad for you, there's a million bad poker puns and I know them all."

I planted my hand on my hip. "You are a mystery, Nikolai."

"Yeah?"

"Yeah. You make a joke when I least expect it." I leaned both forearms on the counter across from him. "Gambling is illegal in Georgia. It's illegal in most states, come to think of it. Where do you play all this poker?"

"Cellars, basements, bars after hours, warehouses…"

"That sounds scary," I said. "I'm picturing a bunch of gangsters in fedoras, pointing guns at each other under the table."

"Nah, they're mostly regular guys," Nik said. "A few criminals now and then, but we're gambling illegally, so…?" He shrugged.

"Is it ever dangerous?"

"I hold my own."

My eyes were immediately drawn to the thick muscles bunched around his shoulders. "I'll bet you do."

I froze, my words hanging in the air between us. Still leaning on the counter, I covered my eyes with one hand.

"Yes, I actually said that out loud…"

I peeked out to see Nik smiling down at his food then forking a bite.

I coughed. "So when's your next game?"

"Tonight," he said. "First of two."

"Why two?"

"Most games run over several nights, eight or ten hours per night. Or more…"

My eyes widened. "You play for ten straight hours?"

"Or more." Nik leaned back.

"Sounds like a long night," I said. "How do you get up to work the next day?"

"I make my own hours."

"You're a night owl."

"I don't sleep much," Nik said. "Or very well."

*He slept well last night,* I thought and heat colored my cheeks. *Because we wore each other out.*

I looked up to see Nik watching me so intently, I wondered if I'd spoken those words or only thought them.

I reached for my coffee. "You were telling me about playing for two nights…?"

"Yeah, I play one night just good enough to break even or lose a little, if the stakes are high enough. The next night, I clean them out."

"Always?" I asked, arching my brow. "You just win if you want to win? Every time?"

He met my gaze steadily. "Yeah, I do."

With shocking immediacy, a flush of heat crept over my chest, hardening my nipples, and stealing my breath. I took a sip of coffee, but it was hot and did nothing to help me.

"That's impossible," I managed, still feeling as if my emotions were written all over my face. "It's impossible to win every time. How do you do it?"

"I can read people," he said slowly. "It's this…talent I have. Lots of players have it; we read other players' tells."

"Their tells?"

"Little things they do to show how good—or shitty—their hand is."

"And that's how you win? By reading people?"

He nodded, his eyes on mine.

"What about luck? Surely your cards can't be great *every* hand."

"They're not," he said. "But when the other players have something good and I've got a shit hand, I don't get stupid with my bets."

"You know when to hold them and know when to fold them?" I said, grinning. "Know when to walk away…"

Nik snorted a laugh, nearly spilling his coffee. "You say my jokes are bad…"

I tossed him a napkin to wipe his chin. A giddy sort of happiness filled me knowing that I'd brought out Nikolai's beautiful smile, especially when he seemed so out of practice.

"So you can read people, huh?" I said, still smiling. "What about me? Can you read me?"

Nik's laughter faded. "You're a complete mystery."

I made a face, unable to tell if he was kidding or not. "No...I've been told...I mean..." I tucked a lock of hair behind my ear. "I'm pretty emotional. Heart on my sleeve and all that."

*Gullible, stupid, airhead...*

I shuddered. Someday I would stop being startled by Steve's intrusions into my psyche. In Costa Rica, I thought, where the teeming jungle and crashing waves would fill me up and leave no room for his insidious whispers. There, he would be silenced forever.

But I could swear that in the split second before I flinched, Nik's head shot up with a sharp look in his eyes. I took an involuntary step back but his gaze turned distant, as if he were looking at something beyond me. Then his eyes met mine. He blinked and his face reverted to neutral.

"There's nothing wrong with being emotional," he said, his voice low.

"No?" I said. I wiped an invisible crumb off the counter. "I was under the impression that most men don't like emotional women."

"Most men are fucking idiots."

I looked into his steely blue eyes. Despite the harsh tone in his voice, the sense of feeling safe and at ease in Nik's presence returned. We hardly knew each other, but I felt no scrutiny from him. No judgment.

*Of course not. We're not anything to each other. A night of pleasure. Using each other...*

The sense memory of Nik's mouth on me rose up, and the heat dashed across my cheeks again. My lips parted in a small gasp and I quickly turned my gaze away, to the counter, my coffee mug, the window...

"The rain is crazy, isn't it?" I said. "Do you have to get back out there soon?"

"I have some time," Nik said, his voice drawing my gaze back to his like a command. Now the heat was in my lower belly, between my thighs.

"You do?"

"I make my own hours, remember?"

I nodded faintly.

*You said one night. That's it. That was the rule.*

My body was desperate for me to break the rules.

Nik held my gaze while he sipped his coffee; while he wiped his mouth on a napkin; as he stood up. I was helpless, unable to look away; not pinned down but pleasantly trapped. He moved around the counter to stand before me, to press me—without touching me—back against the wall. I could feel the heat of his body all along mine, his inked muscles coiled and tense with power. And need.

He stared down at me, a question in his eyes. I answered.

*Kiss me.*

He did. Nikolai's lips covered mine and I tasted warm coffee, and the clean taste of him as his tongue slid along mine. My body reacted as if we hadn't spent all night being wracked by pleasure. One arm went around his waist, to feel the heat of his bare skin and the muscles moving beneath, and the other around his neck, to bury my fingers in his short, silken hair.

We kissed until we needed to do more than kiss. Nik lifted me off the ground effortlessly and carried me to the bed.

"You might be late for work," I whispered, my tongue darting to taste him, my teeth grazing his lips.

"Worth it," he said, and moved his mouth to my neck, dragged his tongue down my skin.

My shirt vanished, his pants came off, and Nikolai showed me that all we'd done in the heat of the night, he was capable of in the light of day. He took me down to the bed and kissed my body until there was no room for thought. Only sensation, and the delirious ecstasy of his body on mine, inside mine, moving in tempo to mine until we both shuddered our releases, like an exchange of gifts.

After, we lay in silence, my head on his chest, his fingers playing in my hair. We listened to the pattering rain count the minutes until he had to go. Because he had to go. This was my territory and I needed it back. The walls and barriers that had come down for one night were resurrecting themselves because no matter what Steve said, I wasn't a stupid girl. I could be an adult about this. I could have a fling and say goodbye, even if the guy was more than anything I'd expected.

*I'm not going to fall into another trap...*

In that same instant, Nik extracted himself from the bed. With my arm propped up, my head leaning on my palm, I watched him pull on his jeans, boots, and a plain t-shirt. He grabbed his black leather jacket off the floor where it had lain all night and dug out his motorcycle keys.

Nik didn't say anything; didn't fill the silence with awkward words and I somehow managed to keep my mouth shut from doing the same. He bent over me, and I took his kiss—a deep, intense kiss; not a goodbye peck—and then watched him go. He went to the door, and opened it. The pouring rain was like a drum and I hated that he had to go out into it.

*One night,* I thought. *That was the deal.*

Nikolai hesitated at the door but didn't look back.

"Goodbye, Fiona."

"Goodbye, Nik."

He shrugged on his jacket and went out, closing the door behind him.

As soon as the door clicked shut, I fell back on my pillows, a sigh gusting out of me. I was naked, my skin marked by him, my body thrumming, a sweet ache pulsing between my legs.

"Nikolai," I murmured into the quiet space. There was no answer, only rain and the growl of his motorcycle—roaring loud and then driving away.

# Chapter 6

*Fiona*

After a shower and a change of clothes, I couldn't stand the silence of my place a second longer. I could still smell the clean scent of Nik's cologne on my sheets, tempting me to lie around in bed all day, my face buried in the pillow. I grabbed my phone and shot a text to Opal.

**Lunch at Panera?**
Her reply came a few seconds later.
**In this storm?**
**I'm pretty sure they have indoor seating.**
**Smartass**
I bit my lip. **Do u want to hear about my horizontal mambo or not?**
**Be there in ten.**

At Panera on the outskirts of Savannah, Opal sat across from me at a small table, bowls of broccoli cheddar soup in front of each of us. My friend scrutinized me through narrowed eyes for a moment.

"I can't believe you went through with it and I'm so happy that you did. If it was good…" She cocked her head at me. "Was it good? You look like it was good."

I pretended to be thoughtful, tapping my fingernail to my teeth. "Was it good? Let me think…"

Opal huffed. "Oh, hell…"

I laughed. "Okay, okay. Do you remember that scene from *Thelma and Louise*, where Thelma—who's married to a serious douchebag—has crazy, epic sex with Brad Pitt in a hotel room?"

"Yessss," Opal said, slowly, dragging the word out.

"And remember how the next morning, Thelma showed Louise the epic hickey on her neck that came as the result of the epic sex? And how she said, 'I finally know what all the fuss is about'?"

Opal sat back. "You didn't…"

My grin split my face as I tugged my shirt collar down to reveal Nik's bite marks on my skin. "I finally know what all of the fuss is about."

Opal's eyes widened, and a laugh burst out of her. "High five, girl. For real…"

I clapped my hand against hers. "Oh my God, Opal, it was insane. He was so…"

"Hot?"

"Beyond hot. Tattoos, wicked piercings, and this other guy was being an ass to me at the club, but the way Nik handled it…I mean, he just *handled* it."

"Nik?" Opal said. "I like Nik…"

"Short for Nikolai," I said proudly, as if I'd named him.

Opal's eyebrows shot up. "Oh, look at you taking an international lover."

"Oh my God, don't say lover. No one says lover anymore."

"Fuck buddy?" she said, drawing a huffy sniff from the older lady sitting at the next table. I covered my giggle with my hand. Opal sniffed right back. "Semantics, schemantics, tell me the details."

"He's a salesman. Motorcycle parts," I said. "I know I shouldn't have but I sort of poked around in his wallet and found his business card. He's legit."

"His business card," Opal said. "With a phone number…"

I ignored that. Hard.

"Anyway, he rides a motorcycle too, cross country. He's only in town a few days and then he's off again. One town to the next and the next."

Opal nodded thoughtfully. "Okay. Give me a visual. Tall, dark, and handsome?"

"Not too tall, but taller than me. He's…"

*Beautiful.*

"…ridiculously handsome. Dark hair, blue eyes, and he's almost entirely covered in tattoos." My blush deepened. "Almost."

Opal gave me a sly look. "Damn, girl. Tell me more."

"He plays poker. Underground games, while he's on the road, and he's really good at it."

"How do you know?"

"I can just tell." I toyed with my straw. "He's got…something about him that screams confidence. Or intelligence, or I don't know what. He doesn't talk much, but I can tell he's a lot deeper than he lets on. He sketched me at the club, on a napkin. And it was incredible."

Opal opened her mouth to say something then shook her head. "Nope, save that for later."

"Save what?"

"Nothing. Go on. You're almost at the good part."

"I didn't know what the hell I was doing but he made me feel…comfortable." I said softer, my cheeks on fire. "He followed me to my place and we…"

"Had Brad Pitt and Thelma sex…"

I leaned over the table. "Yes, and I'm telling you, Opal, my body feels *awake*. For the first time in years. The things Nik did to me…" I shook my head. "If it wasn't for the storm, I'm sure all the neighbors in the entire building would have heard us. Griff and Nate…and maybe a few people in the next town over."

Opal fanned herself with a napkin. "Wow, your night was so different from mine." She held up her hands as if weighing two options. "Bingo at Shriners…hot sex with a tattooed stranger."

"I win," I said with a laugh.

"You totally win." Opal sipped her lemonade and looked up at me from over her glass. "Are you going to see him again?"

I sat back. "No." I reached for my drink "No, I… No. Why would I?"

"Didn't you say he's in town for a few more days?"

I did say that. Why did I say that? Why did I tell her that when it would only lead to that question?

*Because it would lead to that question?*

I frowned. "They don't call it a *one*-night stand for nothing." I shrugged. "That's all it can be. One night."

"Says who?"

"Says me," I said with a sigh. "I can't get involved with anyone,

Opal."

"Why not?" Opal asked. "And don't tell me it's because you're leaving for Costa Rica soon. If you meet someone special, you adapt. That's what people do. Do you think I planned to marry Jeff? No! I was happy as a clam as a single gal, with a plan that said marriage wasn't going to happen until age thirty *at the earliest*. Then that sneaky bastard spills coffee on me at a café in Savannah and four months later I'm engaged."

"But that's sweet," I said. "Jeff is sweet…"

"The point is, my careful life plan got blown to bits and I adjusted. I made room for that kind of happiness. I gave it a chance. Now here you are, having a great time with a guy who—mind-blowing sex aside—makes you feel comfortable, who's got a lot going on upstairs, and protects you from unwanted advances from strangers, *aaaand* you've got his phone number! Are you telling me you're not going to use it because of your plans?"

Her voice softened and she leaned over the table to cover my wrist.

"This guy, Nik? He might be nothing. He might be good for sex and not much else. I'm not saying he's your Forever, but he's here Right Now. For a few more days anyway. Why not see what happens?"

I realized then that all that I hadn't told Opal about Steve was standing in the way of her good advice. Of our friendship.

"I can't 'see what happens,'" I said slowly. "I fall hard, Opal. I fall hard and blindly, and I get swept away by the smallest hint of kindness. And then next thing I know I'm…"

"You're what?"

"Trapped." I could barely say the word but now that I had, the rest was ready to burst out.

Opal folded her hands on the table, slowly. A move that meant she was pissed off. "Steve?"

I nodded.

"There's more?"

I nodded again.

"Tell me."

I sucked in a breath and let it out. "He took my money, Opal. I had $10,000 from my father when he died and Steve kept it in our 'joint account' that he never gave me access to. He stole my money, he stole my self-esteem. No, he didn't steal it, he chipped away at it and just when I thought I'd crumble, he kissed me and cried over me and told me he'd die without me."

Opal sat back in her chair as if my words had pushed her. "Fiona...All this time I thought...But no, that's abuse. That's *abuse* and I never knew. You never told me..." Her eyes widened and she lowered her voice. "Honey, did he hit you?"

I shook my head. "No, never. He wasn't violent, just...insidious."

"Bad enough, but why didn't you tell me? I thought you had a bad ex. Hell, we all have bad exes..."

"It's too humiliating," I said. "It was like I was locked in a prison, except the door was unlocked the whole time and I was just too beat down and stripped raw to walk through it."

"But he took your money..."

"And moved us away from all my family and friends..." It was on the tip of my tongue to tell her I'd married him but it was too much. "He cut me off, and it took..." I swallowed. "It took a lot to work up the courage to leave."

*It took more than courage. Five weeks of planning, two of which were done from a hospital bed...*

Steve had never been violent, that was true, but he still managed to hurt me with his betrayal and lies all the same, scarring me forever...

I buried that pain fast and deep. Some secrets didn't deserve the light of day, no matter how well-intentioned the friend who heard them.

"I feel so stupid about the entire ordeal," I said. "I can't be stupid anymore."

"You're not stupid," Opal said fiercely. "I feel stupid for not seeing it or asking more questions..."

"You ask plenty of questions," I said with a laugh, though it faded quickly. "But that's why it has to be only one night with Nik, even though..."

"Even though...?"

I turned my water glass around and around. "Even though I wouldn't necessarily *mind* another night like last night." I held my head in my hands. "Oh my God, Opal, does that make me terrible? Like I'm just using Nik for his body?"

Opal smirked. "This is outside my purview. I was at Bingo last night, remember?"

"It's a little bit terrible," I said, staring into last night. "His body is drool-worthy and he's an absolute beast in the sack, but he has such a sweet face. He doesn't say much, but I know he has a sense of humor, and he looks at me…"

"Yes?"

"Like I'm beautiful."

"Honey, you are beautiful." Opal slapped the flat of her hand on the table. "Jesus, just what did that Steve do to you?"

"Ssshh!" I hissed, glancing around. "And anyway, who cares? I shouldn't need a man to make me feel pretty, but that was part of Steve's awfulness. At first he wouldn't stop telling me I was beautiful, how much he wanted me. A year later, he was making offhand comments… 'You're wearing *that?*' or 'Those pants make you look like a boy.' And then the comments became insults, how I had no boobs, I was too thin. He got annoyed if I didn't order big meals at restaurants and would order for me. I've always been skinny and self-conscious and picked on in junior high about it. He just dialed right into that. He'd insult me one minute and then tell me I looked like an angel the next."

"Keeping you off balance."

"Yes, always. And I'm still off balance. I don't know how to get my equilibrium back. I don't know how to trust what I feel about anything. I was so wrong about Steve…"

"You were not," Opal said. "You did everything right. You trusted him and believed him because why wouldn't you? You had no reason not to."

"But there were plenty of reasons not to."

"Hindsight, sure. But at the time? You did what anyone would do."

I smiled. "Thank you for saying so."

"But you don't believe a word of it."

"Whether I was right or wrong, it's what happened and I can't let it happen again. I need to know that the person I let in after Steve isn't going to be like him. I have to protect myself."

"I know you do," Opal said, her shoulders wilting with a sigh. "And if you need more time, I'm not going to tell you not to take it. But please let me be here for you. Please don't shut me out. If you ever want to talk more about…him."

"Thank you."

"In the meanwhile, there's the matter of one stolen business card." She arched a brow. "No rule against making a one-night stand a three-day fling."

That damn blush crept over my cheeks again. "I haven't decided yet. But…no, I won't call him. Probably. He's working all day and playing poker all night."

"*All* night?"

I laughed. "Anything after eleven p.m. is a straight-up bootycall and you know it."

"So make that bootycall," Opal said. "Enjoy yourself. He makes you feel good, right?"

*More than good,* I thought and the memory of Nikolai putting his mouth between my thighs rose up, unbidden.

"Yeah, he does," I said faintly, toying with my napkin.

Opal held up her hands. "I don't see a downside here."

I smiled and said nothing, but tore my napkin in two, right down the middle.

Back at my little apartment, I watered my houseplants and checked on Lemony's water and birdseed.

"How are you, sweet boy?" I cooed. I let my fingers trail over his cage. "Are you tired of looking at these bars? I know. But if I let you out, you'll panic and fly all over. You'll head right for the first window you see, thinking it's freedom. But it's not. It only looks that way, and you can't tell until it smacks you right in the face."

I folded my arms on the counter and rested my chin on them. "When we're in Costa Rica, I'll let you go and you'll be free. We both will. In the meantime…"

In the meantime, I had Nik's business card in my purse.

"He makes me feel good. Is that wrong? Can I have that for one more night?"

Lemony *cheeped* from inside his cage. It sounded like a happy little chirp but how would I ever really know?

# Chapter 7

## Nikolai

The rain was constant. My leather jacket helped but the jeans that had spent all night drying in Fiona's kitchen were soaked by the time I got back to my crappy little motel.

I peeled out of them and headed to the shower. I stripped naked and turned the spray on hot but didn't step in. I could smell Fiona on my skin, on my hands and still taste her on my mouth. I didn't want to wash her off of me. I wanted to keep a little bit of that strange calm a little longer, as if it were in her scent that still clung to my skin.

*Stupid.*

As soon as I'd stepped off Fiona's porch that morning, the world had come rushing back in.

*We had one night. That was her deal and I took it.*

I got in the shower.

After, I changed into one of my other pairs of jeans—I had two total—and a black t-shirt. Dinner was fast food, eaten in my motel room as I watched the nightly news blare murder, death, accidents and misery until I came to my senses and shut it off.

At quarter to nine, I headed out. It was time to play.

I checked my cell phone—the only tie between me and the world of normalcy—for directions to the poker game *TMoney1993* had invited me to.

The rain had started up again, a light smatter against the visor of my helmet as I rode to the game site. The warehouse clung to the river's edge with a dozen more just like it—old and wind-torn, not likely used in months, if not longer. The chain link fence around it sagged in more than one place with a rusted KEEP OUT sign falling askew.

It was a ridiculous location for a low-stakes underground game—someone's office after hours would have sufficed—but when I muttered the password to the guy at the door it was obvious that the rest of the players were all like Tim—big shots at their banks or investment firms in the city, who played at gangsters, risking it all if the local law caught wind of their seedy operation. I could have told them the FBI wasn't going to waste time on these bums. Poker plus guns or poker plus drugs, sure. Just poker? With a $100 buy-in?

I kept the smirk off my face as TMoney—Tim, in the real world—introduced me to the group of six other guys sitting in the center of an overgrown storage shed—wood-paneled, dirt-floored, flickering fluorescent lighting—with the poker table in the middle.

*Fish, every single one.*

I was supposed to be the noob; it was going to take a serious acting job on my part to play worse than these guys.

After three hours I had them lulled into submission, but I was bored out of my mind. I won enough to keep them involved, and lost enough to make them think I wasn't a threat. The stage was set for the next night.

I played on autopilot, my mind preferring to live in the memories of last night. Fiona with the pink hair, and the pink halo of sweetness surrounding her...I could taste that sweetness on my mouth, feel her wrap her thighs around me as she brought me to release.

*And her peace...*

I wanted it. Her. All of it, one more time.

A phone rang.

All eyes that were focusing on cards a moment ago looked up, all hands grew still, and all shit-talk was silenced. It took me a second to realize what I was hearing and then it came again. My phone was ringing.

My phone never rang...unless it was from the nursing home my mother was rotting away in.

*Oh, shit. Is this it? Is this the call?*

Talking to anyone but other players at the table was against all the rules, and even these two-bit chumps knew it. Suspicion coiled around me like rank soot.

"Sorry," I muttered, rising to my feet and digging my phone out of my leather jacket that was slung on the back of my chair. "I have to take this..."

I glanced at the number, expecting the St. Louis area code but it was a local number. I hit the green answer button.

"This is Nik," I said, turning away from the table.

"Nik, hi, it's Fiona."

I froze. My balls tightened in my jeans at the sound of her soft voice and my damn heart tripped over itself at the same time.

"Fiona..." she said into my silence. "From last night?"

"No, hi....uh..." I said. "How did you get my number?"

"From your business card. One fell out of your wallet." A pause. "Is this a bad time? No, I'm sorry. It's late. I should go—"

"No, don't go," I said louder than I wanted. I coughed and lowered my voice. "What's up?"

*What's up? Fucking hell.*

I heard Fiona take in a breath, and I imagined her in her little place, a warm yellow light glinting in her pink hair, and the storm raging outside. And here I was in an overgrown storage shed, robbing a bunch of idiots blind because I had nowhere else to go.

"I made some cookies," she blurted.

"Cookies..." A strange warmth flooded my chest. "Okay."

"Yeah, I do that sometimes when I can't sleep. I bake. And I couldn't sleep and so I made some chocolate chip cookies. My aunt's recipe. They're really good. I use way too many chocolate chips, and...so I was wondering if you wanted any."

I checked my watch. Cookies at 2:10 a.m. I didn't need the *ken* to know that's not all she was offering.

"Yeah, that sounds good," I said. I lowered my voice just for her. "I'm really fucking hungry."

"Me too," she said on a slow exhale. "Um, okay great. I'll see you soon."

"See you soon."

I hung up the phone and turned back to the table where the guys were grousing and shooting me dark looks.

"Sorry, guys," I said, tossing my cards into the pot to show I'd folded. "Cash me out."

"What the hell, Nik?" Tim said, holding out his hands. "We got a game or not?"

"Tomorrow night," I said, quickly scanning and counting my chips. "I'll finish out tomorrow night."

*I'll put you out of your misery.*

"A woman," one of the other guys said with an amused snort. "Our boy, Nik, here is going to get himself a piece of ass."

I stiffened and nearly knocked over a chip stack for the way this guy talked about Fiona.

*Fuck's sake, it's true, isn't it?*

Yeah, I was going to be in Fiona's bed again in less than twenty minutes, and the idea turned my blood to fire. But a part of me I had thought was dead and gone flared faintly with its own color and light. Something beyond pure lust. I liked being with her. And stronger than anything else, that peace that she exuded to quiet the *ken.* I wanted more of it. *Needed* it.

The rain-slicked roads swept underneath my bike as I hit the throttle, tearing through the night like a junkie heading for his next fix.

No sooner had I parked at Fiona's apartment complex, the rain came down in sheets. I rolled the Bonneville behind her little Prius, under the carport, and went to her door. I took off my helmet and sucked in a breath of humid, summer air that not even the rain could cool.

I knocked.

A muffled, "Come in," answered.

I did and nearly sagged with relief. It felt as if I'd been carrying a heavy boulder and the second I stepped across her threshold, I set it down.

The apartment was dim but for a small light at Fiona's bedside table. There was a rich smell of warm chocolate, and the oven ticked as it cooled down. The bird in its cage was still on the counter, a plate of chocolate chip cookies beside it.

Fiona was in bed. Naked. The ribbons of her long hair only partially covered her breasts and she made no move to hide them when I shut the door behind me. She had a book in her hand.

I could hear her heartbeat from the door.

"Hi," she said, her voice sweet and soft.

"Hi," I said. I stripped out of my leather jacket and hung it on the hook by the door, inhaling and exhaling. I had to calm myself, to make this last.

I went to the counter and took a cookie. It was still warm and melted on my tongue in sugary chocolate perfection. I couldn't remember the last time I'd had homemade cookies. Since I was a kid, I guessed.

"Good?" Fiona asked from the bed, watching me.

"Yeah," I said. "It's really fucking good."

The heat of her desire burned red in the eye of the *ken* and was hot on my tongue, mixing with the chocolate; the best thing I'd ever tasted. Fiona set her book down on the nightstand and settled herself against the pillows. The air around her wavered, as if I were looking at her through fire.

I finished the first cookie and took another, taking my time, feeling the wait build between us and grow heavy. My jeans were tight beneath my belt.

Fiona bit her lip. "Tease."

I ate the second cookie and brushed the crumbs off my hands, then moved—slowly—to stand beside her at the bed.

The bright blue of her eyes met mine and held on, unwavering, as I kicked off my boots and stripped down to my boxers. Her eyes dropped to my erection and I saw them flare with want, and then back up to me. She turned back the covers, her body naked and almost glowing in the pale light of the room and the otherworldly light that only I could see.

"Come here," she said.

I took off my boxers and her want flared brighter, hotter. My own eyes filled with her naked body and brief thoughts flickered in my mind of which part I was going to indulge in first. I climbed in and lay over her, my erection like steel, pressing against her thigh.

But once there, in Fiona's arms, naked with her, my lust melted into something softer. Being with her, I realized with a strange jolt, was enough. I could have done nothing more than hold her and fall asleep and I would've been perfectly content. The peace of her wrapped around me, drew her to me, and goddamn she looked so beautiful...

Fiona felt it too and her arms went around me, holding me close to her, our lips a hair's breadth apart, waiting for the kiss that would start this night and let me do what I came here to do. Instead, I settled against her, let her watch me, and touch me in ways that had nothing to do with sex.

She trailed one finger along my jaw, tracing the outline of my lips, then along the other side, to my ear and the heavy piercing.

"How was poker?" she asked softly, like a woman might ask her man how his day had been.

*I'm not her man. She's not my woman...*

But I was staring at her eyes, her feathered brows, the soft curve of her cheek. "Good," I said.

"Did you win?"

"Broke even," I said. "I'll clean them out tomorrow night."

Fiona nodded, and uncertainty slowly crept over her. I wasn't there to hold her and be held. That wasn't part of her plan.

"Kiss me," she said.

I did, hard. I felt things fall into place for her. And for me. I couldn't stay. I wasn't part of her plan. This night wasn't supposed to be about soft looks and touches, but about sex, so I made it about sex.

"You've been waiting for me," I said, almost a growl against her neck. My hand found one small breast, the nipple hard.

I pinched. She gasped.

"Yes," she breathed. "All night."

"Are you ready for me?" I asked, my hand trailing down the flat of her stomach, past her navel, and lower.

She arched into my touch. "Yes," she hissed. "So ready…"

My fingers found her wet and soft and I groaned at the same time she did at the touch.

She kissed me, hard and deep, and I thought she was going to guide me inside her but she jolted to a stop, as if remembering her own rule.

"Condom," she said, and her hand snaked out to the nightstand drawer.

I rolled it on. Then she took me inside her, and the world fell away in a perfect peace. The rest of the night was lost in her. I brought her to one screaming orgasm after another, until we were both exhausted.

Then she slept and I held her the way you hold something you know isn't yours to keep.

# Chapter 8

## Nikolai

Fiona lay across my chest, her breasts pressed against me, her naked skin touching mine in a hundred places. The gray light of midmorning struggled through storm clouds that wouldn't subside. Rain speckled the window. I lay back on the pillows, my body feeling spent and heavy. Outside, the storm hadn't abated, but in Fiona's space, the thick calm surrounded me and made me drowsy.

Fiona's fingers trailed along the tattoos on my chest, up my shoulder, down my arm, to my hand.

"Make a fist," she said. "Make two fists."

I brought over my other arm that had been lazily playing with her hair, and did as she requested.

"Pawn and hoax," she said, her fingers trailing over the letters inked between my knuckles. Her gaze lifted to meet mine. "What do they mean?"

"That's life, right? We're pawns in some cosmic game. Either that or it's all a hoax; a big fucking joke."

*Or a mistake. I'm a mistake.*

She frowned. "Sounds a little grim, don't you think?"

I shrugged.

Fiona laced her fingers in mine—her skin softly pale against the dark of my ink. "If I were to get letters tattooed on each of my fingers, do you know what they would spell?"

*Love and hope.*

I shook my head. "Can't guess."

"Love and hope," she said. "That's life to me. Love for all the good that happens to you and the people you care about, and hope that any pain will be bearable or lessen in time."

*Who do you care about and who cares about you, Fiona?*

The *ken* couldn't tell me that, and the real world offered no clues. No pictures on the walls, no calls or texts from her phone, no mention of family. The only evidence I saw of contact with the outside world was one photo on her nightstand. Fiona was laughing and smiling in between the embrace of an African-American woman and two guys about my age. They looked to be at the state fair—in the background of the picture was a Ferris wheel—and one of the guys was holding a cone of cotton candy the same color as Fiona's hair.

Asking a personal question was so foreign to me I felt like I was struggling with a second language.

"So…how long have you lived here?"

"Two years," she said. "The view is pretty but this place is smaller than I'd like. It's okay for now while I save up for my big move."

"Where to again?"

Fiona's delicate features drew tight with uncertainty. Hesitant. Through the *ken* I felt the dark edges of an old memory—no, *years* worth of memories—gather around her like storm clouds. Her moving out of Georgia was tied to these bad memories. The *ken* showed me a blurred image of her running toward some destination, her hair streaking out behind her, her arms reaching while a thick black line tethered her to a storm. She ran and ran, and the line attenuated but held tight. I knew she wouldn't stop running until it finally snapped, and she was free.

It took less than a second for the *ken* to show this to me, and I gritted my teeth against stealing it from her. For the violation of her innermost self.

"You don't have to tell me—"

"Costa Rica," she said. "Wow." She gave a short laugh, shaking her head. "I don't really tell people that…"

For half a second, she doubted herself and then shook it off as those two words drove back the cloud of dark memories. Fiona's eyes brightened, backlit by years' worth of dreaming and planning as she looked into mine.

"Yeah, I'm moving to Costa Rica. I want to live off the grid, you know? Get a little house in the middle of all that beautiful greenery."

Her fingers traced a dreamcatcher tattooed all down the left side of my body. "It's perfect. It's everything I want."

"Sounds remote," I said.

"That's what I like about it. I want to grow food and maybe have some chickens…walk along the beach whenever I feel like it, or swing in a hammock and listen to the jungle, and just be."

"Just be…what?"

"I don't know," she said with a small smile. "Just be. Just live and breathe and be whoever I am without…stuff getting in the way. Do you know what I mean?"

"Yeah, I do," I said. "I know exactly what you mean."

She rested her chin on her hand. She still lay draped across my chest, as if she belonged there.

"Do you ever dream of a place like that, Nikolai?" she asked.

"No," I said.

"No?" She cocked her head. "If you could go anywhere in the world, where would it be?"

*Anywhere there is no* ken. But the *ken* was in me, like a disease I carried with me wherever I went.

*Except here, with Fiona.*

"I don't know," I said. "Haven't really thought about it."

"You travel so much already," she said. "Is that why you get so many tattoos? One for each place you've been?" she asked, resuming her examination of my skin. "You're covered from neck to waist, as far as I can see." Her smile turned coy and she flipped the cover back to glance at my naked body. "Still some blank real estate on your legs. None on your penis, thankfully. You have a magnificent penis, Nikolai."

I coughed a short laugh. "Thanks."

She flipped the cover back. "But for real, why so many tattoos?"

"Expression, I guess," I said.

"There is so much variety," she said, her fingers trailing up my arm, over skulls and harpooned fish and a straight flush—ace high—and Old English calligraphy next to a scantily clad pin-up girl from the 40's.

"Don't get me wrong, they flow nicely. I'm just trying to get a sense of the message here. It's like a…"

*cacophony*

"…cacophony of ink. Lots of different symbols and ideas clamoring for a piece of your skin."

I stared. She could have been describing the *ken.* Thoughts and feelings came at me like a tidal wave of sound and color and confused words that begged to be put in the right order. I considered it a theft—an invasion of privacy of the worst kind—but sometimes it felt like they were unconsciously seeking me out. As if this mental robbery wasn't a robbery at all, but a desperate giving. A cacophony of souls crying out and only I could hear them.

*What would Fiona think if she knew what I was?*

I watched her for a moment, her beautiful open face and her easy smile, and I imagined how fast she would shut down—shut me out—if she knew I had touched some darkness in her past she was desperately trying to outrun.

"You have some nice ink too," I said, diverting her thoughts.

I ran my fingers along the hibiscus on her shoulder and down to the wildflowers on her back. She shivered and squirmed as my trailing finger tickled her skin. I brushed her long hair off her back so I could do it again.

"Oh my God, stop." She laughed. "You know what it does to me when you touch me there."

"I know *exactly* what it does to you…"

Her cheeks were dusted pink and she gently moved my hand away. "We're having a civilized conversation," she reminded me. "A getting-to-know-you talk while lying around naked."

"Seems normal," I said, with a grin.

She stared at me, her face softening. She reached out and touched my lip with her fingertips. "You do have a sweet smile, Nikolai. It's such a rare sighting, though."

The moment settled between us, our eyes met, and her blush deepened. The pink aura around her brightened and the peaceful calm of her fell over me like the world's most comfortable blanket.

"Anyway," she said, letting her hand fall. "I wasn't planning on ever getting a tattoo. Or coloring my hair either, come to think of it. But I made a promise to myself that I would do what I wanted, always, so long as it didn't hurt anyone."

"Your bucket list," I said.

"Right," she said. "My never-to-be-written-down bucket list. If I feel like doing something, I do it." She bit her lip and smiled at me. "Like taking you home."

"Oh yeah?" I said. "I was on your bucket list?"

"Sort of. Does that sound terrible? It's been a long time since I've been with anyone, and since I'm moving away…" She cleared her throat and couldn't meet my eye. "Nothing wrong with a little fling… I mean, you have to hit the road again tomorrow, right?"

I felt it as a tentative reaching, like a hand to a fire, seeing how close it came before getting burned. She needed me to say yes. Part of her wanted me to say no.

"Yeah," I said keeping my voice neutral. "I have to keep going."

"Do you have girls in other towns?" she asked. "You don't have to answer that if you don't want to but I can imagine you must."

"No, no… I don't have girls in other towns," I said.

"No? And here I thought I was your Savannah girl."

*My Savannah girl…*

Fiona propped her elbow on the bed and let her fingers resume their trek across my chest. "It's almost noon. Your work's not missing you right now?"

I shook my head. "Decided to take the day off."

"But for your poker game tonight," she said.

"Right. Seven idiots are waiting for me to take their money."

She laughed. "Nooo. Are they that bad?"

"They're not good."

Fiona grinned, then cocked her head, her brows coming together. "Do you really work all year? I just can't imagine it."

"It's what I do for now," I said. "I'm not sure what comes after."

That was the most truthful thing I'd said since we met. It felt good.

"What about you?" I asked. "Where do you work? At a bakery, maybe?"

"No, I work in a garden center. Flowers, soil, and seeds… I love green things…watching them grow. I love animals too, like little Lemony over there. This place would be overrun with dogs and cats if my lease would allow it."

"I can see that about you," I said slowly.

"The whole universe can, apparently," she said. "I took a personality quiz on Facebook once, and it's the only silly quiz I ever took that was 100% right."

"And what are you?" I asked, only half teasing. *Why is everything so quiet around you?*

"I'm a nurturer," she said. "It's accurate. I volunteer at an animal shelter a couple of times a month, too. I help walk the dogs and calm them down. They're so scared when they first arrive. They had a life before they were on the street or were dumped somewhere, and now they have to start all over again."

The darkness was back, hovering, ready to pounce. I ran my fingers along her back, making her laugh instead.

"Fiend," she said, swatting my arm. "That's you. A fiendish sex god." She watched me a second, and then lay her cheek on my bare chest. "Aside from being a sex god, what would a Facebook personality quiz say about you?"

I frowned. "Sex god's not enough?"

Her laughter was music and a pink mist curled around her.

"Despite all evidence to the contrary, there's more to you than that," she said. "I think a quiz would say you're a strong silent type who defends women, and has a sense of humor that not too many get to see."

"Not too many," I said, shifting under her.

Fiona cast her gaze down. "I'm sorry if I get too personal. I don't have much of a filter. But that's part of my plan too." Her colors dimmed. "My days of saying nothing are over."

I wondered if that was entirely true. I wondered if she would tell me the truth about the dark cloud I saw hovering over her if I asked. I could ask her about...him.

*Him. It's a him...*

Like a dream that fades upon waking, I could just grasp the shadows that chased her, and they suddenly took on a shape—a faceless man who was responsible for the pain Fiona ran from. Anger boiled in my veins and I fought for calm.

*Who is he...?*

I sucked in a breath. What did it matter? There was nothing I could do and I was leaving the next day. I was already too addicted to the inexplicable peace this woman brought me. The last thing I needed was to get close to her, to feel anything more than lust, though part of me wondered if I were too late. I had an almost primal instinct in me to protect her and it had nothing to do with the peace and everything to do with her.

The doorbell rang over and over, disrupting the quiet of the morning. It was followed by a knock, then a child's voice calling through the door.

"Fiony? Are you there?"

More doorbell ringing followed, and Fiona's face lit up, the light around her flaring pink and gold.

"That's my neighbor's daughter, Hailey," she said, hurriedly drawing on a silky bathrobe. "She's an angel. I babysit for her almost every week."

I pressed myself back in the bed and the angle was just narrow enough so that I wouldn't be seen from the door. The bell clanged again. The rainfall grew loud as Fiona opened the door wide enough to kneel. A little girl, about four years old with blonde curls, threw her arms around Fiona's neck.

"Fiony!"

"Hailey, girl!"

"I'm sorry, Fi," said a woman's voice from behind the girl. "She thinks the doorbell is a toy."

"No worries, Nance," Fiona said and held the little girl by the shoulders. "This little Georgia peach is always welcome."

"I just wanted to say hi and goodbye to you," Hailey said. "We're going to Grandma's this weekend where it won't be raining and I can play at the park…"

"Okay, okay," said the girl's mother. "Fiona's busy, I'm sure. Let's get going. Maybe a week from Friday, Fi? Are you free to watch this little bugger?"

"Wouldn't miss it."

"Bye, Fiony-balogna!"

"Bye, Hailey-baley! Have fun at Grandma's." Fiona got to her feet. "Bye, Nance. Drive safe."

She closed the door and stood for a moment in silence, looking almost snuffed out. A pain so deep it was almost physical pummeled me through the *ken,* as if someone had punched me in the gut.

*The hell…?*

Nothing like this had ever happened before and I knew that nameless shadow—the *him*—was responsible.

*Doesn't matter,* I thought. *You shouldn't know this. You shouldn't be prying into her life like this…*

"That was my neighbor, Nancy…" Fiona shook her head. She hugged herself in her robe and smiled faintly. "I said that already, didn't I?"

The shadow clung to her.

"I have to go," I said, throwing off the covers and reaching for my clothes.

Fiona's head shot up, and a jolt of her shock made the air tighten. She laughed nervously. "Right now?"

"Yeah. I have work…"

"You said you were taking the day off…" Fiona waved her hands, cutting off her own words. "No, never mind. It's fine."

"It's not you…"

"It's me," she said, leaning hard on the small counter. "It's not you, Nik. It's me. Right?"

I yanked on my jeans and stopped. "Fiona, listen…"

My words trailed. Fuck, she was too beautiful, too goddamn kissable in her silky bathrobe and her hair tousled from our sex…And that intangible quality was there—the one that was like a promise of euphoria to an addict.

*If I were a normal person, I'd take her out on a real date and just talk to her.*

I let the shirt fall from my hand and sank down on the bed. She stayed at the kitchen counter, watching me.

"I don't stay," I said. "It's not what I do."

"I know. I always knew that." She thrust her chin out. "But you don't have to make like a thief in the night. Wait out the storm. Or if not, go, but don't be a jerk about it, okay? I deserve better than that, and I've worked really hard to get to a place where I can say it: *I deserve better than that.*"

"Yeah, you do," I said, the truth falling out of my mouth and if I wasn't careful, more truth would follow. I could see she'd gotten out from under the shadow of *him* and was trying her best to stay in the light.

Fiona let go of the counter and crossed to me. She pushed my knees aside and stood between my thighs, her hands resting on my shoulders.

"We don't know each other," she said, her fingers sinking into my hair. "You're leaving town tomorrow and I'm leaving the country in a few months. Let's just have this time. No pressure. No promises we can't keep. Okay?"

I put my hands on her hips, rested my forehead against her stomach. She stiffened slightly with surprise, then rubbed my back and my shoulders and dragged her fingers through my hair. And through that touch, more of her thoughts came to me.

She wanted me to go, she wanted me to stay, in equal parts. But above all that, stronger, was Costa Rica. Freedom.

*Endless sunshine…*

That's what she wanted. What could I possibly give her? If I told her the truth she would only hate me. I'd had enough of people hating me for what I was; people like my mother and father who were supposed to love me…or the doctors who knew and treated me like a lab rat.

I couldn't let myself get close to Fiona, or build something with her, and watch it all burn to the ground when she learned the truth. I could only keep going, across the country and back again, trying to outrun my own dark cloud.

"I'm fucking tired," I said against the silk of her robe. "Exhausted in my goddamn bones."

"Then rest," Fiona said, her hands soft on my skin. "Just be."

# Chapter 9

## Fiona

Nikolai slept for hours. Deeply. I banged around in the kitchen to make lunch, and he hardly moved. No tossing and turning, his face smooth and free of the hard edges of stress he carried around with him. As the afternoon gave way to early evening, I wondered what came next. And not just in the hours to follow but in the days and weeks after that.

*He's leaving Savannah tomorrow,* I reminded myself as I tried to read a book on my little couch in my little living room. *There are no 'days and weeks.' There's only tonight…*

Tonight.

My body shivered pleasantly and that sweet ache of longing bloomed deep in my body, while a different kind of ache entirely tried to take root in my heart.

*Tonight. Our last night.*

I snipped that little regret like a weed sprouting among the flowers at Garden City Greens.

*Be a grown-up about this. You wanted a fling and you got one, and now it's ending.*

Nik stirred in my bed, and a frown marred his handsome face for a moment before smoothing again. My book fell slack in my hand as I watched him sleep. I could easily imagine him as a little boy, before the tattoos and piercings. He had an innocent-looking face, as if he'd been forced to grow up too soon and now needed to protect himself with heavy ink and sharp metal.

I wanted to ask him about his life before the road, but I was too afraid the answer would hurt. And I couldn't let myself hurt over a man.

*But you can fuck him like the whore that you are...*

I jolted and the book fell from my lap. Nik came awake, sitting upright and blinking.

"Oh, uh, sorry, to wake you..." I bent to retrieve my book.

He looked at me strangely, his brow furrowed in confusion and worry. "Are you okay?"

I frowned. "Yes, of course. I'm fine. Just reading."

Nik tore his scrutinizing gaze from me and glanced around as if he were looking for someone, then shook his head with a heavy sigh. His features returned to the mold of stress and wariness.

"Sleep well?" I asked. "If you need more, feel free."

"What time is it?" he asked.

"Quarter after four."

Nik rubbed his eyes, and reached for his shirt. "I should probably get back to my motel," he said, and I didn't miss the note of reluctance in his voice. "Gotta get cleaned up and eat something before the game tonight."

"Oh right," I said. "I forgot about your poker."

A silence fell in which Nik pulled on his jeans, and I struggled for what to say next.

*Stay for dinner?*
*Thinking about making tacos*
*I want you for one more night.*
*Tacos and sex? How does that sound?*

The doorbell rang, followed by a knock, and then Nate's voice through the door. "Fi? You decent?"

"Coming," I called, and waited until Nik put on a shirt. "That's one of my neighbor friends. Do you think he'll believe me if I say you're a distant cousin just passing through for a quick visit?"

"I wouldn't bet on it," Nik replied.

A laugh burst from me, and I opened the door. "Hello, Nathaniel."

"You're alive! Fabulous," Nate said. He stepped inside and talked while kissing both my cheeks. "We had a few too many cocktails after that horrendous show and ended up staying overnight in Savannah—"

He froze and his eyes widened comically at Nik who was leaning on the kitchen counter.

"Oh my," Nate said, his eyes darting between us, then spearing me with a questioning gaze. "I'm so sorry, I didn't realize you had a *friend* over. I'm Nate Miller," he said to Nik. "Fiona's nosy neighbor. The kind who gets all up in her business and doesn't apologize for it." He took in Nik's tattoos and piercings with all the subtlety Nate possessed—which was none at all. "And you must be…?"

"Nik Young," he said. "I'm Fiona's distant cousin, just passing through for a visit."

Nate barked laugh. "Sure you are. Cheeky. I love it." He backed to the front door that was still open and called over his shoulder, "Hey Griff, come over and meet Fi's new friend. *Right now.*"

I rolled my eyes and exchanged a helpless glance at Nik. One corner of his lip turned up in a smile. Griffin appeared at the door a moment later, casually elegant as usual, in jeans and a sweater.

"Hello, love," he said, kissing my cheek. He spied Nik over my shoulder, and while he possessed a million times more tact than his husband, his eyes widened with obvious interest. He approached Nik too, hand outstretched. "Griffin Miller."

"Good to meet you," Nik said. He shook Griff's hand and I caught a tiny wince in Nik's face, as if he'd been jolted by a small shock.

The four of us stood in a short silence, my neighbors screaming questions at me with their eyes.

Finally Griffin elbowed Nate. "Well, we should get going…"

"No, it's cool," Nik said, pushing off from the counter. "I was just leaving."

"Oh, are you…? Okay," I stammered, a hundred different words and emotions tangling up in my mouth. *This isn't how I want to say goodbye.*

My place was too small for four people to be gathered at the door. Nik squeezed through my friends to get to his leather jacket, before Griff tugged Nate out of the way, leaving Nik and me face to face.

"Will I see you again…before you leave Georgia?" I asked, painfully aware we had an audience.

"I'll stop by," Nik said.

*Tonight? Tomorrow?*

Echoes of Steve's mind-games tried to creep over me—him being purposefully vague and leaving me waiting. I thrust my chin and forced a casual smile.

"If you can. I know you have a schedule."

Nik looked down at me, his hard features softening. "I'll see you,

Fiona."

My steely resolve wilted under his warm attention. "Okay. Bye."

He held my gaze a second longer, then turned to my friends. "Good to meet you both."

"Likewise, I'm sure," Nate said, his arms crossed.

"A pleasure," Griff said, elbowing his husband.

I shut the door behind Nik and waited for my exuberant friends to pounce.

"Well, well, well, Fiona Starling," Nate said, examining his nails. "Anything you'd like to share with the class?"

Griff wore a soft, thoughtful smile that I didn't like. He came from the Opal Crawford School of worrying about my personal life. I know he and Nate wondered why I didn't date, but while Opal knew a little bit about Steve, the Millers knew nothing. I figured the fewer the people I brought into my shady situation, the better.

"Who is he, Fi?" Griff asked.

I shrugged and moved away from the door. The words *No one* almost escaped me but I caught them back. Fling or not, it felt wrong to call Nik 'no one.'

*God, don't get stupid now...*

"I met him at Club 91," I said. "We got to talking and we sort of...hit it off."

"Is that the slang for sex these days?" Nate said, tossing a glance at my bed's rumpled sheets on his way to the fridge. "I thought it was 'Netflix and chill.'"

Griff sat at one of the stools at my counter, and whistled at Lemony in his cage. "This bird has seen some X-rated shenanigans, hasn't he?"

Nate emerged from my refrigerator with a bottle of water. "You mind? We're out and I'm not touching tap."

"Help yourself," I said with a smirk as Nate already had the cap twisted off.

"Have you seen some naughty sexy times?" Griff cooed to the bird, then looked to me sweetly. "So you and Nik...? Is this a thing or a fling?"

"Yes, that. A fling," I said, plopping down on my couch and facing them. "He's only in town for a few days. Traveling salesman..."

Nate choked on his water. "What's he sell? Whips and chains?"

I laughed. "Motorcycle parts."

Nate placed both hands on the counter. "Honey, if that boy is a salesman, I'm the Pope."

I frowned. "Of course he is. He said he was. I have his business card..." I shook my head. "Anyway, he has to travel constantly for his job. He plays poker while he's on the road. Underground games."

"Oh, a criminal element," Nate said. "He's a bad boy."

"Are you going to see him again?" Griff asked, leaning one arm on the counter. "After he 'stops by', I mean."

I plucked an invisible piece of lint off the couch. "Probably not. He's going to hit the road and I'm leaving the country in a few months so..."

Nate rolled his eyes. "Ugh, don't remind me."

"Anyway, what's up with you guys?" I asked loudly. "How was the play?"

"Awful," Nate said at the same time Griff said, "A work in progress."

I smothered a laugh as Griff shot Nate a withering glance that Nate returned with a shrug. "I only speak the truth."

Griff turned to me. "It was the right thing to do, to support my friend, and it paid off big time."

"How so?" I asked.

"We drank a wee bit too much and got a hotel," Nate said. "The next morning, Griff wanted to do some house hunting. In a hurricane. As one does."

"It was hardly a hurricane, and by house hunting, he means that as we drove back here, I caught sight of a For Sale sign on a gorgeous little Victorian-style house." Griff's blue eyes were lit with happiness. "I just got this feeling about it, Fi. It's a little run-down but I could see through the chipped paint and the sagging rain gutters." He shook his head. "I knew this house was It."

"It?" I asked. "The one?"

My friends had been house hunting since I moved in to the complex two years ago. Griff was an attorney—just starting out—and Nate worked in a gallery. They lived in our dinky complex to save money for a down payment on their dream home in Savannah.

"We found it," Nate said, his usual snippy tone softening and warming. He reached out and Griff wordlessly took his hand. "I had my doubts but..."

"But the owner didn't care that it was raining buckets," Griff said.

"She let us in for tea and we talked for hours. By the time we left, she agreed to take her sign down if we agreed to sit down with a broker next week and make it official."

"So we are," Nate said.

"Oh my God, I'm so happy for you guys!" I flew off the couch to hug Griffin, and then I moved around the little island to Nate. "I'm so happy and so sad. When will you move?"

"Hopefully in a month or so."

I socked Nate in the arm. "See? You guys are leaving me before I leave you."

"Yeah, to *downtown Savannah*," Nate said. "Not Central America, for crying out loud."

"Even so, I'll miss you so much," I said and suddenly found it hard to keep a smile.

"You have to visit us every weekend when you're not babysitting Hailey or walking stray mutts around the shelter," Nate said.

Griff took my hand and gave it a squeeze. "The house has three bedrooms. Plenty of room for you and a *guest*."

I squeezed his hand back and let go. "So," I said, flouncing back down on the couch. "You said the house is a Victorian? Tell me every detail."

Griff and I prepared tacos and guacamole while Nate drank wine and supervised. We ate and talked and laughed, and they went home close to ten o'clock at night. No sooner had I shut the door then the silence descended.

My place felt empty. My bed was empty.

I wondered how thick the silence would feel when Griff and Nate moved away.

*And how cold the bed will feel tonight when there's no one in it but me?*

Nik had said he'd stop by, but he didn't owe me anything. For all I knew, his hurried goodbye at the door was the last time I'd ever see him.

I tried to shake all these negative thoughts. My plan was intact.

Costa Rica. There would be no silence in the little house I planned to rent. The teeming jungle would be the soundtrack to every dark night, and the ocean waves crashing at my feet during the day would eat any silence that tried to remind me I was alone.

I was going there alone.

*Alone. Lone. Lonely.*

"Oh stop," I said, to break the silence.

Lemony was no help, fast asleep on his perch. I hung his cage back on the hook by the window. The storm had lost its power and the news said it would be blown out by tomorrow.

I checked my phone for a text from Nik. Since I'd called him, he had my number. He hadn't used it.

*I'll stop by,* he'd said.

When?

"*Tonight after I get off work, I'm taking you to a fancy restaurant.*"

"*Oh...but I made plans with Janice. The neighbor? I don't know anyone here. She's the first person I think I might become friends with...*"

"*Cancel it. I want to take you out. Someplace fancy. Put on a pretty dress for me and I'll pick you up at eight.*"

"*It's been a long time since we've gone out just you and me. I guess I could cancel...*"

"*Trust me, sweetheart. I'm going to sweep you off your feet tonight.*"

"*That sounds amazing, Steve.*"

"*You're* amazing. *I love you...*"

I blinked to dissolve the memory that had played before my eyes like a bad movie. I'd put on a pretty black dress that night. I hated wearing a lot of makeup, but I painstakingly followed the instructions from a YouTube tutorial. I twisted my hair into an elegant French twist since Steve was always complaining I looked like a high school kid with my long hair.

And I waited.

For hours.

Steve didn't come home until well past midnight. I'd taken off my dress, removed my makeup and climbed into bed hours earlier. I kept my back turned and pretended to be asleep as he slid into the bed beside me. I waited some more. For a touch or a whispered, *I'm sorry.*

Nothing. And I was too ashamed to ask Janice to hang out ever again...

I blinked rapidly to banish the tears, and started for my closet, to change into something to sleep in—something slouchy and unsexy and comfortable because I could wear whatever the hell I wanted...

My phone buzzed a text. Nik.

**I'm sorry I bailed earlier. Done in a few hours. Too late to come by after?**

My body reacted as it usually did to the idea of Nik touching me—a wildfire of heat raced through me and my breath caught. A smile broke over my face and then tapered away as I sent my reply with nervous fingers.

**Not too late.**

A pause, then, **CU soon.**

And I knew he meant it. I stayed in my sundress.

I was on the couch, trying in vain to read but the anticipation sent tingles down my limbs and made it hard to concentrate. The rain had come again, a last hurrah, but gentle this time. It tapped on the glass and the wind whispered in the trees instead of howling like before.

At quarter after two, Nikolai came back. He knocked at the door.

"Come in," I said softly.

He strode in carrying the harsh scents of smoke, liquor, and the gentler smell of warm summer rain with him. He shut the door and stood before me, motorcycle helmet in hand, staring at me. The rain glistened and rolled like mercury over the black of his leather jacket and dampened his dark hair to black. The blue of his eyes was like the hottest part of a flame, radiating desire. Pure, unfiltered want. I'd never had a man look at me how Nik did in that moment—as if I were everything he'd ever wanted in the world and all he had to do was come and take it.

My body reacted instantly—a flush of heat. A sweet ache between my legs.

"Still raining?" I said, trying to organize a coherent thought.

"Yeah, it is," he said, watching me.

"They say the storm is going to blow over tonight," I said. "Clear skies tomorrow."

He nodded. "Tomorrow."

Tomorrow, he'd leave with the storm.

The understanding passed between us, giving us permission to have this night. One last night.

"So," I said, slowly setting my book on the coffee table. "How was the game?"

"I won," Nik said, his voice almost a growl.

His eyes swept up and down my body; I could feel where they landed on me: my bare legs tucked under me, the flimsy summer dress I wore. My breasts were outlined against the material because I'd neglected to wear a bra.

"So it was a good night?" I said. "You got lucky?"

"It's not luck. I win when I want to win."

"Every time?" I unfolded my legs, then spread them slightly.

"Yeah." Nik's gaze was intent on my thighs. "Every fucking time."

His heated words tore through me like a current. I inched my dress up to show him more, my entire body screaming for him. His eyes widened, nostrils flared. He dropped his motorcycle helmet, stripped off his jacket, and crossed my small living room in three long strides. In front of me, he dropped to his knees and shoved my legs apart.

"Oh God," I breathed, shocked and relieved, both. "Yes…"

His hands slid up my thighs and came back down with my thong. It stretched to the point of breaking around my spread knees, and Nik tore it off me and flung it away.

"I'm going to go broke replacing underwear," I said, my heart pounding now.

"Then stop wearing them," Nik said.

His hands slipped back under my dress, gripped my hips, and hauled me to the edge of the couch, my dress riding up. I fell back with a sigh, as another flush of heat swept through me.

With a final, lust-ridden glance at me, Nik thrust my knees further apart and bent his head to me. A cry tore out of me at the first touch of his mouth between my legs, his tongue relentless and hard from the start, his mouth sucking, teeth grazing.

I reached up with both hands and gripped the top of the couch, holding on for dear life, as Nik's mouth worked over my most sensitive flesh with a hunger that stole my breath. My body tensed, then bucked, nonsense sounds and words fell from my lips, my eyes fluttered, stars bursting behind closed lids as the first orgasm ripped through me.

"So sweet," Nik said, his voice rumbling against me. "So fucking sweet…"

His words were like a whip, driving me to higher highs, even before the first climax began to wane. I wreathed his neck with my legs, my heels digging into his back, dragging, pulling him tighter to me.

Nikolai stayed with my bucking hips and kept his mouth on me, his tongue delving. I felt delirious as the first orgasm tapered away and a second roared up in its wake. I arched my back into it, my hands releasing the couch to drop to either side of me, my palms pressed into the cushions, offering myself to him.

"Oh God, Nik…"

My body tensed as the climax shuddered through me, and I collapsed on the couch, my head rolling against the back, my legs going slack on his shoulders. Waves of warm pleasure rolled through me, and I sucked in sweet draughts of air as Nik gently set my shaking legs down. He sat on his heels, looking as satisfied as I felt, and I watched, with a tired, heated fascination, as his tongue—that had worked such incredible magic on me—rolled slowly over his lower lip.

"Oh my God," I said. "If this is what happens when you have a good night at the tables…"

"I'd have done the same thing had I lost," he said. "But I never lose."

"Never?"

He ignored that, his eyes raking over my body. "I spent the entire game winning and wanting you. Wanting you so fucking bad…"

"You did?"

"I did." He rose to his feet, pulling me with him. His gaze never wavered from mine as he lifted me up to carry me to the bed.

"Are you going to throw me over your shoulder like a caveman?" I asked, lacing my arms around his neck.

"You want me to?" he asked.

I grinned, shrugged one shoulder. "That's one for the bucket list."

But my place was too small; we were already at my bed. He set me down, stripped my dress off and then I became lost in him, a delirious tangle of arms and legs; biting kisses and his hands…God, Nik's hands were everywhere. My entire awareness became only the sensations he created in me and the fierce desire to create the same for him.

At last, he collapsed on top of me, where I melted into the bed, satiated and heavy and every part of me thrumming. I held Nik close, my fingers sunk deep into the damp hair at the back of his head, our breaths gusting out of us like bellows.

*Who are you?*

Who the hell was this man who could turn me on with a look? He exuded danger like a vapor and yet I felt completely safe with him. His body was attuned to mine in a way I couldn't understand.

Nik started to lift off of me but I held him tight. "Stay."

*Stay here...*

"I can't," he said, the words sounding like they weighed a thousand pounds. "I...I'm too heavy."

I held him as he shifted a little so that his left side was mostly on the bed, but I hooked my leg over his hip and pressed close to keep us joined. He buried his face in my neck, his breath hot and short on my neck until he caught it, then he exhaled. His body expanded under my arms with a sigh.

"Tell me something, Nik," I said, settling myself over his chest, his hand playing in my hair.

"Tell you what?"

"Anything. Something about you." *Something I can keep after you go...*

He shifted beneath me. I turned to rest my cheek on his chest, looking at him.

"Tell me about your art," I asked. "Where did you learn to draw?"

He shrugged. "Don't know. Just did it. Painted mostly. I liked...working with bright colors."

"Do you still paint?"

He shook his head, once. "No."

"You're very talented," I said. "You don't do it anymore? Besides cocktail napkins?"

"The last time I touched a brush was in high school, but..."

"But...?"

"But I got sick. I was in the hospital for a long time. When I got out, I didn't want to paint anymore."

An ache bloomed in my heart. "I'm sorry." I was going to ask what he'd been sick with, but bit the words back.

"What about you?" Nik asked slowly. "What did you want to be? A gardener? A baker?"

"No," I said, the ache flowering into something barbed and sharp.

"I wanted to be a kindergarten teacher."

"But now you don't?"

I turned my head the other way, to watch the rain streak the window, like tears. "I still do." I squeezed my eyes shut. "Maybe someday. But Costa Rica comes first. Once I'm there, and get settled, I can…decide how I want everything else to be."

The old pain tried to take deeper root and I braced myself for another question. Stupid of me to even start this conversation. Why had I asked about something so personal? He was leaving and I couldn't talk about my own dreams; they were shattered and gone.

But Nik didn't speak. His hand found my hair again, his fingers winding and unwinding, stroking the lengths and letting them fall. The old ache faded away under his silence and his touch.

I slept with him under me, warm and solid and unwavering.

When I next woke, the rain had stopped.

The wind quieted.

The storm was over.

In the silence, Nik raised his head to look at me, his blue eyes full of unspoken thoughts, mirroring my own.

*Stay,* I wanted to say again, but the word was caught my throat, trapped by fear and tangled in a hundred emotions, none of which I trusted to be real.

*I can't,* Nik said, not with words but in the pain that edged every beautiful feature of his face.

I knew—somehow—he had his own unconfessed secrets that were going to take him out of Savannah, and away from me, more urgently than any duty to his job.

Nik kissed me softly, then harder, and we again gave in to mindless want and heat, to greedy touches that left us sweaty and breathless and were satiated for only a handful of minutes before reaching for each other again. We spent our last hours together in a desperate clutch until finally falling into a stupor of spent ecstasy. Neither of us slept.

Morning light streamed in clear and gold from a cloudless sky that was an empty canvas painted bright blue. The heat had already begun to seep in.

Nik stirred and then silently moved to sit at the edge of the bed.

"Coffee?" I asked.

He slumped, his muscled, inked shoulders rounding. "I should go."

*He should. Because this is my house. My rules...*

For two years, those rules were my only defense against the aftermath of Steve's abuse. Now, as I watched Nikolai Young pull on his jeans, I thought I could hear my ex snickering in triumph.

Nik finished dressing. I slipped on my silky robe and walked him to the door.

"My route takes me up the East Coast, and then back down this way," he said, drawing on his jacket. He yanked at the sleeve, not looking at me. "You going to be around in a few months?"

My heart clanged a heavy beat from within the cage of my ribs.

"I...I don't know—"

"It's okay," Nik said quickly. "I get it."

*You do?* I wanted to ask, because I had a thousand different thoughts that sent my stomach into flutters or dropped it to my knees; blaring defensive warnings designed to protect my heart, and the whispered pleas to take a chance, one more time.

Nikolai opened the door, and the humid heat of Georgia in summer enveloped us both. He hesitated, looked as if he were going to say something, then took my face in his hands and kissed me. A deep, intense kiss that I felt in every recess of my body, even the shadowy cracks Steve had left in my heart.

Nik broke away, still holding me. His handsome features were tense, his brows furrowed. "Okay, see you around," he said quickly and let me go.

"Yeah, see you," I said faintly, feeling the absence of his hands on my face like a chill.

I watched him straddle his motorcycle and pull on a helmet that shielded his face from me. He revved his bike and I knew he was watching me; I could feel his gaze all over, like a pull or yearning. He nodded once, then backed up and tore out of the parking lot.

I clutched the doorframe and didn't move as the last of the exhaust from his motorcycle thinned and dissipated until there was nothing left.

# Part II: The Doe

# Chapter 10

## Nikolai

"It's not working."
    "The treatment takes time."
    "It feels like it's burning me out of my body."
    "What does that mean, Nik?"
    "You see those movies where a house is on fire and a person is trapped? And the fire is getting hotter and the smoke is getting thicker, and the person has to escape but he can't? That's what it feels like."
    "It hurts? You should be asleep during—"
    "It burns the whole time. And a headache after. So bad."
    "Only a few more."
    "How many?"

"Can you sense me right now?"

...

"Nik?"

"Yes."

"What am I thinking?"

"It doesn't work like that."

"What am I feeling?"

"Curious."

"I'm always curious. That's my job. What else?"

"You'll get mad."

"I won't, I promise."

"Like you're better than me."

"What does that look like?"

"Doesn't. It smells. Like perfume covering up a rotten stink. And now you want to pinch my arm—"

"When did this start, Nik? The first time?"

"You keep asking. I don't remember."

"Try."

"I was small."

"How small?"

"Papa was a giant. An angry giant."

"Was he the first person you sensed with the ken?"

"No, Mama. She was warmth on a cold day and the first bite of food when you're hungry."

"And your father? What was he like?"

"Smoke. Heat. Burning. Like a house on fire and we can't escape."

"Did he hurt you, Nik?"

"Sometimes. Mostly Mama."

"Do you hear voices?"

"No. I hear thoughts. Only sometimes."

"What's the difference?"

"Hearing voices in your head is make-believe. The thoughts I hear are real... Now you're disappointed. I'm not getting better."

"I think we'll do another treatment."

"When?"

"Today."

"No! Why...?"

"What do you want, Nik? If you had one wish?"

*"I wish Mama would look at me. Touch me. She used to hug me when I was scared. I'm scared all the time..."*
*"What will make her hug you again?"*
*"If the* ken *goes away?"*
*"Bingo. That's what we want too. Okay?"*
*...*
*"Nik?"*
*"Okay."*
*And then they set the house on fire and I couldn't get out...*

I drove the Bonneville into the Forever Sunrise Assisted Living Facility in St. Louis, Missouri. The city was breathing down my neck and my nose had leaked as I rolled into the parking lot. I wondered why the fuck I was doing this to myself.

I'd left Fiona and an inexplicable deep ache sank into my heart and wouldn't let go; a vague, pathetic wish to be with the only other person on the planet who gave a shit whether I lived or died.

*Except Ma hasn't looked at you for longer than three seconds in more then ten years.*

But here I was, like one of those dumb bastards who keep stepping up to the table even though the house has him beat.

I signed in the visitor's log, trying desperately to ignore the lives around me, flickering at the end of their wicks. Once, during a visit, someone had died. I'd felt their life snuff out, leaving only a little wisp of smoke behind. I'd barely made it to the bathroom in time to vomit.

I went upstairs to my mother's room, and knocked, then opened the door. Her place resembled more a hospital room than a residence. She lay on the bed, her head turned to the window, looking frail and gaunt, as if even the sheets over her body were weighing her down.

"Hey, Ma," I said.

She didn't look at me, but she knew I was there.

I moved to sit beside her, took her hand in mine. It felt like lighter than last time and dry and thin as rice paper. The *ken* showed me a muddled mirage of scattered thoughts and memories. A flash of my father's face twisted in rage and the sting of his backhand that whipped her head to the side. My jaw tingled and I dropped her hand.

"Nikolai," my mother said on an exhale, then squeezed her eyes shut against me.

That felt like a slap in the face too.

"How have you been, Ma?"

Nothing.

"They treating you right?"

The clock ticked on the bedside table.

"You need anything?"

A strange, prickly cloud materialized around her, like a swarm of bees and she looked at me, her dark eyes suddenly sharp and clear.

"What I need? I tell you what I *don't* need. The curse. Why you bring it to me?" she demanded. "It's worse now, da? It darkened your skin and you stick yourself with metal…"

"Okay, Ma…"

"Those doctors, they were no good. They let you out and you come here, bring the curse with you to me. A sick old lady…"

My jaw clenched. "I'm your *son*…"

"Bah." She shook her head on the pillow, her brittle hair like a nest around her head and then her eyes widened in a sudden panic. "My son, my son? Where is my son?" she wailed, her lucidity slipping away like a flipped switch, leaving her frantic. "My sweet little boy is gone. Gone…"

An orderly strode in with a condescending smirk on his face. "Okay, Mrs. Young. There, there. Getting a little upset, are we?" He shot me a look, his eyes flickering over my tattoos.

I rose from the chair. "I'm going. Don't know why I bother."

The orderly agreed without saying a word.

My mother was still shaking her head, murmuring in Russian, her eyes closed, lips pressed together. Her memories were filled with me as a boy, before the *ken*. Her hugging me; laughing with me as we played under the sprinklers in the backyard under a hot Texas sun; kissing my cheek at bedtime and telling me not to worry, Papa wouldn't stay mad for long and besides, we have each other, don't we…?

*Those days are long fucking gone,* I told myself. *Why do you do this to yourself? This is the last visit…*

I stopped at the door to my mother's room, wishing with everything I had I could go inside the memories my mother was living in and live in them with her.

"Bye, Ma," I said. "I'll see you soon."

I drove out of town, to the outskirts and found a motel. Yet another shit motel in the long string of shit motels in my life. I sat on the bed and held my head in my hands.

*Now what?*

I lay back on the stiff bed and stared at the ceiling. A pale yellow water stain colored one corner. That was real. I saw it with my eyes. Through the *ken,* a black ichor of pain and misery seeped through the wall like a spreading ink stain. The occupant of the room next to mine was on the verge too. Maybe he had a gun or a bunch of pills. Or maybe he had a motorcycle that tended to veer toward oncoming traffic and visions of being mercifully splattered all over the road. Anything to end the pain.

*Anything to end the goddamn* ken.

"Fiona," I whispered to no one.

*Tough shit,* no one answered back. She was moving out of the damn country. She had a plan and didn't include giving some desperate freak a fix of whatever it was she had that kept the onslaught of life at bay. Made it bearable.

Made it livable.

*She made life livable.*

The inexplicable peace Fiona had given me seemed like a memory, one that I was remembering wrong. It felt impossible that she stilled the voices and washed the sour tastes out of my mouth with her sweet kiss. She was beautiful and sexy, and sleeping with her had been hotter than it had been with any other woman in my life. Ever.

*She was an infatuation, not a miracle.*

Except that the peace I'd felt was real no matter what I tried to tell myself, and made the *ken* that much harder to take. And beyond her peace, I couldn't stop thinking about her. Her beauty and smile, and the inherent goodness of *her*...

I jerked up off the bed and took a shower, then dressed in a black t-shirt and jeans.

The cure for forgetting Fiona, I thought with a desperate hope, lay between the legs of another woman.

The motel had no one manning the front desk to tell me where the local action was, but Summerville was small. I rode to downtown and found a little jazz bar. It wasn't as loud as the dance club I wanted, but it was packed with people. The snare drum, sax, and piano worked in concert to dull the throbbing cacophony of life, and the dim light helped to calm the *ken* that insisted on showing me the colored mists and halos of everyone around me.

I shouldered my way to the bar, next to a brunette with a reddish glow around her. She wore a tight black dress that showed her cleavage and I tasted pepper on my tongue when she turned on her stool to give me an appraising glance.

"Hi, there." Her gaze traveled up my arms, following the trails of ink, to my piercings and then to my eyes. "I'm Lydia."

She offered her hand and the entire night played out in my mind in an instant: I buy her a drink or two, watch the low-grade heat of her interest flare to full-blown fire, and then when I know she's ready, we go to her place or my motel and I fuck her senseless. Or rather, I try to fuck her until *I'm* senseless. It doesn't happen. Her orgasms swamp my own until all I can see or feel or taste is her getting off. I roll off of her immediately; use the summer heat as an excuse for keeping to my side of the bed. She falls asleep. I take off. Even if it's my own goddamn motel room, I pack up and leave and hit the road and do it all over again some other night, in some other town…

Lydia's eyebrows rose and she dropped her hand that'd been hovering in the air between us into her lap, like a bird that'd been shot out of the sky.

"Hello? Penny for your thoughts?"

I jerked my gaze to her and blinked. Lydia. She was dark and red; chocolate, spice, and velvet. Any man would be drooling to take her home.

*Fiona was soft and sweet, and when I kissed her, the world dissolved like spun sugar on my tongue…*

I turned to leave the club with Lydia's, "Weirdo," tossed at me like a parting shot. It bounced off of me and I hit the street, racing back to the motel. I packed up my belongings, checked out, and settled on the road by eleven p.m. As the road flew by, my mind spun in circles. If I went on like this, something was going to give. I didn't just sense that guy in the motel room next to mine. I was him.

*Take a few weeks. That's all. A break. And then you leave her alone.*

A plan formed immediately. Win some money. Enough to live off of for a few weeks. Hang out with her and just…be.

*Use her, you mean. Dig deep into her personal pain and dark shadows while you take what you need from her, like a psychic vampire, and then watch her go. Great fucking plan.*

I slowed the Bonneville and pulled over. "Fuck."

I killed the engine. "*Fuck.*"

I climbed off and ripped at my helmet and hurled it to the ground. *"Fuck!"*

I screamed it to the night sky, my thoughts and memories filled with her smile, her sense of humor, her fearlessness, and her kindness that radiated pink light, like her hair must look under the sunshine.

But she'd been fucked over and had to protect herself. When I'd said goodbye, I'd felt equal parts reluctance to see me go and a grudging pride that she'd kept her end of the bargain. *He*—whoever that asshole was—had stolen something from her, and though I couldn't see what, I knew it left Fiona afraid to trust a man ever again.

*Can you blame her?*

I grabbed my helmet from where it'd rolled in the dirt, plan scrapped. Fuck it, I'd find another poker game in another town…

The helmet dangled in my hand by the strap.

And then…

Then I was that guy in the room with a gun and nothing left in the tank. Or nothing but brains and guts splattered all over the road after the Bonneville crossed the yellow lines.

Or I disappeared.

*She's my last chance.*

Hope flowed through me like cool water, washing away the blood-stained visions of my future. I put the helmet back on and turned the bike around on the two-lane road, back the way I had come, back to the shabby motel at the edge of town.

I parked the Bonneville at the entry, and ran inside the dinky-ass lobby. My body went still, listening and looking; the *ken* stretching out like a voice calling a name.

He answered.

I blinked in surprise and jerked in a gasp of air. I'd never done that before. Never controlled the *ken* because I didn't know it was mine to control.

*Another goddamn plot twist.*

Hurriedly, my gaze darted around and landed on a pad of paper and pen on the motel's version of a concierge desk. I scribbled a hasty note; nothing professional or clinical. One soul reaching out to another with the first words that came to mind.

*Sleep on it. See another sunrise. Ask for help.*

I ran up to the room next to the one I'd vacated earlier and tucked it under the door. Maybe it would help. Maybe it wouldn't, but it was all I could do.

I hit the road again, this time east, at three in the morning, toward Jacksonville, Florida. The idea of contending with another big city made me nauseated, but aside from Atlantic City, which was too far, Jacksonville had the biggest casino with the highest stakes. I had a couple grand to play with and needed to parlay it into something I could live off of.

I was going to live. Not exist.

*Unless Fiona tells you to fuck off.*

That was my deal. I'd stay if Fiona took mercy on me. And if not…

I squeezed the throttle and the motorcycle tore through the remnants of the night and into the first light of morning. The highway was a dark snake with yellow stripes down its back. Endless. They glowed when the headlight of my Bonneville hit them, taking me into one more sunrise.

# Chapter 11

## Fiona

"Fi? You still with us?"

I blinked and lifted my chin out of my hand where it'd been resting on the register desk at Garden City Greens. "Hmm? Sorry, yes, I was just…thinking."

Opal pursed her lips. "Something tells me you weren't pondering where to put the order of extra zinnias that just came in."

"That's exactly what I was thinking about, as a matter of fact." I said with a small smile. I straightened and brushed my hands down the front of my overalls. "I'm having some very deep thoughts about shelving."

"Hmmph." Opal gave me a soft look that belied the wry twist to her lips, and left me at the register while she helped a customer.

She'd already given me the third degree about Nikolai but there wasn't much to tell. He'd hit the road, as planned, and I was moving to Costa Rica, as planned. Life had resumed its course after a slight detour.

Except I couldn't stop thinking about that three-day detour. It invaded my thoughts every minute of my life—my body remembering Nik's heated touches, and my heart holding tight to the surprising glimpses of his humor, and the way his blue eyes warmed whenever he looked at me…

*I never should have gone to the club that night.*

I sighed and rested my chin back onto the heel of my right hand. My fingers on the left made little trails in the dusting of soil on the table.

Earlier, a customer had purchased a croton plant with broad, shiny green leaves, marbled with red and yellow striations. A little bit of its dirt had spilled as the customer had set it on the counter. Crotons were my favorite, and I thought Costa Rica must be filled with them. Whenever a customer bought one, my spirits lifted, reminding me how close I was to seeing for myself if that was true.

Now, the vibrant colors I imagined in Costa Rica were washed out, as if someone had taken the brilliant photo I had pinned to the wall of my imagination and laid a dull tint over it.

My shift ended at four o'clock, and Opal gave me another one of her looks as I readied to head out.

"Any big plans tonight?" she asked carefully, rifling through receipts at the register.

"Yes," I said, shouldering my embroidered canvas bag that served as my purse. "Lemony and I are going to eat homemade brownies and watch *Sex and the City* reruns until dawn."

Opal smiled faintly. "Sounds enthralling."

I sighed and crossed my arms over my Garden City Greens apron. "Go ahead. Say it."

My friend was too direct to pretend like she didn't know what I was talking about

*And maybe I want to hear it.*

"You're twenty-three and yet I never hear you mention hanging out with friends." She held up a hand. "Flings with tattooed strangers aside, I'm talking about you, being young, having fun, going to parties…Doing what young people do."

"I have friends," I said slowly. "Griff and Nate. And you…"

"I am your friend and I love you to pieces, but the only reason we know each other is because you work with me. Griff and Nate are your friends but they were your neighbors first."

I shrugged, tucked a lock of hair behind my ear, my gaze cast to the ground. "It's just…how it is right now for me."

Opal sighed. "I know, honey." She dropped her voice. "And now that I know more about Steve, the angrier I get. If he were here, I'd put his balls in a sling…"

"I don't doubt it."

"But I can see it now," Opal said, "how you've cut yourself off, and I'm just afraid that Costa Rica is a really monumental step toward disappearing altogether."

I raised my head, tried to find a smile. "That's the plan."

Opal's gaze was hard and soft at the same time. "Have you called Nik?" she asked. "Have you even thought about it?"

*Only every other minute...*

"I think you have," Opal said before I could answer. "And I think you should. Or better yet, postpone your move and call one of the counselors I know. Talk to them, honey." She fished a card out of her wallet and pressed it into my hand. "I don't want you to disappear."

In my apartment, Lemony Snicket *cheeped* a greeting from the window as I came in. It was nearly five but the sun wasn't even thinking about setting. I watched the sunlight glint on Lemony's yellow feathers...and the faux-gold bars of his cage.

"Costa Rica is the right thing to do, isn't it?" I asked. "I still want it. I want those beaches and the mountains, and the beautiful jungle. But now..."

*I don't want to be alone.*

Which was stupid since that was the whole point of moving to Costa Rica in the first place.

"Dammit, this sucks," I said, tears filling my eyes and spilling over. I swiped them away angrily. "I'm stronger than I look, aren't I?"

Lemony cocked his head and hopped from one bar to the next, his little wings only fluttering, not expanding. Not stretching and catching a current.

Not flying.

I dropped onto the couch and opened my laptop that was on the coffee table. In the Google search bar, I only had to type the first letter of the name and it auto-filled.

The article from the *Duluth Courier* was the same as it had been last I checked. No updates. No new news.

"She just disappeared," I murmured.

I switched over to my email. It was filled with the usual junk. The only personal message was from Claudia Araya, my contact in Costa Rica who was helping me to secure a work visa at an animal shelter in the little town of San Josecito, in Uvita. While I'd told Opal, Griff and

Nate—and now Nik—that I was moving, the only person on earth who knew exactly where in Costa Rica was Claudia.

**From**: Claudia Araya caraya@migracion.gov.cr
**To**: Fiona Starling FionaStar357@gmail.com
**Sent**: Friday, June 1 9:19 AM
**Subject**: Almost here!

*Buenos Días, mi dulce niña,*
*I've attached a few listings as potential residences for you, all close enough to the town center for you to ride a bicycle, as requested. The animal sanctuary requires an address with proof of a signed lease, and then we can submit the entire package to the Embajada for final approval and visa issuance. I know picking a house sight-unseen is less than ideal but after one year, the lease is up and you will be free to choose your own 'forever home' as you Americans like to call it. Please let me know which of the attached you feel might be suitable to rent, fill out the application, and I will forward both to Sylvie at the realty agency.*
*I hope you're brushing up on your Spanish!*
*Muy atentamente,*
*Claudia*

I clicked through the listings for three secluded little houses tucked into the jungle greenery. They were all one-bedroom homes with beach views to the west, rounded green mountains to the east, and a jungle wildlife refuge just north.

"Perfect," I said. And it was, but I couldn't get the word to stick.

I dug through my bag and found the business card of the therapist Opal recommended and set it next to Nik's business card on the coffee table, both next to my open laptop.

Three choices. Three roads to take; two of which were detours from my carefully constructed escape plan. My fingers reached out and landed on the plain, creased card with Nik's number on it.

*I miss him. It's okay to admit that, isn't it?*

There was no answer; even Steve's poisonous commentary had gone silent, as if to drive home the fact that the choice of which road to take was mine and mine alone.

I shut my laptop without replying to Claudia, or calling either number, and flopped down onto my bed. My bed felt ten times bigger and wider than ever before. I burrowed my face into the pillow and inhaled deeply but Nikolai Alexei Young was long gone.

He was gone and he'd taken something with him, some piece of the foundation that left the entire structure wobbly.

"I'm fine. This is stupid," I said, surprised—and a little pissed off—to find myself on the verge of tears again.

The apartment walls were thin; I heard Griff's hearty, bellowing laughter from the other side of my kitchen. I grabbed my phone and shot Nate a text.

**You guys around?**
**Watching a flick in 10,** Nate texted back. **Come over?**
I bit my lip. **Don't want to crash a hot date.**
**Hot date is tomorrow night. Tonight it's Al Pacino and pizza. Come over.**
**U sure?**
**Price of admission: Fi's Famous Brownies**
**Deal.**
**We'll hold the movie. <3**
**<3**

I let out a shaky sigh. I could envision Steve's condescending smirk. I busied myself mixing flour, chocolate and sugar, eggs and butter. Forty minutes later, I had a hot pan in two mitts and was standing in front of apartment #5. I elbowed the doorbell and Griff answered, in plaid pajama pants and a wife-beater. He was a fit guy who spent every morning before work at the law firm at the gym on 5$^{th}$, but his arms looked less toned than I'd remembered, and pale without a drop of ink.

*Oh stop it.*

"Fi!" Griff said. "Those smell heavenly. Come in, love."

"Thanks for having me," I said in a small voice. I hurried past him and set the brownies down on their kitchen counter. "These have to cool."

Griff frowned. "You okay?"

"She's having epic sex withdrawals." Nate waved from the couch. "Fiona, darling. Come sit. Tell Uncle Nate all about it."

"I am not having sex withdrawals," I muttered.

"Tattooed biker boy withdrawals?"

"No, I'm fine," I said, plopping down on the couch. "I'm…fine."

Griff sat on the other side of me, and I felt concerned looks pass over my head. Without a word, Nate took my hand in his and Griff put his arm around me.

"What's the flick?" I asked before they could ask me anything else.

"*Dog Day Afternoon*," Nate said. "Griff, honey, would you...?"

"Got it," Griff said and reached for the remote.

We watched Al Pacino's bank heist go from bad to worse, and stuffed our faces with pizza and brownies. I sat wedged between them, buffered by their love for each other, and feeling more and more lonely as the night went on. My friends touched one another—a hand squeeze or brush of fingers—as plates were passed or drinks were poured. Little brushes of familiarity and affection that were as natural to them as eating. It was beautiful to watch, but every time Nate finished one of Griff's sentences, or when Griff handed Nate a napkin just as Nate opened his mouth to ask, my heart ached a little bit more.

"Chris Sarandon in a bathrobe," Griff said as the actor came onscreen.

"Here we go," Nate said, and they both quoted along with the movie, "Red, blues, uppers, downers, screamers..."

The movie passed through me without me seeing it; the dialogue morphed to a lone voice in my head, repeating the same line over and over.

*I want.*

I wanted what they had. I wanted inside jokes and casual touches that said 'I'm here, with you.' I wanted someone who knew me so well, he could finish my sentences. Or knew when to say nothing at all.

I wedged myself deeper between my friends, my cheek resting on Griff's shoulder and Nate tucked against me. By the time the movie ended, Griff had fallen asleep. I nudged Nate. His smile when he looked at his husband was warm, and free of prickly edges.

"Baby's all tuckered out," Nate whispered. "Carbs work on him the way Valium works on me."

I extracted myself from the couch and Nate walked me to the door.

"Thanks for the brownies," he said. "They were bakery-worthy, as usual."

"Thanks for the company," I said and kissed his cheek.

He pulled me in close. "I know we're no match for Mr. Young, but..."

"Oh hush, love you. See you tomorrow."

"Fi…"

I slipped out of his embrace. "Goodnight, Nate."

"Sweet dreams, Fiona," he called softly.

I ducked out and went back to my place that was so much smaller than Nate and Griff's one-bedroom, and stale. Quiet. Empty.

I fell into a fitful sleep, filled with strange dreams about a road at night, and a man kneeling next to a dark shape in the rain…

Sunlight streamed over my eyes. I blinked awake, reaching for the dream but it slipped away the more I came awake. My glance landed on the clock.

"Shit."

---

"You're late," Marco, the stock boy, said as I rushed into the backroom of Garden City Greens to throw on my apron. He gave me a perplexed look. "You're never late."

"First time for everything," I said with a tight smile.

But after my hurried arrival, my shift dragged. I idled all morning, then played catch up all afternoon under soaring temperatures and humidity that felt like ninety-nine percent.

"This is bullshit," I muttered in the stock room. I tossed a twenty-pound bag of topsoil onto a wheelbarrow to take to the grounds, sweat and grime streaking my face. I swiped the back of my gloved-hand over my brow, and grabbed another bag. "I had a plan. No, I *have* a plan. I don't need this aggravation."

*You're not as strong as you look after all,* Steve sneered.

I dumped the bag on the pile and lost my balance. My boots tangled and I landed on my ass onto a short stack of fifty-pound bags. Hot tears stung my eyes.

*Steve is right.*

I wasn't strong. I'd let another man into my world and he'd completely rearranged it. Nikolai infiltrated every thought; my body remembered every intense, physical moment we'd had; and my mind replayed—over and over—how a sudden smile at something I'd said would bloom over his face, as if it had been a long time and he'd just remembered how.

*So call him,* came another thought, this one wearing Opal's voice.

But what good would that do? Nik had a job that kept him on the road all year and I had a plan. I was stuck; unable to go back and undo those three nights and unable to let them go.

*Maybe I don't want to let them go. Or him…*

"But I did. I let him go," I whispered, as a tear dripped off the end of my nose to darken a spot on my coveralls.

"Uh, hey?" Marco said from the door. He wore the uncertain look of a teenage boy when confronted with feminine emotion. "You okay?"

I hurriedly wiped my eyes with the rough, canvas gardening gloves I wore that no doubt left more streaks of grime across my cheeks.

"Yeah, fine. It's hot as an oven in here." I sniffed and stood up, resumed my work.

"Ms. Crawford wants you to get on the register while she takes a call from a wholesaler," Marco said, stepping into the stock room. "I got this."

"Thanks."

On my way out, I glanced down at my sweaty, disheveled, dirt-streaked appearance. *I'm a total mess, inside and out.*

A middle-aged woman was already at the register waiting to pay for a box of puffy white alyssums and a trowel.

"Hi, sorry." I hurriedly slipped behind the register.

"You have pink hair and a green thumb, eh?" the customer commented. She raised her brows at my dirt-smudged overalls.

"Yeah," I said, with a short, polite laugh. "I throw myself into my work."

The woman paid with cash. I reached my hand out to give her the change and Nikolai Young appeared at the entrance to the shop.

My eyes took inventory, like an instant photograph: Nik in jeans, a black t-shirt, boots. His black leather jacket hooked on a finger and slung over his shoulder. Brilliant sunlight glinting off the silver barbs in his ears…

My heart stuttered at the sudden joy that blossomed there.

*Nikolai…*

My hand holding the customer's change opened after completing only half of its journey across the table, and a small cascade of quarters, nickels and dimes rained onto the wood table, where they bounced and rolled.

The sound jolted me. "Oh shit, sorry!" I told the customer. "And sorry for saying shit! Gah, I did it again..."

Nikolai strode forward to help, and the three of us bent to retrieve the coins that had fallen to the floor. I straightened quickly, staring at Nik through the pink locks of my hair that had escaped my loose ponytail. A short silence fell.

The customer stood between Nik and me with a bemused smile. "I'll just leave you two alone..." She hefted her tray of little white flowers and headed out.

"Have a nice day," I murmured faintly, my eyes glued to Nik.

*Was he this beautiful two weeks ago? Impossible...*

Nik ran a hand through his short brown hair. "Sorry to just show up..."

"What are you doing here?" I asked, suddenly conscious of every streak of dirt on my cheeks and clothes, and the sweat that beaded my skin. *Gods of deodorant, please don't fail me now...*

"Fiona!" Opal materialized next to me, making me jump. "Are you going to introduce me to your friend?"

My cheeks flushed pink. She knew perfectly well who *my friend* was. "Sure. Yes. Opal Crawford, this is Nikolai Young."

"A real pleasure," Opal said, extending her hand.

They shook hands and I saw Nik's jaw muscle tick when his skin touched hers.

*You're staring too hard...*

But I couldn't drag my gaze from every nuance of Nik's face; his broad mouth that had lit fires across my skin, and his strong jaw covered with faint stubble that had burned me so deliciously with his raw kisses...

Opal elbowed me in the side. "Fiona..."

I blinked. "Sorry, what?"

"I was just telling Nik that you have the day off tomorrow." Opal stared at me hard, her eyebrows practically vanishing into her hair. "In case he wasn't in town long, I just thought..."

"Opal..." I said through gritted teeth.

Awkward tension hung in the air as thick as the humidity.

Nik glanced at Opal and then back to me. "Can we talk for a minute? Privately?"

"Yeah, sure," I said, willing my pounding heart to slow down. "Follow me."

I shot Opal a parting glare and then led Nik out onto the grounds, to walk in silence amid the rows of potted trees and banks of flowers. The sun blazed down, its heat trapped in the sticky air.

We reached the succulents and cacti, toward the back end of the grounds, and Nik stopped beside a cluster of dark purple and green succulents in a large clay pot on the table. He let his fingers trail over the thick, fleshy leaves that fanned out like an open artichoke and ended in a barbed hook. It felt as though Nik was observing me intently, even with his eyes still on the plant.

"That's an echeveria," I said into the silence. "We have many varieties but that one…" I nodded at the purple and green plant. "They call it the Black Prince."

"Oh yeah?" Nik asked, raising his eyes to me.

"Yeah," I said faintly. "You came back." It was supposed to have been a question, but the words had rearranged themselves and came out sounding more like a sigh of relief. It felt good to look at him again. To be looked at by him.

"Yeah, I did," Nik said. "I was wondering if we could hang out tomorrow. Go somewhere and talk."

"We can talk now," I said.

"No, I mean really talk."

"Oh," I said. My heart stopped then tripped over itself to catch up. "What about?"

"About a change of plans," Nik said, his voice heavy. "I'm tired of the road. Just damn exhausted."

"I know you are," I said softly, remembering Nik's arms around my waist, and his forehead resting against my stomach, saying those words into the center of me.

*We're doing this backwards. He's a stranger and yet we've already shared so much.*

His glance went past me, to the parking lot at the far end. "So I was thinking of taking a break."

"You are?" A surge of happiness lifted me up, followed immediately by a confusion of uncertainty, like a hand squashing me down.

"Yeah," Nik said. "I want to take you out tomorrow and…talk about it."

"Okay," I said slowly. "Sure. If you want to."

"No, Fiona," Nik said, his voice low. "If *you* want to."

Steve had never asked me what I wanted to do, or how I felt, or even my opinion on anything. Nik's simple gesture felt like a precious gift.

*Be smart here,* I warned myself. *Remember what happened last time you let a man in...*

I straightened to my full height—level with Nik's shoulder. "Yeah, okay. To talk, right?"

"Right," Nik said. "Just to talk. I'll pick you up at your place. Tomorrow at ten?"

"Ten in the morning?"

"Yeah, I was thinking we could spend the day together." A small smile touched his lips. "I heard you had the day off."

Despite my attempts to hold myself back, a laugh burst out of me. "You heard right." I tucked a lock of hair behind my ear. "You must have a lot to talk about."

Nik's lips drew down. "Yeah, I do."

*Talking is good. Maybe this is what you need to get unstuck. Sort out all these feelings...*

I felt myself nod. "Ten is fine."

"Cool."

We headed back to the front where Nik said brief goodbyes to Opal and Marco who'd joined her, and he roared out of the parking lot on his motorcycle.

"So that was Nik," Opal said, trying to look innocent and failing miserably.

"That was Nik," I said.

"Who is Nik?" Marco asked, looking between the two of us.

*A mistake? A possibility? A bad idea? A fling...?*

"A friend," I said absently.

"I thought *your friend* was on the road over the next six months," Opal said.

I bit back a smile. "He had a change of plans."

# Chapter 12

*Fiona*

The next morning I was up with the first light, unable to lie around for another minute. The night before, my mind turned over and over the prospect of having Nikolai in my life. Because wasn't that what he wanted to talk about? Him taking a break from the road to settle in Savannah or Garden City? And if not, why bother finding me? My old protective instincts rallied, and I'd composed a speech in which I told him thanks but no thanks; I had a plan to keep and didn't need the distraction.

Then I'd tossed to the other side of the bed, and my speech fell apart under memories of his kisses and strong arms around me that made me feel safe.

*He used you for sex, dummy,* Steve reminded me.

The jibe didn't sting because I'd used Nik right back. More than that, beneath the strong physical connection that consumed us, Nik held me in his cool, blue-eyed gaze as if I were the answer to a question he'd been asking himself for a long time.

*And he's a billion times better in the sack than you could ever hope to be, Steve-O.*

Steve shut up after that.

My thoughts had kept churning and twisting, until I finally fell into an exhausted, fitful sleep, and the dream came again—a darkened road, and a man standing over a dark shape on the ground. Car headlights splashed yellow against the pouring rain like a spotlight on a silver curtain. The man turned...

The alarm blared like a horn, and I was wide-awake.

I showered, then put on baggy cargo pants and a salmon-colored tank top. Not romantic or pretty in any way. Because this wasn't a date. It was a talk, and nothing else. I ate a quick breakfast while the clock ticked closer to ten.

"Is this a huge mistake?" I asked Lemony. "What can come of this? I'm going to Costa Rica..."

A knock came at the door, and I realized I wanted to open that door more than I wanted to keep it shut.

*I'm going to hear Nik out. Have a good time with him. Find the sunshine.*

I opened the door with a smile on my face. "You're quite punctual, Nikolai Alexei."

"It's my best quality," he said. He wore his leather jacket, jeans, boots, and a plain t-shirt in deep blue that made his eyes look like sapphires. He hefted a motorcycle helmet up between us. "Have you ever ridden?"

My eyes widened. "No, never."

"Is it on your bucket list?"

"Hmmm..." I looked up at the ceiling, tapping my finger to my chin. "It is now."

I grabbed my bag and locked the door behind me to step out into the June heat that was already thick, though the sky was overcast.

"Where are we going?" I asked.

"I thought we'd take a drive down the coast, find a beach and have lunch."

"Weren't you trying to take a break from the road?"

"My road trips involve sitting around dingy cellars and basements at night, playing poker with a bunch of cigar-smoking bank managers," Nik said. "I don't do much sight-seeing."

We arrived at his motorcycle and my heart thudded, kicked by nerves.

"I won't go fast," Nik said, then smiled. "Unless you want me to."

"How will you know if I'm having the time of my life or if I'm scared shitless?"

"I'll know," Nik said, his expression unreadable, then he added quickly, "We'll have a system. Squeeze me once to slow down or stop, twice to go faster."

I nodded, my heart still clanging madly, though now I wasn't sure if it was from adrenaline or the idea of having my arms wrapped around Nik.

"The beach I scoped out is a forty-minute ride. If that's too long, or if riding's just not for you, we'll do something else, okay?"

My heart warmed at his gentle consideration. "Sounds good. But where is lunch?"

He nudged a boot at one of the two large leather bags strapped on either side of his motorcycle around the back wheel.

"You packed us a lunch?"

Nik pursed his lips. "Is it hard?"

"No, it's just…thoughtful."

"It's not all that thoughtful," he said. "It's store-bought."

"It's still thoughtful."

He smiled and took up his helmet, which was black and scraped by wind from months or years of riding. The one in my hand was shiny blue with white stripes. I started to pull it on when my nose was filled with something reminiscent of new-car smell.

"Wait," I said. "You bought me a helmet?"

Nik's eyebrows rose in confusion. "Yeah," he said slowly. "It's the law. Not to mention, for your safety."

I swallowed down tears. *Ridiculous! Get a grip.* But such simple considerations from a man were completely foreign to me.

"But it's new," I said when I trusted my voice not to waver. "That's expensive, isn't it?"

He grinned. "You'd prefer a smelly old used one instead?"

"I guess not. But…thank you."

"It's nothing more that you deserve, Fiona," Nik said, and I had the strangest certainty that he wasn't just talking about the helmet. "Shit. Your arms," he said, his glance going to my bare skin.

Self-consciousness swooped in like a vulture and I hugged myself automatically. Nik's expression darkened and he shook his head as if angry at himself. "No, I just meant…do you own any leather?"

"I'm not really a leather girl," I said. "I'm more of a natural fibers, hemp-and-cotton, hippy chick."

"Here." Nik slipped out of his leather jacket and handed it to me.

I took the jacket gingerly and my arm dropped under the weight of it. "What about you?"

"I'll be fine," he said. He jerked his chin. "Go on."

I slipped the leather on. Nik's jacket smelled of him, and the wind, and gasoline, and everything masculine.

"Thank you, Nikolai." I held my arms out to the side where his jacket flapped over my hands. "It's a little big."

"It works," Nik said. He moved to stand in front of me—so close that I could smell the clean bite of his aftershave. My eyes watched his face as he zipped the jacket up, and I swear I could hear every individual tooth as it linked to its pair. When his hand moved up my chest, a tingle spread across my shoulders and climbed my neck in a swath of red.

Nik's eyes met mine with the same hungry look he'd often worn during our three days together. My breath caught, sure that he was going to kiss me, and that kiss would lead back to my apartment, and Nik's hands would *un*zip the jacket, and our road trip would be entirely forgotten…

"You're all set," Nik said and turned away quickly.

I sucked in a breath to cool my blood. "Okay, so how does this work?"

Nik straddled his motorcycle and patted what was left of the black leather seat behind him. "This is you. Once we're on the road, we can't talk to each other. I don't have a Bluetooth set-up."

"Your company won't spring for it?" I asked, straddling the bike to sit behind him.

"Yeah, no…they wouldn't," Nik said. He cleared his throat. "You ready? Remember, one hard squeeze to slow down, two to go faster."

"Got it." I put on my helmet and he put on his. Then I slowly wrapped my arms around his waist, nerves dancing all up and down my skin. I could feel every tight muscle in his abdomen through the cotton material of his shirt.

*Oh my God, you did a lot more than give him a hug several weeks ago,* I reminded myself. *A lot more.*

But this was different. All of this felt completely different and new.

"You ready?" Nik shouted, his voice muffled through his helmet.

I gave him a thumb's up, and then held on tight as the motorcycle engine came to life beneath us. A small cry escaped me, and my nerves turned to pure adrenaline as Nik maneuvered the bike out of the complex, out of Garden City, and onto the coastal highway. The road was a blur and I felt like I was on a speeding roller coaster only with no rails to keep us on track. Exhilaration tore through me like the wind, leaving me breathless.

When we hit a stretch of empty road, I squeezed Nik twice, and the engine roared. I held on tight, my legs clenching around his hips so hard I knew they'd be sore as hell the next day. The road curved and Nik expertly leaned the bike into it. A scream of half-thrill, half-fear escaped me but there was no chance I was going to tell him to slow down.

The gorgeous coast zipped past on our left as we headed south, and the vast blue of the Atlantic stretched out for miles to meet a horizon that disappeared into a low overlay of heavy clouds. I squeezed Nik twice again, and his chest shuddered under my arms in a laugh. He shook his head under his helmet. I laughed too, feeling more alive than I'd had since…

*Since Nik was in my bed, making me feel like this with his mouth and hands, and powerful body…*

After forty minutes or so, Nik followed signs that took us across the highway, to a zigzagging road that led east, to the ocean. He slowed the motorcycle down and I loosened my death grip on him. We came to a secluded spot where the road ended and the beach began with miles of smooth sand, and dead and dried trees lying half-buried. My imagination conjured some ancient dragon that had fallen here and burned, leaving only its charred bones behind.

Nik stopped the bike and shut off the engine. I peeled myself off with a groan of stiffness and pain in my arms and thighs, and then tore off the helmet.

"Oh my God, that was the most incredible…holy shit…I mean…" I fought for the words and finally just shook my head.

"I wondered if it would be too long for a first ride." Nik chuckled. "Guess I was wrong."

I grinned. "Could not have been more wrong."

Nik unpacked a blanket from one of the bags on his bike. From the other, he pulled out a bag from Gigi's Place, a gourmet deli in Garden City I knew well.

"I hope the lunch is okay. I didn't know what you'd like …"

"It's fine," I said. "It's lovely."

Then he reached in his motorcycle bag again and pulled out a small bottle of lemonade and two plastic cups.

"I'd rather have a beer," he said, "but I don't want to drink while we're riding."

"Thank you," I said softly. "I appreciate that."

He gave me a strange look, hard and soft all at once, but it felt as though the hard part wasn't meant for me.

We trekked out across the beach, over soft sand, winding between the branches of the sun-charred trees. The sun played hide-and-seek behind cloud cover, and a cool breeze off the ocean kept the heat from being unbearable. A mile further south, I saw the colorful specks of people enjoying the sand and water, but here we were secluded. A marshy bog cut off the shore to the north, and the fallen trees and another boggy inlet kept the crowds south. We were alone.

The old defenses and fears climbed up from where I'd buried them and into my heart like zombies from a grave.

*Why did you agree to this? You're letting him in...*

Nik knelt to lie out the blanket and abruptly looked up at me.

"We don't have to stay," he said. "Whatever you want..."

I frowned, and hugged myself. "What? No...why would you say that?"

"You looked...doubtful."

I toed a hunk of charred wood with my canvas shoe. "No, I just..." I sighed. "It's really good to see you again, Nikolai. And the motorcycle ride was amazing. This picnic idea is super sweet but...What are we doing?"

"Just talking."

"And then what?"

*Costa Rica. That's what's next. You're going to mess up your plan—*

"I don't want to mess anything up for you, Fiona," Nik said. "But I had to come back. I had to—"

My gaze jerked to where he knelt in the sand. "What did you say?"

"I said I had to come back. To talk to you." Nik tilted his head at a place on the blanket for me to sit. "Let's eat and talk and just...go from there. Okay?"

I nodded slowly and brushed off the coincidence of his words matching my thoughts, and my instinctive defenses switched on, searching for signs of insincerity in Nik. But it was a silly, impossible task. I wasn't good at reading people like he was. Not by a long shot. I had to trust, and the trouble with trusting people is either you did or you didn't. There were no guarantees you'd be rewarded or punished for that trust in the end.

The sun came out from under the clouds just then, warming my skin and casting a gold light over the sand. I knelt beside Nik on the blanket and my shoulder brushed his.

"Okay. Let's eat."

# Chapter 13

## Nikolai

Fiona and I ate in an easy silence, settling in to being in each other's presence again. She'd kicked off her shoes and buried her feet in the sand, leaning back on her elbows, her face turned to the sun.

I tried to keep from staring.

*She's a miracle after all.*

The inexplicable calm of being in her presence hadn't been an illusion. I'd felt it standing in the entrance of the garden shop and again today. She'd wrapped her arms around me on the bike, and her peace wrapped around me just as perfectly. The relief from the onslaught of life was so profound, I didn't want to stop the motorcycle.

And beneath the peace, was something clean and pure and simple.

*I missed her. Her. Fiona.*

She was more beautiful than I'd remembered with the sun shining in her pink hair, and the innate goodness of her glowing almost as bright. She'd tried to dress down for this outing, wearing a tank top and baggy pants, but it didn't work on me. My eyes kept straying to the curve of her neck, or the small swell of her breasts. I'd already been everywhere on her body. There was no part of her that wasn't fucking perfect, and my own body hummed like a live wire for wanting to touch her; to fuck her hard, or take her slow and deep, like she liked.

And another desire, just as potent—to simply lay with my head in her lap, her fingers running through my hair while we watched the ocean in perfect silence and peace.

*What the hell is that?*

I tore my gaze from her and concentrated on pouring us each a cup of lemonade.

Fiona touched her plastic cup to mine. "Cheers."

She sipped hers, while I downed mine in one long draught and wished for something hard to deaden the bundle of nerves that had settled into my gut.

"So, Nik," Fiona said, set her cup down, and twisted it into a groove in the sand. "Tell me about your change of plans. Doesn't your company have you on a schedule?"

*Be careful,* I told myself. *Don't fuck this up.*

"I don't work for any company," I said. "That's just a lie I tell people because the truth sounds pathetic or strange. Or both."

"You don't...?" Fiona said slowly. She sat perfectly still and pulled away at the same time. "What is the truth?"

"I'm a grinder," I said. "I play poker for a living. All that traveling I do is for the games. And when the other players ask me what I do, I tell them the same thing: I sell motorcycle parts. I don't want them to know I'm a grinder either."

Fiona nodded, absorbing this. "I thought your business card looked a little plain."

"I'm sorry I lied to you," I said. *I'm sorry I have to keep lying to you.*

"It might have bothered me more but...You tell everyone the same story?"

"Everyone."

"Okay." The tension that shivered the air around her eased. "I don't mind that you're a grinder," she said. "It's kind of fascinating, actually. How did you get into playing poker in the first place?"

I glanced down, made circles in the sand with my hand with the HOAX tattoo.

"When I was a kid, I had...emotional problems." The soft warmth of Fiona's concern wafted over me. "My dad was an asshole. He couldn't deal with me. Or didn't want to. Took off when I was ten."

"Nik, I'm so sorry..."

"I'm glad he did," I raised my eyes to Fiona's, met her open, kind face head-on, and the words fell out. "He hit my mother. Not a lot. Few times a year. But just once is too fucking much."

Fiona recoiled in the eyes of my *ken*; the darkness of *him* swooping over her. Anger flared in my chest, burning my own pain away in the face of hers.

*Did he hit you, Fiona? I'll kill the fucker...*

But no...the air shifted around her like a coiling snake, and I knew without knowing that *his* abuse of her was sinister but not violent.

*Tell me, Fiona. Tell me before the* ken *does...*

But she said nothing, shut her own memories out, and waited for me to continue. And I did. I never told my story. Not to anyone since my time at the hospital. But here I was, spilling my guts out into Fiona's lap.

"My mother had immigrated to America from Moscow when she was twenty," I said. "She spoke more Russian than English and when my dad took off, she was a little lost. She didn't know what to do with me. I was fucked up—"

*...sick in the head...*

I flinched and turned it into a shrug. "Yeah...Anyway, Ma couldn't handle it."

"What happened?" Fiona asked softly.

"She took me to a bunch of psychiatrists, but none of them any good. My case was rare, they said. I spent three years in a shitty, third-rate hospital being poked and prodded, drugged and shocked—"

"They *shocked* you?" Fiona asked, her eyes wide. "How old were you?"

"Fourteen when it started. Seventeen when it stopped. When I escaped."

Fiona was sitting up now, her long legs crossed under her, leaning toward me. "You escaped? From the hospital?"

The dark memories that hovered over her reached for mine. A connection.

*I escaped too...*

I blinked. "Yeah, I escaped. I couldn't break out, though God knows I tried. No, I pretended I was better. I got with the program. Stopped fighting the orderlies. Stopped spitting out the meds. I told them what they wanted to hear. It took six months, but it worked. They let me go."

"You tricked them?"

"I read their tells," I said dryly, then shook my head. "It was a cheap hospital. Sub-standard. My mother couldn't afford a doc that might've given me real help."

"So they let you go."

I smiled ruefully. "Cured."

"But you're not cured?" Fiona asked.

"No, I have severe…agoraphobia and claustrophobia."

Fiona's concern softened and warmed around her, spilled over to me. "Agoraphobia…that's a fear of large crowds?"

I nodded.

"They locked you up for *that*?"

"Being around big crowds causes panic attacks, and if they're really bad, I get visual and auditory hallucinations." I cast my gaze away from Fiona's open, trusting face. "The docs said they'd never seen anything like it."

Sounded good. Plausible. A digestible combination of reality and the bullshit diagnoses the docs tried to pin on me. The truth rose up in me, wanting to spill out along with my father's abuse and my mother's apathy. But Fiona would hate me if she knew what I was, and I couldn't fucking take one more person I cared about hating me for what I couldn't control.

"That must've been so hard for you," Fiona was saying. "But you're better now?"

*No, I'm on the verge…*

I shrugged. "More or less. I avoid crowds. Being in a big city just about wrecks me."

"Where does the poker fit in?" Fiona asked.

"Not picking fist fights with the orderlies left me with a lot of time to kill. One of the guys—Angelo—ran a game afterhours. I don't sleep much, and Angelo knew it. He let me sit in on a game, and someone else thought it would be funny to let me play. But it turns out I had a knack for reading people."

"Their tells," Fiona said.

"Angelo told me I should do it for a living. He was kidding, but when I got out of the hospital it was all I had. I took it."

"What happened to your mom?" Fiona asked softly.

"She went downhill pretty quick," I said. My fingers found a small rock in the sand. "Mentally and physically. She's in a home in Missouri."

"Do you still see her on your road trips?"

"Yeah, I stop in every time but she doesn't remember me. I sit with her and try to talk but she just cries and babbles in Russian." I chucked the rock at a pile of seaweed twenty feet away. "We aren't close."

"I'm sorry, Nikolai," Fiona said.

The aura that lined her body flared brighter pink, as the sweet kindness of her was seeping into my bones. She reached out to lay her hand over mine.

"I'm not close to my family either," Fiona said. "My aunt and uncle raised me but they weren't terribly happy about it."

"What happened to your parents?" I asked. My hand itched to turn over and grasp hers, but she withdrew to trace lines in the sand with her finger.

"My mom died when I was a baby and my dad got sick when I was thirteen. Lung cancer. Took him quick."

"I'm sorry," I said.

She blinked hard, chasing the memories away. "I miss him. He was warm and kind and my aunt and uncle were cold and aloof. When I turned eighteen I lived…up north for awhile," she said and *he* was right there. So fucking close I could reach out and touch the inky black of his shadow.

Fiona shivered. "I was there for three years and then moved away from the cold to Savannah, where it never snows. And pretty soon I'll be in Costa Rica where there's hardly any cold at all." She said with a forced smile, desperate to change the subject. "And you… You've been crisscrossing the country, playing poker since you were seventeen?"

"'Traveling salesman' sounds better," I said.

Fiona drew her knees to her chest, hugging herself, and turned her gaze to the ocean. "No, it makes sense. I can see why a life of solitude on the road would appeal to you."

"Yeah, it did. At the time."

"But not now?"

"It's not working anymore," I said. "I'm burnt out. That's why I came back."

Fiona faced me and rested her cheek on her knees. "Tell me."

"I've thought of settling down someplace," I said. "And I have a pile of poker winnings sitting in a bank account. I guess that's what it's for. To settle down."

"You don't know what it's for?" Fiona asked.

"I feel like it has a purpose, only I can't see it yet." I waved a sand fly and the notion away at the same time. "Anyway, that burnt out feeling has only gotten stronger lately, and I've known for months I have to quit. Or take a break. But I didn't know where. Until I met you."

Fiona clutched her knees a little more. Wariness tightened the air around her.

"I know you have your own plan," I said. "I don't want to interfere, but..." *But I don't know what the fuck else to do...*

Fiona turned her gaze to the ocean. "Interfere," she said softly. "I think it's too late for that but I have to be honest Nik, I've been thinking about you a lot. Missed you."

Hope burned in my chest and then was extinguished by her sigh.

"But what happens at the end of six months when I have to get on a plane to Costa Rica? Because I am going. It's something I promised myself. And before I met you at that club, my plan felt perfect. I've had some dark days and Costa Rica is where I'm going to leave them behind. Forever."

She had pulled herself into a ball, making herself small, and *he* leaned over her, reaching. Costa Rica was her escape and I was fucking it up.

"I'm sorry," I said tightly. "I shouldn't have come back."

"No, I'm glad," Fiona said. "After you left—and after hearing an earful from my friend, Opal—I've been having...second thoughts. Not about leaving, but about how I want my life to be before I do. Opal told me that sometimes you have to let life in. Make room for happiness when it shows up. I'm always saying *find the sunshine*, but you can't do that if you stay inside, shut away, can you?"

I shook my head, hope struggling to rise again.

Fiona sighed, hugged her knees tightly. "I don't know what's supposed to happen next."

"I'm at a motel right now," I told her slowly. "I'd rent my own place and stay for a few weeks. If that works out, maybe I'll stay for a few more."

"You don't need my permission, Nik."

"Yeah, I do," I said. "You're the reason I came back, but if you're not okay with it, I'm gone."

Fiona held my gaze for a minute then propped her chin on her knee, watching the ocean beat at the shore and retreat, over and over.

"Remember back at the club when we first met?" she said. "You told me the same thing right before we went back to my place. All I had to do was say the word and you'd disappear."

"I remember."

"Just now, when you said the only reason you'd stay was because of me, my first reaction was to kiss you," she said with a rueful smile. "But I didn't. That's where I'm at. My heart is telling me one thing and my mind is telling me another and I don't know which to believe. Story of my life."

A mist of melancholy, like morning fog, materialized around her.

"But I keep going back to the moment I saw you yesterday, at Garden City Greens. I was shocked and embarrassed, considering I was covered in dirt, all sweaty and gross…"

*You looked beautiful…*

"But mostly I was happy. I felt really happy to see you again, Nikolai." The mist evaporated, leaving her pink and bright again. She turned her blue-eyed gaze to mine. "I don't want you to disappear."

My chest tightened as my heart tripped over itself at those words, grabbing on to them and holding on tight.

"Fiona…"

"I guess that means I want you to stay. To try…I don't know, to be together? Is that what you want?"

*I want you, any way you'll take me.*

The *ken* showed me her confusion—longing tinged with a deep pain she feared would never go away.

"I don't know what I want," she whispered, tears standing out in her eyes. "And it's an awful feeling, you know? To not be able to trust yourself."

*She needs to be in her home, in her own place that she worked for. Safe.*

"Come on," I said, sitting up. "Let's go back."

Fiona started to protest, then reluctantly nodded. "I'm sorry…"

"No, Fiona," I said. "You have nothing to be sorry about. Not one thing."

*That asshole who hurt you, on the other hand…*

We packed up the picnic and headed back to the bike.

On the road, Fiona's dark memories clung to her until I felt her inhale against my back. She exhaled and her arms tightened around me twice. I gunned the Bonneville. The shadows were blown to tatters—for now—and the surge of her excitement and exhilaration surrounded me. Her happiness.

Of all the emotions I'd experienced through the *ken,* Fiona's happiness was the most beautiful.

At her apartment, I walked her to the front door.

"I did some thinking on the way back," she said. "I imagined what it would be like if I said no to you. To…us. Whatever that might be. And I didn't like it."

"Okay," I said. I tightly clutched my leather jacket she'd returned to me.

"I…was in a relationship several years ago," she said slowly, through a stiff jaw, as if each word physically hurt. "I don't like to talk about it. Ever. But it messed me up pretty good, and now I have no idea what I'm doing."

I offered a smile. "That's okay. Neither do I."

Fiona laughed a little. "Maybe we can…figure it out. Together. Or try to. I want to try."

My heart thudded in my chest. "We'll take it slow, okay?"

"Are we going to date?" She wrinkled her nose. "Is that weird? We're doing it backwards."

"We don't have to do anything except…"

She tilted her chin. "Just be?"

Christ, she was beautiful. "Yeah. Just be."

A smile curved her lips and everything I felt told me it was the right thing to walk away. To let *her* just be without touches or kisses to muddy up her feelings.

Fiona held up the helmet I'd bought her. "I keep?"

"Actually, I need that back," I said. "I have to hit the next town. There's another girl waiting for me—"

She socked me in the arm. "Very funny."

"You keep."

"Okay, thanks." She opened the door behind her. "And thanks for the picnic. It was perfect, Nikolai."

She craned up to lightly brush her lips against my cheek, and it took everything I had not to turn my head and kiss her hard.

But I didn't kiss her, so that I could see her again.

# Chapter 14

## *Fiona*

I shut the door and leaned against it, listening to Nik's motorcycle engine roar and then fade as he drove out of the parking lot of my complex. I closed my eyes, inhaled, and waited for the snide commentary from Steve I knew was coming. I exhaled. Silence, and the warm glow in my heart and the lingering warmth of Nik's skin on my lips.

*Is this right? It feels right.*

I didn't want to, but I cast my memories back to when I met Steve, to compare what I felt then with what I felt now, as if I could search the rubble of that horrible relationship for clues that would tell me if this one was leading to the same disaster.

Looking back, I realized I never had time to fall for Steve. He swept me up in his world and carried me off, and I went along with it, a little bit drunk from the notion of a man being so enamored with me. Since I was little, I loved the fairytales where the prince slays the dragon to rescue the princess. My dragon was the death of my parents; my castle was my aunt and uncle's cold, unaffectionate house. I believed Steve had rescued me; only to find out he was carrying me off to a colder winter. A different kind of prison altogether.

I prayed it wasn't my imagination or the hopeful beat of my heart, but how I felt when I was with Nik was nothing like what I felt when I was with Steve. Steve didn't love me except in the way a man loves his car or his boat. As a possession that served a purpose. I had a role to play: the little wife who was always there when he came home to cook his food, and warm his bed, and who had no life outside of him.

With Nikolai, there was no pressure, no constantly feeling like I was on the edge of saying or doing something wrong or stupid. With Nikolai, I could just be.

*And what happens between us when the time comes to go to Costa Rica?*

"I don't know," I murmured, and that was the truth. And for now, that was okay.

At work a few days later, Opal practically jumped out of her skin for news. She met me on the grounds where I was hosing a stand of blue hydrangeas with a spray nozzle set on low pressure.

"So? How was the date? What did you do? Where is he now?"

I smirked. "The date was lovely, we had a picnic at the beach, and right now I don't know where he is. House-hunting, probably."

Opal gaped. "For the two of you?"

I gave her a look. "*No.* He's getting his own place. He has his place and I have my place. It's perfect."

"But you're seeing him, right? You two are together? That's why he's staying? For you?"

I couldn't keep the smile from spreading over my face. "Has anyone told you that you ask a lot of questions?"

"My husband. And don't change the subject."

I laughed and drizzled the spray toward her feet.

"We are just dating. I'm trying to be an adult about this. To have him in my life without completely upheaving it. That's a big step for me."

"I know it is, honey," Opal said. "And I'm very proud of you. You're making room for the happiness. You look happy, Fiona. You've always been cheerful, but now it's a little bit deeper, isn't it?"

I shrugged one shoulder. "Maybe. Let's not jinx it, okay?"

That afternoon, I was on the grounds again sweeping up dead leaves and making sure all the large potted trees had enough water. Eventually, I worked my way to the far end where the cacti and the succulents lived. My gaze found the echeveria that Nik had been drawn to a few days ago.

"The Black Prince," I murmured. I plucked the pot off the table and carried it to the register where Opal was sorting through receipts and invoices.

"Another one?" she asked as I plunked it on the counter. "Girl, your apartment is going to look like a jungle."

"What good is an employee discount if you don't use it?"

*And it's not for me, anyway.*

When my shift ended, I drove home, showered and changed into a flowing summer dress in pale blue, then plopped down on my couch with my phone, my fingers hovering over Nik's number. It had been three days with nothing more than little check-ins and hi-how-are-you's.

I bit my lip, and shot Nikolai a text. **Are you busy?**

**No**, he sent back. **I need everything for my new place so I'm doing nothing.**

I grinned, bit my lip. **Want some help?**

**If you don't mind the mess.**

**Are you kidding?** I texted back. **Have you seen me at work? I want to see you right now.**

I could practically hear Nik's voice deepen over those words.

**Address?** I texted. He sent it, and my fingers flew in response. **I'll be right over**.

The apartment Nik was renting was in a small, plain complex at the end of a block of similar plain complexes, some dilapidated as if they were withering under the heat; some with fresh paint and bright flowers in the front. I pulled my old Prius into the driveway space behind his Bonneville. I grabbed the echeveria pot in one arm and climbed the exterior cement steps up to the second floor.

Nikolai answered my knock wearing jeans, a plain white wifebeater that made his arm muscles look ridiculously sexy, barefoot on the hardwood floors.

*Holy hell, this man...*

Nikolai stared at me and blinked as if coming out of a reverie. He glanced at the plant under my arm.

"That looks familiar."

I put it in his hands. "It's a housewarming present."

"Thanks," he said. "It'll look great on my living room floor."

I laughed and he stepped aside to introduce me to his place. A small kitchen that was little more than a cube of formica and white cabinets, that opened on a living area unfurnished. Aside from a few random utensils that lay on the counter, there was nothing in it but a coffee maker and a sleeve of plastic cups. A hallway on the right presumably led to the bedroom and bathroom.

"You said this place was a mess." I leaned on the kitchen counter and gave him a wry look. "You have to have stuff in order to make a mess."

"I know it," Nik said, leaning his hip against the stove. He gestured at the utensils strewn on the counter. "I have no clue what I need. I was at the damn appliance store, just grabbing shit that looked useful."

I held up a whisk in one hand and a honey dipper in the other, my smile wide. "Just the essentials."

"Everything I need," Nik muttered, his eyes raking me up and down. "You look beautiful. I want to take you out to dinner."

My smile faltered under the weight of the deep ache of desire that bloomed deep in me at those words, his hungry look that had nothing to do with food.

"A date?" I asked.

"A first date," Nik said.

I laughed though my blood felt as if it were on fire. "A first date, yet we've already done all the sex things."

"We haven't done *all* the sex things," Nik said, his words teasing while his voice was low. "I can think of at least eight sex things we haven't done yet, just off the top of my head."

"Oh yeah?" I swallowed hard. "Name one."

"Just kiss," he said. "We haven't ever just kissed."

I sucked in a breath, and my stomach fluttered with that 'first kiss' feeling—a giddiness of anticipation and want and nerves.

*But I've already kissed him a hundred times...*

Only I hadn't. Not like this.

"You keep surprising me, Nikolai."

"In a good way, I hope."

"The best way..."

*Kiss me...*

No sooner had the thought flitted in and out of my mind, Nikolai pushed off the stove and moved to me. His eyes locked on mine as he took the utensils of my hand, one at a time, and dropped them to the floor. My breath caught as his nearness awakened my body to every moment of our three nights together. His thumb brushed my lower lip as his hand curved around my cheek and under my neck.

"Thanks for the echeveria."

"You remembered its name," I breathed.

He nodded, his eyes holding my gaze so that all I could see was him and then his mouth descended. A gentle sweep of his lips over mine, a soft touch and then retreat. My mouth parted in a little sigh and he kissed me again. Deeper. He kept his hands on my face, my neck, then slipped one around my waist, holding me close.

My fingers wound into his hair and a tiny sound of want escaped me as our mouths moved in perfect tandem, tongues sweeping softly. He tasted so clean and good; and the softness of his lips contrasted to the scratch of his stubble.

*That's what he is...Soft and hard, sweet and rough...*

I'd never kissed a man like this. I knew I never would again.

We broke apart with reluctance, breathless. Nik's eyes were dark pools of want, but he held my face in both hands gently.

"Just kissing," he said. "Dinner first."

I blinked. "Dinner—?"

"I'm taking you out."

"Oh, that's really not necessary," I said, running my hands along the dark ink on his arms. "We can order pizza..."

Nikolai's eyes raked over me again, and I swear I could feel the heat wherever his gaze landed. He shook his head.

"This feeling right now?" he said, his voice low. "Do you feel it?"

"Yes..." *God yes...*

"I don't want it to end. Not yet. I want to take you out and sit across from you and know that in an hour later you'll be in my bed." He searched my eyes. "If that's what you want."

Heat flushed my cheeks, and I clung to his wrists as the muscles in my legs turned to sand. "That's what I want."

"Our first date." His thumb brushed my lower lip. "I want to do this right."

I swallowed hard. "You're doing everything right."

A flicker of a smile flitted over his lips. "I'm on a heater."

"A heater?"

"A winning streak. And you don't do anything to wreck a winning streak."

He kissed me, slow and long, and then went to his room to change.

I sucked in a breath and fanned myself as I waited, and a fervent idea struck me. Before I could talk myself out of it, I slipped out of my panties and tucked them into my purse.

"That's one for the bucket list," I murmured with a laugh.

*Such a little whore...*

I cringed. "Leave me alone," I whispered.

"You okay?"

I jumped. Nik was in the hallway, watching me.

"Yeah. Fine. Perfect."

He joined me in the kitchen. He wore his boots, a black t-shirt and his black leather jacket. He looked dark and dangerous, and drove Steve's insidiousness away with his very presence. The ground beneath my feet felt solid again.

"Thank you," I said, as we headed for the door.

Nik nodded grimly but didn't ask what for.

Outside, the cicadas and crickets were loud as twilight fell. The quiet little street was cast in yellow light. The night was thick with heat and possibilities.

"I didn't bring my helmet. We have to take my car. Besides," I airily tossed over my shoulder as we headed towards my Prius, "it wouldn't be prudent for me to ride a motorcycle without underwear."

Nikolai stopped dead in his tracks, and the look on his face would have been almost comical had not been so heavy with need.

"You're not...?"

"Nope." I smiled coyly. "I seem to recall a request from you that I stop wearing them. I figure I'm saving money not having you tear them off me."

"I changed my mind," Nik said. "We're ordering pizza."

I laughed and unlocked the car with my key fob. "No, no, no. You wanted to take me out, so we're going out."

"Dumbest idea I ever had," Nik muttered.

I snickered and tossed him the keys. "You drive. I don't know where we're going."

"I don't know where we're going either," Nikolai said, climbing behind the wheel. He settled into the driver's seat and sat for a minute, staring at the dashboard. "The hell? This is like an overgrown golf cart."

"Oh hush." I showed him the start button and he got the car going. "It may not have a ton of horsepower, but it's good for the environment."

"If you say so. Where to?"

"I know a cute little Italian bistro in town. I love it. They keep it dim, with those little red glass candleholders on every table, and red-and-white-checkered tablecloths."

I didn't add that I'd grabbed dinner there with Nancy and Hailey, or Nate and Griff a hundred times, and each time part of me wished I'd been on a date like this, on a night like this.

Nik glanced at me with a soft expression. "Sounds perfect."

He revved the engine, or tried to, and then pulled out of the driveway. At the first stoplight the engine went quiet.

"Shit, it stalled," Nikolai searched the dashboard panels for distress lights. "Did I do something wrong?"

"It's not stalled; it switched to the electric to save energy."

He scowled. "I'm going to get you another helmet to keep at my place."

I snickered, but in truth, Nik's frustration with my car was sexy. The tattooed biker in a Prius. A lone wolf who spent all his time on the road renting an apartment he had no idea what to do with. All for me. It was on the tip of my tongue to tell him go back and order pizza after all, but he was right: the anticipation was giving me a heady feeling, like I'd drunk a glass or two of bubbly champagne.

I directed him to Café Roma, a tiny little place in Garden City's version of downtown. We took a small booth in the back and a waitress handed us laminated menus.

"Drinks?"

I ordered a glass of house wine, Nik ordered a beer.

"I like your new place," I told him as we waited for the waitress to come back. "Are you thinking of getting a job too?"

"Don't know yet. I won some money in Jacksonville before I came back. The plan is to live off of that and see what happens."

"Jacksonville," I said. "Isn't that a big city?"

"Yeah, it was," he said in a low voice. "Too big."

I slipped my hand into his. "Was it hard?"

He shrugged. "I took a gamble." He looked at our locked fingers and then up into my eyes. "It paid off."

The air between us seemed to vanish, and the physical need I'd felt earlier came again, this time in harmony with something sweet and quiet too; the desire to be in bed with him, and the desire to simply be *with* him.

"I like being with you, Nik," I said, because feeling something for someone wasn't the same as saying it out loud. "I like it very much."

"Me too," he replied. "But I don't know how to do romance. Part of me wants to grab you and throw you over my shoulder…"

"Like a caveman."

"Hell, yes. But I also want to tell you how beautiful you look in this candlelight, along with every other romantic thing you deserve to hear. I don't want to mess this up."

"You just told me I look beautiful in the candlelight. That's romantic. You're a secret romantic, Nikolai Alexei."

"I'm not," Nik said, his voice like a growl. "I'm fighting the urge to find out if it's true that you're not wearing underwear."

"Quite the dilemma," I said, my heart crashing against my chest. I took his hand and laid it on my thigh under the table. His jaw clenched. I moved his hand deeper under my dress, to the juncture of my thighs. "I never lie about underwear."

I pressed his fingers to my naked flesh, still holding his gaze. Our eyes widened at the same time, our breaths caught at the same time. His pulse jumped in the tattooed hollow of his throat, while mine sent blood rushing through my body.

Nik's eyes were blue fire. "Fiona…"

"Fiona! Darling!"

Nikolai and I jumped apart as if we'd been shocked. He jerked his hand from under my dress and I busied myself with my napkin, composing myself before I faced Nate and Griffin standing over the table. The former wore a sly, shit-eating grin, while his husband wore his customary friendly smile that politely pretended he hadn't seen anything.

"Fancy running into you here," Nate said, his eyes glued to Nikolai. "You're back? When did this happen?"

"I'm staying in town for a while," Nik said. "Taking a break from the road."

"You two are shacking up?" Nate asked, and was rewarded with Griffin's elbow in his side.

"No," Nik said. "I have a place. On Mulaney Street?"

"Very nice," Griffin said. "It's good to see you again, man." His eyes found mine. "Really good."

A short silence fell in which I grappled with being polite and asking them to join us, and wanting to be alone with Nik.

*No, I'm desperate to be alone with Nik.*

Nate rocked back on his heels. "So! Since you *asked,* we've finished dinner and now are heading back to our soon-to-be former apartment. We've already begun packing up the kitchen. I refuse to cook one more meal on that dinky little stove."

I gave him a dry look. "Since when do you cook, Nathaniel?"

"Since never," Griff answered. "But he's not telling you the best part. We closed escrow," he said smiling as if he couldn't stop if he wanted to. "Yesterday. We're officially homeowners."

I gasped. "Oh my God! That was so fast!"

"My sentiments exactly," Nate said. "Every time he says 'homeowners' I have visions of bursting pipes and the roof caving in."

"Don't listen to him, he loves it," Griffin said.

"Anyway, we're going to have a party at the new place in two weeks."

"You're moving out already?" I asked, deflating a little. "That's fast too."

"We won't move until some renovations are done," Griffin said. "The party will—"

"—be an adventure in shabby chic," Nate said. "The house will be done up in lights, little tables, catering, a dance floor in every empty room…It's going to be—"

"—fabulous." Griffin looked between Nik and me. "You have to come. Both of you."

"As if I'd miss it." I glanced at Nik. "What do you think?"

"Sounds good," Nik said. He looked to Griffin. "Can I bring anything?"

"Yes, hard liquor," Nate said before Griffin could answer. "Something rough that's all the rage amongst the bikers."

I covered my eyes with my hand.

"What?" Nate said. "I just want him to feel welcome. It's not every day we have a poker-playing motorcycle man in our midst."

"You need to stop talking now," Griffin said. He turned to us with an apologetic smile. "We'll let you get back to your dinner." He bent to kiss my cheek. "Call soon, love."

"I will."

Nate blew me a kiss and then bickered with his husband as Griffin hustled him away from the table.

"Is that okay?" I asked. "About the party, I mean? You don't have to if you don't want to—"

"I want to," Nik said, moving close, his hand slipping back up my dress. "I want you. Now."

I swallowed hard. "I thought we were taking it slow."

"This is me," Nik said, "taking it slow."

I bit the inside of my cheek as his fingers found me again, touched me again, sending licks of fire deep inside me.

The waitress came back, but Nik didn't pull his hand away. He casually gave the woman his order—chicken Parmesan—while his fingers circled me slowly beneath the table.

"And for you, honey?" the waitress asked me.

"Fettucine Alfredo," I said, my voice hardly more than a whisper. "And we'll need that to go, please."

Nik drove my Prius back to his place as fast as the engine would allow. I carried the bags of food into the house and set them on the counter. An instant later, Nik was all over me. His kiss was hot and hard, and I sagged with relief into it, needing his hands on me, needing to feel his naked skin against mine.

He trailed open-mouth kisses down my jaw, down my neck to my collarbone. I clung to him as shivers skimmed down my skin, hardening my nipples, until the desire descended lower, to coalesce between my thighs. I moved my mouth around his earlobe, my tongue feeling the contours of his piercing. The cold bite of sharp metal. I grazed my teeth over it, then bit down and pulled gently.

Nik groaned.

"Please tell me you bought a bed," I whispered.

"That's the first thing I bought."

I gasped as one hand slipped over my breast; his other lifted my dress, skimmed up my thigh, teased me with his fingers. I needed more.

"Oh God, Nik," I whispered. "Hurry."

He released me to strip off his jacket and shirt, and then pulled my dress over my arms and let it fall to the ground. He stopped to stare at my nakedness. I hadn't worn a bra either. I watched his eyes drink me in.

"Goddamn, Fiona," he whispered, and then I was in his arms again. We kissed, a blind, desperate mashing of mouths. My hands tore at the buckles on his belt. "Bedroom," he growled, his teeth grazing my lower lip.

He half-carried me to the darkened room that was empty except for a large bed, a small nightstand with a small desk lamp. Nikolai stripped off his clothes and lay over me. Silvery moonlight streamed in from the window, shining in his eyes and glinting off the silver in his ears. The rest of him a dark shape of hard muscle that moved over me and pressed against me.

I wanted so badly to take him inside me, and feel all of his skin with all of mine, but the remnants of my old life would not let go.

"Condom," I whispered.

He nodded and reached beyond me to the nightstand drawer. I heard a tearing of foil, and a moment later he was sliding into me. It felt like it had been much longer than a few weeks since I last had this hard heavy sensation of him inside me.

"God, Nik," I whispered as he began to move. "This. I want this…"

"You," he growled into my neck. "Just you."

There was nothing gentle about Nik's rough hands or his punishing thrusts except the intention behind them. I felt how much he wanted me; not as a man wanting a woman, but as *him* wanting *me*.

I came screaming his name, my nails clawing his back, my heels digging into the backs of his thighs because I didn't want anything gentle either. I wanted him and his body making mine feel alive.

And I wanted *his* release. The pain of his former life on the road and before, in that awful hospital…Now that I knew that piece of him, I wanted it. I wanted him to give it to me. To exchange the pain for ecstasy, because that's exactly what he gave me. Everything that came before in my life vanished under Nik's touch, washed away by the sweat of our bodies. There were no insidious words, only kisses and whispered pleas of want that made me feel cherished no matter how rough he was, or how hard the headboard banged.

After, he brought the food—still warm—into bed, and we ate from each other's forks, and when we were done, we gave ourselves up to the night, to each other, until I'd lost count of how many times my body shuddered against his.

In the last hours before dawn, I buried my face in his neck and held on as he brought me to a final, crushing orgasm that left no room for thought except for one.

*God help me, I'm going to fall…*

And another, as sleep came for me after…

*I'm falling.*

# Chapter 15

## Nikolai

The first night in my new place and Fiona was in my bed. She lay on my chest, still sleeping. She slept across me like a shield, protecting me from the onslaught of other people's lives. My sleep had never been deeper.

I let my hand trail over her back. Her skin was slick with sweat from last night. We'd kicked the covers off since my place didn't have air-conditioning, and the summer heat left us in a drowsy haze.

*My place...*

It wasn't much to look at, cheap. Not a motel but not a home, either. It was mine for $150 a week. With my poker winnings, I could afford to stay for months without breaking a sweat.

*And then what?*

I glanced down at Fiona. I had no answer for that, but I had peace. Quiet. A reprieve from the road and I had this woman. It was more than I'd ever had before.

Fiona came awake and rolled her head in my direction, a small sleepy smile on her face.

"Good morning," she said.

"Morning."

"Have you been awake long?"

"A while," I said. "It's too hot to move."

She grinned. "You didn't seem to have that problem last night."

I smiled lazily, basking. My hand played in Fiona's hair, and I let the long, waist-length strands fall through my fingers. Pink, like cotton candy. I closed my eyes and the color was still there, radiating off of Fiona.

*Goodness, compassion, kindness…*

"Why?" I asked sleepily.

"Hmm?"

"Why did you dye your hair pink?"

"There's a little bit of a story there."

"I want to hear it."

Fiona shifted off of me, her stomach on the bed, and propped herself up on her elbows.

"When I was in third grade, my teacher gave us a writing assignment. She told us to pick two colors and write a poem for each. The poems would describe what we thought the colors represented. Like, blue is the color of my tears when I'm sad. Red is the color of a sun when it sets… Stuff like that."

I sat up a little bit higher against the bedframe, suddenly awake as if someone had dashed me with cold water. Fiona traced the whorls and designs of the tattoos on my chest with a finger, not seeing my slack jaw or wide eyes.

"Which colors did you pick?" I asked.

"Pink and gold."

"Do you remember what you wrote about each color?"

She scrunched up her face in thought. "I do. Don't know why, but they've stuck with me almost word for word."

"Tell me."

Fiona's fingers traced along my dreamcatcher tattoo on the left side of my torso; over the feathers, the beads, and along each strand of the net as she spoke.

"Pink is the excitement you get just before opening a birthday present. Pink is the happiness you feel when you are sitting alone at recess and another kid comes over and asks if you want to play. Pink is how you feel when you hug someone who is crying and make them feel better."

I clenched my jaw against the sudden rush of emotion that swamped me. A strange, potent sense of déjà vu like nothing I'd known before.

*The hell….?*

"Kind of cute isn't it?" Fiona said, oblivious to my turmoil. "When

I decided to dye my hair, I remembered what I wrote for pink and it sort of… I don't know…jibed with where I am in my life. Simple things that make me happy."

"What about gold?" I asked, my throat tight.

"Gold, according to my seven-year-old self, is the smell of McDonald's French fries." She laughed sheepishly. "It's kind of true, isn't it?"

I nodded faintly. "What else?"

"Gold is the color of the morning on a new day that is still perfect. And gold is…" She broke off, shaking her head in that shy, sweet way she had.

I felt myself leaning toward her in every way, all that was rusted and broken inside of me reached for all that was good and pure inside of her.

"What is it?" I asked.

"Gold is the color of love." She rested her cheek on my chest. "Not the love between family members, or mothers and their children. I mean the fairytale love, where the prince would do anything for the princess, even if it meant his own life. And the princess would sacrifice herself to the dragon if it would save the prince. The kind of love that…transcends, though I didn't have that word at the time."

She smiled to herself. "Funny how pure a child's thoughts are. Just simple truths, you know? No fancy metaphors, no big words that try too hard."

I stared at the woman lying over me. Her fingers roamed and trailed over the ink I'd worked into my skin in order to feel something that was real and mine. Pain. Not love. Never love.

Fiona kissed the dreamcatcher. "Of all your tattoos, this one is my favorite."

*Tell her the truth. Now. Do it now…*

But she was already peeling herself off of me and rising from the bed. Fiona slipped one of my T-shirts on over her head, and leaned over to kiss me.

"Come on, lazybones. I have to go to work. I'll make some coffee in this empty kitchen of yours…"

I took her hand and held it tight. "Fiona…"

"Yes?"

The moment held still, the words danced on the tip of my tongue.

"I…I want to see you tomorrow."

*Coward.*

Fiona smiled that shy smile, the one she wore when she was trying to hide her happiness. But she couldn't hide it from me. Silver sparks danced in the air around her.

"You do?"

"Yeah, I do."

She tucked a lock of hair behind her ear. "I usually spend an hour or two at the animal shelter on Saturdays. You could come by after that. If you want."

"Sounds good," I said.

She was radiant. "Coffee sounds good too." She kissed my temple and went out.

I fell back on the pillows, a sigh gusting out of me.

My thoughts drifted back to Fiona's color poems. *It doesn't mean anything…It's just a coincidence.*

Except that pink was exactly as she'd described: how the *ken* translated kindness.

*And gold?*

I'd never seen gold.

---

"I have a pretty good walk-of-shame happening here," Fiona said in the parking lot of my complex. She smoothed down her wrinkled dress. "If I get into my place without Griff or Nate seeing me, it'll be a miracle."

"You look good," I said.

More than good. She'd been in my bed all night, and left it with swollen lips and messy hair. She looked fucking perfect. I pulled her to me for a kiss.

"You're a man of few words," she said against my mouth. "The Lost Paws Animal shelter's on the south end of town near the highway we want. Meet me there tomorrow around ten?"

"Sure."

"Sure," she mimicked in a low voice and laughed before kissing me softly. "See you then."

I touched my cheek where I could still feel her kiss, then touched my fingers to my mouth. A deep longing settled like lead in my gut to watch her go. It would've been easy to chalk it up to the peace she gave me; as Fiona's car pulled away, the world came back. The guy taking out his trash across the street; the occupants of every apartment on the block—they invaded my senses. Or maybe I invaded theirs.

But the longing I felt to be with Fiona had nothing to do with what she gave me and everything to do with who she was.

"Christ."

I turned back into my empty apartment. I supposed I needed furniture but I could hardly unpack my clothes. I ran my hand along the counter, touched the coffee mug that Fiona's lips had touched. This wasn't a home. It was a place to bide my time before she left.

*Go with her.*

I froze. It was the first time I'd allowed myself to even think it.

"She hasn't asked me," I told no one, even as a warmth filled my chest in a way I hadn't felt since I was a kid. "And she'd hate me if she knew how I robbed her."

As if to punctuate that thought, the sour taste of my neighbor worrying over her bills filled my mouth, reminding me how the *ken* had stolen every shred of happiness I'd ever had.

I leaned against my chair-less counter near the succulent plant Fiona had brought me. Each of the echeveria's thick leaves had a barbed point on the end. I pressed the pad of my index finger to a needle-like tip until the pain came, puncturing my skin, deflating me, bring me back down. I watched the blood well. A single, bright red drop. The color of life.

*Fiona knows the colors too,* a small, desperate voice cried, sounding like my ten-year-old self. *She brings you peace. It means something. Tell her the truth...*

My father scoffed. *You're sick in the head.*

My mother wailed. *Nechistaya sila...*

I wiped my finger on my jeans and the red disappeared.

The next morning, I dressed and showered, grabbed breakfast at a local diner since my fridge was bare bones, then rode the Bonneville south, to Lost Paws.

It was a smallish place with a desk to the left of the entry, a waiting area to the right and then a wide hall lined with doors on either side. The echoing barking of two dozen dogs bounced around the floors—some deep and loud from the bigger dogs, and the high-pitched barks of smaller dogs that sounded as if they'd go on forever, barking their fear in a constant, never-ending chain of sound.

I stopped in the lobby area and watched as Fiona and a family of four came out of one of the doors on the left side. Fiona wore baggy jeans, a button-down, sleeveless shirt and her pink hair tied up in a ponytail. She had a small white dog on the end of her leash as she stood talking with the parents. Their two little girls—maybe six and eight years old—knelt and tried to pet the dog who cowered behind Fiona's legs.

Fiona knelt down to the girls' level and took two dog treats and placed them in the girls' palms. The dog ate from both girls and let himself be petted.

After a few more exchanged words I couldn't hear, Fiona handed the leash over to the father of the family. A shimmering mist hovered over her as she gestured the family to the front desk. The little girls were bright as sunflowers.

Fiona watched them go, a wistful smile on her face, and then she spotted me. The flare of her happiness was like a gift she didn't know she'd given me. She waved and met me halfway.

"Hey you," she said. She cocked her head. "What's that look for?"

"What look?" I asked.

"You looked like…I don't know. Like you haven't seen me in a long time instead of just yesterday."

*Poker face, dude. Where's your poker face?*

"I like how you are with the animals," I said, and inwardly rolled my eyes at my clunky words.

"It's easy. I love them. Seeing them find homes is the best feeling." Her eyes went to the family at the front desk, filling out their adoption paperwork. "Anyway, let me wash up and I'll be out in two."

A few minutes later, Fiona said goodbye to the office staff and we headed to the parking lot.

"I was going to take you for a ride if you're up for it," I said.

"I'd love to, but I don't have my helmet," Fiona said. "I should've had you meet me at my place instead."

"It's fine," I said. "I'll follow you. We'll leave from your place."

She craned up on her toes to kiss me. "Race you."

A short laugh burst out of me. "If you insist."

I gave her a three-minute head start, and then rode the Bonneville to Fiona's place, and parked it out front. Fiona was a careful driver; I wasn't surprised that I'd beaten her home. I leaned casually against her front door until her blue Prius pulled in. She climbed out and gave me an arch look.

I crossed my arms. "Too easy."

"Smartass," Fiona said, then stopped, her eye raking me up and down. "Damn. They must pull you guys aside in school to teach you that."

"Teach what?"

"The lean," she said, flapping her hand at me. "Arms crossed, shoulder to the wall…giving me that look."

"There's a look too?"

"There is," Fiona said, opening the front door and then slamming it shut behind us. "The look that's a casual hello on the surface, but underneath…"

"Underneath?"

"Underneath it says, 'I can't wait to get you in bed.'"

I hauled her to me. "I can't wait to get you in bed."

I bent my head to kiss her, when a knock came at the door, followed by a child's high-pitched voice. "Fiony! Fiony!"

Fiona smiled coyly. "Hold that thought."

She opened the door and knelt just as Hailey flew in her arms. The happiness that glittered around Fiona was brighter than anything I'd seen before.

"Hailey, girl!" Fiona kissed the little girl's cheek

The girl's mother—Nancy, I remembered—filled the door. A tall brunette in smart slacks and a blouse, the kind of woman who looked like she'd played field hockey in college. Tough and no-nonsense.

"Fiona, hi, I'm so sorry to spring this on you but I was wondering…" Nancy's voice trailed off as she saw me. "Oh, I'm so sorry. I didn't realize you had company."

Fiona rose to her feet, Hailey clinging to her arm. "Nikolai Young this is Nancy Davis."

Nancy offered her hand and I braced myself for the jolt that always came with snatching some piece of the stranger's life. She had a strong grip and it came with a whiff of distrust and a protectiveness of Fiona.

"Good to meet you, Nikolai," she said slowly, her eyes roving over my tattoos and piercings.

"Likewise."

Nancy dragged her gaze from me to Fiona. "I'm sorry if this is a bad time but I have an emergency meeting in twenty minutes. It'll only take an hour or so but if you're busy…"

"No, it's fine," Fiona said. "We can wait an hour, can't we, Nik?"

"Sure."

Nancy hesitated while her daughter turned her large brown eyes up to me, and asked the question Nancy was too polite to ask herself.

"Why is your skin covered in so many drawings?"

"They're called tattoos," I said. "It's art that you wear on your skin."

"How did you do it? With pens and markers?"

"No, needles."

Hailey's curiosity morphed to wariness. "Did it hurt?"

Nancy's attention wrapped around me like a vise. As far as she was concerned, I had one right answer here.

"Sure did. It hurt a lot."

"I hate shots with the needle," Hailey said. "They are the worst. Is it like shots?"

"Something like that," I said.

The tight band of Nancy's attention relaxed a little and she turned to Fiona and fished some money out of her purse. "I appreciate this so much, Fi. Just an hour, I swear."

"Put your money away…" Fiona said, but Nancy ignored her and stuffed a twenty into her hand.

"You're a life-saver," Nancy said, and shot me one more look. "Nice to meet you, Nikolai. Bye, Hail. Be good."

She kissed her daughter's cheek and went out.

"Nancy is a great mom," Fiona said, twisting a lock of hair around her finger. "But very protective."

"I get it," I said, with a small smile. "I'm not exactly ideal babysitter material."

"What are those?" Hailey asked, pointing at the piercings in both my ears. "Earrings?"

I chuckled, and knelt in front of the little girl. She reached her fingers to touch the talons in each ear, and I held still to let her conduct her examination. Hailey smelled clean, like fresh laundry and daisies.

"They're heavy!" Hailey said, her little fingers tugging on the talons. "Are they sharp?"

"A little bit," I said. "Don't push too hard on the pointy parts."

"Did it hurt to get them put in your ears?"

"It doesn't hurt anymore," I told her. "But it hurt a lot at first," I added, wanting to do right by her mom.

Hailey cocked her head. "Why do you do things to yourself that hurt?"

"I..." My mouth formed words but no sound came out and then the little girl held my face in her small hands.

"No more hurting, okay?" she said, and then wrapped her arms around my neck.

I froze as the full force of Hailey's affection—like white clouds, and cotton and baby powder—enveloped me. I closed my eyes, inhaled the pure goodness of her.

*No more hurting...*

For a few seconds I knew a different kind of peace than what Fiona gave me, and then Hailey shattered the spell with a high-pitched squeal right in my ear.

"Lemony!" She bounded to the window and climbed on the chair to wave and coo at the little bird.

I got to my feet, rising out of Hailey's calm and into Fiona's storm. "Fiona?"

She was turned away from me, her shoulders rounded. The blue mist and the dark shadows both converged around her. I stared. Inside the mist and shadow—like a mirage—I saw Fiona on her knees, tears streaming down her cheeks. She clutched her stomach, rocking back and forth, her mouth open in a silent agonized scream.

Rage tore through me like a wildfire to see her in such pain. I reached for her. "Fiona, what's happening...?"

"It's nothing," she said, pulling away from me. Her voice was muffled against her hand and her throat was choked with tears. "I'm fine. I'm...fine."

The vision wavered as she struggled as hard as she could to bury it down deep. My hand still reached for her but I didn't touch her. If I touched her now, I'd know everything. And even without that touch, the *ken* would eventually give me her story, piece by piece. I was torn between wanting it—to know who had hurt her like that so I could hurt him just as bad—and protecting her privacy.

*Tell me, Fiona… please. Give it to me before I take it from you.*

"Fiony?" Hailey asked from the window. "Are you crying?"

"No, I'm fine, honey," Fiona said. She wiped her eyes and dried her hands on the seat of her jeans. "I was about to sneeze and I didn't. Made my eyes water." She didn't look at me but went to the window with Hailey. "Want to help me feed this little guy?"

I stared after her, blinking, trying to reconcile the agonized image I had seen and the woman standing before me, helping Hailey pour seed for her bird. To know she carried that much pain in her…

*I'll kill him. Whoever he is, I'll fucking kill him.*

I forced myself to calm down before I gave too much away. Fiona had recovered and all that was left was shame she didn't want me to see.

I shouldered my jacket. "I should go. I have a lot to do at my place," I said. "Rain check on the ride today?"

"Okay, maybe that's best," Fiona said, still averting her eyes, though her gratitude was palpable. "In case Nancy runs late…"

"Sure," I said, and went to the door.

"Nik?"

I stopped and my heart broke to hear the tears lingering in her voice. I turned and her eyes met mine from across the room, heavy and apologetic, as she stood with her bird and Hailey, with her green plants all around her—the little forest she tried to make for herself until she could live in the real one, and a child who wasn't hers. Fiona didn't want me to go, and she didn't want to tell me about *him*; what the bastard did to her to cause her so much fucking pain. But I knew it was somehow connected to the children and the animals and the goddamn plants…everything she cared about. It was all tainted by *him*.

She smiled tremulously at me, now scared she was fucking things up with *me*.

"Call me," I told her. "Any time you're…" *Ready.* "Any time you want."

"I will," Fiona said faintly. Her gaze caught and held mine. "Thank you."

I offered her a smile though it had to break through the anger toward that nameless bastard that had hurt her. Making Fiona happy was easy. Who had been so goddamned bad at it?

"Bye, Nik!" Hailey said, waving at me from on top of the chair, a small bag of birdseed in her hand. "See you soon!"

"Bye, Hailey." I looked to Fiona. "See you soon."

# Chapter 16

## Nikolai

Three days later and no word from Fiona. My apartment was still empty and without her, it felt hollow too. Airless and stale. I was supposed to buy furniture. Get 'settled in.' But without Fiona, what was the fucking point? She was all the color and light in my life.

"I miss her," I said into the silence. I missed her colors and her smile…the way she tasted in my mouth when I kissed her, and the way she looked at me. Like I was fucking worth something to her.

Maybe I could be. Maybe I had a purpose beyond poker and the road. Maybe the damn *ken* had a purpose beyond torture…

A whisper of a memory tugged at my thoughts. I stood in the quiet stillness of my apartment. Sweat trickled between my shoulder blades and I closed my eyes.

*"What do you want to be when you grow up, Nik?"*
*"Nothing."*
*"I'm sure that's not true. Everyone wants to be something."*
*"A mechanic."*
*"You want to be a mechanic when you grow up?"*
*"No. But Papa said I need a real job. Painting is not a real job."*
*"Painting? You want to be a painter?"*
*"I did. Not anymore."*
*"Why not?"*
*"Because…"*

*"You can tell me."*

*"Because the painting helps how I see people. And I like it. But every time you give me the treatment I want it less and less. And now you wish I hadn't said that—"*

*"You said your father wanted you to be a mechanic. Can you do both? Be a mechanic and paint on the side."*

*"I told you, I don't want to paint. Not anymore."*

*"You said the painting helps how you see people. What does that mean?"*

*"If I tell people what I see, they get scared. If I paint them, it's just art. Creativity. It's safe."*

*"You like painting people? Portraits?"*

*"Yes."*

*"Who have you painted?"*

*"My teacher. My friends. Mama, once."*

*"And what did she say when she saw her portrait?"*

*"She burned it."*

*"She...burned it?"*

*"And then she brought me here."*

I opened my eyes and the hospital faded out, my empty place faded in.

*The painting helps how I see people...*

"Stupid..."

But it had been true. If I put the paint down it made the *ken* less something that seemed so insane and unreal, and gave it form. It helped.

Before I could talk myself out of it, I called up a local art supply store and placed an order, same day delivery.

I paced in my empty space and waited for the knock on the door. When it came, I paid the guy, and took my supplies—an easel, a three-feet by four-feet canvas, and a set of professional grade oil-pastel crayons—to the empty space in the living room where a couch and chairs were supposed to go. I tore the plastic wrap off the canvas as if it were suffocating it, and set it on the easel.

My hand shook as I took up an oil-pastel in deep pink.

I inhaled, closed my eyes for a moment. I was on the Bonneville with Fiona behind me, her laughter and exhilaration enveloping me. Her arms around me squeezed, twice, I opened my eyes, and began to paint.

# Chapter 17

## *Fiona*

I lay on my bed, my phone in my hand, fingers hovering over Nik's number. It took me three days—three damn days—to trust myself enough just to get this far. I missed him—too much—but every time I started to call, the vision of him with Hailey rose up: Nik kneeling down to her, and her putting her little hands on his face...

*No more hurting.*

It had almost been too much. Like a caged animal tearing at its chains, the agony had nearly escaped as my aching heart recast Nik and Hailey as father and daughter. And me...?

*You'll never have that...*

And now Nik was suspicious. Everything I'd been trying to run away from kept chasing me and lately it felt as if it were catching up, snarling and nipping at my heels, and ready to devour me when I fell.

"No," I told myself, phone in hand. "I'm stronger than I look."

**I'm off work today,** I texted Nik. **Are you free?**

His reply came quickly. **Come over.**

I sucked in a breath. **I'll be right there.**

I threw on cargo pants, and a small t-shirt, then drove to Nik's apartment a little before noon. The heat was already intense, the humidity making the air sticky.

*This is practice for Costa Rica,* I reminded myself, but there was no answering the thrill that the departure was getting closer.

Nik answered the door, looking devastating in a simple dark shirt and jeans.

"Hi," I said.

"Hi," he answered, and then kissed me gently. The tight coil of tension in my belly eased as I somehow knew he wasn't going to ask me about my tears the other day. In fact, Nik always seemed to know when I needed him and when I needed space; what to say to make me feel better, and when to say nothing.

*It's what he does. He reads my tells.*

We broke the kiss and I wreathed my arms around his neck, a smile spreading over my lips. "I missed you."

"Me too," he said. "Come in from the heat. I got an AC unit. I'm halfway civilized."

I started to laugh but as I entered Nik's place it was clear the AC unit was the only thing he'd bought. The living space hadn't one piece of furniture in it and the kitchen was still bare but for plastic plates and utensils, mostly still in their boxes and sleeves on the counter.

Nik noticed my furrowed brows and rubbed his chin. "Okay, maybe less than civilized."

"You need…everything," I said.

"Yeah, I guess I'm not used to staying in one place," he said slowly.

*That makes sense. He's been on the road for years.*

"Well…I can help," I said brightly. "There's a swap meet a little ways south of here. Want to check it out?"

"Sure," he said.

That time, I read his tell. He didn't care one way or another and I wondered if maybe he didn't want to stay long after all.

*Can you blame him?*

"Or maybe…we don't have to go to the swap meet…" I stammered.

His lips quirked up in a smile. "A chair. I need at least one chair."

I laughed lightly. "I think the Prius can hold one chair."

Nik smirked. "No comment."

I noticed a smudge of pink on his fingers. "What's that?" I teased. "New tattoo?"

"Oh, uh…no. I was…painting."

"You were? Where?" I glanced around. "Can I see…?"

And then I saw it in the living area that was still empty but for an easel, a small table of pastels, and a canvas. I gasped. On the canvas was a portrait of me, rendered with perfect accuracy and yet with a swirl of impressionistic color and abstract strokes. I saw myself, a wide smile on my face, my eyes a shocking blue, and my hair fell around my shoulders in a glowing cascade of gold and pink.

In the background, golden sunbursts over a jungle at midday. The vibrant greenery that spilled down to a beach upon where silver waves crashed. Amid the sunbursts was the laughing face of a child, who might've been Hailey, but to my eye could have been the essence of *any* child—round cheeks, bright eyes, a guileless smile.

I turned to Nik who stood behind me, running his hand through his hair nervously.

"Nik…" I shook my head. "This is incredible. It looks like me but…it's more."

He stuffed his hands in the pockets of his jeans. "It's okay…"

"Okay?" I blinked back strange tears. "It's like looking at a mirror but…" I looked to him. "Is that how you see me?"

He hesitated. "Yeah…I do."

"It's…beautiful," I said with a small laugh. "Am I allowed to say that? I mean…your talent is incredible."

My smile froze as my gaze caught what I'd missed at first glance. At the bottom right corner of the canvas, like a blight that threatened to take over the color, was a swath of pure black with a bluish mist at its edges.

"It's not done yet," Nik said, shuffling his feet. "There're some details left to finish…So…ready to go?"

I dragged my gaze from the portrait. "Yeah, sure…"

We headed out but I stopped at the door for one more look at that dark stain. *It's not done yet,* I told myself. *He hasn't finished that section of the canvas yet.*

But that darkness seemed to me like it belonged there as much as the pink of my hair or the green of the jungle.

I turned to Nik and kissed his cheek. "It's perfect. Don't change a thing."

We took the Prius and drove south and inland, through green country and across flat fields, until we came to the country road that led to a cluster of barns that had been turned into warehouses for antiques. I'd only been once with Opal and the Millers, and remembered it as being a small affair. Now, the makeshift parking lot that took up a flat stretch of land on one side was nearly full. Colored balloons and streamers could be seen on some of the barns. A Ferris wheel and a carousel rose up behind the smaller structures, their organ music carrying to us across the grounds.

"It looks like the little country fair is here," I said as I parked the car. "I'm sorry I didn't know it was happening this week, or I would've checked."

"What's to be sorry about?"

"I was thinking about your agoraphobia. I don't want it to be hard on you."

"It's an open-air place," Nik said. "I should be okay."

"Are you sure?"

He grinned. "I'll take my chances."

"Okay, this could be fun," I said, and tucked my arm through his as we headed to the grounds. "I want to eat junk food and cotton candy… Will you play a game and win me one of those gigantic stuffed animals, like they do in the movies?"

"If that's what you want," he said, "I'll get one for you."

I shivered dramatically. "I love it when you say things like that—so confident and manly and sexy."

"Whatever you want, Fiona," Nik said, his tone serious.

*What I want…*

I looked into Nikolai's blue eyes that never regarded me with contempt or irritation. His hands roamed my body at night with greed, never disdain that I was too thin or flat-chested. His lips never formed insults; he never belittled me or made me feel stupid, or small.

I took one of his hands in mine. "I want to walk in the sunshine with you."

Nik and I strolled hand-in-hand through the fair, over hay-strewn ground that itched our noses, and the sound of carnival music filling the heat-thickened air that was already heavy with the smells of cotton candy, hot dogs, cinnamon buns and popcorn. I worried the crowd of running and laughing children or groups of kids trying their hand at the different carnival games would be too much for Nik, but he walked easily, holding tight to my hand.

It was on the tip of my tongue to tease him for being a hand-holder, but I wondered if maybe it helped. If I helped. I had read once that sometimes touching another person helps a claustrophobic to pull out of their anxiety and remind them that the world was bigger than it felt. A touchstone. I'd been the tagalong at the end of Steve's coattail.

I'd never been anyone's touchstone.

We stopped for hot dogs and lemonade, and ate them at a small table under a little umbrella. Nik had two hotdogs stacked on his plate each loaded with mustard, ketchup, onions and relish. I didn't want to keep thinking about Steve, but I couldn't help compare the two men.

Steve was a tall red head; not unattractive, but after everything that happened I couldn't think of him as anything but a shape-shifting snake.

Nik was dark and dangerous-looking in a way that made me feel safe instead of threatened. Protected. There was nothing unsexy about Nikolai, including the way he sat hunched over, his elbows on the table, shoulder muscles bunched and straining his plain T-shirt, as he took a huge bite from one hotdog. I stared at his mouth as he licked a stray bit of mustard from one corner.

*Good God, this man. He's a walking orgasm.*

A slow, amused smile spread over Nik's face as he contemplated his next bite, and I nearly clapped my hands over my mouth.

*Did I say that out loud? No...*

Nik said nothing, only polished off the last bite of hot dog, and washed it down with the last of his drink.

"Finished?" Nik asked, tossing his napkin onto his empty plate. "Let's win you a prize."

The fair was small but had a small collection of games and a few rides. We strode through the games area, Nik's hand holding mine tight as the crowd thickened around us.

"How are you doing?" I asked.

"I'm good," Nik said. "See anything you like?"

"Not yet, but can you smell that?" I turned my nose to the air. "Cotton candy."

Nik jerked his chin. "There."

He led me to a cart where a vendor swirled a cone inside a spinning bin of wispy pink sugar until a cloud formed.

"I'll take one," Nik said, reaching for his wallet.

"Thank you," I said, taking the cone from the man. I tugged a piece of pink cotton candy—the same shade of pink as my hair—off the cone. "Try?"

Nik turned me away from the crowds, and took the puff of sugar from my fingers to hold it to my lips instead. My heart thundered at the look in his eye and my lips parted without a thought. Nik laid the cottony sugar on my tongue where it started to dissolve, sticky sweet and good. I took his thumb in my mouth before he could withdraw it, swirling my tongue and sucking the sugar residue from it.

"Jesus, Fiona…"

He bent to me, using his thumb to open my mouth wider, and laid his lips to mine. I gasped as Nik's mouth tasted me and the melting sugar in a kiss that I felt deep in the core of me. My eyes fluttered open to catch his brows furrowed with intensity, almost as if he were in pain. The candy melted away and still he kissed me, his tongue sliding against mine, a small sound of want rumbling deep in his chest.

"So good," he whispered as we broke away for air. "God, Fiona…That's you. Everything you are…"

He was standing so close to me, the clear blue of his eyes full with my reflection and nothing else. I swallowed hard. "What do you mean? What am I…?"

Nik blinked and looked away, sucking in a breath. "Nothing, sorry," he said. "You're too damn sexy, is what I meant. I'm having a hard time controlling myself."

"Maybe no more cotton candy," I said.

"Good idea."

I hated waste, but I didn't want to eat it without sharing it with Nik and his luscious mouth delving into mine. *This is a family place*, I thought with a giggle and took a breath to calm my racing heart.

"We were going to win you something," Nik said, surreptitiously adjusting his groin.

I grinned to myself, and ran my tongue over my lip. *Yep. Walking orgasm…*

"How about here?" Nik tilted his head at the prizes offered in the games that lined a wood-slatted wall. Stuffed teddy bears seemed to be the norm, ranging in size from puny, to the kind that were so big they were hung from the roofs of the game booths.

"Anything you can't live without?" he asked.

"They're all the same," I said. "Not a huge select—"

Nik stopped walking so suddenly that I took a step ahead of him and his hand holding mine jerked me back. I followed his gaze to see what had stopped him but he stared straight ahead, at a young couple walking our way, holding hands.

The guy wore a red baseball cap on backwards and a heavy metal concert t-shirt with the sleeves torn off. The woman's dark hair was in two short braids that brushed her shoulders, and she wore a red plaid shirt tied at the midriff and Daisy Duke shorts. Her eyes looked straight ahead, the man's face blank, his lips drawn down.

The couple passed us and Nik stood stock still for a moment. Then he dropped my hand, did an abrupt about-face, and stalked after them.

"Nik...?"

The couple rounded a corner, Nik following. I hurried to catch up, to a semi-secluded juncture between the wooden wall that surrounded the games area and a small shed. Over Nik's shoulder, I saw the man had the woman pinned against the wooden slats, his face inches from hers, one hand lying flat by her head. The woman's features were twisted in fear.

"You think I didn't see that?" the man was seething in her face. "Stupid bitch, you should know better..."

I stopped cold as the blood rushed to my ears.

*Stupid bitch...*

*You should know better...*

The man's hand smashed into the wooden wall beside his girlfriend's head, jolting me. Nik never slowed his stride but walked up and tapped him on the shoulder.

"Hey."

The guy turned. "What the fu—"

Nik slammed his fist into the guy's face. His head whipped back, the baseball cap flew, and the guy landed on his ass in a cloud of dust.

"What the hell are you doing?" the woman shrieked, flying to kneel beside the man. "Baby, are you okay?"

The guy pinned Nik with a venomous gaze and jabbed a finger at him from his prone position on the ground. "You're fucking dead." He spat a wad of blood into the dirt at Nik's feet. "Dead man. I'll sue you for everything. I'll call the cops..."

"Go ahead," Nik said, his hands still in fists like he was itching to hit him again. He sounded deadly calm but I saw the fire in his blue eyes. "Call the cops. Let's get them over here and show them the bruises you put on her."

The man's eyes widened, and fear mingled with his shock and anger.

The woman's face was a spinning wheel of conflicted emotions, from anguish to fear, to something like hope, all in a split second. She settled on defiance and thrust her chin at Nik. "You don't know what the hell you're talking about. You don't know us. You don't know our business…"

"Forget him, babe," the man said, getting to his feet. He stabbed his finger at Nik again while backing away, the woman clinging tight to his arm. "Come near us again, asshole, and I'll fuck you up. Big time."

He spat another wad of red and slung his arm around her waist. The woman shot us a dirty look over her shoulder but it was a weak mask. A sham. A cover-up.

*He doesn't mean anything by it*, I heard myself say. *You don't know him like I do…*

I shivered in the ninety-degree heat. Steve had never hit me, never spat these words in anger like this man did, but tossed them off with casual disdain, marveling at my supposed stupidity instead of being enraged by it. I wondered if he'd been volatile instead of insidious would it have been easier to fight back? Would I have walked away if he'd been violent?

Or would I have knelt in the dirt beside him to help him up?

"Fiona?"

I blinked, and unclenched my hands from my arms. My fingernails left little half-moons on my skin. "Yeah, sorry, that was…intense."

"Are you okay?" Nik asked.

"Me? Yes, fine. Why?"

He said nothing but stared, not at me, but seemingly at something above my head, his face drawn tight with anger. He inhaled through his nose and exhaled, as if fighting for calm.

"Sorry you had to see that," he muttered. His jaw clenched and his eyes tuned to follow where the young couple had gone. "My father hit my mother…

"I know. It's okay," I said, moving to stand beside him. His hand found mine immediately and held on. I held on just as tightly, my hands shaking. "That asshole deserved it. They all do…"

Nik whirled to look at me, a thousand different thoughts behind his eyes. I felt the air tighten and realized with a pang of fear I was on the verge of cracking open and spilling everything at Nik's feet on the dirt of the county fair. All he had to do was ask and I'd tell him everything.

*I can't. Not here. I'll fall apart…*

Nik snapped his mouth shut and the moment withered and blew away.

We headed back onto the game's area in silence. Nik scanned the booths, and then marched up to the Test Your Strength game as if he'd been looking for it all along.

It was a bright red pole shaped like a thermometer, with degrees from 0 to 100 painted in vibrant yellow along one side. The higher the degree reached, the bigger the prize. For five bucks you got a shot to ring the bell at the top and win a giant stuffed bear.

We waited wordlessly in line behind a guy who looked bulkier than Nikolai, in ripped jeans and a white t-shirt with a pack of smokes rolled up in the sleeve. The guy hefted the mallet and slammed it down. The metal can shot up to 80°.

"Pretty hot, pretty hot, but no fever." The carney handed the guy a medium-sized stuffed bear from a bin. "Next? Who's next? Step right up. You, young man. Let's see if you've got any muscles hidin' under all that ink."

Without a word, Nik paid the five bucks, and gripped the mallet in both hands. He swung it up and then down, all in one smooth, powerful motion. The can rocketed up to 100 degrees and clanged loudly against the bell.

A smattering of clapping from the fairgoers around us, and the carney stared for a moment before whistling through his teeth.

"You see that, folks? A giant among us. It can be done, oh yes, it can be done."

I watched Nik toss the mallet down. There was no happiness or triumph written on his features, only a haunted look and shadows flitting across his eyes.

The carney hauled a giant stuffed bear out of a bin; pale yellow, about three feet tall and half as wide. It felt as if it were stuffed with little plastic pebbles.

"I'll give it to Hailey," I said.

Nik nodded. We walked away from the game, his eyes were straight ahead, his jaw tight.

"I think I'm done here," he said. "Crowd's getting thick."

"Okay," I said. "Sure, of course."

He saw me struggling awkwardly with the giant bear, and took it out of my hands. He held it over his shoulder by one arm, while his other hand kept mine, and we silently walked across the fairgrounds.

At my car, Nik stopped, his gaze back the way we had come.

"She didn't leave him," he said. "Why didn't she leave him?"

I wondered if he meant the girl back at the fair, or his mother.

Or me.

I was about to shrug. To tell him I had no idea. No frame of reference. No experience…

"Because she was afraid," I heard myself say. "Afraid to leave, afraid to stay…So much fear that you become paralyzed by it. You can't move."

Nik stared. I was saying too much. I couldn't stop.

"They say it's fight or flight, but really it's more like the proverbial deer in the headlights, the fear locking you in place and so you either hope the car misses and you bound to freedom, or that it's over quickly."

Nik's hard stare softened, pleading. *Tell me everything…* he seemed to be saying. But the words were locked behind my lips, tangling with questions and confusion.

*Silly little airhead. You can't let me go. You never can and you never will.*

"That's my guess anyway," I said abruptly, turning away, shame burning my cheeks. "Who knows what that girl's life is really like?"

Nik opened his mouth and then seemed to bite off the words before speaking. He nodded reluctantly and we drove home, him behind the wheel.

We were halfway to Garden City when a small itch in my mind grew more insistent; clinging like a burr that wouldn't be dislodged.

"How did you know?" I asked finally.

"How'd I know what?"

"That he was going to hurt her? They were just walking past us. Hand in hand. Just like us."

Nikolai was silent but his hands clenched tight around the wheel, the hand with *hoax* tattooed on his fingers closest to me.

"He wasn't holding her hand," Nik said. "He was gripping her around the wrist so tightly that his fingers were digging into her skin."

I frowned. "He was? No…I thought—?"

"Yeah, he was," Nik said. "I saw that and the look on her face. Her tell. I've seen it before. My mother used to wear it when my dad was getting ready to blow. Like a storm was coming in, she'd batten herself down. Go blank. Pretend she didn't care what was going to happen next. Like it was no big deal."

"You said he put bruises on her…"

Nik's gaze slid to me then back to the road. "I took a guess. He didn't deny it."

"No, I suppose he didn't…"

*But they were holding hands. Weren't they?*

But the man's name-calling and the way he slapped the wall by her head weren't my imagination.

"I'm glad you saw that something wasn't right," I told Nik. "Even if that girl didn't act on it today, she knows it's not right. Someone else, besides that voice in her head, *showed* her it wasn't right."

Nik pursed his lips. "Fiona…"

"This heat is getting to me," I said. "I'm getting a headache. Do you mind if I nap a little?"

"No, of course not."

I rested my head on the side of the door and pretended to sleep. I'm sure Nik knew I was faking. I was sure he knew a lot of things.

He was really good at reading people.

# Chapter 18

## Nikolai

We rolled into Fiona's complex just before dusk. She'd hardly said a word the rest of the drive, but pretended to sleep while her thoughts flared. I tasted sour memories on my tongue like lemon juice, while the shadows hovered over her, dimming her colors and stealing her happiness.

"Thanks for the bear," Fiona said as I walked her to her door. "Hailey will love it, I'm sure."

"I'm glad."

Fiona didn't want to be alone. The last thing she wanted was to be alone, but she wasn't ready to tell me about *him* either. She was cloudy with the incident at the fair and it tied her more tightly to her past.

"Hey," I said. "We never had that second motorcycle ride."

The barest flicker of a smile touched her lips. "That's true…"

"Come on. Pack a bag."

"Pack a… Where are we going?"

"I don't know. We'll figure it out when we get there."

"Just…get on your motorcycle and drive somewhere?"

Christ, she was beautiful. *Find the sunshine, Fiona. That's all I want for you.*

"Grab everything you need for the night," I said. "I'll be back in twenty minutes."

Her laughter was silver coins sliding together. Her colors brightened and shimmered; the pink came back. "Um, okay. I'll see you soon."

I kissed her lips softly. "See you soon."

We hit the coastal road going south, the same route we'd taken for the beach when I'd first come back to Savannah. We passed that inlet and kept going as twilight thickened to gold and orange along the horizon, and the setting sun ignited the dark green of the forest on the west with a blaze of color.

Fiona, wearing my leather, wrapped her arms around me tight and squeezed twice. I gunned the Bonneville and heard the squeal of her laughter through our helmets. Her exhilaration radiated out of her to saturate me and seep into my blood and my bones, until I felt like laughing or crying or both for the pure exultation of it.

As darkness fell, I spotted a sign for a small inn tucked into the woods along the highway. I took it, and followed the high beam as it lit up a winding path through the forest to a quaint bed and breakfast, painted cream yellow and white. Lights glowed in the windows and a sign proclaimed it The Marling Inn.

I took off my helmet. "How's this?" I asked, idling the Bonneville in the parking lot.

Fiona removed hers too, and goddamn, the way her blue eyes lit up, drinking it all in—the inn tucked amongst the greenery, and the fireflies that danced along the path that led up to the front door…I'd never seen anything so beautiful in my life.

"It's perfect," she breathed, then frowned, looking to me. "But maybe expensive?"

I shot her a wink. "I got it covered, baby."

A laugh burst out of her. "Nikolai Alexei, did you just *wink* at me?"

"It was on my bucket list."

She laughed harder, and then softer, and the warm glow of her feelings for me limned her face—sweet and pure, but tinged with the shadows of her past, like the whitest paper charred at the edges.

"Nikolai…Thank you for this." She leaned over and kissed my cheek.

"Thank you for coming with me." *And for everything good in my life, Fiona...*

But the words stuck in my throat and she climbed off the bike.

In the inn, the woman at the front desk lifted her silver-haired head to watch us come in, her eyes widening for a moment at my ink and Fiona's hair. Then her face broke open in a welcoming smile.

"Hello, you two," she cooed. "Aren't you something? Welcome, welcome. My name's Helen Marling, owner and proprietor. And you are...? Honeymooners?"

Fiona blushed. "No, we're just here for one night."

"That works too!" Helen laughed.

We checked in and Helen showed us personally to our room, the Lobelia suite.

"Every room in the Marling is named after a different Georgian flower," Helen said.

She led us up a curved, wooden staircase. The wall curved with the stairs, and was papered in pale yellow with blue flowers, and photos dating as far back as the turn of the century. On the second floor, Helen unlocked the door to our suite with an actual key and then placed it in my hand.

"Dinner's at eight. I do hope you'll join us."

We unpacked our small bags in a room that was flower overload; the wallpaper, the rug, and even the bedspread were covered in tiny purple flowers. A throw pillow on an antique chair was embroidered with a larger spray.

"When Helen said this was the Lobelia suite, she wasn't kidding," Fiona laughed. "And hey, a balcony."

She opened the double doors and I followed her out onto the balcony that faced east. A dense copse of woods spread out below, dark in the falling night. Beyond, the ocean stretched on and on, streaked with moonlight—a spill of silver on the dark water.

"I'll bet this looks amazing at dawn," she said.

"We'll have to stay up all night to find out," I said, slipping my arms around her waist.

"You have a plan as to how we do that?" she asked, leaning into me.

I nuzzled her neck. "I have a few ideas."

She laughed. "I'm sure you do."

I took a quick shower, and while Fiona took her turn, I put on jeans and my one and only black button-down dress shirt. Fiona emerged from the bathroom wearing a pale green dress that flowed to her ankles and draped elegantly over her thin frame.

I stared and let the *ken* see her without fighting it. I took Fiona in, all of her colors and light, her clean scents, and the taste of her on my tongue that was sweeter than the cotton candy at the fair.

"God, Fiona..." I murmured.

She approached me, laid her hands on my chest. "You clean up pretty good yourself, Nikolai." She slid her hands up around my neck, a waft of perfume, soap, and the warmth of her skin rising around me. "More than good. You look..." She cocked her head. "How do you say 'devastatingly handsome' in Russian?"

I thought for a second. "Razrushitel'no krasivyy."

"You look razrushitel'no krasivyy," she said, her accent wobbly. But holding her in my arms and hearing her speak my mother's language... It felt like the purest acceptance. God willing, she'd gift that same acceptance to me when I finally worked up the goddamn courage to tell her what I was.

*Not tonight. This night is for her.*

"How'd I do?" she asked.

"Perfect," I said, gruffly. "Too perfect. If we don't leave for dinner now, I'll never make it."

She laughed. "Then I guess you'll just have to wait and see if I remembered to pack underwear."

I groaned in mock anguish, but the truth was her colors were coming back and that meant more to me than anything else.

We descended the stairs and entered a small dining room behind the front entry. It was as if we'd stepped back in time by half a century, and into a rich old lady's home. A fireplace, dark for the summer, was the centerpiece, its mantel heavy with ceramic knickknacks. An antique clock marked the time with a brass pendulum above the mantel, and a gramophone near the window played some gentle piano music I didn't recognize. Ten or so tables were set with china and frilly tablecloths, each filled with diners, the youngest of which couldn't have been more than fifty.

All conversations ceased as they turned to stare at us, eyes wide. Wariness went up like a brick wall; they were concerned that we'd be loud or inappropriate and ruin their quiet dinner, but Helen swooped in and knocked it all down.

"Ah, there you are! So happy you could join us." She ushered us to a small table smack in the center of the room and handed us menus. "Steak salad is our specialty tonight, served with grilled zucchini, and of course peach cobbler for dessert."

I glanced at Fiona. "Sound good?"

"Perfect."

I handed the menus back to Helen. "We'll take two."

"Done and done! Annie will be by to get your drinks." Helen leaned over the table. "And can I just tell you it does my heart good to see young people here? And it might not look like it now, but it'll do them good too," she said, jerking her thumb over her shoulder to indicate the other diners. She winked. "Enjoy yourselves, sweethearts."

Fiona and I exchanged smiles, then she put her napkin on her lap, and rubbed her chin on her shoulder discreetly to get a look at the room.

"They're all staring at us," Fiona muttered under her breath.

"They're staring at you," I said.

"It feels a little tight in here. How are you doing?"

I reached across the table and she put her hand in mine. The whispers and colors of everyone in the inn dimmed, and the peace of Fiona intensified around me.

"Better now."

She squeezed my hand and didn't let go.

*I can't let go of this. Of her...*

The suddenness of this thought took me by surprise. It scared the shit out of me, and I pushed it aside, vowing to have this night with Fiona; to give her everything she needed and wanted, everything she deserved that had been denied her. The image of her screaming in howling agony was burned into my psyche. I couldn't erase it from her, but I could give her better memories to turn to when the pain roared up in her.

We ate steak salad and zucchini, both cooked to perfection. It tasted better than anything I had ever had on the road.

"It tastes home-cooked," Fiona said. "You probably haven't had much of this on the road, have you?"

I glanced up in surprise to hear my thoughts spoken back to me. "No, not much."

"Do you miss it? The poker?"

"Not even a little."

"Do you think you might...quit playing?"

*Do you think you'll stay?*

Like an echo behind her spoken words, her thoughts came to me on the conduit of our clasped hands.

"I want to," I said slowly. "I want…something else for my life than the road and dingy basements and card games."

Visions of green jungle and a blue ocean coalesced around Fiona. *Costa Rica…*

My heart pounded in my chest for what might come next. But the tension of an unspoken confession—the story of *him*—coiled in Fiona. There was too much pain locked in her and this quaint little inn couldn't contain it.

*No more hurting…Not tonight.*

"Let's dance," I said.

She blinked. "Dance? Here? We aren't conspicuous enough?"

"For your bucket list," I said. "Have you ever danced in a full dining room in front of a bunch of strangers?"

She laughed, her tension loosening. "Now that you mention it…"

I rose to my feet and held out my hand. She glanced around at the diners who'd turned their attention back to us.

"Really?"

"Don't leave me hanging," I said.

"I thought you didn't dance," she said, giving me her hand and slowly rising. "When we first met at the club…"

"I don't," I said, and pulled her close, held her hand to my chest, wrapped my other around her waist. "But for you…"

Immediately, she rested her head on my chest, and her contentment and relief seeped into me like warm water into aching bones.

The other diners murmured and I felt their smiles as I closed my eyes to turn Fiona in a small circle.

"Nikolai," she said against my chest. "I've never done this before."

"Neither have I."

"Not the dance," she said. "I mean, this. Us. I've never…had this before."

"Neither have I."

I felt her inhale and exhale a ragged breath. "I've told you that my last relationship was…bad."

"Yes," I said, holding her tighter. "You told me."

"But I didn't tell you everything."

"I know." I swallowed hard. "I haven't told you everything either."

Fiona raised her head to look at me. "I'm scared."

"Me too," I said. "I'm scared shitless, Fiona."

Her surprise colored her expression and then she nodded. "This place is so quiet and sweet. Like we've stepped out of time. Can we have this night without anything ugly and bad getting in the way? I'm so tired of being confused and unsure…But right now, I want to…"

"Just be," I said. "That's why we're here. That's what I want for you."

She rested her head back on my chest, her body expanding under my hand with a sigh. "You always seem to know exactly what I need. Even more than I do."

I said nothing to that, but held her and danced. She thought she was weak but the strength in her hummed under my hand and glinted brightly in the eye of the *ken*. A core of steel carried her out of the 'ugly and bad' that haunted her…and into my arms on that night.

*And she protects me from the* ken. *I'll protect her from everything that hurts her, if she'll let me.*

After dinner, we went back upstairs, a quiet anticipation trailing behind us. Inside the room, I shut the door and leaned against it, watching Fiona move into the space and turn on a dim lamp by the bed. Yellow light suffused the room, and she turned to me.

"Nik…"

"Yeah, baby?"

But I didn't need to ask. Everything she wanted was there on the surface. Me. She reached for me with her entire being.

I crossed to her and took her face in my hands. We held each other's gaze and I knew what was coming. Her past. My affliction. They stood in the way of this. Us. And as scared as I was to lose her, I knew I would have to tell her. I'd never felt this way about a woman. It wasn't only her peace or the relief she gave me; it was her.

"You," I whispered. "You, Fiona…"

She nodded as if she knew exactly what I meant. Her eyes searched mine, equal parts fear and want…

*Love and hope…*

"Kiss me," she whispered.

I lowered my mouth to hers, gave myself to her in that kiss. I made promises in that kiss, to try to do right by her. That I would tell her what I was in a way she could hear and not hate me, because I was hers completely.

*And she's mine,* I thought, as her mouth opened for me, as her hands wound into my hair. *She makes me whole.*

Why else did the noise and cacophony of the *ken* fall silent with her?

A bright flare of hope rose in me as our hands gently undid buttons and tugged at zippers. Fiona wouldn't hate me. I'd tell her what I was and instead of being repulsed, she'd stay. Her innate kindness and compassion—the sweetness of her that filled my mouth as I kissed her—would save me. And in return, I'd do whatever it took to keep her safe and make her feel as cherished as she deserved to be.

Our clothes melted away and I lay down with her on the bed, touching and kissing slowly, no fiery need to satisfy, only us as we were, two broken people holding on to one another in the dark and making our own happiness.

She whispered for me to get a condom, almost apologetically—another piece of her past that lay between us. I slipped it on and slid inside her, closing my eyes at the perfect sensation of her around me; her body, her arms and legs, her mouth that kissed me over and over.

I braced myself on one elbow over her, my hand holding her face, her hair splayed on the pillow in a pink halo. She held my hips, drawing me tighter to her, while my free hand slipped beneath her, pressing her into my thrusts. I could not get deep enough in her. She couldn't take enough of me.

"Nik," she breathed. "So much. I want this so much…"

The pleasure coalesced from a thousand different touches into one potent wellspring between us, and she looked so beautiful, coming undone beneath me while I lost myself in her at the same time.

After, we lay in our usual position, her lying across my chest and my hand lazily playing in her hair. Fiona…My shield. Protecting me and giving me rest. And I lay beneath her, strong and unwavering. A foundation she could rely on.

We woke just before dawn. Wordlessly, I drew on my jeans and she pulled my dress shirt over my shoulders, and we went out onto the balcony.

Gray haze was slowly burnt away by a gold fire in the east. The sun crawled out of the ocean, casting embers along the water. Below, the forest was waking up with birdsongs. A mist hovered low over the ground.

Fiona clutched my arm as a deer stepped into a small clearing near the rear of the inn's property. The deer—a doe—raised its head, listening, its dark eyes looking in our direction. It sniffed the air and gracefully stepped along the tall grasses. A moment later, a fawn followed, its brown back speckled with white, its step more nervous and quick than its mother's.

Fiona's hand slipped down into mine, squeezing tight. I squeezed back and tried to siphon the deep longing and ache in her heart so that she wouldn't hurt.

*What happened, Fiona? Tell me first…*

A car revving in the parking lot on the other side of the inn startled the deer. Both their heads came up, ears forward. Then the doe bounded away, the fawn following, swallowed up by the forest.

"That was lovely," Fiona said, turning away, bottling the pain back up. I let it go too, pretended not to see the tear that slipped down her cheek.

Sometimes I wondered how things would've been different for us if she'd told me her dark secrets on that quiet moment on the balcony. Or if I'd asked. Or if I'd taken a chance and confessed to her what I was. If I'd made that wager instead of keeping my cards close to the vest, waiting to see how the round would play out.

But most days I didn't have to wonder at all.

Keeping silent that gray morning would forever be the greatest mistake of my life.

# Chapter 19

## Fiona

"I'm going to ask Nikolai to come with me to Costa Rica."

My heart flip-flopped to hear myself speak the words out loud, and my stomach fluttered like it did when I was a kid on my birthday, opening a present and not knowing what it would be. An infinity of possibilities…

Opal stopped walking and stared. We were strolling the boardwalk in downtown Savannah, along the waterfront early on Monday morning. Quaint shops lined one side, the Atlantic Ocean opened up on the other. The hour was early yet, and the walk was nearly empty of pedestrians. Her face broke open in a smile and actual tears shone on her eyes.

"Oh, Fiona! I…I'm so happy. And so *relieved*. God, the idea of you going down there alone…It's kept me up at night. How did this happen? When?"

"He took me to a bed and breakfast down the coast over the weekend, and it was perfect. Everything about it was so perfect, and *he* was perfect, and I knew then that…"

"That you really like him?" Opal offered.

I shook my head. "More than that. I want him in my life. I hate not waking up next to him. And when I think about him maybe saying yes…I get impossibly happy in a way I didn't think I'd ever know."

"I'm so happy for you, Fiona. Truly."

I smiled faintly. "I'm scared. What if it's too soon? Part of me feels like I'm being stupid again, jumping into deep waters with another man, not knowing if he's going to lift me up or drag me down, the way Steve did. But Nik...he's *nothing* like Steve. I know that in my heart...I just can't get my mind to let go."

Opal nodded solemnly. "That's the abuse, honey. It's not you. It's not Nik. It's *him*."

"I know. Nik is so wonderful. Being with him is so easy. And we have a connection. It started out as just a physical one, but now it's so much more. I feel like he understands *everything*, you know? I don't have to say a word and he knows exactly the right thing to say or do to make me feel so..."

"What, honey?"

"Special." I scoffed and wiped my eyes that stung with tears. "God, I feel so pathetic just saying it, but it's true. When he looks at me, it's pure. Like he doesn't need anything more than what I am."

"Next time I see him, I'm going to hug that boy until he can't breathe," Opal said. "And maybe slap his ass too, if that's okay with you."

I sniffed a laugh then sighed. "He's so good to me, Opal. But not only that. He...he makes me feel like I'm good for him."

"You are, Fi," Opal said. "I know you are."

"I hope so. After that first year with Steve, I became nothing. I cooked his meals and was there to listen to him talk endlessly about his day, his job, his friends, his 'opportunities.' But I could have been anyone. I was a body. A soul he could drain dry." I shook my head. "But Nik...He's had a rough, lonely life. He hasn't told me all of it. I know there's more to his story and his time on the road, and he's so weary of it. But with me, he can just be. It doesn't sound like much..."

"It's everything," Opal said. "Acceptance. Empathy. To live without judgment. And you, my dear, are the least judgmental person I've ever met. You let people just be and you take care of them."

I nodded, the tears flowing again.

Opal frowned. "Is it...are you scared, honey? Afraid he'll say no?"

"No," I whispered. "I think he might say yes. I think Costa Rica would be perfect for him too. He has...a hard time with large crowds. But there, he could rest and have the peace he wants."

"Then why the tears?"

"I...I haven't told him about Steve. Not in detail, but I think Nik knows or is suspicious. Things keep coming up...situations that bring back so many horrible memories and it's messing us up."

"Why? Is Nik giving you a hard time?" Opal demanded. "Because you don't have to tell anybody what you don't feel comfortable telling. Including me."

I glanced at my friend out of the corner of my eye. She wore a bright yellow shirt and her face was open and full of concern, her dark eyes full of love. *You haven't told her everything either.*

"I want to tell him. But…"

Opal frowned. "Tell him what you told me, Fi. You had an ex, he was emotionally abusive, and you're trying your best—"

"There's more to it than that," I said in a small voice.

Opal stopped walking. "More…? More than stealing your money and—?"

"He stole so much more than that," I said. "So much…"

My friend stared a moment longer, then snapped her gaze around, searching. "You want to go somewhere else?" she asked. "Somewhere private?"

I shook my head. "If we leave to go somewhere else, I'll change my mind. I need to get it out."

"Come on."

Opal led me to an antique-looking bench with smooth wood slats and ornate wrought iron. Smooth sand and the pale blue of the ocean stretched at our feet.

"Tell me, honey," she said as we sat down. "Tell me if it helps."

*Tell her. Tell her before the poison of it eats away at you even more.*

I sucked in a deep breath.

"In the last year before I left him, Steve and I hardly ever had sex. He withheld affection from me, even hugs and kisses, only doling them out just as I thought he hated me. To keep me off balance or to reel me back in when I thought he was done with me."

"Asshole," Opal muttered.

"But one night he was a little drunk and wanted me, and dammit, I was so happy," I said, shame and humiliation churning in my gut. "It was so over between us and yet I was still holding on to nothing. So I slept with him. It didn't last long and he fell asleep right after. But it was a start, I told myself. It was the beginning of a new beginning."

The boardwalk and Opal and the bench we were sitting on faded away and I was back in Duluth, in that little house at the edge of a street. Isolated. Alone. The snow fell outside the window…

"It was winter," I said. "A big snowstorm hit and we were practically snowed in. I began to have pains, deep down. It burned when I went to the bathroom. I told Steve I needed to see a doctor but he told me to drink some cranberry juice and get over it. But I got worse and worse. Like a switch flipping, Steve became so considerate and sweet; it was almost like it had been back in the beginning. But it was only because he was scared. And the pain…"

I clutched my lower stomach, hugging myself.

"It felt as if I had swallowed fire and it sunk down to the bottom of me. I got a fever that wouldn't go away no matter how much aspirin Steve gave me. On the third night, I tried to go to the bathroom and nearly fainted. I screamed and screamed, and fell on the floor. I begged him to take me to a hospital. I thought I was dying."

Opal made a sound in her throat but said nothing, let me get it out.

"Steve finally gave in and took me to the hospital. He looked like a thief walking back into a bank after robbing it. Scared. While I felt as if I'd been stabbed by shards of fiery glass. They gave me antibiotics and painkillers and ran a bunch of tests that showed I had an infection. Steve had cheated on me," I spat. "He cheated on me and gave me an infection and that became pelvic inflammatory disease."

"Oh my Christ," Opal said, in a low voice.

Tears flooded my eyes and spilled down my cheeks. "The PID almost killed me. One more day and it might have. And in those first days I almost wished that it had."

"No, why…?"

"It left scarring. A lot of scarring." I fought to hold back the sobs that were balloons in my chest, ready to burst. "And…because of that scarring, the doctor said…He said I have a ten percent chance of ever having a baby. Ten percent, Opal. Ten percent."

The memory of the doctor giving me that number replayed, slamming into my heart again and again.

"I've never had a real family," I said around sobs. "My parents died and my aunt and uncle had no children of their own. I decided a long time ago I would make my own. A big family with lots of beautiful children, sitting around a dinner table that was full of love and laughter instead of cold silence." I lifted my tear-streaked face to Opal. "I was going to be a kindergarten teacher. Did I ever tell you that? It's what I wanted for as long as I can remember. To be surrounded by sweet little faces, and sing songs with them…I wanted children. So much. But I can't and now the thought of teaching hurts too much. So I have a bird, and I take care of plants and I walk dogs and I..."

Sobs tore out of me, and I clung to Opal like a buoy tossed on a turbulent sea. She held me, stroked my hair.

I drew in a shaky breath. "I'll never feel my own baby grow inside me. He took that from me. He stole it..."

Opal held me, rocked me. "I'm so sorry, honey. So very sorry."

I cried out a few more tears from what felt like a never-ending well, and then I sat up. I sucked in a breath and exhaled, feeling clearer. Cleaner. I still hadn't told Opal everything about my escape from Steve, but that was for her safety. And mine.

"I feel better," I said. "But you can see why I can't tell Nik? Asking him to come to Costa Rica is hard enough. Maybe too much. To then add all this talk about having babies or not... He'll think I'm crazy."

"Stage-Five Clinger," Opal said with a small smile.

I snorted a laugh.

"I'm teasing you, honey," Opal said. "You're being honest. And if he agrees to move out of the country for you, he'll want to know the whole story. He deserves the whole story. And you deserve his."

*The whole story...Including that I was married? That technically I'm still married?*

I brushed that aside. Fiona Starling had never been married.

"He'll appreciate the honesty," Opal continued. "It's better that he know now than move with you and find out later, when he's deeply entrenched." She shifted on the bench to look at me. "Do you think he might want kids some day?"

"I don't know. He was so good with Hailey last week. It came so naturally to him and he didn't even realize it. I saw them together...and it just hurt so bad. He should have that someday, if he wants it. But he can't...he can't have it with me."

The tears came again. My face ached trying to hold them back.

"He might," Opal said. "And you never know what might happen. The doctor said you have a ten percent chance of having a family. I know that's not much but it's more than zero."

I shook my head. "The doctor said it would be 'medically significant' if I were to become pregnant and a miracle if I kept it. A miracle, Opal." I wiped my nose. "There are so many children in the world who need families. I can adopt. I will. But I wanted so badly to be pregnant. I wanted to feel the baby growing and kicking…I even wanted the pain of giving birth because I feel like it's an experience I was meant to have."

The boardwalk was starting to thicken with summer tourists. Opal put her arms around me. "Come on. Let's get you home."

She drove me to Garden City and walked me into my apartment. I lay down on the bed, wrung out. Opal sat with me, grazing her fingers through my hair.

"When are you going to ask him?" she said gently.

"I don't know," I closed my eyes. "I'm scared to do it, and scared I'll get hysterical telling him about my ten percent. You're the only person I've told this to, and now I'm exhausted. But the pain is still there. I have so many tears left to cry."

"Have you ever thought of sitting down with your ex and having it out with him? Get some closure? In a court of law, preferably?"

Blood drained from my face and my body went rigid, curling tighter into a ball. "*No,*" I said, like a door slamming shut. "I never want to see him again. Ever. I don't want to tell Nik about him either. As little as possible."

"Why?"

"It's humiliating," I said, opening my eyes to look up at her. "I'm still haunted by that asshole's voice. How do I explain to the new man that the old one still has a hold on me without sounding obsessed with my ex, or just plain pathetic?"

"You just explain it. You tell it like it is. He'll understand. If Nik's everything you say he is, he'll understand."

*He will. If anyone can, it's him.* My eyes fell shut again. "I'm so tired."

"I'll bet." I heard the smile in her voice. "Being in love is exhausting."

A jolt shot through me, but a warm one, like a hot drink on a cold day. "Oh hush. I'm not…I mean…I can't even right now."

"I know it." Opal laughed and I felt the bed dip as she stood up. "Talk soon, honey."

"Talk soon," I said, already drifting…

Distantly, I heard the door open and shut, and then I was alone. I slept and when I woke, twilight had fallen, golden and warm, through the window.

I climbed out of bed, my body aching and tired, as if I'd run a marathon. My phone lay on the bedside table, a text from Nik waiting.

**Want to see you.**

"A man of few words," I said. My smile slipped when I saw another notification on my phone of an email from Claudia, my contact at the Embassy in Costa Rica.

I grabbed my laptop and opened the email.

**From:** Claudia Araya  caraya@migracion.gov.cr
**To:** Fiona Starling  FionaStar357@gmail.com
**Sent:** Friday, June 21 9:19 AM
**Subject:** Pack your bags!

*Dear Fiona,*

*Good news times two! Your visa has been approved! A friend of a friend bumped you through processing as a favor to me, and the realty company accepted your application. If you want, you're able to move in the first of July!*

*I know you probably have much to arrange on your end so if this is too soon, I can have them hold the property. Let me know your plans and in the meanwhile, look for the paperwork in your mail next week.*

*Muy atentamente,*
*Claudia*

I shut the laptop with a shaking hand. Freedom. I was so close. And instead of dread or nerves, I had hope. Hope that Nik would say yes, and we'd begin a new life in that paradise. Together.

"Love and hope," I murmured to the quiet apartment. "Love and hope."

# Chapter 20

## Nikolai

It had been four days since we'd been back from the bed-and-breakfast. Fiona and I spent as much time together as possible, mostly in bed, stripping ourselves naked and raw, giving everything we had with our bodies instead of confessing our secrets. It was as if we had an unspoken agreement that the time was coming soon but we didn't know when or where. We dawdled over those four days and then the night of Nate and Griffin's housewarming party arrived.

I bought dress pants, a shirt, and tie for Fiona's sake, but when I put the entire outfit on that night I felt like a fraud.

*You can be civilized for one night,* I thought staring around my empty apartment. Beyond one chair in the living room and a couple of cheap stools at the kitchen counter, I'd bought nothing. Fiona noticed. Of course she did, but instead of concern or even curiosity, I felt from her a growing excitement that I wasn't putting down roots here.

*She's going to ask me to go to Costa Rica with her.*

The happiness of it stole my goddamn breath. A future unlike anything I had ever hoped for myself stretched out before me. Before us. I just had one obstacle to climb over—telling her what I was—and I prayed to God she'd still want me when it was done.

I rode to Fiona's place under a golden twilight, and she answered the door looking fucking stunning in a deep blue dress that highlighted the pink in her hair and the hibiscus tattoo on her right shoulder. The dress was silky and low-cut, and my first inclination was to tear it off of her and forget the party.

"You're dangerously handsome," she said, breathing heavily after we broke our kiss at her door. "I like this. A lot." She smoothed my tie.

"No human man should have to wear a tie in a Georgia summer," I said.

"But you make it look so good," Fiona said. "My God, Nikolai…Give a girl a heart attack, why don't you?"

"If you're not feeling well," I told her, my hands sliding up and down the silky skin of her back, "maybe you should lie down."

She laughed against my mouth. "Nate and Griffin will kill us if we're late. Or actually, Griff will understand. Nate will kill us."

I captured her lower lip in my teeth. "Worth it."

She sighed and parted her lips to take my kiss deeper, and then we were in danger of losing the night. But she pushed back, breathless, with her blue eyes backlit with thoughts and possibilities. And hope. Tonight was the night we'd reveal everything. We both felt it. After the party, after we celebrated her friends' first step towards a better future, we would take ours.

"Let's take your motorcycle," Fiona said.

I glanced down at the strappy black shoes she wore and the way her dress threatened to slide up her thighs at the slightest gust of wind. Then I imagined rolling into the party in downtown Savannah with her on the back of the Bonneville.

"Done." I slipped out of my black leather jacket and put it over her shoulders. "You don't mind the helmet messing your hair or something?"

"I don't care about stuff like that," she said.

"I know you don't," I said and kissed her again. I wanted to keep kissing her, having her keep smiling at me in case this was the last night.

*It can't be the last night. If anyone can accept me, it's Fiona. She's the only one.*

We rode fifteen minutes into downtown Savannah, to the address Nate had given her. A three-story Victorian, pale blue with white trim and ornate detailing. Lights glowed in the windows, and laughter and music seeped out as we approached the front door.

Fiona knocked and before anyone could answer, I gently pulled her to me and slipped one hand around to cup her cheek.

"What are you doing?" she asked.

"Looking at you," I said. "Just looking."

She melted into my hand. "I love how you look at me. And I don't want you to stop." She swallowed hard. "Nikolai..."

The door opened on a cloud of sound and noise and people. It washed over me like a tide. I staggered back a step and then Fiona's hand slipped into mine, bringing me back.

"You're here," Nate crowed and kissed Fiona on the cheek. "You look stunning as always." He turned to me, his eyes widening as he took in my suit and the tattoos that peaked over the collar of my dress shirt. "Mr. Young, looking dashing and dangerous as always. Most of the guests are fuddy-duddies from Griff's law firm, but you..." He shook his head and pretended to confide in Fiona. "Prepare yourself: every straight woman here is going to hate your guts. Come, come. Entrez-vous."

Fiona held me back, her hand squeezing mine. "Are you okay? Is it too much?"

"I'll be okay," I said.

The house was exactly as Nate had promised; completely empty. The hardwood floors were brightly polished and the smell of fresh paint and plaster lingered in the air to mix with the scents of grease and bread from the mini chicken and waffles circulating around the room on caterers' trays. Little white lights hung in garlands around the windows, and the only pieces of furniture were small, rented tables and folding chairs, draped with tablecloths. Candles flickered in pale blue glass cups on each. Fifty or more guests talked and laughed over the swing music a DJ played from one end of what would be the living room.

All the men were wearing suits, and the women were in cocktail dresses, none as beautiful as Fiona. They had fancy jewelry, perfect make-up, salon hair. Fiona was a wildflower amidst a garden of perfectly pruned roses, her pink hair flowing in soft waves down her back, and her only jewelry was the woven bracelets that adorned her arms.

"I'm so glad you could make it," Griffin said, snatching two flutes of champagne from a passing waiter and handing them to us. "Please come in and make yourselves at home." A smile broke over his face. "I said that, didn't I? Home. Our home."

"Oh jeez, here come the waterworks," Nate said, linking his arm in Griff's. *"Again."*

"It's beautiful," Fiona said. "I'm so happy for the both of you. I know you're going to have so many wonderful memories here."

Nate beamed, then saw some friends he needed to greet. Fiona's friend Opal, and a tall man with pale skin and a receding hairline, took his place.

"Here you are," Opal said, with a half-hug for Fiona. "So nice to see you again, Nik. This is my husband, Jeff."

"Good to meet you," I said, and braced myself for Jeff's handshake. But my other hand was clasped tight in Fiona's, making the brief jolt of Jeff's nervousness easier to take.

"Glad you made it, Jeff," Griff said warmly. "I know this isn't really your thing."

"No, sir." Jeff chuckled and tugged at his collar. "Give me a boat, fishing pole, and a beer, and I'm a happy man."

Opal rolled her eyes. "Or a bingo game."

Jeff squinted. "Huh?"

"Nothing. We're going to mingle," Opal said, giving Griff a pat on the cheek. "I have exactly one hour before this one starts complaining."

Jeff grinned. "You need more than an hour to have the same conversation with half a dozen people about the weather?"

"The weather has been unseasonably hot, now that you mention it," Fiona said.

"That's one," Jeff said.

Opal sniffed. "Don't encourage him."

Jeff laughed as his wife dragged him away. "Good to meet you, Nik."

I nodded faintly and tugged at my collar. I wouldn't have minded a boat on a cool lake with a breeze either; the damn tie felt like it was trapping heat in my shirt. Fiona mistook my discomfort and tightened her grip on mine.

"How are you doing?" she asked me in a low voice. She glanced at the front door where Nate loudly greeted two more couples as they came in. "It's getting crowded in here."

Griffin, with his customary good grace and tact swooped between us before I could answer. "I haven't given you the grand tour. Just the two of you. No one else allowed."

"Oh? What makes us special?" Fiona asked.

"I want to show you your room for when you come and visit." He waggled his eyebrows at both of us. "*Your* room."

"Someone's been celebrating early," Fiona said out of the side of her mouth as we followed Griff out of the front room and up a winding staircase to the second floor.

"Honey, I've been tipsy since noon," Griff said over his shoulder. "I still can't believe this is ours. Somebody pinch me, I'm dreaming."

Fiona reached out and pinched his ass. Griff laughed and swatted at her hand. "Nik, you flirt, I'm happily married."

Griff led us down a short hallway, over more hardwood, to a small bedroom that overlooked the street. It had a rounded window with a seating area and nothing else. The sounds of the party reverberated from below.

"Any time you want to visit, this is yours," Griff said, his eyes soft as he looked at Fiona. "I know it can't compete with wild jungles and mountains, but I hope it's enough to tempt you back. Frequently."

Fiona's eyes glistened. "Of course," she said and hugged her friend. "Thank you."

Griff held her tight, then broke away, blinking hard. "I'd better get downstairs before Nathaniel starts screeching." He gave me a knowing grin. "Take a minute, but behave you two."

Fiona gave her friend a playful shove. "No promises."

Griffin retreated, leaving us alone in the small room.

"It's a beautiful view," Fiona said, moving to the window. "Come sit with me."

I joined her and we sat on the wooden bench, built into the window nook, and watched the night fall over Savannah. Fiona slipped her hand in mine.

"This night is so perfect. It's like a kind of magic, isn't it? To think this house is the start of a new chapter in life, not knowing where it will lead but feeling so…happy and hopeful?"

"Yeah, it is," I said.

"Nikolai…"

*Here it comes…*

"I feel so close to you. And I think about you all the time. Every minute, actually, and what we have…it feels real. For the first time since I decided to go to Costa Rica, I know what I want, and that's a kind of magic too." She took my face in her hands, tears in her eyes. "I want you to come with me. Will you?"

"I want to, Fiona," I said, my voice thick. "So fucking badly, you have no idea."

She was radiant. So fucking beautiful in her happiness I could hardly look at her. I couldn't stop.

"You do?" she breathed, not daring to hope.

"Yeah, baby. I do." I held her hands in mine, brought them down from my face. "But I have to tell you something..."

"I know," she said, her radiance dimming slightly. "I do too. And it's going to feel like way too soon—what I have to tell you—but you deserve to know the whole story."

"So do you," I said and a weight wrapped itself around my heart at the impossibility of it. How outlandish and fucking *insane* it would sound. The only way I had a chance was to do it calmly. Quietly.

"Not here," I said. "I should tell you at your place. Alone."

I felt Fiona's sweet care and consideration waft over me, like spun sugar. "Oh. Is it serious?"

"Yeah, baby. It is, but..."

"What is it?" she asked slowly. "You can tell me, Nik. You can tell me anything."

God, I hoped that was true.

"Fiona..." I swallowed, the words sticking in my mouth.

I felt her pull away from me before she leaned back against the sill, her concern withering to wariness.

"Tell me now," she said. "Please. I can't go downstairs and smile and make small talk and pretend to celebrate my friends' happiness with this feeling in my stomach. So please, Nik. Just tell me."

I raised my eyes to her, imploring. "I'm afraid you'll hate me for it."

"Why...?" She swallowed and tried again. "Why would I hate you? What could you possibly say...?"

I shook my head and stood up to pace the empty room.

"I've never talked about this so I don't know how. The right order of words. And maybe I shouldn't. Maybe this will be a huge fucking mistake. But I can't go with you to Costa Rica until I tell you."

"Okay," she said slowly. "I'm listening."

A silence fell between us but the beat of the music, the trumpets and piano, and the half hundred voices rising and falling in laughter and conversation rose up beneath the wooden floor.

*I can do this*, I thought. *I can make her understand.*

"Do you hear that? Can you feel it?" I asked her. "The party below us? How it sounds and feels...that's my life. A stream of noise and color, everywhere I go, constantly."

Fiona frowned warily. "What do you mean?"

I ran my hands through my hair and then gestured to the window. "Out there, it's loud and bright, not to my ears or eyes but to something inside me. Some…intuition or empathy. I call it *ken* for lack of something better. The ability to feel what every person around me is feeling."

"You feel…?" Fiona's words trailed. She tried again. "You feel what other people are feeling?"

"Yeah, I do," I said. "I feel or see them in colors, and sounds; sometimes a taste in my mouth or echoes of words I can hear as if the person had spoken. I can *perceive* everything, all the time. And it's loud. It's so goddamn loud. And bright. Too many words and colors; other peoples' emotions—their lives cracked open to me like an egg, spilling out in front of me. I don't stay in any one place because I know too much. The longer I'm around someone, the more is exposed to me. And they never know. They have no fucking clue I'm sitting beside them at the poker table or in the next motel room over, stealing their most private emotions right out of their goddamn heads."

Fiona stared, but now that I'd begun, the words poured out.

"So I keep moving. I play poker because I can read people; their cards may as well be laid out on the table for me to see. I can feel a bluff or hear an excited pulse over a good hand; feel the itchy nerves of some poor, desperate guy who just went all-in with the rent check. I hang out at clubs where the music is so loud; the energy of everyone around me is a muted, low pulse in comparison. I get tattoos…I get so many fucking tattoos—any tattoo—because it doesn't fucking matter what I get. The only thing I want is the pain. I want the bite of the needle in my skin because only then do I know it's mine. *My* pain. The buzz of the needle and the sting drown out the rest of the world—even the tattoo artist—and for a few minutes, I belong to myself. No one else. And these tattoos…"

I held up my hands, with the lettering on my fingers.

"These matter. Because what am I, if not a hoax or a pawn? I'm the butt of some fucking cosmic joke. A hoax perpetrated by some sick bastard who gave me the ability to feel everyone but never told me why, or how to stop it, or what to do with it. Or I'm a pawn in someone's game. As if I have a destiny that this *ken* is a part of, but I can't see the other players or even the board I'm standing on. I'm just…lost."

I gritted my teeth against Fiona's doubt and fear.

"Sometimes, in the hospital, I'd hope that I was crazy, and that this fucked-up ability was just the byproduct of synapses in my brain going haywire like they said. But they tried to drug and shock it out of me and it didn't work. Because it's real. I fucking hate it, Fiona, but it's real."

I turned then, slowly, raising my eyes from the floor to meet Fiona's. Her brilliant blue eyes caught and held mine, searching for some clue that I was bullshitting her, or worse—that I believed the crazy words I was saying and that she was in the presence of a madman.

"The world out there is full of pain and misery and I have to take it, every single day. Choke it down," I told her. "Until I met you, Fiona. I don't know why, but you're the only person who can silence the noise. And in you, the *ken* is beautiful. *You're* beautiful…"

I fell silent under the onslaught of her doubt and mistrust. And fear. She was afraid.

"You're telling me," she said flatly, "that you can…*feel* other people's lives? Their thoughts and feelings?"

The yearning in her drifted across the room, but it wasn't to believe me. It was the desire that I would say something else that she could actually accept and not feel so helpless or stupid. So that she wouldn't feel like she'd been duped by some psycho who thought she'd be gullible enough to believe him.

The dark shadow of *him* gathered around her.

"It's true, Fiona, I swear it," I said, knowing that argument wasn't enough but I didn't have the right words…*any* words that could make her believe the impossible. "I've had it since I can remember. I thought everyone had it. But they don't. It's just me and it's ruined my fucking life. Until you. You are the only peace I've ever known."

She frowned, clutched herself tighter. "I'm…peace?"

I nodded, my hope scrabbling to hold on. "Yeah, Fiona. It's loud out there, like I said. In here? With you?" I covered my heart with my hand. "In here, it's quiet."

"You mean… you can't read me or *perceive* from me like you can anyone else?"

"No. The *ken* sees you too. But it's okay. For some reason, with you…it's okay. And everyone else seems so fucking far away."

"Why?" she demanded. "Why can you do this? How?"

"I've been asking that question my entire life."

Fiona swallowed hard, clutched her arms tighter. The shadow

around her thickened deeper and hovered over her...

"I'm trying....*so hard*...not to be gullible anymore, Nik." she said, her voice wavering. "I want to believe you but... You're telling me you have an ability to...to read minds?"

"I can't read your mind," I said. "I get impressions of thoughts. Feelings. Intuitions...I can see and taste and smell them all."

"You can...*taste* them?" she asked, and shook her head. "God, Nik...I don't know what to think. Or *how*—"

*Stupid little airhead.*

The words came, like a whisper, between us.

"Who said that?" I asked.

"What?" Fiona stared. "Who said...?"

*Only you would be dumb enough to believe a story like that...*

*Him. He* was right here, in the room...

I gritted my teeth "Who is that?" I demanded. "Who...? Who calls you stupid?"

"What did you say?" Fiona's eyes widened and she stared, the color draining from her face. Then she shook her head, and rose on shaking legs to walk past me. The cloud was thick over her and smelled of blackened rot. "No. I'm not...I'm not stupid. I don't know what's happening, but I can't—"

I snaked my hand out and caught her wrist, to keep her safe, to keep her from walking deeper into that blackness...

The empty room dissolved and I was in a bathroom—white with wildflowers on the shower curtain and blue tile. Men's razors shared space with women's face cream. A pink rug on the floor...

A scream ripped through the small space.

I staggered back against the wall between the toilet and the vanity, staring. Fiona lay curled on the rug, holding her stomach, writhing. Her pale blond hair stuck to her cheeks in sticky threads. Sweat drenched her face that was contorted in agony.

She screamed again, the sound reverberating in the small room, cutting my eardrums, tearing through my heart.

"Fiona..." I reached out a hand.

"Steve!" she cried, reaching for the door. "Help me...Please..."

So much pain. Goddamn, it radiated off of her in waves, hot and yellow, stinking of pus and bile.

The door opened and *he* was there. Tall. Pale. Red hair. Dead blue eyes.

"Dammit, Tess, really?"

*Tess? Her name is Fiona...*

"Steve..." She lifted her tear and sweat-streaked face to his. "I'm sick. I'm so sick. I'm scared. Help me."

I pushed off the wall, to drop to my knees beside her; to lift her and carry her...

I couldn't move. I tried again. Stuck. Helpless.

"Help me," Fiona whimpered.

"*Help her!*" I screamed.

Steve rubbed his chin. "All right, Tess. Jesus, let's go. Come on."

He bent to help Fiona to her feet. Another scream tore out of her when her legs straightened, and she collapsed back down into a tight curl.

I raced to her side, to hold her in my arms...

I didn't move.

"Fucking bastard, do something!" I raged.

Steve sighed, unhurried, and bent to pick Fiona up. She clung to his neck, sobbing hard, her breath coming in deep gasps, as if she were drowning.

She *was* drowning. In pain and fever and fear.

Steve carried her out of the bathroom and I followed...

A car. Backseat. He bundled her in the front and took the wheel. The night was black, headlights lit up banks of white snow, and flurries danced across the windshield.

Fiona shivered and whimpered inside her blanket.

I reached my hand over the seat to touch her. "I'm here, baby."

My hand moved and stayed where it was. My words came back to me, like a playback on an audio recording.

"It's not a big deal, okay?" Steve was saying. "When we get there, don't make a scene. It's a private matter between us, right? No one needs to know our personal business, Tess."

*Tess. Why is he calling her Tess?*

Fiona said nothing, only cried softly and cried out now and then when the car lurched.

The hospital. Steve got out at the emergency room drive, leaving her alone in the car. With me.

"Fiona. Fiona, can you hear me? I'm right here..." I reached my hand to her and nothing happened. "God, baby, I'm so sorry this is happening to you..."

The door opened, and hands reached for her, pulling her out...

A hospital room. Fiona on the bed, her blond hair pale and brittle, hanging lifelessly around her shoulders. Tubes in her arms, a machine beeping her pulse, IV bags suspended over her. Her sunken eyes followed the doctor as he took the chair beside the bed.

"The ultrasound wasn't very encouraging," he said gently. "The infection moved swiftly and did quite a lot of damage."

"What kind of damage?" Fiona asked, her voice hardly more than a whisper.

I hurried to be by her side.

I was stuck in the corner of the room.

The doctor took off his glasses. His hands folded in his lap, as if to show they'd done all they could and were done now.

"Scarring," he said. "The infection scarred your fallopian tubes and a good portion of the upper quadrant of your uterus."

Fiona's body, limp from pain and exhaustion, went rigid. "What does that mean?"

"It means that the chances of your becoming pregnant and carrying a child to term are very low. I would say in the realm of ten percent, if I were being optimistic."

"Ten percent," Fiona said, staring. "Ten..."

"I'm very sorry. I wish I had better news. I've already informed your husband..."

*Her husband. That fucker's her husband?*

He said a few more words, answered a few more whispered questions, and then disappeared. Fiona and I were alone.

I watched in horror as the gulf of the pain in her widened and deepened, and the *ken* mercilessly revealed to me her deepest wishes and dreams curl up like burnt paper and blow away...

Fiona, her belly swollen with life and kicking inside her, more radiant than the sun. Fiona gritting her teeth against pain that would be forgotten the instant the baby was put to her breast. Breakfast table chaos as children hurried to get ready for school. Dinner tables full of laughter or bickering, skinned knees and bedtime stories, and piles of laundry...A home that resounded with running footsteps and cartoons and a baby's hungry cry...

Gone.

It hollowed her out. A gaping wound. A blackness.

Fiona's beautiful face crumpled and broke. Her mouth opened in a silent cry, and then silent sobs tore through her painfully, bending her in two. And still no sound. Only agony and tears and her lying small and alone on the bed...

*Nikolai...*

She was calling for me. I tore my stricken gaze from the figure on the bed...

"Nikolai..."

I blinked. Nate and Griff's house. The empty room. Fiona stared at me, her skin radiant with health, her hair pink and long...but now fear hung over her like a pall. Fear I had put there.

She struggled in my grip. "You're hurting me..."

I glanced down to where I held her wrist so tightly, my fingers were white. I let go at once, and she snatched her hand back but not before I could see the marks I'd left.

"I'm sorry," I said. "I'm so sorry for what that fucker did to you..."

Rage at Steve for all that he'd taken from Fiona clouded my vision red, muting the stark fear and shame that wrapped around her.

"What is happening?" she asked tearfully, backing away, her fear growing more potent with every passing second. "How did you...those things you said. How did you know...?"

"The things I said..." I stared at her. A sinking feeling hit me. I must've spoken during the vision. I must've looked—and sounded—like a goddamn lunatic. "Wait, Fiona...Wait..."

But I had no words. I'd never been thrust into someone's memories like that. Ever.

Fiona's eyes darted around the empty room, filling with tears. Her voice cracked under the weight of her heartbreak. The betrayal. "Is he here? Does he know where I am?"

A cold knife of dread slid into my heart. "What? No..."

"He's coming then, isn't he? You know him. How else...? How else can you know that? My name... That I was married..."

*Jesus, what had I said?*

"No, Fiona...I swear. It's not like that. I have an ability—"

"An *ability*," she scoffed, tears streaming down her cheeks. "And I'm supposed to choose? You either have this *ability* to read people, or you're lying to me." She shook her head miserably. "God, you know him...all this time..."

I reeled at the fear and betrayal and pain that radiated off of her, put there by me. "I don't know him, I swear to you, Fiona."

"Opal wouldn't have told you about the ten percent," she said, her face so pale. "She wouldn't. And Tess... You said that name. I never even told Opal that name. Never spoke it out loud in two years..." Her blue eyes bored into mine and through them I saw her heart break. "I trusted you."

"I would never lie to you, Fiona." I shook my head. "The *ken*, it's real. It's fucking real and I hate it. I hate that I stole this from you...I swear—"

"Shut up!" she screamed. "You *did* lie to me. About your job. And now you're telling me that you know about my past because you can read minds? You're *psychic*? And you expect me to believe that? I'm not *stupid*," she cried, the word laden with years of pain and shame. "I'm not fucking stupid! I'm not. Not anymore..."

I took a halting step forward.

"Please," I said, hauntingly aware that our time was slipping away and our future in Costa Rica was burning up. "I don't know what to say to make you believe me. I see things because of the *ken*. I saw things about you that no one knows—"

"*Except Steve*," she screamed. "Did he send you here, to what? To fuck with me? Is that his revenge?"

I dragged my hands through my hair. "No, Fiona... listen..."

"No, it's impossible—"

"It's not impossible, it's my life!" I shouted back.

Fiona recoiled. "It's *impossible*," she said, her voice low and trembling. "I never told anyone my name. No one." Her voice rose again on a current of hysteria. "Why? Why are you doing this to me?"

I staggered back, my hands up. Her pain and fear and shame were too much. It was no longer important that she believe me, only that she didn't feel like this anymore. She was so fucking scared...

"I promise you, Fiona," I said, my throat thick with tears. "I swear on my life he doesn't know where you are. I haven't told him anything. I don't know him—"

"Get out," she whispered, her back against the far wall and then screamed. "*Get out!*" A sob tore out of her after and she hugged herself. "Leave me alone. Leave me..."

I staggered back, as if the floor were tilting under me.

I heard footsteps on the stairs, voices, and then Opal was there, and Griffin. Fiona slid to the floor, sobbing. Opal knelt beside her, whispering soothingly to her, glaring daggers at me.

Griffin was in my face, shouting. Demanding. He shoved me toward the door. I didn't shove back.

"Fiona..."

"No magic," Fiona was saying, crying softly in Opal's protective embrace. "There's no magic anywhere..."

# Chapter 21

## Nikolai

I stumbled out of the house through the crowd of people whispering and watching me, their emotions battering me with curiosity and suspicion. I staggered out into the street, chased by Griffin and his anger and Fiona's pain. God, Fiona...I'd touched her wrist and the conduit opened up like nothing I'd ever experienced before. And it fucked everything up.

Everything.

Griffin stood at the front door of his house, his arms crossed, not satisfied until I was out of his sight. My soul cried out for Fiona, burning to make things right; to tell her how sorry I was for making it impossible to believe me.

With shaking hands, I climbed on my motorcycle. Her helmet was still attached to the side bag and the pain smashed me in the heart all over again.

I fucked it all up. The goddamn *ken* fucked it all up.

*No, I have to try again.*

I wanted to go to her place but that would've been another mistake, to hover outside like a damn stalker. I fucking hated to do it, but I went back to my shitty, empty apartment and paced in front of the portrait I'd painted of her. The vibrant colors were now slaps to my face. Her smiling, beautiful face already a memory...

*No! I'll fix this.*

The hours crawled until enough had passed that I felt it was okay to send her a text. Just a text.

**I'm so sorry. Please talk to me. I can explain everything.**

I hit send and waited. No answer. Another hour oozed by.

**Please talk to me, Fiona. Please send me one word that says we can talk later. When you're ready. Please.**

It was rambling and pathetic but I sent it anyway, desperate for her to answer. Silence.

I lay on the bed but sleep wasn't coming. Not for hours. I tossed and turned, and when the yellow light of dawn slunk across my bed, I grabbed my phone. Nothing.

**Fiona, please. I have to see you. I have to try to make this right.**

No answer. The morning crawled. I thought about going to Fiona's place in the light of day but was too afraid of scaring her. Of all that swirling emotion I'd felt from her, her fear broke my heart.

I needed one word from her; one text, one phone call. Just to hear her voice, even if it was to tell me she wasn't ready to talk yet.

Yet.

I couldn't let myself believe she would never speak to me again.

Just before noon my phone rang. My heart leapt out of my chest and my stomach dropped to my knees. I scrambled and grabbed it, catching a number that was vaguely familiar as I hit answer and put it to my ear.

"Fiona?"

"No, sir. Is this Nikolai Young?"

I slumped onto the bed. "Yeah. This is Nik."

"Mr. Young, I'm Mike Gasparo, manager of the Forever Sunrise Assisted Living Facility. I regret to inform you that your mother is in a bit of a decline. We felt it would be prudent to alert you to her situation immediately."

"She's…dying?"

Gasparo cleared his throat. "The doctors have evaluated her, and we believe she is coming to the end of her journey, yes."

"My mother is dying."

The words sunk in, one at a time, like knives. She was old; she'd been sick for a long time, and she could hardly stand to look at me. I'd told myself all those things a hundred times to keep the pain of her rejection from digging too deep. But in that instant, none of it mattered. She was my mother.

"I'm very sorry, Mr. Young. Are you able to visit her and…make some arrangements?"

I slumped over my knees, silently holding the phone to my ear. I raked my other hand through my hair.

"Yeah," I said. "I'll be there."

"Very good. I'll let the staff know—"

I hung up and then both hands gripped my hair.

My mother was dying. And Fiona…

I sucked in air so sticky and hot it stuck in my throat. I felt like I was drowning. I grabbed my phone to book a flight for St. Louis and remembered I couldn't handle airplanes. They made me feel like I had a plastic bag over my head and the oxygen was leaking out.

"Fuck," I ground out through clenched teeth.

I mapped out the drive time to St. Louis. Almost twelve hours.

"Fuck everything."

I packed a few things in a small bag, the futility of it all dragging my every move. If I drove straight through, I'd make it by night but I'd have no fucking sleep. If I slept first, my mother might not hold on. And then Fiona. How could I leave her now?

I finished packing and called Fiona. I listened to it ring, praying she would answer.

Voicemail. Goddamn, her voice sounded so bright and cheerful.

*"Hi, you've reached Fiona. I'm not able to take your call right now but leave me a message and I'll get right back to you, I promise. Thanks!"*

The beep came and I swallowed hard.

"Fiona, it's Nik. I'm sorry. I fucked everything up. I told you in the worst possible way. I wish you could believe me, so much. More than that, I need you to know I would never try to hurt you. I'm so fucking sorry if I did."

I drew in a shaky breath.

"My mother is sick. I have to go to St. Louis. Please wait for me. Please talk to me when I get back. Please—"

The *beep* cut me off.

I sat for a long moment holding my phone in my hand, willing for it to ring again this time with Fiona's number and her voice on the other end, telling me she'd wait.

It never did.

# Chapter 22

*Fiona*

*"Please wait for me. Please talk to me when I get back. Please—"*

The *beep* cut him off. I hung up, played the message again. And again.

And again.

I lay in bed, sweaty and sticky with the blankets bundled around me. I was cocooned with the phone in my ear and tears streaming down my face, and Nik—his voice was so heavy with pain…

My heart was torn in half. Part of me wanted to believe him and to believe that everything we had shared was real. The other half told me I'd been made a fool of all over again. That every emotion I'd had over the last weeks had been the product of someone else's manipulation.

The things Nik knew were impossible for him to know unless he'd spoken with Steve. Were they friends? Steve had always told me if I left him he would find me. He would hunt me down, *for my own good;* to keep me safe because I couldn't survive on my own.

Or had Nik been telling the truth…? What about all the other things he seemed to know about, like the man at the fair?

I hunched deeper in my stifling blankets, recalling how good Nik was to me, how considerate; how he made me feel beautiful with every touch, and important to him with every word. I couldn't imagine it had all been an act.

"It felt so real…" I whispered.

*So had all the sweet promises Steve made…*

"No." I threw off the covers and lay flat on my back. Nik was nothing like Steve.

*Then how did he know?*

After Griff had forced Nik out of the party, I hysterically demanded that Opal tell me if she had told Nik about my hospital diagnosis. She'd sworn up-and-down she'd told him nothing, that she would never betray me.

But Nik knew my name. That I'd been married. Because he was psychic? That's what he was asking me to believe?

*Stupid, silly girl. You* want *to believe him, don't you?*

Steve. Panic rocketed through me. God, he could be on his way right now. He might already be in Garden City…

A knock came at the door, and the phone jumped out of my hand.

"Fiona?" Griff called. "It's us, checking in."

"I'm okay," I said, cringing as my voice came out sounding like a croak.

"Talk to us, honey," Nate said. "Please."

"I need a shower," I called. "Badly. Then I can talk. I'll come over when I'm done."

"Promise?" Griff said dubiously.

"I promise," I lied.

"We're going to be back in twenty minutes," Nate said. "Twenty."

"Thank you, Nate." Tears filled my eyes. "I'll see you soon."

I picked up my phone and listened to Nik's message again. How could I believe him? How could I believe anything?

*The beach. Go to the beach.*

I couldn't think. Not here. I needed the beach where Nik had taken me when he came back to Savannah. I needed the wide ocean and the wind. I needed to bury my feet in the warm sand and close my eyes and think. Find the sunshine. Just be.

I grabbed my bag and slung it over my shoulder. I yanked my tangled hair from under the strap and then froze as I caught a glimpse of my reflection in the long mirror by the closet. My eyes were swollen and red from crying, and shadowed from lack of sleep; my dress was wrinkled and sweat-stained.

"Oh God…"

I grabbed my keys, blew Lemony a kiss, and slipped out of my apartment, shutting the door quietly. I climbed in my car and started it up, scared that Griff and Nate would catch me. But the Prius was a quiet car and I carefully made my way out of the complex unnoticed.

At the stop sign just outside Garden City, I turned on the radio and Fiona Apple's "Criminal" was playing. That had to be a sign. I felt better. A little more like myself. A sigh eased out of me. I followed the route through Savannah that still hadn't woken up this early on a Sunday morning, driving along the tree-lined boulevard that would take me to the coastal highway.

At a red light, I noticed a tall, red-haired man was crossing the street a block ahead and my heart jumped into my throat. He turned in my direction and I swallowed a hard. It wasn't Steve.

*But I'm coming for you...*

The light changed, I crossed the intersection and reached to turn up the music with a shaking hand, to drown out his incessant, insidious commentary. I glanced at the knob for a second to crank up the sound and then it happened.

Brown hair, a blue blouse, tan skirt flashed in the windshield, followed instantly by a hideous, sickening *thump* and the crumpling of my hood. I hit the brakes with both feet. The car screeched to a halt, throwing me forward and then back against the headrest.

*Oh my God...I hit someone.*

I hit a woman and now she was lying in the street ten feet in front of my car, her lap on backwards, her legs splayed, one bent the wrong way, as if she had three knees.

The blood evaporated out of my body, cold fingers crawled over every inch of my skin, leaving a tingling, numb sensation behind. A heavy pall of dread fell into my gut and my heart beat lurched sluggishly against my chest.

My hands shook so badly I could hardly put the car in park. I managed to get the door open and stumbled out of the car, toward the woman.

*Oh my God. Oh my God. Oh my God.*

My eyes searched her for signs of life, feeling as if I were out of my body, because something this horrible couldn't have just happened. The woman was young, younger than me, maybe, and her eyes were open, fluttering. Her chest rose and fell, and small groans were issuing from her throat.

A man sprinted over from seemingly nowhere, dressed all in black—black polo shirt, black pants, black boots. He looked between the woman and me, and then knelt beside her.

"I'm sorry," I whispered. "I just looked down for a second. I'm so sorry…"

Shame and guilt and fear congealed in my stomach. The woman's hips were twisted, and a bone protruded from the sickeningly broken leg.

*I did this. I did this to her…*

"I'm sorry," I said again, jaw trembling. "I'm so sorry…"

The man glanced up at me and gave me a pitying look before his features hardened again. He grabbed his phone and spoke into it. The words made no sense. A rushing sound in my ears deafened me.

Cars had stopped; people were getting out. As if from a great distance, I heard someone say they called 911. I fell to my knees beside the woman, the asphalt scraping them raw though I hardly felt it. She was still breathing. Her eyes were glazed and looked somewhere beyond here, somewhere beyond pain, I hoped.

"I'm so sorry," I told her. "I just looked down for a second…"

I said it over and over again. I was still saying it when the police cruisers pulled up with an ambulance. An officer gently pulled me away so that the EMTs could work on the woman whose legs were mangled and twisted and God I wanted to vomit…

"Have you been drinking, ma'am?" the officer asked, taking in my wrinkled party dress, my disheveled hair…

"N-no," I said, craning to look over his shoulder at the woman. "I just looked down for a second…"

He asked me more questions. I could barely understand him. Was he speaking a different language? I gave him my ID, the driver's license with the name Fiona Starling on it. He had me blow into a tube. No alcohol, no DUI, but my life was over anyway.

They sat me down on the curb, and I watched the EMTs wheel the woman into the ambulance, and the man—a bodyguard?—climbed in after her.

*Please let her be okay. Let her be okay, oh God…*

The police officer conversed with another officer and then they gently helped me to my feet.

"Come on, honey."

They turned me around, put my hands behind my back and one of them read me my rights. Cold metal tightened around my wrists and a hand cradled the back of my head as they gently guided me into the backseat of the squad car.

The door shut and for the handful of moments before the officers came in, I was encased in the heated metal-smelling interior—a cage between me and the front seat and a door with no handle.

"I'm sorry," I whispered. "I'm so sorry."

# Part III: The Black Prince

## Chapter 23

### Nikolai

I hated St. Louis.

When I'd arrived twelve days ago, the hum of the city had skimmed across my skin like electric hands, reaching for me. It got worse when I crossed over into the more urban areas, and into the city. The lives of others swamped me but instead of filling me up, they sucked my energy and crowded me out of my own self until I was numb.

Leaving Fiona wrecked me. The peace she'd given me evaporated with every mile I put between us, as did the hope that she'd ever talk to me when I got back. And I had to get back quickly. I couldn't shake the idea that coming to St. Louis was a mistake but what the fuck could I do? I was torn by duty to the only two people left in my life.

*Ma hasn't looked at you in eight years. Fiona hates you. There's no one left.*

That was the thought that greeted me every one of those twelve mornings upon waking in the hotel near the assisted living facility. On the thirteenth morning, I dragged myself out of bed; I showered and dressed and told myself I had to keep going. Love and hope. Love and fucking hope…

I rode the Bonneville from the motel through a foggy, yellow haze, to the Forever Sunrise Assisted Living Facility, and parked in the visitor's lot. Before I even had my helmet off, I could feel it. A tightening in the air.

Today was different than the last twelve.

I signed in at the reception desk and Doris Walker, one of the assistant managers, welcomed me with a pitying smile.

"Mr. Young," she said. "How are you this morning?"

*My mother is going to die today.*

"Fine."

She handed me a visitor's badge. "I'm sure you're a great comfort to your mother these last days."

*I* was sure my mother was out of it and had no clue I was there, but I nodded and let the woman think she was being helpful.

I took the stairs to the second floor. At #219 I knocked lightly on the door then opened it. Carl, one of the nurses, was already inside. My mother was lying in the bed, bone thin and sallow, her brown hair streaked gray and brittle against the pillow.

"Morning, Mr. Young," Carl said, with a sneer lurking behind his polite, professional smile. He didn't like me. He'd been around for some of my past visits where my mother fell into a panicked delirium where she was half in the present, half trapped in the past. Carl thought I should stop coming.

"She's pretty quiet today," Carl said. "A little bit weaker."

I took the chair by the bed. Carl was right. My mother was weaker than she had been these last twelve days, and I felt it. The separation between her body and her self was growing, minute by minute, second by second, like threads being pulled one at a time.

*Today is the day.*

"Can I get a minute, Carl?" I asked, when he didn't move.

He held my gaze a minute, then nodded. "I'll be right outside."

My mother's head was turned to the window, her eyes looking

through the bland scenery outside.

"Hey, Ma, how are you today?"

Like every other day, she didn't turn or acknowledge me. The *ken* showed her to be somewhere else entirely. It was like talking to someone who was engrossed in a book or movie.

*And she's not coming back.*

"Ma? Can you hear me?"

Her mouth tilted in a small smile, but not at me. She wasn't in the hospital room anymore. She was smiling at something where she was now.

Threads unraveled...

"Hey, Ma, I just want you to know that I...I understand why you put me in the hospital. And I'm not mad. I get it..."

She sighed, and her narrow chest hitched.

I inched forward on my chair. "Ma, I really need you to hear me."

*I need to hear that I'm still your son.*

Her eyes widened at something only she could see. Time was slipping out from under her.

"Ma...?"

Her hand twitched on the bed and an idea took hold out of my desperation.

*Don't do it. The* ken *fucked up everything with Fiona. Don't try it...*

But the part of me that remembered my mother when she loved me, when she looked at me with affection, needed to reach her one last time.

I reached out and took her hand. Bird bones covered in rice paper. The *ken* showed me a muddled mirage of scattered thoughts and memories. I closed my eyes and concentrated. With Fiona, it just happened. I fell into her memories without trying.

*Just be...*

I eased a sigh. The room dissolved and reconfigured itself as our backyard in Waco, Texas. Summer. The grass in the backyard was browned under the relentless sun. My mother turned on the sprinklers, which meant my father wasn't home to shout about the water bill.

My mother was young and beautiful, her head thrown back in laughter as a little brown-haired boy chased her with a bucket of water. He struggled to lug it after her and she ran slow, then pretended to be cornered so he could dump it over her feet.

"Ai, you got me," she cried and picked him up and swung him around.

The sprinklers jetted water around them. Rainbows danced, and I watched.

"My sweet Kolya," she crooned. "You and me, yes? My little partner in crime."

She smiled at him—at the six-year-old me—then kissed his cheek and they danced in the water…

My eyes blurred. "I love you, Ma," I whispered, too quiet to be heard over the shucking sprinklers or the laughter of a little boy.

My mother stopped dancing, held the boy's hand in hers, and looked right at me. At *me*.

"I love you, Kolya. I always have, my sweet boy. I always will."

A sound, a gasp, fell out of me and I could hardly see for the tears. Her smile was radiant, and I blinked hard, to keep seeing her. She raised her hand, put her fingers to her lips and blew me a kiss. Then she took the boy's hands in hers and resumed their dance in the water, under the sunshine. She had found her sunshine and she would live there now, forever.

I closed my eyes as a part of my battered heart mended itself. When I opened them again, I was in her room at the nursing home.

The last thread had unraveled.

"The funeral will be held in four days," the director told me. "She's made all the arrangements."

I nodded, still in a daze. They thought I was lost in mourning. And I did mourn her, but I knew where she was and that she was happy.

Over the next three days, I checked my phone for a message from Fiona. Nothing. Twice I called her and both times it went to voicemail. On the third call, the automated message said the mailbox was full.

*Wait for me, baby. Please…*

On the fourth day, I stood at my mother's grave with a priest and Mr. Gasparo from the nursing home. I buried my mother under a small marble placard that initially was to have only her name and the dates, but I paid for an alteration.

*Nadia Sokolov Young*
*Beloved mother*

The casket was lowered into the ground. I shoveled some dirt over it, the priest said a few words, and then it was over. I set flowers by my mother's grave and laid my fingers to the plaque.
*Enjoy your sunshine, Ma...*
Then I left St. Louis forever.

I drove back to Savannah with urgency propelling me faster and faster with every passing second. I needed Fiona, even if it was for her to yell and scream at me, to hate me. That was better than silence. The incredible joy of what I felt with my mother was giving way to the feeling that I had been gone for too long. It sunk into me with deep claws and would not let go.

I grabbed a few hours' sleep in a cheap motel outside of Chattanooga, then I pushed through to Garden City, arriving at Fiona's apartment at around ten in the morning. Her Prius wasn't in the parking lot.

*No big deal*, I thought. *She's at work. Or her car's in the shop.*

I knocked on the door. Then again. The silence on the other side scared me to my bones. It felt deep and wide. I tried the knob, not thinking it would actually work, but it turned in my hand. I pushed the door open and stepped inside.

No plants. No bird. No furniture.

My heart pounded as I took in her apartment in flashes, like snapshots.

A couple of cabinets were open in the kitchen, the shelves empty. A trashcan stood in the center of the kitchen. A roll of paper towels was on the counter. A vacuum was plugged in near the living room.

*Fiona...*

She left. To Costa Rica. She had fled to find her freedom. The pain was like a knife in my chest, but I took it willingly. She was gone and if all I had left was the pain, then I'd take it. If that's what she needed to be happy, then that's what I wanted for her.

A man's voice sounded behind me. "Can I help you...?"

I spun around. The man was in his mid-40s, in denim and a t-shirt that stretched over his protruding belly. He held a ring of keys in one hand and a bucket of cleaning products in the other.

"I..."

"What are you doing here?" he asked.

"I was looking for Fiona," I said. "Who are you?"

The man's face twisted in sour frustration. "I'm her landlord," he said. "Or was." He moved past me to set the bucket of cleaning supplies on the kitchen floor.

"When did she move out?" I asked.

"Move out?" The guy snorted. "Yeah, I guess you could say she moved out. Got herself a new place. The Savannah County Jail."

Blood drained from my face. "What did you say?"

"I don't know what happened, so don't ask," the landlord said, digging in the bucket for cleaning spray. "All I know is some cop showed up a few days ago with a social worker from the sheriff's office, and a friend of hers, cryin' and talkin' about puttin' her shit in storage, and I don't know what else."

"She's...she's in jail? She's been *arrested*?"

The guy straightened. "That's typically how one finds oneself in jail. Look, I told you, I don't know nothin' except she had six months left on her goddamn lease. Now if you please? I gotta get this place ready to rent."

I took a last look around Fiona's place. Now so empty. Not only of her possessions, but of her.

*There's been a mistake. A horrible fucking mistake.*

Outside, I tried to remember if I knew which was Nate and Griffin's apartment. I pounded on #5 but there was no answer and I realized they'd probably moved into their new place in Savannah anyway. Hailey and Nancy? I had no clue and no more time to waste. I got on the Bonneville and took out my phone, feeling like I was trapped in a surreal dream and couldn't wake up. I punched "Savannah County Jail" into the GPS.

*What the fuck could Fiona have possibly done...?*

At the municipal buildings, I tore around the lots until I found the visitors' entrance for the jail. The building was heavy with the smells of ash and blood, sweat and anger. Two cops walked a hard-looking man in cuffs past me and my stomach dropped. A potent pollution choked my throat and stung my eyes. I tried to imagine Fiona's pink hair and ethereal glow locked behind bars here but I couldn't do it.

I found the reception desk and gripped the edges of the counter.

"Fiona Starling," I told the deputy working the desk. "Where is Fiona Starling?"

The woman gave me an arch look and tapped on her keyboard.

"No Fiona Starling."

"Look again. I was told she was here."

"She may have been transferred, she may have been released. I have no Fiona Starling on my list." She typed some more. "Actually, I have no record of any Fiona Starling being here within the last thirty days. Someone gave you the wrong information."

"Tess," I said, practically shouting. "Try Tess. Her name is Tess."

The deputy sighed. "Tess what? This system doesn't go by first names, honey."

Fuck, I hadn't heard her last name.

"Try Tess Starling," I said.

The woman typed, shook her head. "Come back when you know who you're looking for."

It took all I had not to slam my fist on the counter. I stepped out of the jail, the blood racing through my veins as if it were on fire.

*Opal. Opal will know.*

I took a deep breath and climbed back on the Bonneville. I wove in and out of traffic just shy of being reckless. I tore into the parking lot of the Garden City Greens nursery, dropped the kick, and ran into the interior shop. Opal was at the register helping a customer. Her eyes widened when she saw me and a dark cloud of anger and pain broiled above her like a storm. She shook her head at me once, slowly. A warning.

She finished with the customer and was already saying, "No, no, no," as I walked up to her. "You should not be here," she said holding one finger up to my chest. "You've got no business being here."

"Opal, please tell me what happened. I was at her place and the landlord said she was in *jail*? How is that fucking possible?"

"It's *fucking possible* because she was upset," Opal said. "She never told me what happened at the party, but whatever you said to her...whatever you *did to her,* upset her more than even I had guessed."

Tears filled her eyes. She pressed her lips together hard until she got in control of herself. Her silence was maddening. My hand itched to grab her, to touch her and pluck the information out of her goddamn mind if I had to.

*That's how you lost Fiona in the first place.*

"Please, Opal, I know I fucked up but tell me where she is. Is she really in jail? It has to be a mistake."

"It is a mistake," Opal said. "The whole thing is a goddamn mistake. I never knew the whole story, poor baby. Not all of it. I never knew what she had been through, but now that abusive prick is going to find her."

I clenched my teeth. "Goddammit, Opal, tell me what happened."

Her gaze snapped back to me. "I will not," she said. "For all I know you're just as bad as he is. Or in on it. Why did you leave her? Where have you been? Gone to report back to that asshole, Steve?"

"What? No…My mother…she was sick…" I shook my head. "It doesn't matter. Tell me."

Opal softened slightly, shook her head, her gaze growing distant. "I left her, too. I left her alone after that first day and I never should've done it. She said she wanted to sleep and I said okay. Then she took off."

Opal fixed me with a steely cold glare. "She hit someone with her car. A young woman. She shattered her pelvis and broke bones in her legs. When the police arrived Fiona was distraught. This is what I heard because I wasn't there and I should have been." Her tears were falling again. "She was *distraught,* they said. Still wearing the goddamn dress from the party with music blaring out of her car radio. That's not Fiona. She's a careful driver. She would never hurt anyone. Whatever you said to her…"

Opal's words slapped me in the face.

"They took her down to the station," she said, "and found out her name wasn't Fiona Starling and that she was *married* to that Steve asshole. She was running from so much, and I never knew. Poor baby, and now it's too late. She was charged with reckless driving and identity fraud."

My heart clanged dully in my chest. "Did she have a lawyer?"

*Jesus Christ, did someone help her?*

"Griffin was her lawyer and he was good, but it didn't matter. The woman Fiona hit was some state senator's daughter from Florida. A rich politician who got in good with the judge and they threw the book at my poor girl. The fines for the fraud wiped out her savings and they gave her three years in prison for reckless driving." She fixed me with another incredulous look. "Three *years*."

I reeled. "Three years... Where?"

But Opal wasn't listening. "I was her phone call. She didn't say much except that she wanted me to take care of Lemony. She didn't even ask for a lawyer; I set that up with Griff myself, and I set up getting her stuff put into storage. I was going to take her bird, too but do you know what I found when I got there? He was dead. Lying on his back, legs in the air. He had food and he had water; it wasn't too hot, it wasn't too cold, he just died."

Opal sniffed and wiped her eyes with a tissue pulled from the pocket of her apron.

"Now Fiona's locked up," she said dully. "There's nothing more you can do." Her voice hardened. "Just go away."

"Opal, wait. Please tell me her last name." I carved my fingers through my hair. "I have to see her. I didn't mean to hurt her. I didn't mean for any of this to happen. I need to know her full name..."

"So you can do what? Make it worse? Upset her more? Visit her while she's trapped and can't say no?"

"Please," I said. "I'm fucking begging you. I have to fix this..."

"You can't," Opal snapped. "And everything else you want to know is in the news anyway. Her *husband's* going to find her, torture her with his very presence. Everything she worked so hard for is gone." She shook her head at me, disgust roiling off of her in waves. "I'm not going to tell you one more damn thing. You can look it up yourself, but it won't come from me. I kept her confidence. I didn't betray her and I'm not going to start now. That's the least I can do."

She left me standing there in the heat and thickening air that seemed to choke me.

I walked like a zombie out of the garden center, back to the parking lot and pulled my phone from my pocket. I typed *Tess accident arrest Savannah* in the Google search bar. A local news affiliate article came up first.

*Early Sunday morning, Tess Daniels, age 23, struck with her car and severely injured Margo Pettigrew, age 21, daughter of State Senator Andrew Pettigrew, of Miami Beach Florida. The Pettigrews had been vacationing at Tybee Island and, according to her security escort, Miss Pettigrew decided to take a lone walk in Savannah on the morning of the incident. Daniels was arrested and charged with reckless driving and identity fraud when it was discovered she had been living under an assumed name in Garden City, a suburb of Savannah. Daniels was arraigned and sentenced to three years at the Whitworth Women's Facility. Since that time, Miss Pettigrew has undergone three surgeries and is still recovering at the Mount Sinai Medical Center in Miami Beach.*

Bile rose in my mouth. I felt sick to my stomach and tears choked my throat. Three years. Three years...

The article didn't say whether Fiona had been transferred from jail to the prison yet. I climbed back on the Bonneville and turned it back in the direction of the county jail. Hopelessness dragging at me.

"Tess Daniels," I told the same woman behind the counter. The name sounded like a foreign phrase in my mouth. "I'm here to see Tess Daniels."

The woman gave me a tired look, and typed the name. She shook her head at me.

"Transferred," she said. "Last night. Whitworth Women's." She clucked her tongue. "Today just isn't your lucky day, is it?"

Back out in the parking lot, under the relentless Georgia sun, I pulled out my phone yet again. Whitworth was northeast of Athens. A four-hour drive.

*This is a mistake*, I thought as I put on my helmet. *A huge fucking mistake.*

I headed east on the Bonneville and hit the highway, remembering Fiona's arms around me, squeezing me twice to go faster, the thrill of her exhilaration wrapping around me.

Those memories felt like a dream now and this waking nightmare was all that was left.

# Chapter 24

*Fiona*

It was after ten o'clock at night when we arrived at Whitworth Women's Correctional Facility. I was marched in with the rest of the inmates in orange jumpsuits through the processing center. We were made to strip, then squat; spread ourselves for inspection. I thought the first time it happened in jail was the worst; as if I could get used to it. I wasn't used to it. Humiliation trailed over me with the sweep of the female corrections officer's gloved hand.

The prison was overflowing. That's what I'd heard on the bus ride over. My group of inmates was supposed to be lodged in the minimum-security wing of a min/medium-security prison, but the prisoners all looked much tougher than minimum security to me. For many of these women their faces were hard and stony, as if the difficulty of their lives was slowly petrifying them from the inside out. Showing how bad it hurt was a sign of weakness. I was riddled with it.

When we got off the bus, I tried to look at the rest of the inmates in our line to see if there were any like me: new and scared to death. But we had to keep our eyes forward and say nothing. We were marched to the dormitories. After lights out, the large room seemed to seethe with the breathing of a hundred and fifty women. I imagined a sleeping dragon I didn't want to wake up.

I was assigned to a sectioned-off cubicle with two bunk beds to each side. The last bed available was the top bunk on the left side. I stored my belongings, which had been reduced to a bar of soap, a towel, toothpaste and brush, flip-flops and two pairs of state-issued underwear, both too big for me. As quietly as I could, I climbed onto the second bunk but it squeaked and rattled.

"Shut the fuck up," came the sleepy murmur from one of the women in my cubicle.

I climbed under the thin sheet and curled into a ball around the bag of belongings. I lay still, listening to the coughs and bed squeaks of the one hundred and fifty inmates in the same room. No one was crying. Or maybe they were. Like me—silently, not even letting the bed shake.

*This is your life now, for the next three years.*

Three years with the possibility of parole in eighteen months.

The judge had been a friend of Margo's father, who was a state senator. They golfed together and went boating off Tybee Island. They hustled me through the system so fast, Griffin hardly had time to catch his breath. He did his best, but favors were exchanged and Griff told me Sen. Pettigrew wanted this swept under the rug as fast as possible.

"It's fishy," he'd whispered to me before my arraignment.

Fishy or not, the judge threw the book at me. Three years for reckless driving and 'serious injury by vehicle', and $8000 in fines for my fraudulent social security card and driver's license. The fact that they hadn't found my fake passport kept me from a ten-year sentence. During my one phone call, I'd told Opal to find it, and burn it and take care of Lemony. She'd done the first, but poor little Lemony was already gone.

I lay on the bunk and turned my thoughts to Margo Pettigrew, and her suffering. Over and over I replayed that moment, the sickening crumpling sound as her body hit my car. I hadn't been speeding. I had the music turned up and looked away for just a second and it was almost as if she materialized on the hood of my car. It didn't matter. I hit her. I nearly killed her. I could've paralyzed her and even now she had months of rehabilitation to look forward to. And pain.

*So much pain...*

It felt as if I'd just fallen asleep when the COs marched through the dormitories, whistles piercing the air. We climbed out of bed to stand at attention for a headcount. I got a look at my cubicle-mates. One African-American woman about my age, a Latina woman in her early 40s who slept in the bunk below mine, and a pale girl with half of her head shaved and blue tattoos fading around her neck and wrists. She gave me a sly, calculating sneer.

*Minimum-security,* I told myself. *No violent offenders here.*

I felt the girl's eyes on me as we were marched to breakfast—her nametag said Taggerty.

We were ushered through the hallways to the cafeteria. Breakfast was runny scrambled eggs, a hard biscuit, microwaved sausage, and a cup of juice. I took my tray, feeling like a new girl in high school who had no friends and no place to sit. All of the tables were full. I picked the corner of one that was mostly empty but for three women at one end. I sat down, shoulders hunched keeping my eyes on my plate. I thought if I made myself small enough maybe no one would see me.

"Hey Pinky, who said you could sit there?"

I kept my eyes down.

"Hey. I'm talking to you."

"Look at this girl," someone else said. "Anorexic much?"

"Bulimic," said another. "She's going to waste all that food."

I glanced up at a woman with dark hair and hard eyes. She was sitting beside my cubicle-mate, Taggerty. The dark-haired woman's nametag read Brooks. A third woman, Vasquez, made up the trio.

My nametag said Daniels. Not my new name or my birth name. My married name.

Taggerty slid down the bench and pinched the corner of my tray between her index finger and thumb. "Bulimic," she said with authority and made a *tsk tsk* sound. "This is just going to go to waste. Pinky, here, is going to scarf it down and puke it back up first chance she gets, aren't you? When you think of it that way…" She pulled my tray to her end of the table, "…we're doing her a favor. Keeping her from *the purge.*"

Taggerty divvied up my food between the other women, then slid the empty tray back to me.

"You're welcome," she said.

After breakfast I went to the commissary window. After paying the fraud fines and putting my stuff in storage I had hardly anything left. My Costa Rica fund was gone. I figured Steve would be coming for the rest if he hadn't already.

"Snickers bar, please," I told the woman behind the commissary window. It looked like a mini-convenience store with snack food, toiletries, and stationary. She glanced at my nametag, typed on her computer, and then slid the candy bar through the slot in the window.

I took it back to my bunk and climbed up. The Latina woman was reading in her bunk. She said nothing to me and I said nothing to her. I ate the candy but it sat in my stomach like a lump, doing nothing except amplify my nerves, which already felt raw and exposed.

Another whistle blew and it was yard time. The regimentation of the day—someone always telling you where to go and what to do—felt like a rough hand pushing me around when I just wanted to go somewhere and be alone. I found a quiet corner under a tree by myself and pulled my knees up to my chin, trying to make myself small.

*You can't pretend you don't exist for three years.*

I had to find a way to manage the fear that was wrapped around me like a python, squeezing.

After yard, it was showers. My heart pounded so hard in my chest I could hardly breathe. I took my towel and my bar of soap, and slipped on the cheap plastic flip-flops. I joined the line and a few minutes later Taggerty and her friends were behind me, three inmates back. They snickered and whispered and I could feel their attention on me like a hot wind.

"Hey, Pinky," Brooks said.

"No, she's not Pinky," said the third member of their group, Vasquez. "What's the name of that model from a million years ago? That skinny British chick? Stick? Sticky?"

"Twiggy, dumbass," Brooks said. "Twiggy's taken. Daniels needs a new supermodel name. Piggy. Piggy, are you a supermodel? Is that why you look like you haven't eaten in three years?"

I ignored them and waited my turn.

The showers were stalls closed off by curtains instead of doors. Naked women walked here and there and inspected themselves in the mirror like it was a gym. One totally nude inmate lifted her leg onto the sink to inspect the fungus growing between her toes. I wondered how long you had to be in prison to feel that comfortable. I hoped I would never find out.

I kept my towel wrapped around me tight until it was my turn. In the stall, I shut the curtain and washed myself with the bar of soap that left a chalky film on my skin. I pumped some shampoo from the dispenser on the wall. My hair was too long; I didn't think I would ever get it clean under the weak water pressure, but I hurried to get done, eager to get back to the cubicle to put my clothes back on.

I shut off the water and reached for my towel. It was gone. I peeked through the curtain and saw Taggerty, Brooks, and Vasquez still waiting their turn in line, my towel slung over Taggerty's shoulder.

"Give it back," I said, trying to make my voice as hard as I could. It came out a whispered squeak.

"Piggy is shy," Taggerty said. "Don't be shy. After all, you're a supermodel. Come show us what a supermodel body looks like."

I couldn't stand in the shower, cowering. It took every bit of will I had to push the curtain aside and step in front of Taggerty. I held out my hand.

"Give me the towel," I said.

Taggerty scoffed, her eyes raking me up and down. "Tiny titties. Tiny titty Piggy."

"Jesus, eat a sandwich. Or ten," Vasquez said.

Somehow I managed to keep my eyes on Taggerty even as my skin felt on fire.

"Give me the towel," I said again.

She held my gaze for a moment, then slung it from her shoulders. "Sure." She handed it to me. "Here you go."

I took it quickly and wrapped it around myself. I should've been more alert but I was too relieved. I started out of the bathroom and Brooks' foot snaked out, tripping me. I caught myself but the cheap flip-flop twisted under my foot and I fell forward. My cheek smashed against the hard tile wall.

Pain radiated around my eye socket and laughter went up amongst Taggerty and her friends. The right side of my face throbbed and I felt a trickle of blood drip down my cheek.

A corrections officer appeared at the bathroom entrance. "Keep this line moving, ladies." Her eyes found me. "What happened here? Daniels? You need the infirmary?"

"No, I'm fine," I said.

"Fine, huh? You want to tell me what happened?" The officer's glance flickered to Taggerty, Brooks and Vasquez, all of whom wore perfectly blank expressions.

I moved past the CO, back to my bunk to get dressed. I had to use my towel to stop the blood. It wasn't a lot but my skin was puffy around my right eye and starting to darken.

"I see you met the Rainbow Coalition," Martinez said from her bunk. She'd been so quiet I hadn't seen her.

"The what?"

"The white girl, the black girl, the Latina," Martinez said. "Tag, Brooks and Vasquez. They call themselves the Rainbow Coalition.

They think it's cute."

"Body-shaming bullies," I muttered, dressing quickly.

"Ai," Martinez said. She cocked her head at me on her pillow. "I look at you here, with your pink hair and sweet face and I have to think there's been a mistake. What happened, querida?"

"An accident," I said, buttoning my jumpsuit with shaking hands. "There was...an accident."

I couldn't talk about it without crying and I couldn't cry. Not here. Martinez seemed nicer than anyone so far, but how would I know?

Fully dressed, I felt better and lay down on my bed and stared at the ceiling. For the first time since all of this had happened I let myself think about Nikolai for more than a handful of seconds.

The pain was swift, wrapping around my heart and squeezing so hard that tears came to my eyes. I brushed them off quickly before anyone could see. Nikolai was gone and the hole I felt from his absence went straight through me, down deep. I didn't think it would ever be filled again. It didn't matter what he'd said at the party, or even if he had been sent by Steve. None of it mattered. He was gone, I was in this cage, and I wasn't coming out for a long time.

A corrections officer came by with a clipboard in his hands. "Daniels, you got a visitor."

I swung my legs off the side of the bunk, my heart pounding all over again.

Steve. He found me and now he was coming to see me, to torture me.

"Who is it?" I asked.

"Do I look like your social secretary?"

"Do I have to go?"

The CO gave me a funny look. "You got something better to do?"

Better to get it over with, I thought. See him one time and never again. Maybe then I'd stop being scared all the time.

His voice laughed at me. *You aren't going to last a month here, sweetheart.*

I was led through the main prison area, through processing, to the visitor center. Because I was new, I wasn't allowed face-to-face visits yet, but was ushered to the phone banks where chairs were lined up in cubicles behind bulletproof glass. The visitor and the prisoner each had a phone receiver.

"Number seven," the officer said. "You have fifteen minutes."

216

I counted up the chairs until I came to seven. I nearly fell into my seat because it wasn't Steve who sat there.

It was Nikolai.

He looked so beautiful after the ceaseless ugliness of prison. I drank him in. But his face was so full of pain and regret. His blue eyes held mine, tired and imploring. They were not the eyes of a man who'd been victorious in duping a woman into falling for him. His expression was of loss, and a tiny whisper in the back of my mind wondered if it were possible he'd been telling me the truth.

*It doesn't matter,* I thought, lifting the receiver with a shaking hand. *Have this time and then let him go.*

I put the phone to my ear. "Hi, Nik."

# Chapter 25

# Nikolai

Fiona sat down on the other side of the glass and my heart fucking broke at the sight of her. She looked so beautiful and scared and small, wearing an orange jumpsuit that was too big for her. The tag said Daniels. Someone had given her a black eye; the skin by her eyelid was puffy and a small cut full of congealing blood was dashed across her brow. My hand holding the receiver clenched tight.

"Hi, Nik," she said in a tiny voice.

"Who did that to you?" I asked through gritted teeth.

She smiled sadly. "My new friends."

"Fuck, Fiona…" It took all I had to stay in the chair. I wanted to smash through the glass and take her out of this goddamn place.

"You look tired," she said softly, pink suffusing her skin. "I got your messages. How is your mom?"

"She's gone," I said.

The pink flared, tinged with violet dust. "Oh, Nik, I'm so sorry."

"No, I'm sorry, Fiona. So fucking sorry…"

She stared at me through the glass, and swallowed hard. "There's nothing to be sorry about. I did this to myself. I messed up. I messed up so badly and I hurt that poor woman."

"You wouldn't have done any of that if it hadn't been for me."

"No, I have to take responsibility for what I did to her. But…"

"But what?"

She hunched smaller in her chair. "I wasn't speeding. I was upset and I was playing my music too loud, but I was paying attention. Or I thought I was." Her voice quavered. "I guess I wasn't."

"Fiona…"

"Doesn't matter."

"Don't give up, baby…"

"It's all gone," she said. "Costa Rica. My place. Even little Lemony." Her eyes filled as she turned them to me. "And you."

Dread filled my veins. "No, I'm here. I'm still here." I swallowed hard. "Did I…Did I lose you?"

She held my gaze and I could see her fighting for control. "I don't know," she whispered. "I don't know what to think. I want to believe you, Nik, but I don't know how."

"I know. It's madness," I said harshly. "This…*thing* I have has been torturing me my whole life and now it's hurt you and I'm so sorry."

"You don't have to be sorry," she said. "I'm in here now. Nothing much matters."

"No, Fiona…"

I could feel her slipping away, her hope eroding piece by piece, her light dimming under the dead fluorescents above us.

*She belongs in the sun…*

"I have to get you out of here," I said through gritted teeth. "I'm going to get you out—"

She shook her head. "Griff did the best he could." Her eyes shone. "It's good to see you, Nik. You're so beautiful after all that's ugly in here. I thought I'd be angry with you if I ever saw you again. Or confused. I was so conflicted about what you told me and how I felt, but now I just want to survive."

"Fiona," I said, fighting for control.

"I'm just so tired of being scared. So tired of it…" She cast her gaze down, defeated. "You should go. Don't put your life on hold for me, Nik."

I clenched the phone so tightly my knuckles ached. "My life has been on hold for years. It began again when I met you."

"Mine too," she said in a small voice. "I feel the same way. But…" She raised her eyes to mine. "There's nothing you can do, and I don't want you to get in trouble. Please. Keep yourself safe." Her voice cracked and broke. "Nik."

God, my name, spoken like a plea, a lifeline thrown out that I couldn't catch. She put her hand to the glass between us, pressed her palm flat. I put my hand to hers.

"Don't wait for me, Nik," she said brokenly. "Three years is too long. Too hard. I can't see you in bits and pieces. Once a week for a handful of minutes? I can't…"

"No," I said, shaking my head. "I'll come every fucking day. Every day, Fiona. Don't…"

"I'm sorry, Nikolai," she said, her voice a whisper through the phone. "I'm so sorry. For everything."

A female corrections officer appeared behind Fiona. I could hear her saying, "Time's up."

My gaze frantically flickered to the wall clock. "That wasn't fifteen minutes. Fiona, wait…"

"Let's go, Daniels."

The officer pulled Fiona's hand off of the glass.

I rose from my seat. "Stop! We're not done. We have four minutes left…"

"Nikolai…" Fiona said softly into the phone, her eyes shining, her lips holding a faltering smile.

"Fiona," I said into the phone, my voice strangled. "Wait. Just wait…"

The officer plucked the receiver out of Fiona's hand and hung it up. The click in my ear was like a door shutting and locking tight.

"No…" Anger rose in me like a great red wave. "Wait a fucking minute. We have four minutes."

They couldn't hear me. They were taking her away from me.

"Hey!" I banged the receiver on the plexiglass. "We're not done yet. We still have four minutes!" I slammed the receiver again, hard. And then again. And again. I punctuated every word with a bang on the unyielding glass. "Four minutes! Goddammit, we have four minutes!"

Fiona looked over her shoulder at me from between the officers, her smile sad and sweet. And then she was gone.

Rough hands grabbed me around the shoulders and yanked me away from the table. I was dimly aware of the other visitors staring, officers shouting at one another. They dragged me through the visitor center, through the screening area where one slammed me chest-first against the wall. My cheek hit the cement and pain radiated through my skull.

"Fiona…"

They handcuffed me, and one officer kept me pressed to the wall while others spoke into their shoulder radios, deciding what to do with me. I closed my eyes, recalling Fiona in that last moment. Her bruised eye and the black hopelessness that was dimming her light. She didn't deserve three years locked up, tormented by other inmates. She was suffocating.

But the truth was *I* couldn't do three years without her. I wanted to fucking burn this place to the ground, and take her away. To Costa Rica, where she could thrive with her plants and animals in the sunshine and none of my fucked up shit could hurt her again. I could survive if I knew she was there, safe and happy. That's all that mattered.

"It was an accident," I muttered against the wall. "She would never hurt anyone…It was a fucking accident. A mistake."

*This has to be a mistake…*

The officers hauled me down a hallway toward a back door. The sunlight was glaring and hot in my eyes. They uncuffed me and gave me a shove, like bouncers kicking out a drunk.

I felt drunk. The ground spun beneath me. The door slammed shut behind me, and I heard the bolt slam home with the heavy weight of three years reverberating through it, straight to my fucking heart.

# Chapter 26

## Nikolai

The Bonneville roared under me.

I pushed the machine faster and faster, careening around turns and weaving around cars as night's shadows thickened around me. One highway became another; road signs tried to tell me where I was, but I hardly saw them. I was going nowhere because I had nowhere to go. No way to help Fiona.

**Highway 23 South**

My eye caught the highway sign just as darkness descended completely, bringing with it the rumble of a thunderstorm.

I turned my headlamp on, still riding as fast as the winding road allowed. I was on a two-laner, with tall trees looming around me on all sides; the highway had been cut through a thick forest. I kept going even as the rain came down spattering the visor of my helmet. Even as visibility dimmed and then became dangerous, I didn't stop. The headlamp cast a ghostly yellow light on the silent road ahead. No cars came the other way; none were behind me.

My shoulder muscles complained from sitting in the same position, my hands ached, gripping the handlebars. Then the Bonneville sputtered as if it were as exhausted as I was. It shuddered and lurched beneath me, the engine popping. I thought it was the rain or a malfunction. A quick glance at the gas meter showed that the needle was on E. I fucking ran out of gas.

I coasted the bike to the side of the road as it died completely. The road dropped down into a shallow ravine. I tore off of the bike and shoved it over the side. The Bonneville hit hard with a shatter of glass—the headlamp probably—and slid down the wet leaves to come to a stop about eight feet away from the road. Once upon a time that motorcycle had been my most prized possession. Once.

I paced the road, up and down, like a caged animal trying to escape the madness of all that had happened. Finally I sat on my heels, my head in my hands, gripping my hair, pulling hard as a roar of rage and pain rose up in me.

*Fiona...*

A guttural scream ripped from me and the sky tore open. Rain came down in sheets. The pounding drops sounded like cymbals crashing as the water splattered the leaves in the trees around me. There was a flash and then thunder bellowed. A moment later, lightning crackled again, illuminating the road in front of me for an instant—a winding snake that led deeper into the forest.

I breathed hard, my throat scraped raw. My entire being was scraped raw; I was flayed open and bleeding because the only person who mattered in this fucking world was scared and in pain and I couldn't do a damn thing about it.

I stood for long moments in the rain, until the cool water doused the fire and left me numb. I started to climb down the ravine after it, to sit with it until the rain stopped and then...

Despair washed over me again.

*I have no fucking clue.*

I took one step and then I heard it. A keening sound that raised the hair on the back of my neck. I started to walk in the blackness, my eyes slowly adjusting and aided by the intermittent flashes of lightning that showed me the curve of the road.

I'd only walked a short distance before I could make out a lump on the side of the road. The sound came again, making me shudder. I hurried towards the dark shape, part of me wondering if that horrific wailing was my own heart, crying out for all that I had and hadn't done for Fiona. My failure.

The sound came again, low and tired now. It was a deer, its front legs broken—smashed like kindling. Blood streaked from torn flesh along its chest and mangled legs, and pooled around the animal, thick and black. Congealed. The deer had been lying there for God-knew how many hours in unknowable agony. The car that hit it hadn't stayed to finish the job.

I fell to my knees beside the deer just as the clouds above parted enough to let a sliver of moonlight slant across us. The deer—a doe–stared at me with wide, black eyes that were full of terror and pain. The animal's keening wail had quieted at my approach; maybe she no longer had the strength to make that god-awful sound.

*Or maybe she was waiting for me.*

My chest tightened and my breath hitched out of me as I reached the Bowie knife strapped to my belt at my back. I sat with the blade in my hand resting on my thigh, unable to move. The doe watched me with glassy eyes, her breath ragged in her open mouth.

"I'm sorry," I whispered. The rain dripped off the end of my nose or maybe it was a string of tears. "I'm so sorry I couldn't help you."

The deer dragged her head along the asphalt, pressing her forehead to my knee. My heart clenched. Without thinking anymore I drew the Bowie knife across her throat. Warm blood spilled to mingle with the cold rain.

The same instant the deer's last breath sighed out, the headlights of an oncoming car lit up the road from behind me. A pick-up truck driving from the opposite direction rounded the curve and slowed when its lights fell over me.

The truck pulled over and I stood up, wiping the Bowie knife on my pants. I slid it back into its sheath on my belt. The truck's driver side door opened and a young guy, maybe a little older than me, with blond hair and a denim jacket stepped out and approached.

He looked at me with blue eyes that were warm, his face open.

Without a word to me, he knelt down by the animal and put one hand on her head.

"T'áá íiyisíí ahéhee," he murmured softly.

"What did you say?" I asked the man as he got to his feet.

"There's no direct translation into English," he said, his voice low and smooth. He had a wide-open, friendly face but his blue eyes held a sadness that ran deep, and I realized with a jolt that my *ken* could not see him.

"The Navajo and other native tribes have such a ritual when they hunt," he said. "It speaks of a gratitude greater than thank you to the animal that gave its life so that we might live." He shook his head, as if marveling at his own words. "A gratitude greater than thank you."

I stared at this man who gave nothing to the *ken*. No colors, no tastes, no sounds.

"Who are you?"

"Name's Justin," he said.

"That's not what I asked," I said.

He smiled a quiet smile and looked down the road from where I'd been, shielding his eyes from the rain. "Car trouble?"

"Back that way, about twenty yards. Motorcycle ran out of gas."

"The next town's not far ahead. I'll give you a lift."

We walked through the downpour to where I'd dumped the Bonneville.

"Ran out of gas, huh?" Justin chuckled and clapped me on the shoulder. "Let's get it into the truck."

Justin and I lifted the Bonneville out of the ravine; I took the handlebars and he pushed from the rear wheel cover. Together we got it up the small hill, over mud and slippery leaves, and back onto the road. There we lifted it into the flatbed of his pale blue pickup truck and I tossed my helmet in after. It was an older truck, rusted and dented in places.

I climbed into the cab and turned to face Justin in the dark. The rain smattered the glass, rattled on the hood.

"Who are you? Don't fuck with me."

"I'm here to help," Justin said. "And I don't mean getting your motorcycle off this road either." He started up the engine. "The town I was telling you about is just up ahead. Let's gas up your bike and then grab a beer. I'll tell you what I can."

A mile and a half or so up the road we came to a blink-and-you-miss-it town tucked away from the rest of the world. The rain finally let up as Justin pulled into a gas station, and we filled up the Bonneville. Next to the station was a motel and a small tavern with a flickering neon sign out front. The Pour House.

Inside, it was dim—yellow light gleamed on dark wood. The jukebox played some country song I'd never heard of. A couple of guys lingered at the bar, smoking and drinking. It looked like the kind of place where instead of waiting to use the bathroom you just stepped out into the woods to take a piss.

"It's on me," Justin said. "What'll you have? Shot of whiskey? Or ten? You look like you could use it."

"I'll take a shot and a beer," I said.

I took a seat at a table tucked in the corner, my back to the wall and a full view of the entire joint in front of me. The *ken* showed me nothing of Justin, and while I should've been relieved for the break, it made me nervous too. I surreptitiously pulled my Bowie knife out of its sheath and laid it on the seat next to my leg.

Justin came back holding two bottled beers by the neck in one hand and he palmed two shots of whiskey in the other. He plunked them down on the table and took the seat across from me.

"Cheers," he said, and tilted his beer bottle towards me before taking a long pull.

I said nothing but downed my whiskey and chased it with a swig of beer.

"You got a name?" Justin asked.

"Nikolai," I said. "And your name's not Justin."

"Says so right on my driver's license." He wore a small, strange smile. "But we both know that doesn't mean much, don't we?"

My stomach hardened and my mouth went dry. I let my hand rest on the knife by my thigh.

Justin folded his arms on the table and leaned forward. "You can't see me, can you?"

"No," I answered and then with a jolt, I realized what he'd asked. "I can't. How did you know? How *do* you know…?"

Justin frowned and sat back in his chair, a ponderous expression on his face. A kind face. He was a good man. I didn't need the *ken* to tell me that. I could read his tells. I took my hand off the Bowie knife.

"I'm trying to figure out the best way to tell you so that you don't think I'm fucking crazy," Justin said. "But then again, I get the feeling you've been called *fucking crazy* a time or two yourself, haven't you?"

I nodded. "Do you have it too?"

"What do you have, Nikolai?"

"I can sense people's emotions all the time, everywhere, nonstop. Sometimes I can pick up what they're thinking. But for you. Looking at you is like being partially blind. No…" I shook my head. "If I were to paint you, you'd be black and white. No color."

Justin grinned. "What you see is what you get."

He sipped his beer and I stared, wondering if he'd heard me correctly. He acted as if what I'd said was the most normal thing in the world. Just another piece of information for him to process. My stomach burned with something stronger than the whiskey.

"I call it my *ken*. For twenty-four years all I've *ever* wanted is either to get rid of it or find someone who can tell me what the fuck it is. And now here you are…"

Justin met my gaze steadily. "Yes," he said. "Here I am."

I leaned over the table feeling almost crazy with a wild energy. Like how runners must feel when they see the finish line: exhausted but still hurtling forward, with burning muscles, shortness of breath, and a stomach that feels like it's ready to puke.

"Tell me," I said. Begged. "Tell me what I am."

Justin's expression was kind and patient. "You're like me," he said, "but different. I don't have the *ken*, at least not in the same way. The information I get—information I'm not supposed to have—comes to me in dreams. Dreams that I can't grasp when I wake up but that come back to me in bits and pieces at the exact moment I need them. Telling me where to go, what to say. I dreamt about you. That's why I'm here."

"That's why you're here," I repeated. "You can dream the future…?"

He nodded, once.

"Okay…" I said, slowly. He was so fucking calm while I felt like I was on fire on the inside. "But what does that mean? How can you do that? How can I do what I do? Just what the fuck are we?"

Justin held up his hand and I realized I'd been halfway out of my seat. I sat my ass back down.

"I don't know what we are, Nik," he said heavily. "Sometimes I feel like I've caught a glimpse of myself but it slips away. Like walking past a mirror but turning my head to look a second too late. I get only a flash of…something."

"What do you see?"

"I see someone who's tapped into the energies of this universe in a way that other people aren't, but nothing else. And for the longest time I hated it. I hated when I found out I was the only one. I thought everyone around me was exactly like me."

My jaw clenched again this time with a surge of something deeper than relief to hear my own thoughts spoken back to me by someone else. My pounding heart slowed. The beer bottle was cold in my hand.

"I hated what I was," Justin said. "Until I found out how to use it for good. To help. It saved me. She saved me." A rueful smile spread over his kind face. "I met a girl… Isn't that how the best stories begin?"

"Yes," I said, my throat suddenly thick with tears and regret. I took a sip of beer to swallow them down. "I met a girl."

Justin leaned over the table. "I wish I could tell you exactly where it came from, your *ken*. But I don't have those kinds of answers. All I can tell you is what is true for me. You have a conduit to the energies in this world, and the only way to survive it is to use it to help others."

"Help others? What are we, some kind of goddamn team of superheroes with the most useless, random fucking powers? I can't help anyone," I said, my voice wavering. "I can't help her. I'm too late. I fucked it all up."

Justin shook his head. "It's not too late." He grinned. "Or I wouldn't be here."

The calm surety of his voice washed over me. I took another sip of beer. "Tell me how."

"The dream I had about you was long and expansive, but when I woke all I could remember of it was the name of the highway I found you on, the Navajo prayer for gratitude, and the name Margo Pettigrew." His eyes widened at my shocked expression. "You know her? Is she your girl…?"

"No. Fiona's my girl. Margo Pettigrew is the name of the woman she hit with her car. They gave her three years in prison for it." I looked up to see Justin watching me. "She can't do three years."

"Find Margo Pettigrew."

"And do what?"

Justin smiled ruefully. If your *ken* is anything like my dreams, you'll know what to do when you get there."

"Margo Pettigrew is some rich daughter of a Florida state senator. She's holed up in a hospital that's probably swarming with security guards. I'll never get in to see her."

"You'll find a way," Justin said. "It's important, so you'll find a way."

"And this will save Fiona? Talking to this woman will somehow magically erase her prison sentence?"

*There is no magic in the world…*

"I can't say," Justin said. "I didn't dream that far."

Our eyes held and I felt the weight of his truth settle over me. I realized now how hard it must have been for Fiona to believe what I had told her, because here I was, sitting across from a guy who claimed he dreamt the future.

"You didn't dream that far…" I muttered.

A smile spread over my lips, and then a chuckle, which became a laugh. Deep, bellowing laughter erupted out of me, bringing tears to my eyes.

"Oh fuck," I gasped, and leaned back in my chair feeling as if I had run a fifty-mile marathon and now I could rest, just for a minute, before running another fifty to Margo Pettigrew.

Justin smiled and signaled the waitress over. "Two more whiskeys," he said. "Actually, why don't you leave the bottle?"

I stared at Justin and narrowed my focus on him the way I used to narrow my focus on a tattoo needle for the pain. This time it was for the experience of being in the presence of someone who knew what I was, who didn't judge, who didn't doubt, who wasn't afraid. I had only this night, this round of drinks, because I doubted I'd ever see Justin again.

The waitress came back with the whiskey and poured shots. We clinked glasses and downed them at the same time. I noticed a gold wedding band on his left hand that curled around his beer.

"This girl you met," I said. "You married her."

"Hell yes, I did," Justin said with a laugh. And even without the *ken,* the love he felt for this woman was so potent, it was as if she were sitting right next to him. "Her name is Jo," he murmured, "but that's not on her driver's license either. We're having a baby in a few months."

"Congrats," I said, clinking my glass to his. "Boy or girl?"

"Boy," Justin said with obvious pride. "I can't wait and I'm scared shitless." He jerked his chin at me. "What about you? You want kids some day?"

I recalled little Hailey putting her arms around my neck, and the feeling that went with it—a life experience I hadn't let myself consider because it felt so impossible.

I shook my head, the tattoos on my arms looking darker than they ever had before. "I'm no one's idea of a father."

Justin held my gaze steadily. "You sure about that?" Then he glanced to his beer, watched the bubbles rise. "Women have a way looking past the bullshit to get to what really matters in life. My wife…she looked beyond what I was and so saved me. I saved her too, I guess. So she tells me. We saved each other, and I think that's how it's supposed to be."

I shook my head around another sip of beer. "If I get Fiona out of prison, that's not saving her. That's righting a wrong."

"Everything happens for a reason," Justin said, tipping the neck of his bottle at me. "That's one thing I can tell you for certain."

"She wouldn't be in prison if I hadn't fucked up."

"What did you do?"

"I told her what I was."

Justin poured us two more shots. "She didn't believe you."

I shook my head, downed my shot. The world was getting blurry at the edges. "Because I did it wrong. I scared her," I said, disgusted. "It was the last thing I wanted to do and it's exactly what happened."

"Does she love you?"

The question struck me right in the chest, like an arrow. "I don't know. I think so."

Justin arched an eyebrow at me. "You think?"

"She's never said the words and until she does the *ken* can go fuck itself," I said. "I hate ripping the memories out of people's heads. I wanted so badly for Fiona to tell me everything about her past before the *ken* stole it from her. But it stole it anyway. It…put me *inside* her memory."

Justin's eyes widened. "Holy shit."

"I can never undo that. I can never unsee what I saw." I shook my head, my body feeling loose and my jaw wagging a little with the whiskey. "You said the only way to survive this ability, or whatever the fuck we have, is to use it to help. But how can it help anyone?"

"You never used the *ken* around Fiona before that incident? To know what she was feeling so you could say or do the right thing. To make her happy? To make her feel safe or loved?"

I sat back in my chair. "I… I don't know."

"I'm not a gambling man," Justin said with a grin, "but I would bet that the answer is yes."

"Still feels wrong," I said. "But around her, the world is so much quieter. All those energies you talked about us tapping into? They're fucking loud and bright and sometimes they taste like shit. They don't leave me alone. Except with her. Then I know peace. With Fiona I can live with the *ken*. Without her, I'm fucked. *Ken* or no *ken*, if I don't have Fiona I'm fucked."

"Because you love her."

I opened my mouth to speak but it felt wrong to say the words; I'd failed her so badly. I rubbed my eyes trying to clear my vision. "Fuck, why am I sitting around here? Gotta get to Florida."

"Not tonight," Justin said. "Even without the booze you were in no condition to keep going. You need some sleep. Get some rest and some food in you, and then go."

I hated to admit he was right. It felt like years since the housewarming party and that I'd been awake every minute since.

"Finish a beer with me." Justin raised his glass. "You know, it's not every day I meet someone who's … tapped in."

"It's a fucking miracle," I said tossing back the liquor. "Are there others like us? With my *ken* or your dreams or something else entirely?"

"The way I see it," Justin said, "it's like extraterrestrial life. There are billions of solar systems with planets orbiting suns at just the right distance, like Earth. To think one of those out there doesn't hold life is crazy, right? I think you and I are in the same boat. There are seven billion people on this planet. To think we're the only ones who are special… it's kind of arrogant."

"It's only arrogant if you think it's a good thing," I muttered. "Mine's been nothing but a nightmare for as long as I can remember."

"And now it's time for you to put it to good use."

I shook my head darkly. "I don't know…"

My words trailed as Justin cocked his head, as if he were listening to something only he could hear.

"What is it?" I asked. "Is…something talking to you?"

Justin nodded solemnly. "It's telling me…"

I leaned forward. "What?"

Justin stared straight into my eyes and said in a loud whisper, *"If you build it, he will come."*

I blinked and then sank back in my chair. "You fucker," I muttered. Then louder, a harsh laugh busting out of me. "You *fucker*. A stupid baseball movie? Holy shit, I'm drunk…"

"Yes, you are," Justin said, his shoulders shaking with laughter. "Totally walked into that one."

"Asshole," I said around a chuckle.

"Takes one…" Evan said.

His name was Evan, and I was three sheets to the wind and falling face first onto a motel bed before I realized I knew that. Whiskey-tinged sleep grabbed for me with greedy hands and I slept better than I had in weeks, waking to slants of sunlight across my eyes the next morning.

I sat up, blinking. A mild headache throbbed behind my eyes. Through the motel window I saw my Bonneville parked out front. It had been washed, and the headlamp was replaced. She looked almost as good as new.

My gaze drifted to a note on the hotel room table.

*Nik,*
*I had another dream last night. This is what I remember.*
*Fiona will need a new passport. Look up Del del'Rio in Dolores, Louisiana. Del has a contact. She'll help you. She helped us.*
*Wear black when you meet Margo Pettigrew.*
*Tell Chuck his sister's in labor.*

*Good luck, brother.*
*~E*

I checked out of the hotel and rode my bike to a small diner on the outskirts of town. I ate a huge meal and ordered another one to-go for the road, then pointed the motorcycle south.

"T'áá íiyisíí ahéhee," I said.

I didn't know how I knew to say it, but I knew what it meant. A gratitude greater than thank you. I sent it up to the stars or to the sky or the energies that bind us, and hoped that somehow it would find Evan on his way back to his Jo.

# Chapter 27

*Fiona*

I dreamt of a dark road winding through a forest. Lightning flashed and I saw Nikolai walking alone, head down, shoulders hunched. A relentless rain drenched him. Ahead was a dark shape on the side of the road and a sound like a wail of death, full of pain...

I woke up with a gasp. The dormitory was still dark, not yet dawn. My cheeks were wet and the fear that *I'd* made that keening cry in my sleep sent a flush of sticky heat surging through me. My skin was slick with sweat. I held perfectly still, holding my breath to control the sobs and listened for sounds that I'd woken anyone up. Nothing. There were only the sounds of sleep of the women in the dorm.

I drew in long, deep breaths, fighting to stop the tears.

*Nikolai...*

My hands clutched the thin blanket, wishing they were filled with his shirt, with his warm skin and strong muscles beneath. I wrapped myself around the pillow, wishing it were his body against mine, holding me and keeping me safe.

But he was gone and not coming back. Three days earlier, I'd told him to go and he did. I hadn't heard from him since. That was the best thing, wasn't it? I was too scared all the time, too unraveled. I hardly recognized myself.

*Silly little girl. Got yourself in a heap of trouble, didn't you?*

I squeezed my eyes shut and clenched my teeth to keep the sobs in. I flinched when a soft hand touched my hair. I opened my eyes to

Martinez standing beside the bed, her face level with mine. In the dark, her eyes were soft and caught the dim light in their brown depths.

I held perfectly still, my heart pounding in my chest the only movement as I waited for a pinch or an insult, or for her to belittle me for crying. One harsh word would be too much; I felt as if I were made of glass, cracked in a hundred places. The slightest touch would shatter me.

But Martinez's hand was soft, her voice maternal and warm. "Dry your tears, querida," she whispered. "You aren't going to make it unless you find something to hold on to. To fight for."

Slowly, I let out a breath. "I let him go," I whispered.

Martinez brushed the hair from my forehead; a mother's touch I hadn't ever known.

"You can't rely on anyone else. No man or friend or family. You have to find it in yourself to pull through."

"What pulls you through?" I whispered.

"My books," she said. "They are something to look forward to. The end of every story is something I look forward to, to see how it turns out. And when it's done, I have the next book to look forward to. One after the other. That pulls me through." She brushed her thumb on my chin and I could see her smile in the dark. "You are like my youngest daughter. A sweet little thing who wouldn't hurt a fly, sí?"

"But I did," I whispered. "I hurt her badly."

Martinez patted my cheek. "So get through it, querida. However you can. Find it in yourself to get through it."

"Find the sunshine," I murmured, my aching eyes falling shut.

"Sí, querida. Find your sunshine."

I slept.

A heavier sleep than any before, and woke up to the COs' whistles, feeling sluggish and hung-over from crying.

We were marched to breakfast, and I took my tray—oatmeal, two curves of pale cantaloupe, and one slice of toast—and began the nerve-wracking trek through the cafeteria, keeping my hair over my face to conceal my red and puffy eyes.

I took a corner of an empty table, determined to eat and get out as fast as possible. I'd put one bite of bland, sticky oatmeal in my mouth when the "Rainbow Coalition" descended on the table.

"Piggy, Piggy, Piggy," Taggerty said with a tired sigh. "There are starving kids in China who would love to have the food you're just going to puke into the toilet."

"I'm not going to throw it up," I said, my eyes on my tray.

"Denial," Brooks said. "She needs an intervention."

"I concur," Taggerty said. Her hand appeared in my line of sight to take hold of my tray. "It's for your own good, really…"

I gripped my tray.

"Don't be like that, Piggy." Taggerty tugged again. "Hand it over."

I held on. Taggerty tugged again, harder and I let go just at the right time.

Taggerty yanked the tray towards her and it slipped off the edge of the table. Oatmeal dumped into her lap and watery orange juice splattered her jumpsuit. Brooks and Vasquez—along with several other inmates at nearby tables—burst out laughing.

"You're right," I said, standing up. "I feel better already."

I left the cafeteria with my eyes straight ahead and my hands clenched at my sides to keep them from trembling. My heart hammered in my chest. I'd won a small victory but at what cost? Taggerty wasn't going to let this go…and I still hadn't eaten breakfast.

I turned down the hallway to the commissary window.

"A Snickers bar…" My gaze fell on the stacks of individually wrapped bars of soap. They were industrial-sized bars, and heavy. "And three bars of soap."

The woman behind the counter tapped on her keyboard. "You can't afford it. You're going to zero-out for the week."

"Already? How…?"

"Try eating in the *cafeteria* once in a while," the woman said with a smirk.

*Gee, wish I'd thought of that.*

"How much can I afford?"

"The candy and two bars of soap."

"Give me three soap, no candy," I said.

The woman reached behind her and grabbed the bars. "You know you can't eat that, right?"

I took the soap and went back to my bunk hungry.

Taggerty and her crew suspiciously avoided me for the rest of the day, but I felt retribution coming like a storm on the horizon. Shower time, probably. I wanted to skip it but the dormitories were perpetually hot and sticky, and the fear that had congealed around me was like a heated blanket. I wore sweat like a second layer of skin.

When the call to shower came, I stripped down naked, wrapped myself in the towel and joined the queue for the shower. The three bars of soap I'd bought were tucked under my arm.

Taggerty, Brooks and Vasquez purposely dawdled to get in line behind me. I felt it coming and almost didn't flinch when I felt a tap on my shoulder.

"Hey, Piggy," Taggerty said.

I ignored her. The tap came again, harder.

"I'm talking to you, bitch. Thanks to the mess you made, I need to get extra clean today." She put her mouth close to my ear. "I'm going to need another towel. Your towel. But you don't mind do you, Piggy? You like showing off your supermodel physique."

She tugged at the top of my towel and I spun around. Taggerty's hair fell over one eye; the other was clear and green and hard, like a marble.

"Leave me alone," I said.

"That's cute, Piggy, but I can break you in half with one finger and you know it."

I had nothing to say. No cutting comeback, no threat I could back up. I turned back around, my heart crashing against my chest.

"Don't you turn your back on me." Taggerty shoved me and I stumbled forward, jostling the woman in front of me.

I faced Taggerty. "Don't do that again," I said.

"Or what?" She shoved me.

Heat flushed my cheeks. I was sick of fucking being pushed around, sick of being belittled, sick of being made to feel stupid and weak, and so goddamned scared all the time. I shoved Taggerty hard. She staggered back into Brooks, and before I could think, I ripped off my towel and wrapped the three bars of soap inside to make a kind of bag. I held the towel in both hands, ready to swing.

"*Leave me alone*, I said.

Taggerty laughed. "Oh, our Piggy is all grown up, isn't she? She's been in the clink for four days and now she's a hard-ass motherfucker."

Vasquez smirked but Brooks pursed her lips and glanced toward the bathroom entry.

"Come on, Tag, let it go," Brooks said.

"Fuck that," Taggerty said. "This bitch wants to play. I'll play."

She feinted at me and then lunged, but I was ready. I swung the towel with the three bars of soap up and connected squarely with the side of Taggerty's face. The soap hit her cheek, her head whipped to the side, and she staggered back to fall against the wall.

Adrenaline coursed through my veins and I tightened my grip on the towel.

"I told you to leave me the fuck alone," I said on shaking breaths.

Taggerty's eyes were wide and her hand slowly came up to touch her cheek where a lump was growing. Her fingers came away stained red as blood trickled from a tiny cut on the curve of her cheekbone. A mirror image of the one she'd given me three days before.

She glared at me. "You don't have it in you to do it again."

I gripped the towel tighter, naked and trembling, every muscle coiled and ready. "Try me."

Taggerty stared me down. I stared back, unblinking. Then she laughed and touched her cheek again. "That fucking hurt, Piggy."

"My name is not Piggy," I said.

"No, I guess it's not. What do they call you? Daniels, right?"

I nodded.

Taggerty grinned. "That fucking hurt, *Daniels*."

"Good," I said.

Brooks' eyes widened and she elbowed Vasquez. They all exchanged amused looks and laughs.

A corrections officer appeared. "What's the hold-up, ladies? What happened to your face, Taggerty?"

"Nothing, ma'am," Taggerty said, her eyes on mine, a small smile touching her lips. "I slipped. Whacked myself on the wall. I'm good though. We're all good here."

The CO looked to me, naked, still holding the towel. "Daniels?"

"Yeah, we're good," I said slowly, my eyes still locked with Taggerty's.

"Then get this shower moving. You're holding up the line."

As soon as the CO had gone, Brooks and Vasquez busted out laughing, and it felt as if a balloon filled to bursting with tension slowly let its air out instead of popping in a torrent of violence.

"Daniels, you are one crazy bitch," Brooks said.

"She whacked you good, Tag," Vasquez added.

"Fuckin'-A," Tag said shooting me a grudgingly respectful nod. "She's stronger than she looks."

After the shower, I went back to the dormitories, dressed, and headed to the library. Getting lost in a book—or one book after another—seemed like a solid plan. The front desk of the small library held a bunch of pamphlets and brochures. One that offered general education programs through the local community college caught my eye. It included a program for those who wanted a teaching credential. I wondered with a pang who would ever hire a kindergarten teacher with a criminal record?

*I'll jump off that bridge when I get to it,* I thought. I took the brochure.

An hour later, with a copy of *The Count of Monte Cristo* tucked under my arm, I headed back to the dorm. An officer joined me in the hallway, a clipboard in his hands.

"You have a visitor."

My heart soared. *Nikolai came back...*

"I'm crushed, Daniels," the CO said, perusing his visitor manifest. "You didn't tell me you were married."

I crashed back down so fast and so hard, I could hardly breathe.

He was here.

# Chapter 28

## Nikolai

It took me a day and a half to get to Miami Beach. I wanted to push through and ride all night—every second that ticked by while Fiona rotted away in prison was like a tally scratched on the wall of my heart. But I had to sleep. To focus, I guess. I had no fucking idea what I was going to do when I saw Margo Pettigrew, but I figured it was best to be as sharp as possible.

Miami Beach was swarming. The buzz of the tourists, the heat, and the constant bombardment of the colors, tastes and scents… it was almost too much. Twice I dabbed my nose with a bathroom paper towel, and twice it came back red.

I found an internet café and searched for information on the Pettigrews. It was easy enough; he was a state senator, newly elected and popular. She was his twenty-one-year-old daughter who had been—according to the local newspapers—brutally struck by a frazzled young woman back in Savannah where the Pettigrew family had been vacationing off Tybee Island.

Margo Pettigrew was holed up in a private wing of Mt. Sinai hospital with a shattered pelvis, a collapsed lung, and a left leg that had been broken in so many places the doctors had considered amputating it.

I closed my eyes as a sick feeling turned in my stomach. Fiona wasn't reckless; I had made her into something she wasn't by ripping her worst memories out of her and holding them up for both of us to see.

I let out a slow exhale. Evan had told me the key to helping Fiona lay with the woman she'd nearly killed. I had to trust him. I had nothing else.

I checked into a small seaside motel around six o'clock in the evening. I showered and even though the heat was pushing ninety-five degrees, I dressed all in black: black jeans, black T-shirt, my black motorcycle boots and my black leather jacket.

I rode to Mt. Sinai, feeling as if the entire city were clinging to my back and whispering in my ear. Inside the hospital's air-conditioned interior, the feeling backed off a little but the pain and misery and fear of hundreds of patients and their families coalesced around me like a fog.

I tried to focus, but what the fuck was I supposed to do next? Buy some flowers at the gift shop and pretend I was a visitor? Ask the receptionist where Margo Pettigrew was recuperating? She was a senator's daughter. They weren't going to hand that info over to a stranger.

I stood for a moment in the waiting area, and like I'd done in that motel so many weeks ago, I sent the *ken* out, like a call in the dark. I pushed it through all the waves of other peoples' lives to concentrate on one. One soul with pain in her legs, maybe, or who was haunted by visions of a car striking her.

Margo answered but it was nothing like I'd expected. I sensed a yawning void of nothing, and somehow I knew it was her.

I took the stairs up, letting the *ken* lead me to the fifth floor. I came out onto a wing that was most definitely reserved for patients with money. The waiting area was empty white spaces, flowers on tables, and art on the wall. A gourmet snack cart pushed by candy stripers in neat uniforms moved around the nurses' station. There was a sense of calm here… but for Margo.

Holy shit, it was as if she were a black hole sucking in all the light; sucking me toward her with a desperate need that lived beneath the nothing.

Again, going to the nurses' station felt wrong. Instead, I walked with purpose down the hall towards that yawning emptiness, to a door with a man standing in front of it.

A bodyguard. He was dressed all in black. His badge read Charles Murphy.

*And there's Chuck. Thank you, Evan.*

I put a knowing grin on my face and strolled up to him. "Hey Chuck, time's up."

The guy frowned, trying to place me. "I'm on until midnight, then Spencer has graveyard. Where's your badge?"

I pretended to be shocked. "You didn't get a call? The boss sent me to get your ass out of here. Your sister's been trying to get a hold of you."

"My sister…?"

"She's in labor."

Chuck's eyes widened, then narrowed. "Hold on." He pulled out his phone and checked it. "No one's called me…" He punched in a number and put the phone to his ear, his eyes locked on mine.

I acted casual as fuck, rocking back on my heels.

"Hey, Pats? What's up? Are you…? You are? Where? Southside? Okay…is Brian there? Good, great, I'm on my way…"

Chuck slipped his phone back in his pocket and slapped my shoulder. "Holy shit," he said. "I gotta go…You got this?"

"I got this," I said, easing a sigh. "Go. You're about to be an uncle."

"Holy shit…" Chuck strode down the hall and around the corner, leaving me alone with Margo Pettigrew.

So far, Evan had been right about everything. My hope flared brighter…and dimmed again as I quietly stepped into Margo's room.

It resembled a hotel suite but with every medical machine necessary to monitor Margo's vital signs. IVs hung above her over the bed. Margo herself was a small brunette who looked lost in a sea of white sheets. Tubes ran into her arms, a nasal cannula fed her oxygen, and her leg…

Jesus Christ, her left leg was slightly elevated and scaffolded from ankle to hip in a hideous-looking external fixator. Pins penetrated her bruised and scabbed skin almost every three inches along her thigh and shin, and her foot was swollen.

Worse than the sight of her leg was the yawning emptiness I felt from her. Something deeper than sadness or melancholy; something beneath depression.

*She has no tears left…*

But her eyes were sharp and full of intelligence. They flickered to me as I approached, then looked away to stare out of the window where night was falling. "What do you want?" she asked. "Afraid I'll get up and run away?"

I moved to her bedside. "I need to talk to you."

Her brows came together, dark against her pale skin. "Talk? I didn't think you meatheads were capable of anything but saying 'Yes, sir' to my father."

"I want to talk about the accident," I said.

Margo didn't flinch. Her pulse on the monitor was steady.

"Go away," she said tiredly.

"I can't," I said. "I can't leave here until we talk."

"Did my father send you?"

"No. I'm here on my own."

She turned back to me, her gaze sweeping, noticing my lack of a badge. "You don't work for him." Her lips curled. "Are you here to kill me?"

"No..."

"A pity."

"I need to talk to you about the woman who hit you."

Margo closed her eyes for a moment and I felt a whisper of regret flit in and out of the empty void that encased her.

"All I have to do is call the nurse and have you kicked out."

"Please," I said. "She's in prison. She's doing three years—"

"She nearly killed me," Margo said flatly. "Not to mention, I heard she was living under an assumed name. She's a criminal." She turned her head to look at me more directly. "Is she your girlfriend? Am I supposed to feel sorry for her? I've had four surgeries on my leg. My hip has been reconstructed out of titanium and I can't last longer than twenty minutes without morphine. Except they won't give me the morphine I need..."

The emptiness surrounding the woman swelled and it felt as if the air were being slowly sucked out of the room.

"If you're here to ask me to talk to my father for her, forget it," Margo said. "She made her bed and now I'm lying in it."

"Margo," I said. "I need your help. Fiona—Tess—needs your help. What happened was not her fault, it was mine. I made her upset—"

"Then she shouldn't have been driving," Margo said, and I tasted a lie behind her words. Guilt and remorse swirled around her like damp ashes after a raging fire. "Get out before I call the nurse," she said. "Or security. *Actual* security."

"Margo, please…"

"Stop saying my name!" she whispered in a hiss. "You don't know me. You don't know a goddamn thing about me. Your girlfriend nearly killed me. She's getting what she deserves."

"Then why do you feel guilty?"

She flinched against the pillow. "What? I…don't…" She regained her composure and flapped her hand at her leg. "Take a look at that mess and tell me why the hell I should feel *guilty*?"

"I can't. That's what you need to tell me. Your story. You have a story, right? One that you can't tell anyone?"

Margo stared. It was all right there, but I couldn't grasp it. And if I ripped it out of Margo the same way I'd ripped the secrets out of Fiona, I'd lose. Hard.

*You want something from her, give her something in return.*

"It's okay," I told her. "I have a story too. And the *not telling*? It eats you up inside until there's nothing left. Nothing at all."

She remained silent but I felt how my words were pulling at her, drawing her out. I felt her reaching for me like someone who's reached before, a thousand times, and always had her hand slapped back.

"I'm not a security guard," I said.

"No shit," she said, but it came out shaky.

"I don't really have a job. I play poker for a living. Until I met Fiona, I traveled back-and-forth across the country, from one underground game to the next. No direction, no goals. For six years, I rode, pretending there was a destination that mattered waiting for me in the end. But there was only more of the same. Nothing."

Margo listened, her sharp eyes regarding me intently.

"Sometimes," I said, "when I'd been on the road for eight hours, I'd let the motorcycle drift." I looked at her. "Do you know what I mean? Drift."

"Into oncoming traffic," Margo said.

"Yes. Into oncoming traffic."

A short silence fell and I felt her yearning for more. More words. More connection.

"I got tattoos—dozens of tattoos because the needle's pain was real. It felt like it was the only thing that was real. Pain to remind me that I was still alive. That I was still here."

Margo nodded almost imperceptibly. "I pinched," she said. "I couldn't cut my skin because they'd see, but I'd pinch so hard, I'd get bruises all up and down the inside of my thighs. I pinched hard enough so that tears came to my eyes. Tears meant I could still feel…something." She swallowed hard. "You know what that feels like, don't you?"

"Yeah, I do."

She looked away, blinking hard. "I thought I was the only one."

"It's exhausting, isn't it?" I said.

"God, yes. I'm so tired," she said. "Pretending everything is okay is so much harder than not being okay."

I let the moment distill between us, then gently asked, "What happened? What really happened?"

Margo smiled ruefully, her eyes shining. "Didn't you read the news? Your girlfriend wasn't watching where she was going and plowed into me. Me, a helpless pedestrian. She almost killed me." Her voice became a whisper. "Almost."

I held my breath but didn't speak, afraid of screwing this up with my desperation.

*Just let her be…*

Margo's fingers toyed with the sheet.

"Do you know you are the first person to visit me in four days?" she asked. "My father's too busy and my stepmother is in Paris. She never misses summer in Paris. She prefers it to Tybee Island. Too many mosquitoes, she says. Too many 'hick locals.' She's still there, in Paris. I haven't heard a word from her. And my father's busy with his work, as usual. But he had Angela, his secretary, send those flowers."

Margo tilted her head at the white roses on the table. "Aren't they pretty? They even have a note from him. *Love, Dad,* it says. Isn't that fucking considerate? Except that's not his handwriting."

I felt it coming, the words bubbling out of her on a tide of pain that lurked beneath the nothing and hadn't seen the light of day in years.

"Gregory was my security detail on the day that I got hit. He was assigned to watch me while my father went boating with some friends. I didn't want to go boating but that's all right, I wasn't asked. I'm too quiet. I don't make small talk. I'm morose and unsightly to a state politician who always wants to put his best foot forward. 'Put your best foot forward, Margo,' he likes to tell me. And I want to tell him most days it's all I can do to climb out of bed. It's all I can do to shower and dress and make sure my shoes match."

She turned her head on the pillow to look at me. "They say

depression makes you sad. But I find it makes you not care whether or not you put your best foot forward."

I leaned forward in my chair, swallowed hard. "Margo, why were you in that street?"

Margo cocked her head, her gaze steady. "What is your name? Your real name, and don't lie to me."

"Nikolai."

"Nikolai," she said. "I was in that street putting my best foot forward. One after the other, right into oncoming traffic. Into the path of your girlfriend's car. I had escaped Gregory for a few precious minutes. Just long enough to cross the boulevard and step into the street. Nobody drives the limit on a sleepy Sunday morning. Everyone speeds on the boulevard. That's what I thought. But not your girlfriend." Her mouth turned down in bitterness. "She had one job to do and she failed."

I took a chance. I reached for her hand and held it in both of mine. The great yawning nothing that surrounded her swallowed me whole. And inside there *wasn't* nothing. There was everything...

I braced myself and took it all. I felt everything she felt; the pain, the loneliness. She sat at a family dinner surrounded by talk and laughter, and yet was stranded on a desert island, sending up smoke signals that no one could see.

"They think you're fine," I told her. "They think you can just snap out of it if you really want to. They don't understand why you can't smile and make nice and—"

"And put my best foot forward," she whispered.

"Medication is for the sick," I said. "Sickness is for the weak."

"Pettigrews aren't weak. We are nothing if not strong and healthy and fit," Margo said. "But for me. I'm weak. I don't feel anything anymore and I couldn't take it for one more second."

My own vision blurred, for her pain and Fiona's.

"It wasn't her fault," Margo said, tears gathering in the corner of her eyes. "No one could have avoided hitting me. It was impossible. Gregory knew it but he was ordered to say nothing. My father wanted to cover it up and push the blame as fast as possible on your Fiona. And it was so easy..."

"Because she was upset," I said blinking hard. "That was my fault. Please don't let her suffer for that."

She sighed heavily and I felt the emptiness around her deflate a little, hope and light seeping in.

"How did you know what to say to me?" Margo asked. "I had no words, not for years. Just...nothing. And yet you said them all."

"Does it matter?" I asked.

She stared for a moment then shook her head, the tiniest of smiles spreading across her lips. "I guess it doesn't," she said. "It only matters that someone else understands."

I nodded, thinking of Evan and the profound relief of knowing I wasn't alone.

"You're not weak," I said. "But you need help. Everyone needs help."

"I'm scared," she said, "and it's the first real feeling I've had in a long time. " She shook her head. "I am sorry that Fiona wound up in prison for what I did."

"Will you help us? Help her?"

Margo's hand in mine squeezed weakly, but nurse came in before she could speak. I went to let go of Margo's hand but she held me tight.

"How are we doing here?" the nurse asked, her glance flickering to our hands. "Need anything?"

"Yes," Margo said. "I want to see a doctor. Not the orthopedist...someone else. Someone I can talk to."

"Of course, Miss Pettigrew. Whatever you need."

"I also want to talk to my father. Will you please get in contact with him? And if he tells you that he's too busy and won't speak to me, tell him I'll speak to the press instead. Will you do that for me?"

I saw the weight of the Pettigrew name and how Margo wielded it, maybe for the first time in her life.

"Yes, ma'am," the nurse said. "I can do that. And how is your pain level, currently?"

"Worse," Margo said, her eyes finding mine. "And better."

"It's about time for another dose," the nurse said, and injected a pale yellow liquid into the IV that ran into Margo's arm.

"Rest now," the nurse said, shooting me a look. "It's late."

She went out and Margo looked to me, her eyes already losing their sharpness.

"I'll do what I can for Fiona," she said. "It should be easy. My father will do anything to avoid bad press. The idea of me telling the world that I threw myself in front of a car and that he got a judge to imprison an innocent woman to cover it up will have him making calls in a heartbeat."

"Thank you, Margo," I said on a shaky exhale.

"Thank *you*, Nikolai," she said drifting on a sea of morphine, her voice floating up between us. "Nikolai…whoever you are. A prince all in black, who came to rescue me. The dragon was circling…ready to swallow me whole, and then you came…"

"I'm not a prince."

"You are. The Black Prince. You're saving me."

"You're saving me too, Margo," I said. "By helping Fiona, you are saving my life."

She smiled, sadly beautiful. "I've never saved anyone before," she said, her eyes drifting closed. "It's a good feeling."

# Chapter 29

*Fiona*

I walked to the visitor's center feeling as if it were death row. My heart smashed against my chest and my mouth had gone dry.

*Don't go. There's no rule that says you have to see anyone.*

But one foot followed the other, taking me forward. Closure, Opal had told me once. Maybe that's why I kept walking. I'd been jumping at shadows—and Steve's voice in my mind—for years. It was time to turn on the light.

Still, my legs were watery and my breath seemed to go no further than my chest.

I started for the phone banks but was informed that I'd been approved for face-to-face visits.

*Oh God...*

I was redirected toward the main visitation room where inmates sat across a small table from loved ones. I peeked in the glass window as the corrections officer unlocked the door. The room was full of my fellow inmates and their husbands, children, friends...people they longed to see and touch.

In the center table sat Steve Daniels.

He loomed so large in my memory and had taken up so much space in my mind I expected a giant. A monster.

In the chair sat an ordinary guy, in jeans and a green polo shirt. The fact that he was so ordinary was almost worse because it was harder to justify my fear. His insidiousness was invisible to an ordinary onlooker. He didn't look like a monster, until you looked into his eyes. His eyes were dead.

For a half a second, I couldn't move and then the memory of me in the women's shower, naked and swinging a towel full of soap, came flooding back.

*I'm stronger than I look.*

I stepped into the room and Steve's red-haired head came up. I noticed his hair was longer and unkempt, his shirt stained. The Steve I remembered kept himself impeccable—clothes ironed, hair neatly trimmed. This Steve's leg was jouncing under the table, his arms crossed tight, like a junkie jonesing for a fix.

His leg stilled and his arms fell loose when he saw me. The smile that spread over his lips curdled my blood. I'd seen it so many times early in our relationship, when I was a naïve eighteen-year-old girl. I'd thought that smile was real and just for me; that I was being swept off my feet by a prince.

*He's not the prince. He's the dragon. And now I can see he's not even that...*

"Tess," he said, holding his arms out to the sides, as if to say *What am I going to do with you?*

I moved to the chair in front of him and sank down.

"How are you, sweetheart? It's been so long..." He cocked his head. "Pink hair? It's cute. I like it."

I stiffened. He sounded so sweet and kind, so full of concern. Just like he had in the beginning.

"What do you want?" I asked.

He chuckled. "That's the first thing you say to your husband after two years?"

"You're not my husband," I said. "On paper, maybe. Not in here." I touched my fingers to my heart then clenched my hands in my lap to conceal how badly they were shaking.

Steve's expression hardened, like a mask. "I am your husband," he stated. "I haven't stopped being your husband, no matter how far you strayed."

"How did you find me?"

"I Googled you. Every day for two years. I knew something would eventually turn up—"

I gaped. "Every day...?"

"*Every day*," he said, pronouncing each word distinctly. His eyes fixed on mine, pinning me down. His fingernails, usually perfectly manicured were raw and uneven, and he scraped them lightly across the table.

My heart dropped to hear that sound. Soft and almost imperceptible, but I could *feel* it more than hear it, like a scratch against raw nerves to make my skin tingle unpleasantly... a limb waking up.

Under the table, my hands clenched tighter.

"You searched for me every day. Did you ever..." I swallowed hard. "Did you ever send anyone to find me?"

Steve frowned. "Did I send anyone? I didn't need to 'send anyone', Tess. To be honest, I knew it was only a matter of time before you stumbled and fell. But I had no idea you'd fall so far..."

I hardly heard him. The instant the question had left my lips, I knew the answer. Now, face to face with Steve after two years, it was so obvious. So glaring. Nikolai was nothing like Steve and would never want anything to do with someone like Steve. Nik was alive and vibrant—even in his pain—and the time we'd shared had been rich and full of light. Steve was dead and empty. The only contact Nik would have with a creature like Steve would be to knock him on his ass, like he had done to that guy at the fair.

But if Nik hadn't learned of my hospitalization through Steve, that meant he'd been telling the truth about his special ability. The *ken*. Now wasn't the time or place to process it, but it was enough to know that everything else we'd shared had been genuine. I felt it in my bones, in my blood, in the instinctual part of my being that lived below thoughts and rationale. The words we'd exchanged, the way he looked at me and kissed me and made love to me...it had been real.

"It was magic," I murmured.

"What's magic?" Steve asked.

"Nik. Nik is magic."

He shifted in his seat, crossed his arms like a stern boss who just learned his employee had gone against his orders. "Nik. Who is Nik?"

"He's a real man. He's a hundred times the man you are. He never made me doubt myself. He never told me I was ugly. He never made me feel unwanted or un..." I swallowed my tears. "Unloved."

"Uh huh," Steve said. "And where is this Nik now?"

I had no answer. I didn't know where Nik was, but I wanted him back because I knew my heart now, and it was filled with him.

Steve smiled triumphantly at my silence. He sat up, brushed his hands down his shirt and sat up straighter. "I see how it is. He fucked you and made you think he cared and then he took off, right? You just went from one man to another, didn't you? I always knew there was a side to you that was ... a slut."

I expected the word to hurt. It rolled off instead.

"I am not a slut. I spent two years alone because of you," I said in a low voice, "I pushed Nik away because of you."

Steve cleared his throat, pretending to be taken aback. "I'm hearing a lot of blame being placed on me, Tess. You're saying it's my fault that Nik isn't here? Maybe there's a little something else going on ... like a three-year prison sentence. What random guy is going to wait around for you? It's a lot to ask, especially when the person you're waiting for has been so foolish and reckless. I always knew you were fragile but I didn't think you were this careless. What's the real story? Were you drinking when you hit that poor girl with your car?"

"No. I actually thought I saw you walking down the street and I ... I got flustered for a second."

"Oh, so now I'm to blame for *your* accident? Maybe if you hadn't run away like a thief in the night, you wouldn't have gotten so *flustered* and none of this would have happened. Did you ever think of that? You just vanished, Tess. Did you spare one thought about how I might feel to find you gone? Do you know what it's like to have someone in your life for three years, to provide a home for them, and sleep beside them, and then one day discover that they've disappeared? No word? No calls or texts?"

"I had no phone to call or text," I said flatly. "You took it."

He waved his hand, dismissing my answer, my feelings; dismissing me because what I'd done to him was the only thing that mattered. "For God's sake, Tess, you're my *wife*. I was lost without you. I was a mess. And scared. Don't you think I worried where you were? I thought you were dead in a ditch! I called hospitals; I called the police. I put out a missing person's report, did you know that? So much fear and worry and concern, but no, you just took off ... so you could go fuck this Nik guy."

"Are you done?" I asked.

Steven blinked. "Am I...? Am I *done*?"

"Yes," I said. "Are you done talking about yourself and how *you* feel?"

"Tess..."

"You just said the word 'I' about ten times in your little speech. But let me ask you, how do I feel, Steve? Right now. Can you tell me that? How am I feeling?"

He frowned, his brows knit together. "Shame for hitting that woman and almost killing her…"

I flinched at that, then nodded. "Yes. What else? How do I feel about you being here?"

"Relieved. Relieved that I've forgiven you and you're not alone anymore," Steve said. He reached his hands across the table for mine. I reared back.

"Wrong," I said. "I am not relieved to see you, Steve. In fact, I'm a little bit nauseated that you're this close to me, and if you try to touch me again, I'm going to scream for the guards."

He stared for a moment, his pale blue eyes flat but thoughts churned behind them. "You're being dramatic and silly."

"Silly?" I said, and my chest tightened. "You stole everything from me. Everything."

He blinked. "I stole…? You are the one who stole ten grand and ran…"

"That was my money. My father left it to me. You locked it away so I couldn't leave. I only took back what was mine. Besides, I don't even give a shit about the money. It is nothing compared to what you took from me."

Tears filled my eyes and my first inclination was to blink them away. To make them disappear before he accused me of being weak and emotional. But those tears were mine and they were real, and I let them fall.

Steve sat back in his chair, a chastising smile on his lips. "Here we go. Tess…" he warned. "You know what crying is, right? It's how you hide from the real situation at hand. To make me feel sorry for you instead of—"

"No, that's not what crying is," I said. "The tears are for what I can never have back. The loss I feel is real."

"Is that what this is all about? Is that why you left? Because of that one little conversation you had with a doctor?"

I sat back in my chair, the sheer audacity of his callousness like a slap in the face.

"You cheated on me. You got me sick and I nearly died. Now my body is so scarred—"

"Look, I was never all that crazy about having kids," he barreled on. "You knew that. The way I see it, if it's meant to be, it'll happen. If not..." He shrugged. "We'll do in-vitro or something. Or adopt if it's so important to you."

I stared. "You think...Do you think I'm going to be with you when I get out?"

He stared back, and the fake-y smile vanished, falling away like the mask that it was. His nails scratched the table.

"We're married, Tess. You're my wife. I've been patient for two years. I can wait three more, and then this foolishness ends. When you get out of here, you come back with me." He drew his hand down to the edge of the table, scraping, then back up, to start again. "With me, Tess. Me."

I waited for the fear to come back, to sink in and lodge itself deep. For the time I'd been married to him, Steve had broken me down from a girl who was just finding her way in the world, to a shell who doubted and mistrusted every thought and emotion she had in her head and heart. He used my desire to love and be loved and turned it into a weapon, battering me with it until I cracked into tiny pieces and had no idea how to put myself back together again. Until now. I could have laughed at the irony that I had to go to prison to be free.

I raised my eyes to meet Steve's, and the stifling band of fear that'd been wrapped around me for so long loosened and fell away.

"No," I said.

"No...what?"

"You are an abusive asshole and there is no 'us.' Not ever again."

Steve rolled his eyes. "Abusive? I never laid a hand on you..."

"Not all punches come from fists," I said. "Not all cuts break the skin but I bruised and bled just the same. On the inside."

Steve's eyes hardened to cut glass. "Oh for God's sake, Tess, cut it with the melodramatic shit. It just makes you sound stupid—"

"*I am not stupid*," I said, drawing looks from other inmates. "I escaped you—"

"Escaped," he snorted.

"I *escaped* you," I said, "but was never free. Not really. You were still there, like a shadow I could never outrun. Because I did run away. I ran instead of facing you and so I felt chased, every day of my life. But I'm not running anymore."

"You're right. You're not running. Because you are in *prison*," he said, almost triumphantly. "Prison, Tess. You weren't thinking clearly when you hit that woman, and you're not thinking clearly now. But it's okay. I'm back. I'm—"

"I've been in prison for years. For *years*, Steve. I've been scared for years and I'm so tired of it. You put fear in me. And I thought if I ran far away, out of the country even, I'd outrun it. But I can see it now. It wasn't you. The fear was in me. And now it's crystal clear: you're nothing and I am done being afraid."

He rolled his eyes in a way that I imagined a shark would, rolling its black eyes to dead white. "I have to say, I am quite hurt, Tess. You're making me out to be such a cruel person. Aren't you being a little unfair? Here I am with open arms and you're throwing me under the bus."

"It's over, Steve. We're over. For good."

He held my gaze. I wondered if it were my imagination but I thought I saw a flicker of fear—real fear—flit over his eyes. Then, all I saw was anger. "Nothing's over."

"It is. Us. We're over because there never was an us. You used me to fill a purpose, and I let you use me because I didn't know my worth. I didn't know that I could be good for anyone else. Or myself."

*But I am good for someone else. And he's good for me.*

"You won't make it without me, Tess. You have no one…"

"I have me," I said. "For the first time in years, I have me." I stood up, stood over him. "Goodbye, Steve."

His hand snaked out and grabbed my wrist. Instantly, I felt repulsion and disgust.

"Let go of me," I said calmly.

"I can wait. I *will* wait. As long as it takes. You can't hide from me."

"I'm not hiding. I'm looking you in the eye and I am telling you: Let. Go."

Steve stared. I stared back and held my ground while my heart pounded in my chest. Finally, his hand went slack and then fell away. I turned to go, his voice chased me with rage.

"You can't run from me." I heard a chair scrape and knew he'd stood up.

I kept walking and didn't look back. His voice grew louder.

"It's not over, Tess. It will *never* be over."

I left the visitor's center and let the door shut between him and me. I leaned against the wall, a shaky breath gusting out of me. I clapped a hand to my mouth, thinking I would be stifling a sob. I laughed instead, an aching laugh that began deep in me, like a muscle waking up after being out of use for so long. I'd been living half a life, trying to find the sunshine under a sky full of clouds. But now…

*Now I'm free.*

My world broke open. I wanted Costa Rica for itself, not for escape. I wanted to teach so that I could surround myself with children for the love of them; and a hope filled me that my own children were waiting for me out there, somehow.

I thought of Nikolai.

My silent laughter subsided, the sweet ache deepening to an intense longing.

*I want Nikolai.*

Nikolai had always accepted me for who I was, even riddled with fear and uncertainty. He saw my flaws and fears, and if what he was saying about the *ken* was true, then he saw deeper even than that, and still he wanted me. He let me just be. Had I lost him?

I passed the bank of inmate telephones on the wall on the way to the dormitories. I waited in line and then dialed Nikolai's number. The automated system prompted me to speak my name to tell the recipient that a collect call from an inmate at Whitworth was waiting. But Nik's phone rang and rang. No voicemail.

*You sent him away.*

I sucked in a breath. If he were gone for good, then I'd have to face it, though a lifetime without Nik was far worse of a sentence than three years in prison.

*You don't know if he's truly gone. Keep going. Just keep going.*

I inhaled deeply and dialed Griffin Miller at his law firm.

"Fiona, oh my God, I literally had my hand on the phone just this second to call you." His voice was electric with excitement.

"What is it?"

"Are you sitting down?"

"I'm leaning against the wall. Does that count?"

"Hold on to something, honey. Judge Riley had the governor commute your sentence.

I froze. "What did you say?"

"Commuted. All of it. You're down to time already served and five hundred hours of community service."

I put my hand flat on the wall to steady myself. "How…how is that possible?"

"I got the phone call today. The judge's order is sitting right in front of me. It says new witness testimony was submitted that states you weren't reckless and that Margo Pettigrew provided 'a clear and sudden impediment to oncoming traffic.'"

I nodded slowly. "I...I don't know what to say. What about Margo? How is she?"

"She's recuperating well from what I hear."

"I'm so happy but I still feel so terrible for her. I hurt her so badly..."

"It was an accident, Fi," Griff said. "An unfortunate accident but you didn't deserve three years in prison for it. And the judge saw that. Somehow."

"Somehow..." I murmured, my thoughts going inexplicably to Nik.

"Fiona," Griff said. "You're getting out."

"I'm getting out," I breathed. "Is this for real?"

"It's real, honey. You'll be released in the next few days, after they're done processing the judge's order. I'll keep you updated."

"Thank you, Griff, for everything."

"I didn't do a thing except answer a phone."

"I'm grateful you were there to answer it for me," I said. "And while I still have you as my attorney, can I ask you to do one more thing for me?"

"Name it."

"I need you to draw up divorce papers and have them served on Steve Daniels. Immediately."

Griff's smile colored his next words. "Consider it done."

I gave him Steve's address for our house in Duluth and the name of the company he was working for when I left two years ago.

"I don't know if either of those are current..." I said.

"It's enough to track him down."

I grinned. "Yeah. Track him down, would you?"

I hung up with Griff and walked back to my bunk, dizzy from the chain of events, and my heart full of gratitude...and longing.

My desire to see Nikolai grew into a fierce hunger. I wanted to touch him and tell him how sorry I was; to tell him to come back to me. That he could be with me as he was, in any way that he was...

Martinez was on her bunk, rifling through the contents of a manila envelope.

"A care package from my kids," she said, her fingers trailing over homemade cards and letters.

"That's adorable," I said, kneeling beside her. "How many children do you have?"

"Two girls," she said. "four and eight. They're little handfuls but they're minding their auntie while I'm in here."

"Will you see them soon?" I asked softly.

"Every Saturday," Martinez says. "And in three months. Three more months of Saturdays and then I can go home."

From the pile of treasure, her hand plucked a dreamcatcher made from popsicle sticks, string, beads, and a feather. She handed it to me.

"I think this one is calling you."

"For me? No, I can't…"

"To catch your dreams," she said, pressing it into my hand.

"I'll keep it, but only to remember you by," I said. "I'm getting out in a few days."

Martinez's liquid brown eyes widened and then she cocked her head with a proud smile. "I'm so glad, querida. You don't belong in this cage." She reached out and took a lock of my pink hair and gave it a playful tug. "The Rainbow Coalition is going to miss you."

I laughed. "I think they'll get over it."

Her smile softened. "And do you have someone to meet you when you are set free?"

"I don't know," I said, casting my gaze down. "I let him go, remember?"

She curled my fingers around the dreamcatcher. "So catch him back."

That night, I slipped the dreamcatcher under my pillow. I thought I'd feel silly or stupid, but I was neither. I knew myself. I knew what I wanted.

"Come back, Nikolai," I whispered. "Come back to me…"

# Chapter 30

## Nikolai

I waited in Miami Beach for two days and then Margo called me back into her hospital room and told me it was done.

"I got my father to lean on the judge just as hard as he did the first time," she said. "Tess—or Fiona? She should be out within the week."

I sagged with relief in the chair at her bedside. "Thank you, Margo. What about you? What's next?"

"There's a doctor here, a psychiatrist. She sat down with my father and me, and we did a lot of talking. And then I talked with her some more. I don't want to do anything but talk to her some days." She gestured at her leg and its hideous-looking scaffolding. "Talking's about all I'm good for now," she said. "And the doctor started me on some medication. My father hated the idea at first but he hates the idea of a scandal more. Of being perceived as a terrible father. So…" She shrugged. "I'm not great but I'm better. I've never been able to say that before."

"I'm glad you're better," I said. "And thank you again."

She shook her head against the pillow. "Thank you, Nikolai. And tell Fiona I'm sorry."

"Everything happens for a reason," I said, with a smile. "Or so I've been told."

I left the hospital and leaned on the Bonneville in the parking lot. Fiona was free or would be soon, but what kind of life would she have? Her apartment and savings were gone, her plans to go to Costa Rica were in shambles. She needed money to start over again, or to leave the country if that's what she still wanted.

And I had twenty thousand dollars sitting in a bank account, waiting for me to decide what it was for.

*Fiona. It was always for Fiona...*

But twenty grand wasn't going to stretch very far, especially if she needed a passport that was going to get through customs and the Costa Rican government. I remembered Evan's advice about a contact in Louisiana, and went to grab my phone from the sidebag, to research the going rate for a fake passport. My phone was gone. I searched the other bag. Nothing. It must've fallen out when I dumped the motorcycle down the side of the road.

I rode to the nearest Fed-Ex and jumped on a computer. Illegal passports, turned out, cost upwards of $10,000 if you wanted one that was going to have a prayer of getting past Homeland Security. Fiona couldn't get released from prison only to get tossed back in for a shitty passport. Passport fraud was a ten-year sentence. I had to trust that Evan's contact wouldn't fail us.

"Shit," I muttered. Cutting my savings in half for the passport didn't leave much for her to live off of. I wanted her to have a solid footing.

*Back to the tables,* I thought with a sigh.

I could build up a good chunk of money over the course of a few days, underground, en route back to Georgia.

I played online poker at the Fed-Ex and got in with an underground game just outside Gainesville. It was at a seafood restaurant where ten tables became a poker den after hours. Decent stakes. I showed up at eleven pm that night with my online contact's password.

The place was lively, like a mini-casino. The owner was in good with the local law so they left them alone. There were even a couple of off-duties playing at one of the ten tables. You can always tell off-duty cops doing something illegal; they act as if the entire operation is only happening because they're allowing it to. I guess that was true, except they were just as guilty.

The clouds and mists and unpleasant tastes that stung my mouth were thick, but I battled through them and took my seat at the table and began to play. Aggressively. I didn't have time to fuck around.

By the time dawn started to seep its light through the slats of the windows, I had added $6000 to the ten grand I was playing with, and had cleaned out all but seven of the players in the entire joint. Time to move on.

"Quite a heater you got going on," said the guy handling the bank when I went to cash out. "You coming back tonight?"

"No, I'm done."

"That's what he does," said a voice behind me. "He's a fucking chopper. Except that he cheats to win before cutting and running."

I turned, and there was Will, the shifty little bastard I'd played against in Atlanta before I met Fiona. He looked skinnier than I remembered, and the stench of addiction oozed out of his pores. Will had acquired a little heroin habit since last I saw him.

"That's a bold accusation," said the banker. "You got some evidence for that?"

I crossed my arms. "Yeah, I'd like to hear it."

The other players watched me closely. If there was one constant among poker players, it was that they had a strict sense of honor. If there was even a whiff of cheating (and a chance to get their money back) the retribution was swift and merciless.

Will's yellowed eyes never left mine. "I don't know how he does it," he said, "but the fucker cheats. He cleaned a bunch of us out in Atlanta couple months back, easy as you please, then skipped town. It's his M.O."

The restaurant manager had gathered—they all had. The off-duties looked ready to break my neck.

"Search him," said the manager.

They yanked off my black leather jacket, patted me down, searched my pockets for electronic devices, or the proverbial ace up my sleeve. They found nothing.

There was no law that said I had to stay and play the full three days, and there was no evidence that I had cheated. The banker cashed me out.

"If I see you around here again, there's going to be trouble."

"Don't do it," Will whined. "He's a cheating bastard..."

"Have you considered," I said slowly, feeling the danger coil around me like a black fog, "that maybe I'm just better than you?"

In retrospect, that might've been the wrong thing to say.

I took the money and slipped out of the restaurant with dozens of narrowed eyes following me and eighteen thousand dollars in a small leather bag. I didn't even make it to the Bonneville. Three guys blocked my way. A fourth tapped my shoulder.

I turned and Will's fist slammed into my jaw. My head whipped to the side and then back. I glared. He took a step back and I gave him an uppercut that left him reeling. Then his friends were on me. A flurry of punches took me down and booted feet kicked the breath out of me.

From my position on the ground, I saw Will, blood leaking from his mouth, pick up the bag with Fiona's money in it.

Adrenaline coursed through me but there were four of them and only one of me. I landed solid blows more than once, but the biggest kicked me in the kidney while I was on all fours, and another struck me across the head. Pain burned across my back and the world spun out from under me. I collapsed to the ground, hard.

"We know who you are now," Will said "Us grinders? Coast to coast. You're fucking done. I'll make sure of that."

They left me slumped against the side of the building, my legs splayed, my body aching in a hundred different places. Blood leaked from my mouth and nose, and from a gash above my eye.

*Now what the fuck do I do?*

The underground poker network was a vast system with a thousand arteries. I wouldn't be able to find a game within three states by tomorrow. If I had any hope of winning something for Fiona, I had to hit a casino.

"Fuck," I muttered and spat blood. A casino had bigger stakes, more money. I could get in and out with a good chunk…if I could survive the onslaught of the *ken*.

I had $10,000 to my name, not counting a prepaid Visa with a couple grand for emergencies. I'd use that too if I had to. The largest casino was the one in Jacksonville that I'd used to win the money to stay in Garden City. I recoiled; that place had nearly done me in.

I went back to the hotel and cleaned myself up. I looked like shit: bruises, tired eyes, a split lip, and a gash on my brow. I'd been playing all night and my aching body and tired mind screamed for sleep. I let myself have an hour's worth—a small bite of food to a starving man—and then hit the road again.

Jacksonville was a riot of colors, tastes and sounds. I was battered on all sides, tossed on a sea of emotion that threatened to drown me before I even hit the casino parking lot. I parked the Bonneville and took off my helmet. I closed my eyes and inhaled deeply. As I breathed out,

I imagined Fiona slipping her hand into mine, her smile so damn beautiful and sweet.

*Just be...*

I wanted that peace, but it was impossible. The only times I'd ever come close to knowing my own self were when I was with her. It was then that her peace washed over me, and the *ken* didn't bombard me with life but instead wove itself into my perceptions naturally. Easily. Fiona allowed me to just be.

*Wait for me, baby,* I thought. *I'm coming back to you...*

I approached the casino and signs for a poker tournament greeted me at the front door. There was a tournament that began today with a jackpot of $50,000.

"You're kidding," I muttered. I'd been preparing for a three-day ordeal, praying for high rollers in one of the private poker rooms, maybe. This was a huge break.

*Everything happens for a reason.*

I found the registration line and got in it. It was first come, first served, with a buy-in of five thousand dollars. The line stretched nearly to the door and I was sure I'd miss the cut off. I got up to the desk and the woman gave my piercings and tattoos a cursory glance.

"Just made it. One hundred players allowed. You're lucky number one hundred."

"No shit?"

"No shit." She took my money as I filled out the information form. She stamped it, and handed me a card to exchange for chips. "Good luck, sweetheart."

I took the card. "Thanks," I said, the *ken* already bearing down. *I'll need it.*

I exchanged my card for chips and took a seat at a table. From the first moment I sat down, I knew it would take everything I had to get through this.

The tournament was twenty tables in a conference-like room with a low ceiling. The mists and changing colors of the players hung in the air like thick smoke. I had to fight through the cacophony to focus on my opponents and read their tells—those anyone could see. The *ken* was useless here. I had to play like everyone else, except with my eyes partially blinded by color and light, and with the rushing sound of random whispers hissing in my ear.

Three hours in, I dabbed a cocktail napkin to my nose. It came away red.

*I'm not going to make it.*

It took everything I had to focus on my cards, the community cards, my opponents. I must've looked like a madman. Players were knocked out and the tables condensed; me and the other survivors would be shuffled to a new table where my new opponents snickered at the shifty bastard with the tattoos and the flop sweat broken out on his forehead. They stopped laughing when I knocked them out.

*For Fiona. Win for her.*

After what felt like years, I glanced blearily at the chip counts on the board. Twenty two players left splitting $500,000 in chips. I glanced at my chip stack and did some quick estimating. I guessed I had around the sixteenth biggest chip stack. The top fifteen finishers took home money. Finishing sixteenth would get me $10,000. Not nearly enough. Finishing in the top five was where the real money was, but *fuck*, it felt like climbing a mountain naked, or swimming an ocean without coming up for air.

I blinked the sweat out of my eyes, wiped my nose, and pretended the red didn't scare me.

The day dragged on. Hour after hour, the *ken* grew more relentless as the casino filled up with nighttime gamblers. I was barely holding on. Finally, the floor manager tapped my shoulder and told me the room was being reconfigured again. The final table, and I had a seat with eight other players.

They rearranged the room so that the audience circled us, bombarding me from all sides. I felt like a fish in a bowl and the water was becoming murkier with every passing minute. The nerves and fear of my opponents was ratcheted up so hard I could hardly breathe.

I dabbed my nose and considered my options. If I finished seventh, I would walk away with $25,000. But if I could knock out one more guy, I'd win $30,000. Thirty grand, and I could go back to Georgia, to Fiona…

*If I don't spring a serious leak first…*

We played a few hands, and I got to know my tablemates' play. They were old pros, most of them, who'd been around the pro circuit a hundred times. I was the only newbie, but they all had their tells. Even without the *ken* I could see a tick in the cheek here, a smirk there.

I identified the guy directly across from me—a middle-aged man in a cowboy shirt and bolo tie with black hair that was silver at the temples. He would be my mark. *Take him down, then cash out with thirty and get the fuck out of this casino.*

I focused my attention on him. I had to focus on one thing because the weight of everyone else—the audience watching, the crowds that meandered throughout the rest of the casino, the hotel guests, every essence of life—was like a hand pressing me down. *Focus on this one guy.* The bolo tie guy. He was twitchy. Nervous. His tell was a quirk of his thin mustache when he had something good; he drummed his fingers on the table when he had shit.

Obvious tells. *Maybe too obvious. Watch him.*

After another agonizing hour, Bolo's chip stack was low and mine was a mountainous castle. Time to go in for the kill. The dealer shuffled and dealt two cards to each of us. The cards skimmed the green felt effortlessly and practically slid into our hands.

"Nervous, buddy?" The guy next to me glanced at me and back to the two cards face down in front of him. "Final table. Stakes never been higher."

*No shit.*

I thumbed the corner of my two cards up. King and Jack of spades. "Just how I like'em," I muttered.

The flop showed a ten of spades, nine of spades, and a Queen of diamonds.

*Holy shit.* I'd flopped the nuts with the mother of all draws.

I needed any spade for a flush, a queen of spades for the straight flush, but I wouldn't hold my breath. With a hand this fluid, I could've taken on every other player at the table, but I could hardly focus. The bets came around again. I already had a straight. I called the bet to keep Bolo confident. He led out with $2000 in chips.

The turn came, a Queen of hearts. Bolo's mustache jumped and he raised a thousand dollars.

*He's got more than one lady tucked away.*

He was representing three—if not four—of a kind. My entire win—Fiona's escape money—came down to a goddamn gutshot. If he had trip Queens, I'd already won. But if he had quad Queens, I was dead in the water.

The guy on my right raised. I think he was holding on with a full house. He was toast and didn't know it. I re-raised.

My head was pounding now, like hammers on the inside of my skull. I felt as if I were upside down—all the blood had rushed to my face and the pressure mounted with every passing second. I wasn't going to make it much longer. I dabbed my leaking nose. It felt like an eternity for the dealer to lay down the river.

A Queen of spades. Straight flush. Game over. I win.

My body didn't react at all.

Bolo went all-in. That final Queen gave him quads—I saw the twitch in his mustache like a flashing neon sign. I swayed in my chair, waiting until the bet came to me, the other players' actions barely registering. The guy folded. The guy on my right pushed a bunch of chips into the pot.

I had the best hand and I knew it. No *ken*, no reading tells. I'd won the biggest hand of my life with sheer luck and not a damn thing more.

Poker rules state you have to raise if you have the best hand. Bolo watched me grab a stack of chips—thousands' of dollars worth—and splash the pot.

"Raise."

The syllable left my lips and the tension in the air tightened around me like a noose. The audience, seated in a mini-stadium around us got to their feet, cheering and hollering.

Bolo stood up in front of his chair, disbelieving. "No…You don't have it," he told me, his eyes wide. "I have quad Queens."

He flipped over his two Queens to join the two in the river.

"I *do* have it," I slurred. I flipped over my spades to show the straight flush. "But nice hand."

"Nice hand? *Fuck!*" Bolo raised his hands like he was going to flip the table, but he clasped them behind his head, pacing.

The entire audience burst into cheers and applause, mingled with shouts of surprise and excitement. It wasn't every day a hand as good as a quad Queens was shot down by a straight flush. I'd only ever seen it once or twice in all the games I'd played over the years. Bolo, I knew, would be telling this bad beat story for the rest of his life.

"The gutshot of the century," said a guy to my right. He held his hand out to shake mine. "Well done."

I blinked, shook his hand, and glanced down at the pot. I was right; he'd been angling for a full house, and got it, but it wasn't enough. I knocked him out and two other players too, without even being aware of it.

"Top three finisher," he said. "Not too shabby, young man."

I peered at the chip count and my winnings. There were only three of us left. The third place finisher walked with $40,000.

"Holy shit."

I sagged with relief but no one leaves a poker tournament until the end. I played like shit for two more agonizing hours until I was knocked out. Third place.

I couldn't get to the cashier with my payment voucher fast enough.

"Third out of a hundred. You should be proud, honey," the woman with bouffant hair said around her snapping gum. Her smile fell. "You don't look so good. You're due for some R and R."

She printed out a cashier's check. I snatched it, then staggered through the casino.

Outside, Jacksonville was roaring like a dragon. I got on my bike, blood streaming down out of my nose, and I carefully rode north.

Ten minutes outside the city, I could breathe again. I pulled over to clean myself up and sat with my helmet in my lap and a $40,000 check in my wallet. Every sinew in my body ached and exhaustion lived in my bones. But a small smile came to my lips as I thought about that win.

*Go out with a bang, they say.* No matter what happened now with Fiona—no matter if she kept me in her life or turned me back to the road—I had played my last game. A twinge of nostalgia wafted over me. Then it was gone.

Whitworth Women's was a five-hour drive from Jacksonville. If I left that night, I'd be there at dawn. Every part of me screamed for sleep but something told me to keep going. That if I got there tomorrow afternoon, it'd be too late. I'd lost my phone and had no way of knowing when Fiona would be released but…

*Tomorrow morning. Early. Be there when she steps out.*

I rolled into Whitworth before dawn. I stopped at the gate, and the officer at the booth checked my ID.

"Picking up?"

"Yeah, Tess Daniels. Is that today?"

He gave me a funny look, then checked his manifest. "Sure is."

He directed me to a far end of the visitor's lot, behind the prison.

A door in the gray stone wall was marked *Processing, NO Re-entry.*

Steve Daniels was already there.

I knew him at once; tall, pale, and red-haired, with a strange buzzing about him. He watched me roll up on the Bonneville with flat eyes. I killed the engine and took off my helmet. We regarded each other in the predawn silence.

He was repulsive, like a clay version of a human being. I thought if I cut him open, insects and maggots would spill out instead of blood.

"You're him," Steve said. "Nik."

*He's been to see her. He's spoken to her...*

Rage coiled in me and I wondered if he'd already sunk his claws back into Fiona. Maybe she'd called him to pick her up...*Because if she had called me, I hadn't answered.*

I climbed off the bike and Steve took a step back. He was taller than me, but I had at least forty pounds of muscle on him. My hands clenched into fists.

"She's not leaving with you," I said.

"You think she's going with you?" he sneered. "I'm her husband."

The words were like poison to my ears, making me flinch.

"She doesn't have to be with either of us," I said slowly, "but she's not going with you." I narrowed my eyes at him. "Did she ask you to be here?"

Steve's eyelids flickered. His tell. "Yes."

"You're a fucking liar."

"She needs me. She has nowhere to go. We have a home togeth—"

I surged forward, cutting him off by gripping him by the throat and then slamming him into the wall. His feet scrabbled, his hands clawed at mine.

"You are going to go away now," I hissed, my voice low and hard. "You're going to vanish. You are not going to speak to or even look at her ever again."

He couldn't reply; I was barely giving him air. The sensation of buzzing intensified. I looked into his wide, panicked eyes and there was nothing there. Emptiness and below that, terror...Images flashed and I 'saw' them through the *ken* as impressions.

An empty field with electric wires buzzing overhead.

An ant farm, the little creatures crawling over themselves.

Steve was a perpetual victim, scurrying to fill the emptiness of his soul, and sucking the life out of those around him for his fuel. I itched to hit him hard, again and again, for all he'd done to Fiona, but I knew in that instant, it wouldn't make an impact beyond bruises and bleeding flesh. He'd only feel sorry for himself; wronged instead of punished.

The *ken* dove deeper into him through the physical contact. Down in the center of the void was a soft pink light. A lone speck of brightness in a deep black sea where the sunlight never reached. No wonder he wanted her. No wonder he'd waited two years to get her back. That small piece of her was more vibrant, more breath-taking than anything within him.

"Her," I seethed, disgust so intense, it was all I could do to keep my hand to his throat. "*You* need *her*. All this time…You imprisoned her. Kept her down. Made her feel like shit. You nearly *killed* her, just so you could keep her."

Steve gasped and struggled, and the *ken* showed me his life without Fiona since she escaped him. A desperate man, barely holding on.

"I see you," I growled. "You've been the weak one all along. And without her, you are nothing. Nothing." I forced myself to draw closer, nose to nose. My hand clenched tighter. "*You…are…nothing.*"

I let him go and he leaned heavily against the wall sucking air. My fingers left marks on his throat.

I said nothing more. Nothing else was needed. I'd stripped away the exoskeleton to reveal the craven coward underneath and he knew it. He stared at me with an animalistic instinct to flee darting behind his eyes.

"She's mine," he said hoarsely. He straightened his collar and backed toward his car, keeping his eyes on me. "My wife…"

I clenched a fist at those hideous words. "Not anymore."

Steve's eyes widened. "You can't just…take her from me."

"She's not a fucking possession," I said through gritted teeth. "And if I ever see you near her again, I'm not going to be nice to you like I was today."

Steve's jaw worked silently and I thought he might cry. He pulled himself together and spat at my feet. "Fuck you. You think you're so tough? Go to—"

I lunged at him, fists cocked and he scurried back, nearly tripping over his feet. He fell in the dirt with a thud and Fiona wasn't there to pick him back up.

He climbed to his feet, and carefully climbed back into his sedan and drove away.

As soon as his car was out of sight, I leaned my hand on the wall and sagged, sucking in huge draughts of air to settle my roiling stomach. The events of last two weeks and all the time on the road threatened to come crashing down too, but I dug deep, and pushed myself off the wall.

I went back to my Bonneville, to sit and wait for Fiona. I was ten steps from the wall when the sound of a door opening came from behind me. I turned, just as the sun broke fully over the western horizon behind me. An officer held the door open and Fiona walked out.

She was still there, all of her, and she was *more*. Taller somehow. The colors around her glowed brighter and God, I loved her. I had never loved anything so much in my life as I loved Fiona the moment she stepped out of the shadows and into the sun.

# Chapter 31

*Fiona*

I walked out of prison wearing a pair of jeans that were too big for me, a faded yellow t-shirt, and the sandals I'd thrown on when I left the apartment the morning after Nate and Griff's party. My dress hadn't survived my incarceration. On my arm was my embroidered bag—empty—but for fifteen dollars for a bus ticket the processing officer had given me. My phony driver's license had been confiscated. My apartment keys were gone. I had no apartment. I had nothing.

*I'm going to be okay.*

I smiled at the CO who held the door for me and stepped outside, to freedom.

And Nikolai…

Time stood still. My breath caught in my throat and the only movement in the entire world was my heart crashing against my chest. He was a dream or a mirage…

*He's gold…*

Nikolai stood all in black as the sun rose behind him, lining him in a halo of gold light. He was both luminous and dark, the dense muscles of his body exuding strength while his sweetly handsome face beheld me in a soft, heart-breaking expression of joy and love.

Love. Gold was love, and Nik was radiating it; it glowed from his skin, touched his hair and glinted off the sharp metal in his ears. I felt saturated.

And then the sun rose higher, and the corona around him

brightened and diffused as the sunlight spilled over the edge of the world. But in my heart, that vision of him would live forever.

"Hey," he said gruffly, his voice thick with emotion. "I don't want to make things harder for you. I just...came to see if you needed a ride anywhere."

Tears sprung to my eyes. I didn't want to stop looking at him.

He dug into his wallet and pulled out an envelope. "And this. I came to give this to you." He held an envelope out to me. "It's something to help you start over again."

"Without you?"

His jaw worked and his beautiful blue eyes shone in the morning sun. "If that's what you want."

"What I want..."

I stepped closer to him and moved into the circle of his arms. I inhaled him, remembering. My eyes drank in every detail of his face, reacquainting. He stiffened against me and his heartbeat pulsed in his neck. His expression told me he didn't dare to hope. Slowly, like melting, I lay my head against his chest and wrapped my arms around him.

He was still for half a second more, and then my eyes fell shut as Nik's arms went around me and held me tight, so tight I could hardly breathe. I felt him press his head to mine, inhaling me. His heart pounded under my cheek. We clung to each other, feeling every place we touched and knowing that it was real. I was free and he was here...

He pulled me away to look at me, to brush the hair from my face, his fingers lingering over the faded bruise around my eye. "Are you okay? Did anyone else hurt you?"

I shook my head, and my fingertips touched a little cut on his lip, then at the edge of the deeper one on his brow. "Who hurt *you*?"

"It's nothing."

"No, tell me what happened."

He shook his head. "I can't. There's too much. And right now I...I just want to know this is real."

My heart broke for the pain and hope in those words; the echoes of his past and how he'd been shunned by the people in the world who were supposed to accept him.

I placed my hands on either side of his face. "It's real, Nik. For the first time in years, I know what I feel. What I want. My own heart was a mystery and strangled by fear until I nearly suffocated. But not anymore."

"There's still so much I haven't told you," he said. "About the *ken*..."

"I know," I said. "But right now, all I feel is love." I fought back tears that threatened to swamp me when I needed him to hear me. "I love you, Nikolai Alexei. I love you."

He swallowed hard, and I felt him under my hands, struggling for control. His gaze swept over my face and at the air around me, staring and hopeful, as if he couldn't believe what he was seeing. Then his eyes fell shut, and he pressed his forehead to mine as my words washed over him.

"Say it again," he whispered.

I held his face in my hands, my lips brushing his as I spoke. "I love you, Nik. I'm in love with you. And I think I have been for a while. I just didn't trust myself to know it was real."

He raised his head, bewildered. "I've never seen this before. I didn't know what I was looking at. So beautiful.... But hearing the words..." He stared at me, his blue eyes full. "That's not me taking. That's you giving."

"Yes," I whispered brokenly. "I love you, Nik, with all that I am."

He held my face in his hands, brushing my tears with his thumbs. "I love you," he said hoarsely. "I love you, Fiona, so much that I feel like I've loved you before. That I'll keep loving you long after this life." He shook his head, his expression pained. "I don't know how else to explain why you give me such peace. From the very beginning."

I pressed my cheek into his hand. "I feel it too, Nik. We've known each other before, haven't we? Because this feels so perfect. Like how it's supposed to be."

I leaned closer and laid my lips to his in a soft kiss.

"This," I whispered against his lips. "How I feel right now...is how it's supposed to be."

I don't know how long we held each other; until another car rolled into the parking lot. I shouldered my bag, and climbed on the back of the Bonneville. Nik handed me a red and black helmet.

"This is new," I said. "My other one was blue and white."

"I picked it up on the way over," he said.

"The way over from where?" I asked gently.

"Jacksonville."

"Jacksonville…Florida? And what were you doing there?"

"Buying you a helmet." He gave me a funny look. "Isn't that what we're talking about?"

I swatted his arm. "Smartass." I leaned my chin on his shoulder. "I want to know everything."

"I'll tell you everything, baby. But first, where to? My apartment?"

"Or Griff and Nate gave me their spare room in their house. Gave *us*," I amended, "the spare room if we want it."

Nik grimaced. "I don't think I'm their favorite person right now."

"I'll explain everything to them. As much as they need to hear, anyway."

He nodded. "I expected one of them or Opal to come get you."

"I was told I was getting out late last night. I didn't want to yank them from their jobs."

"Savannah, then?"

"It's four hours away," I told him. "You look tired, honey, and I'm still trying to process my sudden freedom."

"Are you hungry?" he asked. "Prison food has to suck."

"I wouldn't know," I said. "But if I never see another Snickers bar it'll be too soon."

He twisted on the seat to look at me. "I want to know everything."

I smiled. "You will."

"I love you," he said. "And I know where we should go."

"I love you," I said. "Where should we go?"

"Some place nice. A fancy hotel with room service."

"And a private bathroom with a giant bathtub? I'm sort of over showers right now."

"Whatever you want," he said.

"I have everything I want," I said, squeezing him tight. "Let's go be alone somewhere."

Nik drove the Bonneville southward, and an hour and a half later my eyes widened as he pulled into the circular drive of the Ritz-Carlton at Lake Oconee—a hotel that more closely resembled a stately manor house.

"Nik," I said, as we took off our helmets and the valet approached. "I'm not dressed for a place like this."

He gave me a tired grin. "My money is the right shade of green; that's all that matters."

We checked in with a distinct lack of luggage using Nik's credit card. He'd been right. The staff was courteous despite his tattoos and my second-hand-prison-release-wear. Even so, I was happy to be safely ensconced in a hotel room.

"Oh my God..." I stared, turning in circles. "This is...so nice."

Nik sat heavily on the king bed. "No more than you deserve."

The suite was larger than my apartment in Garden City two times over. I peeked into the cavernous bathroom that was all white ceramic and chrome. A jetted soaker tub sat on a small dais at one end, next to a walk-in shower.

"The tub is perfect," I said, crossing the room to the double-doors that led to a balcony that overlooked the lake where afternoon sunlight glittered on the blue-green water. "And a gorgeous view..." I plopped down on the couch by the window and propped my feet on the coffee table. "Our hotel room has its own living room."

Nik yawned and smiled faintly.

"Oh, Nik." I moved to sit on the bed beside him. "You're dead on your feet."

"I haven't slept much lately."

"Why don't you take a nap while I soak in the tub?"

"What about food?" he asked. "And talk. We need to talk about...everything, don't we?"

I didn't have the ability to read emotions as he claimed to, but it was written in his expression how he feared rejection. How, despite my love for him, he still feared it. Or maybe *because* I loved him, he feared it would hurt him all the more if I couldn't cope with the reality of it...if I believed him at all.

*Do you?*

My exhausted mind had no black-and-white answers, but my heart whispered that my love for Nik wasn't conditional. That I loved him entirely as he was. But there were miles and miles of road etched into the tired lines of his face and I needed to decompress.

I caressed the stubble of his cheek and grazed my fingers through the hair at his temple. "You sleep. I'll tub. We'll meet after for food and talk."

He nodded wearily and lay back on the bed. I touched my fingers to my lips and laid them to his. He smiled faintly but his eyes were already closed. I got up and shut the blinds over the balcony doors and the window, cutting the light until it was pleasantly dim.

In the bathroom, I ran a hot bath, and poured in a copious amount of lavender bubbles. While the tub filled, I glanced at myself in the mirror over the double sink.

"Oh God…"

I looked gaunt. My face was thinner after my short stint in prison, my eyes shadowed with dark rings. My hair hung flat and lifeless down my shoulders, the pink color looked faded.

Tears sprang to my eyes but I blinked them back.

"It's over now."

I piled my hair on my head in a loose bun, then slipped naked beneath the steam and foam. I lay back against the ceramic in that giant tub and waited for the stress and fear from the last few weeks to melt away.

The silence of the bathroom was deafening. There was no silence in either jail or prison. No quiet moments in which to put two thoughts together without a sound or a look from another inmate making me jump. And now the events of the last few weeks came crashing in.

I sat up in the bath, and pulled my knees to my chest. I felt small and naked in my sudden silence and solitude. An island surrounded by a vast ocean.

*Stop. You're being ridiculous.*

Nik knocked on the door, then peeked in. "Hey. You okay?"

I sniffed a small laugh. "Just the person I wanted to see," I said softly. "How did you know…?" I shook my head. "Never mind. Silly question. Couldn't sleep?"

He crossed the bathroom and knelt beside the tub. "Couldn't sleep."

"Because of…me?"

"I felt a great disturbance in the Force."

I laughed but it echoed hollowly in the cavernous bathroom, and died out quickly.

The next moment, Nik was tugging off his boots.

"Shove over," he said.

"What—?"

"Come on," he said. "Shove over. You're hogging the tub."

"What are you doing…?"

I scooted forward, and then a laugh burst out of me as Nik climbed in behind me, fully clothed in jeans and a t-shirt. Water and suds sloshed over the side. Then his arms went around me, gently pulling me to his chest. I knew exactly what he was doing, and it was exactly what I needed.

"Feel whatever you need to feel," he said against my hair. "I got you."

My eyes fell shut and I sagged against him in relief to feel his strong body beneath mine. His arms wrapped around mine across my chest, our fingers entwined. The warm water cocooned us both. I lay for long moments, rising and falling with his breath, his cheek against my hair, and felt what I needed to feel. Relief, exhaustion, gratitude…and guilt, because no matter what had happened or why, Margo still had a long recovery ahead of her.

I cried a little, and Nik held me tighter, and the love I felt for him and from him soothed my turbulent emotions. He gave me peace and said I did the same for him, that I calmed the turbulence of the *ken*. That I was the only one.

I turned over in the circle of his arms and lay against Nik, face to face, my forearms on his chest. His jeans were rough against my naked skin. He watched me for a second, and I felt him *see* me with his *ken*.

*Is this real? Can he…?*

"You can see my emotions?" I asked.

He stiffened slightly. "I can see them. And taste them. And sometimes, when I touch you, I can hear a thought."

"What color am I?"

"Pink."

"What do I taste like?"

"Sugar." He brought his hand, dripping, to touch my cheek. "You taste sweet, like sugar."

I took his hand and placed it over my heart. "Can you hear my thoughts?"

Nik's eyes shone and a muscle in his jaw ticked. "Yes," he said. "You love me."

"Just as you are," I whispered. "I love you just as you are."

He swallowed hard. "It doesn't bother you? What I can see…?"

I shook my head. "I thought I'd feel exposed, but I feel relieved. Safe. I trust you, Nik. I trust you with my heart. Besides, I'm the one who should feel nervous, not you. You can see all of me." I raised my eyes to his. "And you still love me…?"

"I love you, Fiona," he said, brushing the damp hair from my eyes. "Just as you are."

Our eyes held for long moments, both of us basking, then a smile broke over my face. "Okay, glad we had this talk."

He laughed shortly, dispelling the vulnerable moment with the rough sound. "That's it?"

"That's it," I said. "There isn't anything wrong with this love, Nik. Not one thing."

I kissed him, sighing softly into the kiss. I made promises in that kiss. Vows to never doubt him or make him feel unwanted or different for what he was. Because he was beautiful in my eyes—a hard man who'd been through hell and back for me. Who'd suffered for me; it was writ in his tired eyes and the blood that dashed his brow. He had seen so much in the last few weeks. I gave him peace but he gave peace to me. He gave me the freedom to be myself. And he gave me his love.

So much love.

"And now you need some sleep," I said, breaking the kiss.

"I do," he said, his hands sliding up my back under the water. "But you're naked…The struggle is real."

I smiled. "We have time now. We have all the time we want."

We climbed out and Nik stripped out of his wet clothes and left them in the emptying tub. We dried off and wordlessly climbed into bed, naked. He lay back on the pillows and I lay against his chest, my head resting there, his hand playing lazily in my hair.

"This is how we're supposed to be," I murmured.

"Yes," he said, half asleep. "Just like this. Always."

"Always." I wrapped my arm around him, burrowed my face into his neck.

He pulled me tight and with the next exhale, I melted against him.

We slept in the perfect silence that was just us. Him and me. I was his shield, guarding his peace, and he was my foundation, unwavering beneath me.

Always.

# Part IV: Magic

# Chapter 32

*Fiona*

When I awoke, late afternoon sunlight—brassy and warm—slipped in between the blinds at the window. I was wrapped in Nik, his arms around me, my leg thrown over his waist. The sleep had revived my tired mind and I was ready to hear about the last few weeks.

But my body needed him first.

I lay kisses along his neck where the tattoos climbed all the way up to his jawline.

He stirred and came awake with a small sigh. His blue eyes were like liquid sapphires, holding my gaze with a potent mix of love and lust that stole my breath.

"Hi," he said softly.

"Hi," I whispered.

He bent his head to me and we fell into each other. Slowly, at first, with long, deep kisses and hands on each other's faces. Like wading into shallow water…and then we dove under.

Our kisses turned hard and urgent; a wet mashing of mouths and clacking teeth and rasping breaths in our noses because it was more necessary to kiss than breathe. Hands became greedy, then demanding. I felt his body coiling with unspent need, and the thought of what he was capable of made my heart pound.

His hands found my breasts, they fit perfectly in his palms, and I arched into his touch without a shred of self-consciousness or shame. This was me—my body—and I felt beautiful in it, in my nakedness, and in Nik's eyes that drank me in.

"Krasivaya," he growled.

He moved lower, his mouth finding one nipple. He bit to the point of pain and then sucked and licked to soothe the ache away. I gasped, my fingers making a fist in his hair as he moved to the other.

"Nik, please," I managed, wondering how we'd waited this long. "I need…" I swallowed hard. "I need you…now."

He reached for his wallet on the nightstand.

"No," I said, pulling him back to me. "I want to feel everything."

"You sure?"

"They were to protect myself. I don't need to protect myself from you."

"No, you don't," Nik said, his voice tightening as I moved up on to him, to straddle him. I caught my breath, fought my own body's hunger to slow down, to make it last.

"I trust you, Nik." I took the hard length of him in my hand. "I want you to have all of me."

"Fiona," he said through gritted teeth.

"And I want all of you," I said, and sank down, taking him in. My eyes fell shut at the perfect, heavy pressure of him, stretching and filling me.

When our skin was flush against one another; when he was buried completely inside me, Nik made a sound deep in his chest; as if he were in pain and ecstasy at the same time.

"Christ, you feel so good," he breathed. "I can feel…everything."

"Yes…"

Nik's heated gaze went to where we were joined, then up to me. I could feel the power in his body beneath me and inside me. I felt the love he had for me like a gentle caress, but the lust that coiled in him was as strong as it had been the night we met, and hot like a licking flame.

Slowly…so slowly, I began to move, rolling my hips, grinding down on him. I could feel the tension in him and see it in the way his biceps bulged. He wanted to move me. He wanted to lift me up and slam me down while he thrust upward. My heart raced at the thought. I wanted that too…but not yet. I resisted him and he felt it. He was strong enough to do whatever he wanted to me ten times over, but he read my want, and bit his frustration back.

"Fiona…" he said, like a warning.

"I know," I whispered. "Just a little more…"

I leaned forward, rested my forearms on either side of him, on the inked muscles between neck and shoulder, still rising and falling on him. His control was hanging by a thread. I felt like a surfer, riding the curl of a wave just before it crashes, knowing it's *going* to crash and take me under…

*Now…*

I kissed him—a trembling touch of my lips to his— and then I invaded his mouth with my tongue and captured his lower lip in my teeth and sucked.

A low groan rumbled up from deep in Nik's chest, and then his control evaporated. He kissed me back, a hard sweep of his tongue along mine, while his arm snaked around my waist. He lifted me without breaking our connection and took me down onto my back, to drive into me, over and over.

The wave crashed and I drowned in him. Sweat and hot skin, the slapping sound of his pounding body into me. I clung to him, my head thrown back, nails clawing helplessly at his shoulders.

"Oh God, Nik…"

"Come," he growled, his mouth hovering over mine, his hips grinding relentlessly. "Come for me, Fiona. Now…"

My body obeyed. I cried out as an orgasm swamped my body, tossing me on a delirious tide of sensation.

"Yes…" he breathed in relief. "Fuck, yes…"

He slowed his punishing thrusts and lowered his mouth to mine for a soft, perfect kiss. I kissed him to breathe, and he groaned his release into my mouth. I swallowed it down, held him as he collapsed on top of me, and felt the heat of his climax spill into me.

We caught our breaths and then Nik's eyes softened, his kisses turned gentle. Still inside me, he kissed me, over and over; long, deep sweeps of his tongue. His hands cupped my face and *God*, the way he looked at me...

"More," he whispered. "I want more."

My head bobbed, my mouth already craning for his. "Yes...God, yes..."

And we began again.

Over and over, we brought each other to one tidal wave of release after another, pausing only long enough to catch our breaths and then reach for each other again, until finally our bodies demanded food and water.

Nik ordered room service and we ate peppered steaks and mashed potatoes in bed, and then shared a cup of chocolate mousse. Nik offered me a spoonful. I took the chocolate in my mouth, my eyes locked on his, then ran my tongue over my lower lip. His widened slightly, and then he tossed the spoon aside, hauled me to him, and kissed me hard and hot.

"Sweet," he growled. "So fucking sweet..."

We dove back into bed, drowned in each other, until finally, in the deepest part of the night, the swells of ecstasy tossed us ashore, gasping for breath and utterly spent.

---

"What is...anger?" I asked.

Nik chuckled. "Is this a quiz?"

We were in our customary positions, me lying over his chest, my fingers tracing the lines of his ink, while his fingers played in my hair or slipped down my back to give me pleasant shivers.

"Yes," I said, undeterred. "Is it red? Like, *I'm so mad, I'm seeing red?*"

"Sometimes," he said. "There are some patterns but it's mostly different from person to person. Anger is sometimes a red fog, sometimes a buzzing cloud, like wasps, and you know to stay the fuck away."

My eyes widened. "Real wasps?"

"Not real," he said. "It's more of an impression. My rational mind knows nothing is there but the *ken* translates it however it wants."

"What is pink? You said I was pink."

"You're *mostly* pink," Nik said. "It varies with your mood but pink seems to be your default setting."

I laughed. "But what does it *mean*?"

"Pink is compassion. Kindness. Caring for others."

I nodded, my thoughts going to Hailey.

"And now you're tinged blue," Nik said. "A mist. It comes when you think about children."

Nik's smile was soft but I could see him brace himself for my reaction.

"You're right," I said, smiling at him. "I miss Hailey."

He nodded, eased a sigh from under me. I brushed the melancholia away.

"What about…sex? What happens during sex?"

"*A lot* of things happen during sex," Nik said, with a grin.

"Like what?" I said with a laugh. "Can you see my orgasms?"

I was only kidding but Nik's answer was dead serious.

"Sure."

I lifted my head to look at him. "What…? Noooo."

"Oh, yes."

"What do they look like?"

"Kind of silvery, like shooting stars, or sparklers on the Fourth of July…"

"You're lying," I said, laughing.

He held up his hand. "God's honest…"

"You're telling me that orgasms are *literally* fireworks? Like how they're sometimes shown in a cheesy movie?"

"I didn't say they're *fireworks*, but that's a good goal to shoot for." Nik walked his fingers down my back. "I'll have to step up my game."

I stared incredulously, and then laughed. "You're lucky you're so cute." I settled myself back onto his chest, facing him.

"There was a lot of pink in that portrait you did of me," I said after a moment. "I love that painting. It feels…honest. Like I was looking into a mirror that saw more than just my physical reflection. Will you keep painting?"

"I don't know," he said. "I thought I was done until I met you. That sketch on the cocktail napkin was the first thing I'd drawn since I got out of the hospital."

"Did you draw before that? As a kid?"

Nik's eyes darkened in the dim light of the lone lamp in our room. "Yeah, I did. It helped, to make portraits like that. It helped me to cope with the *ken*."

I found his hand and pulled it to my lips. "When did the *ken* start?"

"When I was real small," Nik said. "Maybe I've had it since forever, but I only remember talking about it to my parents when I was eight or so. My dad thought I was messing around, as if I'd said I had an imaginary friend."

"And your mom?"

"She was okay with it, at first. She thought I was being imaginative too, until a few years later when my dad's abuse got worse. Then I'd try to protect her, or ask her what I was seeing when she bent to kiss me goodnight. That's when she got scared. Said I had the devil in me. A few years after that, my father left us. He said that I was crazy and that my mother indulged my lies and made it worse. He said I drove him away."

My heart ached for him, to carry so much blame as a little boy. "And that's when she put you in the hospital?" I asked softly.

He nodded. "Everything I told you at the beach that day was true," he said. "They diagnosed me with severe claustrophobia, agoraphobia with visual and auditory 'hallucinations.' It wasn't a first-rate hospital. The doc in charge had no clue what to do with me and I told him things about himself he didn't like. Frequently."

"And they shocked you for that."

"It didn't do anything except scare me and give me headaches." His eyes darkened. "And it killed my desire to paint."

"You're an incredible painter," I said. "I hope you keep going."

He smiled faintly, his fingers twining with mine. "Maybe I will."

"Tell me the rest," I said. "Tell me what happened after Nate and Griff's party."

Nik told me everything, beginning with his mother's passing in St. Louis; his harried ride back to Garden City where he learned about my accident; a race to Whitworth to see me in the prison, and then his anguished, aimless drive south.

As he spoke, I closed my eyes and listened, and my imagination must've been in overdrive as I could see it all so clearly.

I saw a young mother dance in the sprinklers with her little boy.

I saw Nik standing in my empty apartment, shocked and panicked to hear I was in jail.

I felt the hopeless despair as he rode south until his motorcycle ran out of gas on a winding road through a forest in the driving rain.

"You're going to think the next part is crazy," he said.

"The whole thing is crazy. Why stop now?" I said, poking him in the side.

He told me about the poor deer and how he'd ended its suffering, and how Nik had shared a round of whiskey and beer with a man named Evan who claimed he could dream the future.

"He dreams the future?" I asked.

Nik nodded. "It sounded crazy at first, but he was right about everything."

"Magic," I said. "There's magic in the world after all."

His fingers were warm on my skin. "Yeah, I guess there is."

He continued his story, telling me that Evan said Margo was the key to my freedom. Nik drove to Miami Beach and sat with Margo and used his *ken* to touch the loneliness in her.

"Empathy," I whispered. "She confided in you because she knew you understood her."

"Margo was on the verge," Nik said. "No. Beyond the verge. She teetered over the edge. Margo threw herself in front of your car, Fiona," he said in a low voice. "The only reason she didn't fall all the way was because you're a careful driver."

I nodded, my eyes full. "Griff told me something like that. He said there was no way I could have avoided hitting her. But I still feel awful."

"She says she's sorry for that. And for you winding up in prison."

I traced the tattoo of a moon tearing through wisps of clouds under Nik's right pec. "If I hadn't gone to prison, I wouldn't have confronted Steve. He was the boogeyman for so long, and then I sat down with him, face to face, and it was so obvious that he was nothing to me. That my fear had been feeding on itself for so many years..." A small smile came to my lips. "But you want to hear something strange?"

"Why stop now?" Nik said.

"You said it was raining that night your bike ran out of gas?" I asked.

"Yeah, it was."

"And there was something on the side of the road. A dark shape…"

"The deer," Nik said. "It had been hit by a car hours earlier."

"I saw it," I said. "Evan…he drove up to you in the dark. I saw his headlights against the rain…"

"Where did you see this?"

"I dreamt it," I said.

"You did?" Nik's eyes snapped open but then he blinked slowly as the thought washed over him.

"More than once," I continued. "But that's all I can remember."

"You dreamt right."

"I wonder why."

Nik stretched and settled deeper in the pillows, his voice heavy. "Evan said that what he and I do is to tap into the energies of the universe." He smiled sleepily at me. "Maybe you did that too."

"Maybe, but how? Why me?"

Nik reached for me, pulled me up to nestle me against his chest.

"You're part of this too, baby," he said. He closed his eyes and I thought he had fallen asleep when he finally said, "After I killed the deer to end its suffering, Evan said a prayer over its body. A Navajo prayer that the Native Americans used when they hunted. To thank the animal for giving its life so that they might live. Evan said it meant *a gratitude greater than thank you*. But we hadn't been hunting. We didn't use the animal for food. At the time, I didn't know why he said it."

"But you do now?"

Nik opened his eyes to look at me, blue like a deep pool of clear water.

"Evan found me with the deer, and without him I wouldn't have known to seek out Margo. I was planning to sit with my bike and wait out the storm. I only walked that road because I heard the deer's cries. I don't know what would have happened if he had missed me. I don't know what I would have done if I had lost you." He closed his eyes again.

"That deer died for you and me," he said, "so that we might live."

# Chapter 33

## Nikolai

The following morning, I called up the front desk and had them deliver toothbrushes and toothpaste along with a breakfast of eggs, bacon, grits, and fruit. The food arrived on a cart covered under silver domes with a silver pitcher of coffee.

We ate and after Fiona took a shower and then sat on the edge of the bed, wrapped in a white towel. "I need to call Griffin and Opal before they call the Whitworth and worry."

"I'm going to take a turn in the shower," I told her, with a small grin. "So I don't hear the yelling."

She grabbed me before I could climb out of bed. "I'm going to tell them you spoke to Margo and got her to tell her story. They're going to love you for helping me."

"They love you more," I said, kissing her softly. "That's how it should be."

I took a shower and brushed my teeth. I came out with a towel wrapped around my waist and stopped midstride when I saw Fiona sitting on the bed, still wrapped in her own towel with her bag in her lap. Her damp hair fell to curtain her face. The colors around her were a murky mix of joy and nerves, excitement and uncertainty.

"Fiona?"

"What's this?" She held up the check for $40,000 I'd slipped into her bag the night before.

"I told you," I said. "It's yours. To help you start over."

"Forty thousand dollars?" She shook her head before I could speak. "No, I know what this is. It's your life savings, times two. And you were just…going to give it to me?"

"It's your Costa Rica money."

Her eyes shone with the warmth of her love—a deep pink that glowed gold at the edges, like the sky during a sunrise.

"Where did you get it? Poker? I'm no expert but you'd have to play big to win this much. Is that what you were doing in Jacksonville?"

"I won it with the money I'd been saving," I said. "The money I didn't know what to do with until suddenly I did."

Fiona blinked back tears. "Nik… What if…I didn't want to be with you? What if I were still mad or thought you were lying? You'd have been left with nothing."

"It's your money, Fiona. I think it's always been your money." I sat beside her and slipped my arms around her waist. "And I had hope."

"Love and hope," she murmured, sniffed. Then touched my brow near the small gash by my brow. "And this?"

*God, I love her.* Fiona's care and concern for me wrapped around me like warm water. I knew she wanted to hear the whole story but there was no sense in dimming her light over the ugliness of Will and his friends, or the tournament.

"I ran into some old friends," I said. "I'm fine, I swear. It's not a story worth telling."

*The gutshot of the century isn't a story worth telling?* I bit back a smile. *Not today.*

Fiona narrowed her eyes. "I saw how tired you were when you came back. I may not have the *ken* but I know this forty thousand dollars didn't come easily, did it?"

*Make her smile. Keep her in the sun.*

"No, I had a tough time, actually. And the only thing that will help me get over it is sex. Lots and lots of sex."

A laugh burst out of her before she could stop it, and she swatted my arm. "You've had lots and lots of sex. That's all we've done since check-in."

"See? I feel better already."

She rolled her eyes, a reluctant smile on her lips. I pulled her close to me, kissed the curve of her neck.

"It isn't my money, it's *our* money," she said, and gasped as my teeth nipped and sucked lightly. "For wherever we go next. Okay?"

"Okay," I murmured against her warm skin. "Where are we going next?"

She pulled away to look at me. "I still want Costa Rica," she said. "I wanted to run far, to escape Steve, but I chose Costa Rica for a reason. I wanted the beaches and mountains and forest. And I still want that." Hope flared around her, a soft delicate glow. "Maybe they'd let me teach English to little ones. And I think it would be good for you too. Not so many people. Peaceful." She raised her eyes to mine. "Do you still want to go?"

"Yeah, baby, I do." And that was the truth. I'd go anywhere she wanted; whatever made her happy, but I wondered if there was something in that country that was for me too. A purpose.

Fiona's colors flared bright and beautiful. She kissed me softly. "I love you," she said, then pulled away. "But I have two years of a parole from my commutation deal and five hundred hours of community service. I want to do the service, but two years…?"

"Evan told me of a contact who can help get you a passport, but Fiona, it's risky."

"I know," she said. "But I don't want to wait. And I don't want to live with the name Tess Daniels anymore. That girl is gone. I want to start the life we're meant to have."

I held her face. "Are you sure that's what you want to do?"

She nodded. "It's what's supposed to happen. I can feel it. And Evan…everything he told you would happen, happened, didn't it?"

"Yeah, it did."

"Do you trust him?"

I thought about Evan, a man I'd known for a handful of hours. *My brother…*

"With my life," I said.

Fiona's face lit up in a smile and then she kissed me, deep and hard. "Oh my God, is this happening?" she breathed against my lips, her body pressed tight to mine. "Are we really going to go to Costa Rica?"

"Yes," I said, stripping off her towel. "But not yet."

We drove the three hours back to Savannah, arriving at twilight. We tried my apartment first, but my key didn't work anymore. I cupped my hand and peered in the front window.

"They rented it to someone else," I said. "Someone with furniture."

"Oh, Nik…What about your painting?"

I turned to Fiona. "I'll paint you another one. I'll paint you a hundred times over if you want."

"It's not that it was me, it was your art…" Her gaze darted to me. "Wait, you'll paint again? Really?"

I shrugged with a small smile. "Someday."

*But not here.*

We drove into Savannah just as the sun began to sink in the west. Nate and Griffin greeted us at the door. They both hugged and kissed and fawned over Fiona, and then Nate fixed me with a cool look.

"Mr. Young," he said stiffly. "We meet again."

"Drama queen," Griffin said with a roll of his eyes. He extended his hand to me with a warm smile. "Fiona explained everything this morning. I can't thank you enough for what you did for her."

"Just righting a wrong," I said.

"Hmmph," Nate snorted.

Fiona moved to stand beside me and rested her head in the crook of my shoulder. "Behave, Nathaniel," she said. "I love him. And you have to love whomever I love. That's the rule."

Griffin's heart was open and easy to forgive. He beamed at us like a proud parent, but Nate's thoughts were full of Fiona's pain the night of the party.

"No, I get it," I said to him. "And I'm sorry. I never meant to hurt her. And I never will again."

Nate tapped his foot, his arms still crossed, and then threw up his hands. "Well, I'm mixing cocktails and I happened to have made too much, so get in here and help us drink them. Griff, how's dinner coming? It's not like I'm *starving* or anything."

Nate turned into the house, his voice echoing back to us.

Griff leaned in to me. "He offered you booze. All is forgiven."

"I'll take it."

Fiona glanced up at me, smiling, and we followed them inside.

The Millers had decorated their new home in a simple, but elegant style. The dining table was set for six, for Opal and her husband. When they joined us on the back patio, Opal hugged Fiona tight. The two women spoke a few words. Then while Fiona and Jeff said their hellos, Opal took me aside.

"I'm sorry, Opal," I said, before she could speak. "I'm sorry for what happened that night and for making Fiona so upset. I'm glad you were there for her."

She stopped, taken aback. "Oh. Right. Well, I said some things to you that day at the garden shop…"

"You were protecting Fiona. Never apologize for that."

Opal stared at me a moment longer, then narrowed her eyes at me. "Fiona tells me you're a pro poker player." She gave me a sharp look with a smile behind it. "Am I being played?"

"I'm being sincere. I weighed the odds that you were either going to kick my ass or forgive me." I grinned. "I hedged my bet."

She gave me a suspicious look. "Come here, you big lug." She pulled me in for a hug. "She told me what you did with Margo," she said against my ear. "Thank you."

I took her gratitude and relief, but over all that was her love for Fiona. I hugged her tight. "I'll keep her safe, I promise."

She pulled away. "That sounds like a goodbye."

I put on my poker face and said nothing.

"Dolores, Louisiana," Fiona said, watching me pack a small bag. "Never heard of it."

"The contact Evan gave me is there. If I didn't trust him, I wouldn't even consider it."

We were in our room in the Miller's house, a week after Fiona's release from prison. Early morning light spilled over the bed and glowed golden in her hair that was freshly dyed with long pink streaks and tousled from last night's activities. Nate complained every morning we were going to shake the rafters loose in his new house, but still we couldn't keep our hands off of each other.

"It's such a long drive," Fiona said. "I hate being apart from you."

"Me too, baby," I said and that was an understatement. Being without the peace she brought me was going to be bad enough, but I hated the idea of leaving and not being able to fall asleep tangled in her, or not see her face the first thing upon waking.

*I love her too much.*

"It's only for a few days," I said, mostly for my benefit. "I can do one more big road trip for a good cause."

"I wish I could come with you."

The terms of her parole wouldn't allow her to leave the State of Georgia and she'd already begun her five hundred hours of community service at a shelter that housed victims of domestic violence, many of whom had escaped their abusive partner and now had nowhere else to go.

Even if we had a passport ready to go that very minute, Fiona would've stayed to complete that service for those women. She said it was the only way she felt okay about breaking the terms of her release.

"And more than that," she'd told me after her first day, "I want to help. I feel like I can give something back, even if it's just a little comfort and empathy."

"Comfort and empathy go a long way," I'd said.

Now, I kissed her goodbye and she held me close. "I love you. Be safe."

"I love you. I will."

I hit the road just after dawn and drove almost straight through, making only two short stops for gas and food. I arrived in Louisiana at 9:30 that night, and went straight to The Rio. It was a small dive bar on the outside, but on the inside, it was a miniature disco palace. Rainbow flags decorated the wall above the liquor bottles. The person I could only assume was Del del'Rio was behind the bar in full 1970s Diana Ross costume, with big hair and a gold sequined dress. "Ain't No Mountain High Enough" blared on the sound system. The patrons at the bar were all male and a cloud of suspicion and curiosity followed me from the door to the bar.

"What's your poison, sugar?" Del asked me, tossing a cocktail napkin in front of me with a hand covered in costume jewelry and red lacquered nails.

"Whiskey, neat," I said.

She poured the drink and set it down in front of me. "Ain't you something," she said, taking in my tattoos and piercings. Then her dark eyes widened under layers of makeup and fake eyelashes. "Now hold on a minute...Do I know you?"

"No," I said, "but we have a mutual friend."

"And what is our mutual friend's name?"

"Justin," I said with a grin. "That's what's on his driver's license, anyway."

A smile broke over Del's face and then she slapped her hand on the bar with a hearty laugh. "I like that," she said. "*Justin* called not three days ago and told me to expect a tattooed, pierced motorcycle man inquiring about special documents."

"I heard you had the connection."

"You heard right, baby," Del said. "Justin's wife is more dear to me than The Rio. Any friend of theirs is a friend of mine. What's your name?"

"Nik."

"You just get in town, Nik?"

"Just this minute."

"You look tired, sugar. Take a room at the hotel down the road, then call me here with your room number. I'll have my boy get in touch with you tomorrow."

"Thanks, Del," I said. "I appreciate it."

"He don't come cheap," she warned.

"I hope not," I replied. "I can't have any trouble."

"No trouble. He's worth every penny. For you?"

"No, my girlfriend," I said.

Warmth emanated from Del and her colors were brighter than her costume and makeup. I knew—again—that Evan hadn't let us down.

"I should have known," Del said. "For love. And when it's for love, there *ain't no mountain high enough*," she sang along with the music. Del patted my cheek, still singing and sashayed down the bar to help another customer.

I took a room at the motel and it all started to come back to me: the feeling of being in a shitty motel in the middle of nowhere after a ten-hour road trip.

*For Fiona*, I thought. *This is the last time. For her.*

Four days later, Fiona and I were in a back booth at the burger joint, watching a short, wiry young man named James stuff his face was a bacon cheeseburger. Given his cloak-and-dagger phone act, I'd expected a more sinister criminal. This guy looked like he worked at the Genius Bar at an Apple store.

*Maybe that's his day job.*

"It's deep web stuff," James said over a bite of food. He washed it down with a swig of Dr. Pepper. "I can craft a new identity to go behind the name on the passport in case you get checked. That's my deluxe package. $10,000. Five now, five later. I'll need a passport photo and whatever name you want. It'll take me about three weeks to put it all together."

"I can pick my own name?" Fiona said. Her hand clutched mine under the table.

"Yesss," James drawled, annoyed. "I don't do stolen passport photo-swap bullshit. I craft one out of the same material the government uses. It's a fucking work of art. No one's going to be able to tell the difference."

Fiona bit her lip. "I can't use Starling anymore. But I want to keep Fiona. It's who I am now. I don't know another last name…"

James rolled his eyes and took a bite of this burger.

I glanced at him and then Fiona, suddenly nervous as hell. "You can have my name," I said slowly.

The colors around Fiona were brilliant—the most stunning sunrise of pink and gold I'd ever seen. "Your name?"

I glanced to James again who was still chewing and pretending to be extremely interested in something on his phone.

"Yeah, baby. If you want it." I swallowed. "Do you?"

"Yes," she whispered. "I do."

"Settled then?" James said loudly. "Great. So what's the name?"

She looked at me with so much love in her eyes and heart, radiating from every part of her, I swear to God it was all I could do to keep from breaking down like a goddamn baby.

"Fiona Young."

We left the restaurant and she fell into my arms. We kissed and held each other and kissed some more, and it didn't matter that we were standing in the parking lot of some cheap burger joint.

*There is nothing wrong with this love,* Fiona had said once, and she was right.

# Chapter 34

## Nikolai

Five weeks later, Fiona had completed her community service and had received her new passport. I knew it would work perfectly. I compared it to mine; they had the same feel, the same materials, the same look, the same layers of watermarks and colors.

*The same last name.*

The Miller's threw us a going away/unofficial wedding ceremony in their backyard. Opal and Jeff, and Nancy and her little Hailey were the only guests.

I stood beside Nate, our officiant, at the far end of the short, grassy expanse of their yard, with Griff, my best man, to my left. Jeff and Nancy watched from white lawn chairs as Hailey walked from the back door of the house, across the grass in a little pink dress, dropping pink rose petals from a basket. Opal came next in a flowered dress and stood on the other side of Nate as Maid of Honor. She shook her fist at me and then smiled and laughed.

I smiled back but it fell off my face to see Fiona come out of the house.

She wore a simple, slippery dress that draped over her body like liquid and was the same shade of pink as her hair. She carried a bouquet of gardenias, the scent of which mingled with her own sweet scent, and her hair was adorned with wildflowers. My heart stopped at the smile she gave me as she came to stand beside me.

"Hi," she said softly.

"Hi," I replied, my voice hardly a whisper.

"Oh my God stop, you two," Nate scolded. "I'm going to cry before we even get started."

Our little ceremony began.

We spoke vows to protect each other, to keep each other safe; to love each other for who we were in every way.

We exchanged rings made of sterling silver overlaid with polished zebra wood; Fiona's was smaller and delicate, mine was wide and heavy. Fiona slipped the ring over my finger, over the W on my *pawn* tattoo. I'd thought about getting them removed but tattoos are permanent for a reason, to remind you of where you came from and what you had been through. A wedding band from Fiona to break up the word *pawn* felt perfect. I was no longer a hoax or a pawn; the *ken* had a purpose, and every day I drew closer to discovering it as it whispered in the back of my mind. With Fiona, I would.

"And now," Nate said, "with no authority vested in me whatsoever, I declare you husband and wife, or a reasonable facsimile thereto." He inclined his head to me. "You may now kiss the fugitive. Bride! Sorry, I meant bride."

I held Fiona's face, kissed her softly, and in the golden glow of her light, we whispered our own, private vows.

"I've loved you before," I said. "I'll love you forever."

I felt a tear slip down to touch my fingers. "I will love you for all of this life," she whispered. "And I will love you in the next."

There was a smattering of applause and cheers from our handful of guests, and then Hailey flew into Fiona's arms. I watched my wife pick the little girl up and hold her tight, and rain kisses on her little cheek.

*My wife...*

It wasn't official but she was my wife in every sense of the word; in my heart and soul, and I didn't need a piece of paper to validate what I felt for her. It had no boundaries. And I made another vow, a private one, that we would build a family together, somehow. Not only to make up for the cold, emptiness of our pasts, but to create a future that would be filled with warmth and light.

*Fiona has so much to give...*

I watched as she spun Hailey around. The little girl squealed in laughter; Fiona's head was thrown back, her own joy radiating from her in a beautiful light; a brilliant sunrise that glowed with love and hope.

Love and hope.

She had given me so much of both; my heart was full of love for her…and a gratitude greater than thank you.

# Epilogue I

The man walked up the dock in the failing twilight. The woman was up on the top deck of the houseboat, watching him approach. He knew she had been up there every night since he'd left. Six months pregnant, she moved gracefully off her chair and down the ladder.

He met her at the railing of the houseboat, but she stepped onto the dock before he could come aboard. She circled his neck with her arms. Her belly pressed against him gently and he closed his eyes against the sensation.

"You're back," she sighed against his rough denim jacket.

"I'm back." He stroked her dark hair. "I missed you."

"There's a solution for that," she said and held him tighter. "Don't leave again."

"I won't," he said. *At least not until the baby's born*, he thought but didn't say. He didn't know if a dream would call him again, or how urgently, but he knew he'd have to heed it if it did.

But for now, he was home.

The woman pulled back to look at him, to brush back a lock of blond hair that fell down to his chin.

"How did it go?" She smiled archly, her scar silvery in the swelling moonlight. "A successful mission?"

He returned her smile. "Very. They found each other. I think they'll be happy."

"How do you know?"

"Just a feeling I have…"

"Tell me about it?"

"Can I shower first?" He asked, pulling her closer. "I might need some help…Lots of hard-to-reach places."

She kissed his lips softly, then deeper. "I can help."

She led him inside the house, and they stripped naked and stepped into the little shower. She lathered him with a soapy washcloth, to wash the dirt of the road from his skin. He turned in her arms to kiss her.

"I'm so glad you're back," she said. "But I'm glad you went too, if it helped them." She looked up at him from under the rain of the shower. "Will they be as happy as we are?"

The man looked down at his wife, his hand finding the swell of her belly, and feeling the kick of his son beneath.

"They will."

# Epilogue II

*Two years later...*

## Fiona

"¿Cuántas hay?" I asked my class, pointing to the ten sketches of cats on my board. "Contemos. En inglés," I added.

Twenty five-year-olds in blue and white uniforms stared up at me with twenty pairs of dark eyes, and then twenty voices counted in unison as I pointed to each cat.

"One, two, three, four, five, six, seven, eight, nine, ten."

"Very good," I said.

The bell rang and they scurried for their backpacks, some running to throw their little arms around me first. I watched them go, taking their sweet laughter with them, and leaving the schoolroom dim and quiet.

After an hour of prep for the next day, I packed up my bag and headed out of the school. I waved goodbye to some of the other teachers and jumped on my bicycle for the ride home. Our casita lay a mile outside of the village of San Josecito, and over a bumpy path that led east, away from the blue waters of the Pacific, and deeper into the jungle along the Rio Uvita.

The path branched off and I took the right fork to where our little three-bedroom house—all warm wood— was tucked into the forest. I rode my bike to the small clearing in front that Nik called 'the driveway', then walked the bike through my garden, in between the long, low wooden boxes—one filled with flowers, another fruit, another herbs and vegetables.

I leaned the bike against the side of the casita. Above, hummingbirds flitted over the feeders I had hung from the roof. The air smelled of green things, and beneath that, of bougainvillea and the faint salt of the ocean.

Inside, the casita was wide-open spaces, all of the same warm wood that glowed gold at night when the lamps were lit. A plate of fruit was left out for me. I smiled and popped a grape into my mouth. The casita was quiet, which meant Nik had a client out back.

I moved through the living area with its simple rattan furniture and brightly embroidered cushions and pillows we'd bought from local artisans. The walls were vibrant with Nik's work. His art, that was more than paint on a canvas, but life on display.

I went out of the back door and took a path that was bordered by crotons and ferns to the small wooden structure at the edge of our property.

Nik called it the shack. I called it his studio.

There were only two walls, the rest left open to the jungle. I peeked around a corner. A tarp lay spread out over the entire small space, stained in a hundred different places with bright drops of paint.

Today, an older man from the village sat on the stool. Nik, barefoot in jeans and a white undershirt, stood behind a large canvas, three or four oil-pastels in his hand. A tray of fifty more sat on a table beside him. Nik was a restless painter; if his hand wasn't putting color to canvas, he was pacing behind it, then peeking around it to better *see* his subject.

A sweet ache bloomed in my heart at today's portrait. Nik had painted the old man in a halo of brilliant yellow light, and laughing joyfully, his eyes full of life and his smile broad and easy. Subtly, light seeped through the cracks of the man's wrinkled skin, as if he were a source of light himself. His wispy white hair glowed.

Around the edges of the yellow corona, Nik had painted a night sky, which I thought seemed at odds with his subject at first. But as I watched Nik, I saw him take a good long look at the old man, and then choose a gray oil-pastel. He began to draw a moon at night, dashing it with white so that it looked silvery and bright as it emerged from behind wispy clouds. The clouds blended flawlessly with the man's hair, so it looked as if the night sky was the man's dream.

"Tell me about your wife," Nik said as he painted.

The man, smiled, creating more crinkles. I thought he must smile often and easily; those lines were deep.

"Oh, she was...how you Americans say? Una romántica?"

"Oh yeah?" Nik said.

The moon was coming to life before my eyes—Nik painted fast, his hand sweeping and curving over the canvas, then moving in tighter for quick, expert brushes of his paint.

"Sí," the man said. "A romantic. Every night, she called to me. 'The moon is coming out,' she'd say. 'Come share the moon.'"

I bit the inside of my cheek.

Nik finished the moon and in a few sweeping strokes, had rendered a beach of smooth sand bathed in moonlight along the bottom of the canvas.

"She liked me to walk with her on the beach every night," the old man said, and I watched Nik paint footsteps in the sand, as if they were pressed there by the man's words as he spoke them.

The old man chuckled. "She liked to hold hands like we were young lovers instead of married fifty years." He looked at Nik. "You're married?"

"Yes," Nik said.

"You hold her hand every night," the man said. "If you know what's good for you."

Nik smiled and he turned his head subtly in my direction for a quick second. "I will."

I grinned and retreated quietly to let them finish. The man would never know that the paint came before his words. He wouldn't see the canvas until it was done and by then he would believe that Nik painted only what he'd told him.

It had started with me.

Nik painted me to replace the portrait that had been lost in Savannah. I loved it as much as the first; but there were differences. The girl in this portrait was radiantly happy and the pink around her was tinged with gold.

One night, we asked some new friends we had made in the village to come over for dinner. They saw the portrait and one asked Nik to paint her. He did, quietly asking questions of her here and there in his low voice, like small talk; innocuous conversation you'd hear between a hairdresser and a client.

The woman wept when she saw the finished product.

She told a friend and he came for a portrait. Then another. Then people from the village came trading fruit or fish, or a handful of money for a chance to sit for Nik.

Our village of San Josecito was near Uvita, which held a music festival every year. Nik painted there, and the line to see him stretched nearly to the beach.

After that, people began to filter in from all over the world. Not in huge droves but in manageable trickles, some willing to pay hundreds or thousands of dollars. One art critic called him the Marc Chagall of portraitists. But we needed to keep a low profile. Nik declined all press and interviews, and kept his fame at a level of a local curiosity: something not to be missed if you were vacationing in Uvita.

But the clients were steady. I think some suspected there was more going on in Nik's handshake that began every painting session. How could they not suspect? His paintings revealed who they were.

"You see them," I told him after a client left in happy tears. "They feel *seen*."

More than one told him that their portrait sessions were a kind of therapy. And when they saw the finished product, it felt as if a piece of themselves—or many pieces—had fallen into place.

"The irony is, that's how I feel," Nik told me. "With every portrait I paint, I feel a piece of myself coming together. So many broken pieces shattered all over…and now I'm putting them back where they belong."

"It helps everyone. Your *ken* helps."

"Evan told me that was the way to survive it. I just couldn't see how." He turned to me. "It helps them but it helps me too, which is why it feels wrong sometimes to take their money."

But Nik only took what they could afford to pay—what they felt was right. He wanted to do it for free, but it was important to his subjects that they give him something.

And we had an adoption pending.

Araceli was eighteen months and currently living in an orphanage in a northern province. Our adoption agent, Sara, told us we were in the final stages of the adoption. The Civil Registry liked us. They liked Nik's painting and my teaching; how we were a part of the community, and gave back to it, and lived among it, not off it like permanent tourists.

In the casita, a ceiling fan turned above my head as I took down the photo of Araceli that was pinned to the wall above the sink. Dark curls framed her face and large dark eyes peered at me. The process was so slow; she wouldn't be ours for almost another year…if we were approved.

We could wait. From the instant Sara showed me her photo, I knew we'd wait for her forever.

Nik came in and poured himself a glass of orange juice from a glass pitcher on the counter. His fingers left smears of paint on the glass.

"How did it go?" I asked.

"Good," he said, though he looked distracted. "How was your day?"

"Lovely," I said. "Same as the day before and the day before that."

He smiled faintly.

"You okay?" I asked, brushing the hair from out of his eyes.

"Fine," he said. He started to give me his customary handsome grin, but stopped, looking over my shoulder at something.

"Nik?"

He gave his head a shake. "Sorry," he said. "It's nothing. Probably just need a better night's sleep."

I nodded. He'd been restless the last few nights, tossing and turning, and talking to himself.

"Tilapia for dinner?" he asked.

"Sounds good," I said, and pulled him to me for a kiss. "I love you."

He held my face in his hands, his brows knit together, as if he were suddenly perplexed by something. "I love you," he said. "So fucking much."

I grinned. "Un romántico."

A laugh burst from him, and he smiled, the strange, distracted expression fading. "I'm going to shower and start the grill."

That night we ate up on the flat roof of the casita as we did every night the weather permitted. From there, the jungle was a sea of dark green swells that gave way to a golden beach and then a deep blue sea. Insects battered themselves against the old-fashioned lantern Nik had traded from a fisherman in the village—the lantern for a portrait.

In the gold light, Nik's eyes met mine and the distracted look flitted over his face for a moment, then was gone again.

He got to his feet and held his hand to me. "Dance?"

"I didn't bring up any music," I said, rising to my feet.

"We have music," Nik said.

I took his hand and he engulfed me in the protective circle of his arms. The insects buzzed and Nik's heartbeat kept time under my cheek as we turned a slow circle on the roof, all of Costa Rica spread before us.

"Stay," he whispered. "Please, stay."

I lifted my head. "Hmm?"

Nik's eyes, so blue in the amber light of the lamp, held mine and then he kissed me. Softly and sweetly, and then deeper. He kissed me until I was breathless.

"Let's go to bed," he said.

He made love to me that night in every sense of the phrase. I felt worshipped, my body singing under his hands and mouth. He left me humming with waves of ecstasy after.

"I'm going to get some water," I said, starting to rise.

"I'll get it," he said, gently pressing me back down. "Do you want anything else?"

"I think the mangos are ripe," I said, settling against the pillow. "Thank you."

He brought me a glass of water and a plate of sliced mango. Nik fed the fruit to me and I licked the juice from his fingers until we were reaching for each other again. He slid inside me again and came inside me again, all the while telling me he loved me, over and over.

"I love you too, Nik," I whispered, tears in the corner of my eyes though I don't know why. "So much. You're making this my perfect life."

"I hope so, baby. I want everything for you. Everything."

We slept entwined, and I woke to Nik talking in his sleep.

"Ostavat'sya," he said, his brows knit, his expression pleading. "Pozhaluysta. Ostavat'sya…"

I gently brushed the hair back from his forehead and his face smoothed out. He rolled toward me, pulled me tight to him and slept peacefully.

Sunlight streamed into the casita seeming to come from everywhere at once, and Nik was laying kisses along my back, making me shiver with need.

"What's gotten in to you?" I asked with a tired laugh after he'd brought me to yet another delicious orgasm.

He shrugged. "You're beautiful, sexy, and I love you."

"Simple as that, huh?"

"You're still naked," he added. "So there's the convenience..."

I laughed and nestled close to him.

"You were talking in your sleep last night," I said after a minute.

"Oh yeah? What'd I say?"

"Something in Russian. Pozhal..ostavat...something." His arms stiffened around me. I craned my head to look at him. "What does it mean?"

"Nothing. Gibberish. My Russian is rusty." He smiled a little and kissed me on the shoulder. "Breakfast?"

"Sure," I said, frowning. I grabbed my phone and, on a hunch, I Googled the Russian word for 'stay.'

*Ostavat'sya.*

For the next few days, Nik wore the distracted look, but he never said the word *stay* again in either English or Russian, and if he murmured it in his sleep, I was already too deep under to hear it.

One month later, I wrinkled my nose when Nik offered me a cube of pineapple he was cutting.

"Ugh, no thanks," I said.

"You love pineapple," he said.

"I do," I said. "But right now I can't stand the thought..." I cut my words off with a clapped hand to my mouth, my stomach roiling. I ran for the bathroom and just made it. Nik found me kneeling by the toilet, breathing hard and wiping my chin.

"You okay, babe?" he asked slowly, as if straining to be casual.

I nodded, and he helped me to stand. My hand was shaking but so was his. I looked up at him. "Nik..."

"Lie down," he said, taking me to the couch. "Take it easy."

"It's something I ate," I said, my voice tremulous. "Last night...we had those tapas. Maybe they didn't agree with me..."

Nik said nothing. He'd had two plates of tapas and was fine.

*It's a stomach bug,* I told myself, because any other possibility was too precious to contemplate—like the most delicate of glass bubbles. One touch...and it would shatter.

But the next morning and throughout the rest of the day, I threw up or felt like I was going to. After barely making it to the sink to expel the light lunch Nik had made for me, I reached my shaking hand to him and clutched his hard.

"Nik..." I whispered, imploring. "I'm late. Not a lot, but a little. And I can smell everything and I hate food that I normally love, and oh my God, I'm scared. I'm so scared..."

He held me tight and stroked my hair. "Don't be scared," he whispered. "Let's go find out for sure, and if you are..."

"If I am," I said against his chest, my tears staining his shirt, "the chances of keeping it are almost nothing. Being pregnant at all is a miracle..."

My voice cracked and broke on *pregnant*, and I sobbed against my husband.

Nik held me and pressed a kiss into my hair. "I know, baby. I know."

We bypassed the home pregnancy test and went straight to the clinic, where a young doctor named Miguel Jiminez performed a blood test that confirmed I was six weeks pregnant.

"Ten percent chance," I whispered, Nik's hand in mine as I sat on the table in a paper gown. "I only had a ten percent chance."

We told Dr. Jiminez my situation, and he looked serious but hopeful. After a full exam and an ultrasound, he blew air out of his cheeks and shook his head.

"I don't want to get your hopes up but I have to be realistic here. With the amount of scarring on your uterus, I'm not confident of a healthy implantation. I'm going to recommend you go home and rest. Perhaps not full bed rest but as close to it as you can manage for now. Just to be safe."

My eyes locked with Nik's. "Ten percent..."

Dr. Jiminez smiled warmly as he rose to leave. "Let us all hope for the best."

I vowed to do more than that. Every hour, every minute I would send a silent plea or prayer, to God or the gods or the energies of the universe—anything that might be listening that I would keep this baby.

That he would…

"Stay," I said.

The word fell out of my mouth and my glance darted to Nik, wide-eyed and staring. He said nothing but took my hand and didn't let go.

My morning sickness didn't abate, and while I didn't enjoy vomiting my breakfast up every morning, I was thankful. It meant I was still pregnant. Every food craving, every aversion, every bout of nausea were moments to be cherished. I stayed in bed for three solid days, but on the fourth, I threw off the covers.

"I need to walk. I need fresh air and exercise."

"If you feel up to it," Nik said.

"I do. I'm scared shitless but I feel so…happy too. So *content*. It's the strangest thing. In the back of my mind there are whispers that it could all…end. But mostly I'm just happy. Like everything is going to be okay."

That afternoon we got word that the adoption had been approved. Araceli was ours.

We celebrated that night, carefully. We were careful about everything. We took long walks on the beach, our hands locked together, each footprint in the sand a step closer to the goal, counting down the days, for both children.

*Two babies instead of one…*

I could hardly grasp it.

We readied Araceli's bedroom, and Nik cleaned out the smaller, third bedroom we'd been using for storage. I stared from the hallway, not daring to hope that we'd soon have two children when I'd resigned myself to a life of none.

"We need to be ready."

I nodded, while inside it felt reckless, to challenge fate. But at the fifteenth week, I felt the baby move, like a little flutter.

"I felt him," I said, my hand on my slightly rounded stomach. "I felt the baby."

Nik sat beside me on the bed, and put his hand where I'd felt it. There was nothing at first, and then…

Nik's eyes widened, a small, incredulous smile on his face. Love and hope. That's all we had.

The sixteenth week came and went. Then the twentieth. Flutters turned to outright kicks. Dr. Jiminez, pleasantly baffled, performed a sonogram in which he said everything looked normal.

"Would you like to know if it's a boy or a girl?" he asked, a tinge of hesitation still coloring his voice.

"It's a boy," I said, looking to Nik. "Isn't he?"

Nik nodded but the doctor, intent on the ultra sound, thought I'd asked him.

"Sí," Dr. Jiminez said. "Indeed, a boy."

He stayed.

I went into labor the beginning of the thirty-eighth week. I relished the pain that began as a small twinge in the early morning and grew into a monstrous clench by the late afternoon. I relished the pain. The sweat. The squeeze of Nik's hand in mine. I wanted it all, to feel everything.

Finally, as the twilight fell golden outside the window, our son was born.

He came into the world crying the hearty cry of a healthy newborn, perfect in every way. The nurse put him to my breast that was fuller and more round, just for him. He latched on immediately while Nik cut the cord. I noticed my husband's hand shaking a little. The nurse and doctor left to give us time together.

Nik sat beside me looking at our son in my arms with a heartbreaking expression of love and hope and fear and doubt.

"Nik…?"

He cleared his throat gruffly. "What if…he's like me?"

Tears sprung to my eyes. "If he's like you, we will love him hard and tell him he is not alone. That his daddy can do what he can do. That there might be others out there like him too; people who are different in the same way he is. And we will tell him that there might be someone out there in the world who needs him exactly for who he is, and that he will need him or her just as much. And when they find each other, they will be happy."

Nik turned away for moment to bring his emotions under control. "Okay," he said. "Okay."

I put the baby in Nik's tattooed arms and smiled until my cheeks ached. "We never picked out a name," I said.

"Evan," Nik said. "I think we should call him Evan."

"I do too." I kissed Nik's cheek, then gently pressed my lips to the baby's forehead.

"Evan Alexei Young."

Six weeks after we took our son home, Araceli arrived.

Nik opened the door to Sara, our adoption agent, holding the little girl's hand. Araceli was two years old now, and she clutched a hand-woven stuffed rabbit, her eyes wide and dark.

*Our little girl came home...*

I stood, staring for a moment at this beautiful child. A second miracle, standing right in front of me.

Nik moved first and knelt in front of her. "Hi, honey."

"Hi," she said. A little whisper.

"We've been teaching her English," Sara said. "To help her better adjust."

Araceli cocked her head and reached out to touch the piercing in Nik's ear, and then down over his tattoos. In my mind I saw Hailey all over again, only the old ache and longing wasn't there. Not this time.

I moved to kneel down beside Nik. "Hi, baby. I'm...Fiona." I'd almost said *your mommy* but I thought it was better to take it slow.

She reached out and touched my hair. "Candy," she said.

"That's right," I said softly. "Pink, like candy."

Araceli's dark eyes went between us and I could swear I felt her own little flicker of hope struggle to catch. Then the baby cried from his room, and Araceli's guarded face broke open in a smile.

"¿Bebé?"

"Yes," Nik said. "Want to see?"

Araceli bobbed her head. Nik and I exchanged hopeful glances with Sara.

"I'll just wait here," she said, with a knowing smile.

We took Araceli to the nursery. Evan was fussing as he always did right when he woke up. Araceli stood on tiptoe to see, then dropped her stuffed animal and held her arms up for Nik to be picked up.

I covered my mouth with my hand as Nik lifted her and settled her on his hip as if he'd been doing it for years. Araceli wrapped one arm around his neck and together they leaned in to see the baby.

"See?" he said, his eyes finding mine. "That's your baby brother. Hermano bebe."

I moved beside them, and Nik wrapped his free hand around my waist. Araceli beamed at Evan and then at me, and with that smile, I felt the last piece of my life fall into place.

*My family...I have a family.*

It felt like a dream. I glanced up at Nikolai Young who'd come into my life like a fiery storm of lust and passion, and became everything I'd ever wanted.

"I love you," I said in front of our son as he held our daughter. "I love you, Nikolai."

I knew Nik could see my love for him through the *ken*, but thinking the words wasn't the same as speaking them out loud for him to hear. Like a book that's never read, the emotions are lost unless given weight and breath and voice. When I said the words, when I released them into the universe, he heard them spoken with intention and not through some veil of mist or color or light.

He smiled down at me, his handsome face wearing an expression of completeness. Of peace that mirrored my own.

We'd found our sunshine, and now we were free.

The End

# Another Sunrise

Though this is a work of fiction, the struggles and pain some of these characters suffer is all too real for many. If you or someone you know is suffering, there is help.

The National Domestic Abuse Hotline: 1-800-799-7233
Thehotline.org

National Suicide Prevention Hotline: 1-800-273-8255
Suicidepreventionlifeline.org

# Also by Emma Scott

**How to Save a Life (Dreamcatcher #1)**
*Let's do something really crazy and trust each other.*

"You're in for a roller coaster of emotions and a story that will grip you from the beginning to the very end. This is a MUST READ…"—
**Book Boyfriend Blog**

Amazon: http://amzn.to/2pMgygR
Audible: http://amzn.to/2r20z0R

**Full Tilt**
*I would love you forever, if I only had the chance…*

"Full of life, love and glorious feels."—**New York Daily News, Top Ten Hottest Reads of 2016**

Amazon: http://amzn.to/2o1aK1o
Audible: http://amzn.to/2o8A7ST

**All In (Full Tilt #2)**
*Love has no limits…*

"A masterpiece!" –AC Book Blog

# Sugar & Gold

Amazon: http://amzn.to/2cBvM26
Audible: http://amzn.to/2nUprDQ

**Coming Soon**

Darlene Montgomery has been to hell and back…more than once. After a stint in jail for drug possession, she is finally clean and ready to start over. Yet another failed relationship is just the motivation she needs to move from New York to San Francisco with the hopes of resurrecting her dance career and discovering that she is more than the sum of her rap sheet. As Darlene struggles in her new city, the last thing she wants is to become entangled with her handsome—but cranky—neighbor and his adorable little girl...

Sawyer Haas is weeks away from finishing law school, but exhaustion, dwindling finances, and the pressure to provide for himself and his daughter, Olivia, are wearing him down. A federal clerkship--a job he desperately needs--awaits him after graduation, but only if he passes the Bar Exam. Sawyer doesn't have the time or patience for the capricious—if beautiful—dancer who moves into the apartment next to his. But Darlene's easy laugh and cheerful spirit seep into the cracks of his hardened heart, and slowly break down the walls he's resurrected to keep from being betrayed ever again.

When the parents of Olivia's absentee mother come to fight for custody, Sawyer could lose everything. To have any chance at happiness, he must trust Darlene, the woman who has somehow found her way past his brittle barbs, and Darlene must decide how much of her own bruised heart she is willing to give to Sawyer and Olivia, especially when the ghosts of her troubled past refuse to stay buried.

Forever Right Now
http://bit.ly/2shkWsw
Coming Oct, 2017

# Mini Glossary of Poker Terms

Bad Beat: When a hand is beaten by a lucky draw.

The Flop: In Texas Hold'em, the first three community cards dealt after the first round of betting.

Flush draw: When a player has four cards in his hand of the same suit and is hoping to draw a fifth to make a flush.

Gutshot: to hit an inside straight

Inside straight: Four cards which require another between the top and the bottom card to complete a straight. Players who catch this card make an Inside Straight.

The Nuts: the best possible hand one can have in a given moment. For example, "I flopped the nuts" means the player had the best possible hand right from the flop.

The River: the fifth and final community card

Straight draw: When a player has four sequential cards in his hand and is hoping to draw a fifth to make a straight

Trips: three of a kind

The Turn: the fourth community card

Quads: four of a kind

Printed in Great Britain
by Amazon